AFRICA BE DAMNED

Keith Jackson

Book Guild Publishing
Sussex England

First published in Great Britain in 2012 by
The Book Guild Ltd
Pavilion View
19 New Road
Brighton, BN1 1UF

Typeset in Baskerville by Ellipsis Digital, Glasgow

Printed and bound in Great Britain by
CPI Group (UK) Ltd, Croydon CR0 4YY

A catalogue record for this book is available from The British Library.

ISBN 978 1 84624 747 7

Dedicated with love to Natalie
And
For Lorraine and Jason

RHODESIA

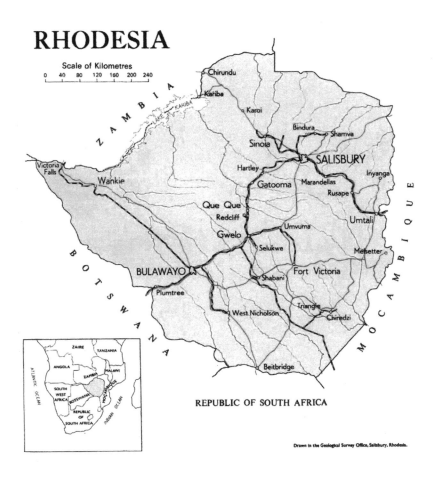

Scale of Kilometres

0   40   80   120   160   200   240

ZAMBIA

Chirundu

Kariba

LAKE KARIBA

Karoi

Bindura

Shamva

Sinoia

SALISBURY

Victoria
Falls

Hartley

Inyanga

Wankie

Gatooma

Marandellas

Rusape

Que Que

Redcliff

Umvuma

Umtali

Gwelo

Selukwe

Melsetter

BULAWAYO

Shabani

Fort Victoria

Plumtree

West Nicholson

Triangle

Chiredzi

B O T S W A N A

M O C A M B I Q U E

Beitbridge

REPUBLIC OF SOUTH AFRICA

ZAIRE

TANZANIA

ANGOLA

ZAMBIA

MALAWI

ATLANTIC OCEAN

SOUTH
WEST
AFRICA

BOTSWANA

MOCAMBIQUE

INDIAN OCEAN

REPUBLIC
OF
SOUTH AFRICA

Drawn in the Geological Survey Office, Salisbury, Rhodesia.

The Rhodesian

The stranger was known as the Rhodesian to the townsfolk who occasionally engaged him in conversation during his infrequent visits to Hluhluwe. The local Zulu community referred to him as *Isithuli* – the silent one. For their part the local constabulary found it expedient to play down the existence of the foreigner in their midst without name or passport.

The Rhodesian blended in well with the hardy outdoor community. Square of shoulder and of solid build, with an unkempt beard prematurely flecked with grey, and shoulder-length hair bleached by the sun. He lived out in the trackless waste of thorn scrub beyond the sisal plantations, in terrain not dissimilar to that covering large tracts of Zimbabwe to the north of South Africa's border. Some said he was a casualty of Ian Smith's bush war, which preceded Rhodesia's bloody transition to majority rule; others ventured to suggest an unsung hero.

A small sun-drenched town in the heart of Zululand, Hluhluwe served a prosperous farming community. The area was unique in that it boasted a sisal-processing factory, to cater for the seemingly endless plantations of spearlike succulents that covered the gently rolling hills from horizon to horizon. It was also credited with a superb game reserve, renowned for the largest concentration of white rhino in Africa.

The local Holiday Inn, which catered for the thriving tourist trade, was situated on the edge of the belt of thorn scrub that separated the town from the sisal and pineapple plantations. In addition to aloes and wild banana palms the grounds featured a particularly large fever tree, adorned with distinctive flaking lime-green bark and menacing ivory thorns. It was beneath this imposing tree that the Rhodesian now sat, alone, at a table placed in conspicuous isolation almost at the extremity of the gardens. Clad in well-worn khaki shorts, short-sleeved bush shirt and *veldskoen* boots, without socks, he stared intently out towards the horizon at the daily miracle of the bush, the setting of the African sun.

As the sun slipped from view and the world was plunged into a mauve haze of retreating shadows, an African waiter, in starched white uniform and maroon sash, weaved between the crowded tables at the poolside. Amos hesitated in the rapidly fading light before setting out across the wide expanse of lawn that separated the lone gentleman's table from the main body of guests. He carried two bottles of beer on a silver tray, held high over his shoulder in true colonial fashion. Without a word or a glance being exchanged he cautiously set the beers down, the bottles already beading with condensation from the lingering heat of the day. Placing a bottle opener on the table he gave a curt bow before departing with indecent haste. On regaining the sanctuary of the busy pool area Amos breathed an audible sigh of relief. He was still congratulating himself on having survived his ordeal when a manicured, ringless hand reached out and tapped him politely on the epaulet.

'Yes . . . yes, Madam?' Amos stammered, as he turned wide-eyed to trace the slender bare arm back to the young lady with vibrant auburn hair and extraordinarily green eyes. She sat with legs sedately crossed on a cane stool beneath the thatched over-hang of the poolside cocktail bar.

'Steward, how did you know what that gentleman out there wanted to drink? And why is his table set so far apart from the others?'

Confused by the very British accent and taken aback by the low cut of the lady's white blouse, revealing more than a hint of her petite – by African standards – but perfectly shaped breasts, Amos could only manage a foolish grin and another, 'Yes Madam,' as he bowed apologetically and backed off into the crowd.

With an exaggerated frown Jodie Knight turned her attention

2

back to the youthful European barman. 'That was rather strange.'

'I'm afraid you're wasting your time, Miss. The locals won't be drawn on that chap out there – be it out of devotion or superstition they all have a healthy respect for his privacy,' volunteered the trainee manager, who was on relief bar duty. Equally in awe of their lovely guest, he too was experiencing difficulty keeping his gaze up and bottom jaw from gaping. It was the iridescent green of her eyes and flawless complexion, save for a barely perceptible scar on her cheek, that held his attention. Absently polishing another glass he tactfully reminded her, 'You were about to tell me of your first impressions of Africa?'

Her curiosity far from satisfied, Jodie obliged half-heartedly. 'Apart from the obvious tragedy of apartheid, I think it's a beautiful country. I found Durban very cosmopolitan, and the Indian market and aquarium were fascinating. The city was also much bigger and cleaner than I'd expected. My only real disappointment has been this *so-called* safari. It's amounting to little more than a guided tour of your game parks in an air-conditioned coach, admittedly with zebra stripes emblazoned down the sides. A far cry from the wilds of Africa I had imagined.'

'We do have more traditional safaris, either in open Land-Rovers or on foot,' Ron said helpfully.

'Yes, well I think that's more in keeping with what Daddy and I were expecting,' she replied wistfully as she eased round on her stool for a better view of the hotel grounds. Her stranger was still out there, silhouetted against the encroaching night, under the tree with the unearthly bark and incredibly long thorns.

Holding another glass up for inspection, Ron broke the silence. 'Would that be your father at the table next to the pool, the gentleman in a tie?'

'Yes, my chaperone for the trip,' Jodie confirmed with a chuckle, recalling her earlier protests that dad was overdressed for the occasion. 'How did you guess?' she asked, still inwardly toying with the challenge presented by the khaki-clad mystery man across the lawn.

'He's nodded your way on a few occasions, while talking to the lady and the other gent at his table; would she be your mother?' Ron was anxious to glean as much as he could about this lovely member of the British aristocracy.

'Heaven forbid! The couple are *Americans*,' Jodie sniggered raising both hands in mock defence. 'They are on our tour and what they don't know about the bush is apparently not worth knowing. Mother was unable to make the trip, due to pressures of work,' Jodie seemed almost apologetic. 'Christine heads up the family brewing business and her time is hardly her own this close to the festive season.'

'Mother runs the business?' Ron prompted, to prolong the conversation.

'Yes. After Daddy lost his first wife to cancer he married Christine, his secretary at the time. Being quite a few years younger than Daddy she took over the reins after he had a mild heart attack. But that's quite enough about me; what is it that compels us to bare our souls to strangers in bars?'

'I guess it's . . .' but before Ron could finish he was loudly interrupted. 'Hey Romeo, how about some service down this end!' one of the local farmers called out in a heavy Afrikaans accent.

Pivoting on her stool as the coloured lights came on around the pool, Jodie checked first on the rugged-looking stranger sitting motionless beneath the acacia tree and then on her father.

Having seen his daughter turn in his direction, Brenton grinned and blew her a kiss.

'A fine young woman you have there partner,' drawled the greying Texan at Brenton Knight's table, adding as he swallowed down the last of his drink, 'What I wouldn't give to be thirty years younger.'

'Watch your mouth Frank,' snapped his overweight wife. 'As for you Mr Knight, you would do well to have a word with that young lady in her mother's absence. Going braless in Soho is one thing, but this is *Africa*.'

Brenton didn't particularly like the American couple but he

craved company, and Frank was more than willing to match him drink for drink, making him feel better about his own excesses. Staring down into his half-empty glass he inwardly bemoaned the years seemingly whiled away. 'One day they are sitting on your knee and the next thing you know they are young adults, turning heads in bars. But time stands still for no man,' he concluded philosophically.

Frank's wife stifled a yawn. 'I really must put my feet up before dinner – my blood pressure you know. Go easy on the whiskies you two.'

Rising unsteadily as his guest took her leave, Brenton noticed the youthful barman making his way back down the counter to continue chatting up his daughter. Christine should be here to see this, he told himself, suppressing his anger at the thought of her last-minute withdrawal from the trip – an African adventure planned over a year ago to coincide with Jodie's graduation and coming of age. They were overdue to spend some quality time together, he thought, returning his daughter's cheery wave as she swung back round to the bar.

'Where were we?' Ron asked, as he resumed polishing glasses opposite the woman who from this day forth would dominate his fantasies.

'You were going to enlighten me about that gentleman out there,' Jodie nodded in the direction of the hotel grounds.

'As you wish, but be warned you may find his antics a little disconcerting,' Ron cautioned as he dabbed his brow with the tea cloth and silently cursed the collar and tie while on duty rule, even in summer.

'I consider myself so warned,' Jodie said, smiling outrageously.

'They have dubbed him the Rhodesian because that's where he originated, a war veteran from all accounts. He apparently lives alone somewhere out there in the bush. He's unemployed and keeps pretty much to himself, as you can see.' Ron was still having difficulty keeping his eyes from wandering.

'Sounds intriguing, so far,' Jodie encouraged, fastening another

5

button on her blouse and tapping the rim of her empty glass.

While Ron poured her another liberal tot of gin, adding a slice of lemon, several blocks of ice and a splash of tonic, Jodie took stock of her day: the magic of the game reserve that morning, followed by a siesta by the pool in the afternoon and now cocktails while watching a brilliant sunset. With a romantic evening beneath a full moon still to follow, subject to her plucking up the courage to approach her mystery man before he disappeared whence he came.

'What does he do for money then?' Jodie prompted as Ron placed her drink on the coaster in front of her.

'I should not be telling you all this,' Ron glanced anxiously about him. Not that the other tourists were likely to believe a word of it, even if they were to eavesdrop, he justified to himself. 'He has an open account in these parts – by that I mean he is not expected to pay for anything. My dad's in the police reserve and he says this guy even gets a free issue of ammunition from the charge office whenever he's in town.'

'Why is everybody so generous?' Jodie asked, turning once more to peer out into the fading light. He was still there, thankfully.

'For services rendered.'

Swivelling back round, Jodie felt her nipples brush against the relative coolness of her cotton blouse. 'Services rendered!' she exclaimed, rapping a well manicured finger on the bar to get Ronald to lift his gaze again.

'He's taken out a good number of insurgents and poachers hereabout.'

Jodie raised an eyebrow. 'Do you mean . . .' she paused, drawing a finger across her throat. In response to Ron's knowing nod she leant over the bar and whispered, 'Ronald, this had better not be a private joke at my expense.'

Delighted that she had used his name, which was emblazoned in gold letters on his lapel badge, Ron continued, 'I wouldn't dream of it. You see, what with poachers, the odd terrorist incursion from Mozambique and the unsavoury element among the migrant labourers who gravitate to the sisal and pineapple estates, we've had more than our share of problems in these parts. There have even been incidents of farmers being murdered, just like north of the border before Rhodesia's independence. Well, since this chap put in an appearance five or six years ago, things have quietened down considerably. Which is probably not surprising given that they say more weapons are accounted for than the actual number of terrorists and poachers handed over to the authorities.'

Having weakened and popped a handful of peanuts into her mouth, Jodie now begrudged the time taken to chew and swallow. 'Surely such extreme measures would only have been resorted to in self defence?' she rationalised.

From the tone in her voice Ron realised the fellow could be Jack the Ripper and she would not have been discouraged. 'I suspect there were extenuating circumstances,' he conceded graciously.

Finishing her drink, Jodie stepped down from her stool. 'Ronald, it has been most interesting but now you must excuse me. I need to freshen up before the barbeque, the *braai* that is,' she corrected.

'Before you go, what is it about this guy that you find so fascinating?'

'Briefly then. I need material for my master's degree in psychology next year and I'm intrigued by our recluse. From what you have told me he certainly would be an interesting case study. Once again, thank you and good night, Ronald.'

Ron could not help noticing the flash of white thigh through the slit in Jodie's khaki safari skirt as she strode confidently back towards the hotel.

Returning the empty bottle to the concrete table that was inlaid with fragments of coloured tiles, the Rhodesian wiped his mouth with the back of his hand. Staring impassively across at the raucous mass of humanity at the pool deck, he vaguely recalled similar scenes from his Rhodesian days. His fellow countrymen had lived it up as if there would be no tomorrow, no inevitable one-man one-vote, no majority rule.

Willing his gaze away from the offending lights, he muttered, 'Enjoy it while it lasts, South Africa; while your blacks seethe in their discontent and future despot leaders plot the nationalisation of your industries and appropriation of your farms.' Another case of too little too late he mused, twiddling a lock of hair in his frustration. The fact that South Africa was unlikely to be spared the fate that had befallen every other post-colonial state in Africa was not all that worried him. Independence would bring change, hastening the end of his days in self-exile. An exile he had indulged in over long. 'Far too long,' he said aloud, staring up at the stars. Too long now even to contemplate the prospects of family unwittingly abandoned in Rhodesia, he thought, slapping his palms against his temples in an effort to quell the pain in his head and the flashes before his eyes. He was finding it difficult to continue ignoring the increasing severity and frequency of the attacks.

Beneath an African Moon

Returning from her room Jodie could sense the excitement around the pool as fellow tourists checked cameras and equipment, and fired questions at one another in anticipation of the evening's entertainment. The programme featured Zulu dancing followed by a traditional *braai*. Steaks, chops and *boerewors* sausages grilled over open coals that were already glowing in the split halves of old oil drums bordering the entertainment area, an oval clearing of compacted dry earth. The sweet smell of wood smoke filled the air. Jodie took a deep breath and closed her eyes. She imagined she could already hear the throbbing of the drums and see the dust rising above the ostrich-plumed ankles of half-naked warriors, as their bare feet rhythmically pounded the earth.

Willing herself back to the present, Jodie looked anxiously at her watch. It was seven twenty; only ten minutes before the show was due to get under way. Having devoted an hour at the bar trying to conjure up a plausible excuse for introducing herself to the Rhodesian, to no avail, she resolved to let fate take its course. Fortified by several liberal gin and tonics, she asked herself how difficult could it be to stroll across a lawn and invite a perfect stranger to be her guest for the evening. After all, what was the worst that could happen?

Finding herself standing at the edge of the lawn, Jodie waved to catch her father's attention. Having returned his smile with a bravado she did not feel, she squared her shoulders and signalled a walking movement with her fingers. Dad responded with a paternalistic tap of his watch, before jovially saluting her departure with his glass.

9

It was dark now and Jodie could barely make out the large thorn tree. Nevertheless, she was convinced by the butterflies in her stomach that he was still out there. She had not gone far before the heady scent of mimosa blossom and the incessant chorus of night insects threatened to overcome her. Her desire to slink back into the protective arc of light from the hotel had reached its peak when a shrill birdlike whistle pierced the blackness. Stopping in her tracks she felt a shiver go up her spine, in spite of the oppressive heat of the humid October evening. The echo of the eerie call had hardly faded when, glancing back, Jodie saw the same reluctant steward as before materialise through the throng and set out across the lawn, two more beers on his tray.

The whites of Amos's eyes stood out like porcelain saucers against a wet coalface, reflecting his terror of the night and the spirits that frequented it. Not to mention the equally disconcerting presence of the all-knowing *Isithuli*, silently awaiting his arrival. Heading in the direction of the solitary table, a startled Amos dropped his tray in response to Jodie's whispered greeting as he passed unseeing within an arm's length of her. He did not cry out, such was his terror, and the unopened bottles came to no harm on the spongy Kikuyu grass.

Reassuring the steward in hushed tones, Jodie relieved him of the tray once he had picked up the bottles. 'I'll deliver these, if you will be kind enough to fetch another chair,' she bargained.

Once Amos had obediently taken his leave, Jodie swallowed hard and continued gingerly on her way, the tray held protectively out in front of her. Stopping abruptly beneath the furthermost reaches of the thorn tree to peer ahead, she could just make out the man's bearded profile. Transfixed, she watched as the Rhodesian slowly turned to face her. Her arrival had been well anticipated.

Continuing to stare wide eyed through the gloom Jodie sought a smile, a gesture if not a word of greeting, to restore her flagging confidence. She was seriously beginning to question what had possessed her to try and impose herself on this secretive individual, of reputedly dubious character.

The nervous warning cough at her back would ordinarily have scared Jodie out of her wits; instead the distraction came as a relief. Her adrenalin pumping anew she remained rooted to the spot while Amos wordlessly positioned the plastic garden chair behind her, departing as stealthily as he had arrived.

Unable to bring herself to sit at such an absurd distance from the table, Jodie remained standing while enduring the stranger's intense scrutiny across a gulf of some ten metres. She was only vaguely conscious of the fact that he was probably better able to make her out against the backdrop of hotel lights, than she could him. Had she known just how acute his practised night vision was, she would have felt even more naked before his gaze.

It was then, mercifully, that the moon rose. The great silvery orb serenely unveiled the night in a wave of diffused, haunting light. The rhythmic boom of a dozen drums resounded from across the gardens, thundering out a welcome. And the piercing wails of Zulu maidens heralded the arrival of the foot-stomping snake of Zulu warriors. It was to the rattle of spears on iron-hard ox-hide shields that the Rhodesian stood and left his table.

Jodie was unaware of any actual movement, only that a tall imposing figure now stood before her, bare muscular legs set astride and hands clenched loosely at his sides. The Rhodesian looked neither pleased nor angry. Confused best described the set expression on his weathered yet still handsome face. Jodie had not dared imagine he'd be quite this captivating. Yet there was something odd about the way he stared at her, with head half cocked, as if seeking recognition. Jodie continued to stand her ground in the gloom, clinging to the tray.

Unable to hide his embarrassment as tears misted his sight, the Rhodesian self-consciously snatched the beers from the tray, still proffered in outstretched hands by the woman in front of him. Chastising himself for even imagining that this tall, beautiful woman, with striking green eyes and auburn hair, might resemble

11

someone dear to him, and cursing the torment of a subconscious that denied him but fleeting glimpses of a distant past, he turned on his heels and strode off into the night.

He had almost reached the point where the manicured lawn merged into thick scrub at the extremity of the grounds when it dawned on Jodie that she was about to lose him; probably for ever.

'Wait . . . wait a minute,' she stammered, struggling to find her voice, 'please don't leave like this. *Wait!*' she hollered.

But there was no stopping him.

'Damn you, *damn men!*' Jodie fumed as she flung aside the tray and dashed after him. She crashed into the bush at the spot where he had disappeared, twigs pulling and snagging at her skirt and blouse as she forced herself forward. '*Please wait,*' she all but screamed – only to actually do so a moment later, a long cry as hundreds of tiny hook-like barbs tore into her flesh in the darkness. The treacherous buffalo thorn held her securely. Jodie's agonising wail died on her lips as the pain took her breath away. She realised that nobody from the hotel would hear her over the pounding of the drums and the high-pitched ululating of the Zulu women. Going into shock her body went limp, and she hung suspended like a rag doll in the grip of the reddish, razor-tipped thorns.

The finely honed edge of a hunting knife glinted in the light of the moon. Deft hands pruned the *wag-'n-bietjie* bush of its vicious vine-like tentacles, until at last it gave up its captive into strong waiting arms.

As she was laid gently down, back on the lawn next to the table beneath the protective shadow of the fever tree, Jodie's eyelashes fluttered and she let out a soft groan. Methodically the Rhodesian set about removing the thorns, following the distinctive raised pattern of blooded welts that crisscrossed her upper body, each thorn silhouetted against the moon as he removed it. Whispering reassurance as he worked he would return to the wound if one had not come out cleanly and continued to press and prod as painlessly as he could until a dark thorn tip, coated in fresh blood, popped to the surface.

'We must get all the thorns out cleanly,' he coaxed apologetically in response to her intermittent groans, 'so the wounds will heal quickly.' It was only as he worked on the firm but particularly sensitive areas beneath her torn blouse that his hands lost some of their steadiness.

'Enough,' she whimpered at last, her nails biting into his forearm as she pulled herself up.

'The worst is over but you will still need a tetanus shot, an antiseptic cream and some painkillers,' he said in a voice reminiscent of a doctor's bedside manner.

Helping her to her feet, the Rhodesian stepped back. The pain in his head, momentarily suppressed by the excitement and the heady fragrance of expensive perfume, had assumed a new intensity. The lights in the distance began to dance and pain lanced in spasms behind his eyes. 'Getting worse, not a good sign,' he muttered between clenched teeth as the migraine took hold.

'Are you all right?' Jodie asked, their roles reversed.

Holding up a hand as if for silence, the Rhodesian nodded without conviction, turned unsteadily and for the second time that night made off towards the bush.

'I don't even know your name. Will you be back?' Jodie called after him, but there was no response and she looked on helplessly, exhausted from her ordeal.

Having called a doctor for Jodie, Brenton Knight contemplated telephoning Christine but thought better of it. He had still not got the full story out of Jodie, and besides Christine could tell when he had drunk too much and would likely blame his derogation of duty for their daughter's misfortune. Having convinced himself that the call could wait until he was able to offer a rational explanation for Jodie's antics, he immediately regretted the lost opportunity to get Christine to fly out and join them.

In spite of the relative coolness of the advancing night the Rhodesian managed less than ten kilometres before dropping to his knees, drenched in sweat. 'No!' he roared defiantly up at the waning moon in a clear sky. He moved into the relative safety of a thorn thicket, while he still had the presence of mind, as his world slipped mercifully into blackness and an eerie silence descended on the bush.

Abduction

Jodie recovered physically in the days that followed but remained emotionally drained. Having solicited the hotel staff and any number of locals for information about the Rhodesian's whereabouts without success, she was becoming increasingly distressed at the prospect of leaving Hluhluwe, and eventually Africa, without seeing him again. Her initial intrigue at the man's exploits and nomadic existence had evolved into a genuine concern for his well-being. Intuition, and three years of studying behavioural sciences, told her that if ever there was a soul in torment it was his.

She refused to go on the game drives, protesting that she had seen her fill of elephant, white rhino, zebra, impala, warthog and giraffe while despairing of ever seeing a lion or a leopard, so the time passed slowly for Jodie. When not interrogating strangers she spent her waking hours lazing listlessly around the pool in the sun, seldom out of sight of the lone table beneath the fever tree.

Brenton's pleas for his daughter to at least phone home and confide in her mother fell on deaf ears. He found Jodie's evening ritual equally disconcerting. At sundown she would sit out under the big acacia in the grounds waiting for Amos to arrive and place two bottles of beer on the solitary table – only to retrieve them the following morning and repeat the process in the evening with cold replacements.

In spite of her father's protests that she was making a spectacle of herself, and acknowledging that she had become the talk of the hotel, Jodie persisted with her routine. The man simply had to put in an appearance, if not for the beer then at least to satisfy himself of her recovery. She desperately wanted to thank him and to have

15

an opportunity to fathom out what it was that so troubled him.

It had become Jodie's custom to return to her room half an hour before sunset to bathe and change for the evening, before beginning her lonely vigil. On the third evening, Amos passed her while she was still on her way back to her room.

'Thursday is my night off, Madam. I hope Madam does not mind me taking the beers early?'

'That will be fine Amos, seeing as how you have already taken the liberty,' Jodie said moodily.

Having bathed and dressed in record time she made her way back through the throng around the pool, noting as she went that the sun was only moments away from sinking completely below the horizon. In spite of the stifling heat she looked fresh and composed in a floral summer dress and sandals, the short skirt accentuating her shapely legs. She had also taken to wearing a bra since her ordeal. Reaching the far side of the patio, she let out an involuntary cry and broke into an undignified run. Arriving breathless at the table she bit her lower lip: both bottles lay on their side – empty.

Jodie could not recall such utter despair in all of her impressionable twenty-one years. Picking up the crown tops lying on the table, she squeezed them until the serrated edges bit into the palm of her hand. Tears filled her eyes as she looked up at the mauve-streaked sky. 'Damn him! Damn these arrogant South Africans . . . Rhodesians . . . whatever!' She voiced her frustration, only to have second thoughts. 'Please don't let it end like this.'

Only partly concealed by the bush, but invisible to an untrained eye, the Rhodesian stood a mere fifteen metres from her. He knew he should not have come. Failing which he should have left after his earlier inspection of her shapely, bikini-clad body had confirmed she had suffered no long-term ill effects from her buffalo thorn mauling. Inwardly conceding that his use of binoculars had been an indulgence as she lay by the pool side, he now guiltily averted his eyes. Three days it had taken to convince himself that he could come and go as he pleased, that the years of bitter self-exile had left him devoid of emotion. Still he stood his ground like an obstinate fool, his predicament all the more unsettling in that a slavish obedience to one's instincts was a prerequisite to self-preservation in the bush.

Unable to avert his eyes any longer the Rhodesian looked up just in time to see the young woman drop down onto one of the chairs at the table, arms folded dejectedly across her chest. Her back was to the setting sun and the light radiated from her hair, framing her bowed head in a reddish-gold halo. He did not recall taking the dozen or so steps that carried him silently to her side, but he knew what he was doing when he placed a hand beneath her chin, which was now wet with tears.

Jodie felt neither alarm nor surprise at the reassuring pressure of the hand gently tilting her face upwards. When their eyes met the Rhodesian was surprised to see that she was smiling up at him through damp wisps of hair. They continued staring at one another, Jodie all smiles in acknowledgement of a silent prayer, the Rhodesian with a worried frown creasing his tanned brow. Both were having difficulty grasping the reality of the situation. Oblivious to the world around them they did not see or hear Brenton Knight, now making his way anxiously across the lawn in the fading light.

'Don't cry,' was all the Rhodesian could manage, for words did not come easily to him these days. Stooping further he placed a hand beneath each of her elbows and gently drew her to her feet. Reaching out he was awkwardly poised to brush the damp strands of hair from her flushed cheeks when a commanding voice broke the silence.

'Let go of my daughter, you . . .' Brenton bellowed from some way off, making heavy going over the spongy grass.

One glance was all Jodie needed to confirm her worst fears; her father was in no fit state to contribute to an already delicate situation. There was still time she thought, turning back to the Rhodesian and placing a restraining hand on his arm. 'Take me with you,' she said. 'Just for a while, a day or so,' she pleaded, tightening her grip on his muscular forearm, for she could sense he was once again about to make a hasty retreat. 'There is something troubling you and I want to help,' she blurted out. Time did not permit a debate on post-traumatic stress syndrome, if indeed he was actually a war veteran.

'I don't need help, and this won't be a stroll through Hyde Park,' he shot back, at the same time grabbing her wrist and leading her off towards the sanctuary of the bush.

'I'm in good hands,' Jodie called over her shoulder as she stumbled blindly after the big man. 'I'll be back soon,' she managed before they were enveloped by the camouflage of the night. 'I hope he understands,' she panted, realising full well that Brenton would already be beside himself with worry. If he returned directly to the bar there was a possibility she could be back by the time he had slept it off. On the other hand he could panic and call Christine, who would go berserk and be on the next flight out to Africa.

A badly shaken Brenton Knight stood wheezing on the spot where his daughter had been a moment ago. Sobering rapidly, he desperately wanted to believe that Jodie knew what she was doing. Having to explain to Christine that he had let her run off with a recluse, some sort of vigilante from all accounts, was not something he relished. Then again, had she come with them in the first place this would never have happened. Still wrestling with his predicament Brenton hurried back to the hotel for a drink, to calm his nerves and help him decide if and when to raise the alarm – and whether or not to involve Christine.

The Rhodesian moved swiftly through familiar habitat, eyes fixed on a star high above a range of hills silhouetted against the horizon. He was now carrying his charge, who had succumbed to the heat and exhaustion after a commendable effort at maintaining the pace. He was grateful that while tall she was slim and not overly heavy.

He tried to switch off mentally, as he was accustomed to doing on arduous marches, but the womanly fragrance of his burden only heightened his awareness and he was forced to brood on the consequences of his thoughtless act. Even with the local constabulary in his debt he knew they would be hard-pressed to ignore a charge of abduction.

As the hours passed his bush shirt became soaked in sweat and he lost all feeling in his arms. 'This is madness,' he berated himself, his head throbbing as he rationalised that his migraine attacks, a legacy from the trauma suffered in his Rhodesian days, were affecting his judgement. The pain behind his eyes became more acute as he slogged on. He was only vaguely aware of the fact that he was going to need help – and soon.

Civvy Street

Tony Longdon gave a start as the motorist behind blasted on the horn; the lights had changed to green. He recalled little of the drive through the tree-lined avenues of Bulawayo, Rhodesia's second largest city, so preoccupied had he been with the disquieting events of his last stint in the army. He parked halfway down the next block, in front of General Mining Equipment (Pty) Limited. It was only 07.00 but he wagered his secretary was already at work, preparing for his first hectic day back at the office in nearly two months.

Jenny was sorting the mail. 'Good morning,' he greeted her cheerfully, 'everything under control?'

'Good morning and welcome home!' Jenny was all smiles and her voice had a ring to it. 'We like to think we managed to keep abreast of things in your absence. Of course everyone will be delighted to have the *boss* back . . . and I'm not being sarcastic. I hope it wasn't too bad this time?' she ventured, following him through to his office.

'Pretty uneventful,' he lied, still trying to get events in the operational area out of his mind. 'The army doesn't change – still hurry up and wait. It just takes a bit more out of you as you get older.'

'Twenty-seven isn't old!' Jenny exclaimed immediately blushing. 'I mean the chaps in the office say there aren't many who can stay the pace with you.'

'Nice thought, even if not entirely true,' Tony acknowledged with a grin. Putting down his briefcase and hanging up his jacket, he sat and savoured a moment of quiet ecstasy as the cold leather of the chair penetrated his cotton shirt. Pivoting in a slow arc he took in the welcome orderliness of the office, pencils sharpened, air conditioner set just right and a new blotter on the desk pad; the cool harmony of his surroundings in complete contrast to the heat, squalor and bloodshed of the past few weeks.

Getting too comfortable, Tony stood and pulled back his shoulders to relieve the tension already creeping into his muscles. Loosening his tie he rolled up his sleeves – it took a while to get used to civilian clothes again after a spell in the bush.

During the pause in the conversation Jenny did not take her eyes off her boss. He had lost some weight, his arms and face were burnt dark by the sun and he was in need of a haircut, but none the worse for wear, she reassured herself. Seven weeks was a long time and she had really missed him. His brisk efficient manner, the permanent sense of urgency and the confidence he exuded had all become part of her life.

'Oh, thank you for the parcel Jenny, most welcome and very imaginative.'

'It was nothing, really.'

'Nothing!' he echoed loosening his tie still further, 'Marmite, condensed milk, shortbread biscuits and even a tin of sardines, where did you get all that stuff? Kathy tells me there's been nothing like it in the shops for ages.'

'Compliments of Head Office,' Jenny conceded modestly, turning to unlock the filing cabinet and take out a neat pile of correspondence. 'Mr Robinson came up from Johannesburg for the day to see how we were managing. I prevailed on him to bring up a few bits and pieces. Which reminds me, you are also the proud owner of two bottles of Scotch whisky,' she nodded towards the cocktail cabinet as she sat down in front of the desk, shorthand notebook poised.

'You just happened to mention that whisky was also hard to come by up here these days!' Tony grinned as he sat down again. 'Before we kick off, how did Reg do?'

'Apart from stepping on a few toes, I believe Mr Taylor

coped very well – considering we had the accountant and credit manager, as well as yourself, all in the sticks at the same time.'

Tony nodded. 'The joys of territorial force peacetime commitments. OK, let's make a start. A run-down, from the day I left.'

'Chronologically?'

'In order of *priority*,' he snapped, 'please,' he added by way of apology, absently twiddling a length of hair at the nape of his neck – a childhood habit picked up from his mother.

Jenny adjusted her glasses and brushed a wisp of hair from her forehead. It had started, but then the first day was usually the worst, she reminded herself.

Ten minutes into the pile of paper in front of him Tony pushed back hard into his chair; it was far too comfortable after the logs and rocks out in the sticks. He'd had a similar problem last night, with sleep only coming in the early hours of the morning. Not that the mattress was entirely to blame – apart from the horrific events of the past few weeks he had returned home with a conscience. No matter that he was a first offender and very drunk at the time, adultery was an ugly word, particularly after seven happy years of marriage. Hell, he had even found himself giving Jenny the once-over this morning. Blame it on the bloody army, he thought, but it was of little consolation.

'Are you all right?' Jenny asked. 'Another cup of coffee, perhaps?' She had not seen him quite this distracted before and it worried her.

'No, I'm fine. Sorry, where were we?'

'We were onto staff matters. Mac is back from his commitment . . . but in hospital I'm afraid.'

Scowling, Tony glanced down at the staff call-up register, ever handy under the glass top on his desk. His sales representative was only due to be demobbed in two weeks. 'What the fu . . . sorry, what happened to him?'

'Landmine,' Jenny confirmed, her throat tightening, for her boss tended to take other people's problems too personally. 'His wife says he is making progress but could still lose an arm.'

22

Tony shook his head, mines accounted for a good percentage of Territorial Army casualties in the operational area these days. Visions of his Lieutenant Anderson resurfaced, cowering behind their wrecked vehicle after they too had detonated a mine just a week earlier. He had been lucky, but Anderson's fighting days were over. For every soldier killed a dozen others were left maimed, crippled or vegetating on the side. This was the ugly side of pre-independence Rhodesia, the hidden cost of denying the black population their right to self-determination.

'I'll call in at the hospital on the way home. Wrap up one of those bottles of Scotch for me. Please,' he added. 'Right, what's next?'

'Still not good news I'm afraid,' she offered apologetically. 'Mr Taylor now has to report to his unit tomorrow and not next month as previously advised.'

Tony glanced at his watch, stood up, and crossed to the window to look down into the all but deserted street. There was a time, before petrol rationing and the extending of military service to all able-bodied men up to the age of fifty, when you couldn't find an empty parking space in front of the building. Now, apart from a few staff cars, the bays were empty. Putting Taylor's call-up date forward was a sign of the times. Returning to the large teak desk he said flatly, 'What the fuck . . . Sorry, I really am trying,' he apologised again. 'What went wrong this time?'

Jenny knew her boss was not expecting a reply. She could also see his mood wasn't getting any better. Neither would it so long as the conversation centred on the war effort. It was as if the whole country ate, drank and slept little else these days.

'If he has to report tomorrow he'll want to hand over and finish up early today. Let's leave the rest of this stuff and I'll see him now.'

As his secretary left the office, quietly closing the door behind her, Tony locked his fingers and forced his arms out until his knuckles cracked. Nine years working his way up to where he was today, a pursuit that had left precious little time for anything else, and all for what? The economy was on the verge of grinding to a halt after thirteen years of sanctions following UDI, and now there was no belt left to take in or workable solution in sight.

A head of close-cropped ginger hair followed a rap on the door as Reg looked into the office. 'Welcome back to civilisation Boss. Jen says it's OK for me to come in now?'

'Yes, for a quick hello and goodbye from the sounds of it,' Tony said walking around the desk to shake hands. They sat in the easy chairs at the coffee table.

'Has Jenny mentioned about Mac?'

'Yes, I said I'd look in on him this evening.'

'I'm surprised to see you back without a scratch,' Reg said. 'Dreadful news about those four chaps in your platoon, from the sound of it the rest of you were bloody lucky to make it out in one piece.'

'Luck or fate, who knows,' Tony shrugged rolling his head to relieve the tension and to shut the deaths of members of his unit out of his mind. 'Don't you find it all a bit unreal at times? I mean, sitting here like this it's hard to believe there's a war going on out there, endless bloody patrols, people dying. One minute you're charging around the bush with a lethal weapon, the next you're behind a desk putting pen to paper as if nothing could be more normal.'

'What I find even harder to fathom, Tony, is you not being willing to accept a commission, particularly with us now spending upwards of four months a year in uniform. It's a waste of talent, your electing to remain an NCO.'

'Forget it my friend,' Tony frowned. 'I don't begrudge you your captain's pips but I have no inclination to be a party to an organised bugger-up. If our territorial army were a private enterprise it would have folded long ago. We've spent years slogging it out in the bush and getting blown up by landmines, with absolutely nothing to show for it.'

'That's a bit unfair! With a kill rate of seventy-to-one ours is one of the most effective anti-terrorist armies in the world. And it's all because fifteen thousand odd national service lads and territorials like us effectively act as the eyes and ears for a much smaller regular army. Sure the regulars get more of the action and most of the glory. But then we don't complain when the shit hits the fan and they move in.'

'Well it's high time someone did complain, what with the locals being picked off like flies. It's no bloody wonder we are losing the battle for hearts and minds,' Tony said testily.

Reg frowned. He could understand Tony being distressed by the recent deaths of his colleagues, but these assertions were over the top. As an employee he knew he would be well advised to drop the issue, but as an officer and loyal Rhodesian he felt obliged to protest, 'Tony, with all due respect there's a war going on and casualties are to be expected, on both sides.'

Staring fixedly at Reg, his senior in age and rank but not at work, Tony challenged, 'Reg, in your position you must be aware these are not simply casualties. Hell you just have to read the bloody newspapers these days – whenever there is a contact dozens of locals are conveniently slotted on the side.'

'Collateral damage,' Reg said. 'It's inevitable that a few innocent people will get caught up in the cross-fire.'

'When it comes to annihilating whole fucking villages, they call it genocide. Desperate measures in desperate times, my friend,' Tony countered.

Reg fell silent. This was dangerous talk even behind closed doors. Turning to the folder on the coffee table in front of him he changed the subject. 'There are a number of issues I need to go over with you before I leave, if that's OK?'

They had barely made a start when Jenny entered the office with another tray of coffee and more mail. 'Sorry to interrupt but this looked urgent.' Picking up on her boss's mood as she crossed to the table she wondered why he didn't heed his own good advice and take a few days off to unwind after a camp, as he insisted on with the other chaps in the office. If nothing else it would give him time to get out of the habit of using four-letter words and being so abrupt. 'The mail,' she offered.

'Just leave it on the desk,' Tony snapped.

'I think you should see this,' she said, a tremor in her voice.

'What is it Jen?' Reg asked helpfully, reaching up to take the registered article slip she was holding. He read, 'Cpl A. P. Longdon, no 37443 9 RR. No prize for guessing what this is, Mr Anthony Longdon.'

Tony surprised them both by calmly signing the slip and handing it back. 'Jenny, have the messenger collect these call-up papers, please.'

Jenny nodded and left the room, unable to trust her voice. Reg shrugged in a helpless gesture.

Tony shook his head. 'It's absurd, absolutely fucking absurd. They must have posted these bloody things before our company was even stood down. It's a case of calling up the dead in respect of those poor bastards who copped it last week. Tell me more about how we have the situation so well in hand, Reg.'

'We should alert Head Office to the possibility of our both being away at the same time,' Reg suggested, electing not to get confrontational.

Nodding, but remaining tight-lipped, Tony crossed to the window, fists clenched behind his back. Staring vacantly down into the half-empty street his thoughts were wandering, back to the Zambezi Valley, to relive the horrors of the past few weeks.

Reg stretched out his legs and lit a cigarette. The paperwork would have to wait.

Massacre

The speed with which the dawn stole through the stillness of the Zambezi Valley was captured by Tony in one of those breathtaking moments that made life so worth living. Cautiously he raised himself on one elbow, still in his sleeping bag. It was 05.30 and Rifleman Wells – Foxy as he was appropriately known – had the 04.00 to 06.00 watch. Nothing stirred, least of all Wells who snored rhythmically, his head covered with his ground sheet.

Scanning the bush for any movement or unfamiliar colouring Tony sat up slowly, positioning his rifle across his lap. Catching a whiff of himself in the warm morning air he shuddered. Sleeping in the same kit for five days on the trot was something he would never get used to. Casting an eye over the three sleeping individuals who made up the rest of his section, he chuckled inwardly as he stretched to pick up a sizeable lump of elephant dung. Aiming at the covered protrusion that was Wells' head, he let fly with the dry, loosely packed missile. It disintegrated on impact, but to no avail. It was incredible, he thought, the stupid bloody things one got up to when in uniform.

Wells stuck his head out at 06.05, peering straight into his corporal's unshaven, unsmiling face.

'Morning, Corp,' he grinned sheepishly, blinking down at his watch. 'Not asleep, just resting my eyes.'

Tony nodded and whispered back, 'Now that they are so well rested keep them peeled while I slip off behind those bushes.' Half an hour longer and he knew that the heat and flies would be enough to make him laugh off this essential part of one's toiletry for yet another day.

As Tony made his way back through the foliage of their night ambush position, Wells placed a steaming mug of coffee next to his bed roll, promptly adding a healthy slug of brandy from a plastic shampoo bottle. Tony shrugged. If you can't beat them, join them, he thought.

'Sorry about guard duty, Corp, I'll watch it in future.'

'Good, you've made my day,' Tony said, suppressing a smile. He had resigned himself to the fact that after six weeks nothing was likely to change the ways of this scrawny, hard-arsed ex-mercenary. 'Get those other two wankers up Foxy, we move out in ten,' he ordered as he squatted next to the radio to report in after their radio silence during the hours of darkness.

The patrol had not been on the move for more than five minutes when a muffled boom rumbled across the valley.

'Landmine!' Wells declared.

Unclipping the handset from his webbing, Tony nodded. 'Either that or the gooks are into bloody artillery now.'

'Zero-One, we heard what sounded like a Lima Mamma in the direction of the old tsetse control road, about seven kilometres from this location. Copied so far? Over.'

'Roger so far.'

'Ask Sunray what's going on. Understood this area closed to civilian traffic and no other military presence in our sector. Over.'

'Copied, Alpha. Wait one.'

The men spread out in some semblance of all-round defence and lit cigarettes while they waited for news from their platoon commander, Lieutenant Anderson. Sitting in the shade of a thorn bush, Wells dug a square-sided hole in the dry earth with his bayonet. He then began his search for scorpions, of which there was an unhealthy abundance in the area, turning over loose rocks and dry vegetation. He had captured a couple of lizards the day before and they had fought to the death in one of his man-made arenas. He was curious to see whether scorpions would also kill one another, if confined and tormented with the tip of a cigarette.

On hearing his call sign Tony scanned the bush once more before turning up the volume.

'Alpha, Sunray confirms no vehicles in your area. If it was a Lima Mamma it was possibly detonated by game. What about rifle fire? Over.'

Wells clicked his fingers urgently to get his corporal's attention, he was nodding affirmatively.

'Negative, the road's too far for shots to have carried. Over.'

'Copied Alpha. Sunray says check it out anyway.'

'Roger. Out.'

'I tell you I heard something, you bloody know-all,' Wells muttered indignantly under his breath as he smashed a rock down on the luckless scorpion in his tiny arena; there being no time to unearth a challenger.

Having found a game trail that headed in the general direction of the old road, the four rugged individuals, in combat shorts, cutaway camouflage t-shirts and wearing their face veils as sweatbands, made good time. The path took the patrol past several small villages in overgrown clearings. Occasional wisps of smoke spiralled up between the dilapidated huts, to which the inhabitants had only recently returned. Many more locals were even now making their way back to the homes of their ancestral spirits. They trekked through the inhospitable tsetse-infested forests, carrying their sparse belongings in bundles on their heads, the odd chicken dangling unceremoniously upside down on thongs at their side as they drove their scrawny goats before them. They were poor people but at least they were free – free from the confines of the Protected Villages into which they had been herded *en masse* like cattle years before.

Closing the gap between him and his corporal, Wells asked, 'Hey Corp, how come we're letting these bloody oxygen thieves out of the PVs?'

Shaking his head at Wells' sick humour Tony explained, without looking back, 'Officially the Protected Villages have served their purpose. Impounding the locals in those fortified kraal complexes meant we denied the terrs access to food and information, and perhaps even more importantly, beer and women. As a result the gooks have given up and are all heading back to the good life in Mozambique.'

'Crap!' Wells spat. 'Give it to me straight, man.'

'The truth, unofficially my friend, is that the gooks have overrun the Tribal Trust Lands. The PVs have been infiltrated to the point where it's pointless continuing with an expensive, and now futile, exercise.'

'Jesus, no shit! What the fuck happens now?' Wells asked in all seriousness, disregarding the need for tactical distance and falling into step at his corporal's side.

'We're now tasked with containing the so-called guerrilla fighters in the very rural districts we tried so hard to deny them. The trick now is to keep them out of the white farming areas and urban centres – *at all cost.*'

'Fuck, now I've heard it all!' exclaimed the ex-Congo mercenary as he dropped back into file. Tony was about to turn and reprimand Wells again for carrying his rifle like a duck hunter, cradled in the crook of his arm, but then thought better of it. Wells had more contact experience than the rest of them put together. The only thing preventing him from joining the regular army was his inability to pass the aptitude test.

As they closed in on their destination Tony noted that more and more of the recently re-occupied kraals had hastily been abandoned. The uneasy feeling he was experiencing was not helped by the eerie throb of invisible drums, which had started up earlier that morning out of nowhere, their tempo increasing as the day progressed.

Dennis Smith, the hefty scrum-half who carried the section's main firepower, the lethal if cumbersome MAG machine-gun, sidled up to Tony when he stopped to check the map. 'Corp, do you think it was that explosion that scared the locals off?'

'It'd take more than a bloody landmine to scare the shit out of the whole fucking population,' Wells volunteered on his corporal's behalf.

Returning his attention to Dennis, whose shirt was encrusted with white salt patches, Tony offered, 'Here, let me relieve you of that bloody thing for a while.'

Dennis gratefully handed over the heavy machine-gun, accepting Tony's rifle in exchange.

'Thanks, Corp, just for a couple of kilometres. Much appreciated.'

'Hey Corp, buzzards.' Wells pointed to the sky at a spot about a kilometre ahead where scores of sandy-coloured vultures circled effortlessly on enormous wings.

Tony motioned Wells on in the direction of the birds, bringing up the rear with the MAG. Once on the move Tony frequently turned to check their back trail – with sweat evaporating before it had a chance to bead on their bodies it was easy to become preoccupied with thirst and the need to conserve precious water. He got his first warning that something was amiss when Wells pulled up short in his tracks at the head of the patrol. Immediately going to ground he watched as the plucky little ex-mercenary dropped to one knee, bringing his rifle smoothly up to his shoulder. The next moment Rifleman Don O'Connor, the fourth and youngest member of the patrol, took a few faltering steps backwards down the narrow path. It was all the prompting Tony needed. On his feet once more he could just make out the conical thatched roofs of the huts through the thorn trees beyond Wells' position. 'Dennis, let's go,' he ordered, wrapping the MAG sling around his forearm and starting forward at a brisk awkward trot, the machine-gun bouncing against his right hip.

With adrenalin flowing and their hearts pounding the two big men broke cover to the left of where Wells still knelt, exposed but vigilant, at the edge of the clearing surrounding the village. It was here too that they checked their advance, taken aback by the sheer number of the huge scavengers their charge had put to flight. Dozens of vultures were now bounding away between the mud huts in ungainly hops, beating the air in a frantic bid to launch their engorged bodies. The sky darkened as the birds slowly gained altitude, to begin their patient vigil high above the carnage.

There were some twenty huts in the kraal and the compound was strewn with the already bloating remains of what looked to be most of the population. Men, women and children lay where they had been shot. Several dead dogs, their legs jutting grotesquely from their mangy torsos, were interspersed with the bodies. The corpses were alive with blowflies, shining an iridescent green in the sunlight. The ground between the bodies was littered with cartridge cases from Soviet-made AK-47 assault rifles and RPD medium machine-guns. Chickens feasted unperturbed on maize cobs from upturned grain bins.

Wells had been right about the sound of rifle fire earlier. Tony realised he should have given him the benefit of the doubt. Now the best he could do was get an idea of numbers and the direction the terrorists were heading, and request stop groups be choppered in to cut the spoor.

Wells had a smirk on his grimy face as he finished the body count.

'What did you make it, Foxy?' Tony asked as Wells sauntered back through the village, upwind from the sickening smell of death.

'Twenty-seven won't be qualifying for any one-man one-bloody-vote, Corp.'

Ignoring Wells' insensitivity, Tony voiced his own misgivings, 'Reprisals are one thing but it makes no bloody sense for terrorists to destroy an entire village on which they depend so heavily for food and information.'

'Kaffirs will be kaffirs,' laughed Wells, scratching his crotch as he joined the extended line to sweep the area to pick up the terrorists' spoor.

It was Dennis who located the old road beyond the village and Wells who verified his findings, pointing out where the long grass on the overgrown track had recently been flattened by a heavy vehicle. 'Corp, a vehicle definitely passed this way earlier today.

We should find what's left of it down the drag,' Wells chuckled, making no effort to disguise his exuberance at the prospects of more carnage.

Tony watched the men move off down the track in staggered formation, each keeping a tactical distance from one another. Bringing up the rear with the MAG he might have been impressed, had it not been for the arms lashing out at the mopani flies – minute bees in fact – which thrived on the moisture from the corners of one's eyes and mouth. Even he found it impossible to ignore the torment.

The patrol located the Mercedes truck a few hundred metres down the overgrown road. Mine-proofing had reduced the damage but the explosion had rendered it immobile. Tony noted it was one of the new Unimogs, modified for the defence force and exclusive use of regular army units.

It was again Dennis who drew Tony's attention to the three sets of tracks that led away from the truck, off through the bush in the general direction of the village.

'What's up, Corp?' Wells asked, giving his corporal a nudge. 'You still with us sport?' he prompted as he followed Longdon's fixed gaze, now focused on the tracks.

'I'm fine,' Tony said before adding after a deliberate pause, 'Do you know what we have here? Another My Lai.'

'A what?' spat Wells, cuffing the perspiration from his brow.

'A My-Lai-type massacre,' Tony repeated for the benefit of all.

Wells shrugged and crossed to where Dennis was beckoning him aside and into cover.

'The US Marines wiped out an entire village back in the sixties, killing some five hundred Vietnamese civilians. They did it to avenge the death of their buddies,' Dennis explained.

Wells looked at the truck, then at the tracks, and then back down the road in the direction of the village. 'I see,' he nodded slowly, a smirk on his grimy unshaven face. 'Man I dig this fucking My Lai stuff.'

Moving his men off to higher ground, Tony established radio

33

communications directly with Company HQ, electing to bypass Lieutenant Anderson. Major Young was on a reconnaissance patrol and Captain Williams, the company 2IC, was called to the set.

Had the urgency not demanded it, Tony would not have bothered with Williams who he considered an incompetent apology of a man who exploited his rank to get back at the world. He had no doubt that Williams, a middle-aged non-achiever, was equally inept as a clerk on the Rhodesian railways as he was as an officer in the territorial forces.

The set crackled and Williams came on the air, annoyed at the audacity of a section leader bypassing his platoon chain-of-command. It was typical of Longdon; an arrogant troublemaker who thought the army should be run like a bloody public company.

Tony gave his position and the number of dead in shackle code before proceeding with his report. 'I say again, a massacre. The tracks from the military vehicle that detonated the mine lead directly to the village. Copied so far?'

'Roger. Any sign of the gooks?'

Williams was either not listening or had simply not picked up on the inference. Tony took a deep breath. It had to be said, 'Negative, this was a military operation.'

For once Williams was not slow on the uptake. 'Zero-One-Alpha are you out of your fucking mind! Return to base and await further orders. Copied? Over.'

'Copied,' Tony confirmed, following up with his own demands. 'I need to know who else is operating in our area and where they are now.'

'I'm giving the bloody orders, is that clear, *Corporal?*'

'Quite clear, *Captain*, and I repeat, the call sign of the other *so-called* friendly forces in this sector, before we move. I don't want a band of rogue Selous Scouts taking us out by mistake. Over.'

'Corporal, I'll see you court-martialled for insubordination. Now move out.'

'Go to hell. Get the information or I'll be laying a few charges of my own, incompetence for one,' Tony replied, casting caution to the wind.

Static followed his outburst and the rest of the patrol stared at their corporal in disbelief. The radio handset shook perceptibly in his clenched fist. Wells was the first to recover and ambled across to the sparse shade where his corporal was lighting a cigarette. 'Hey Corp, do you really think it was the walking armpits who took out that village, or were you just pulling Williams' chain?'

Exhaling with a deep sigh Tony addressed them all. 'There's only one regular army unit that travels out of convoy, operates in twos and threes, and is issued with captured communist weapons as standard equipment. Our illustrious Selous Scouts.'

When Company Headquarters eventually came back on the air, Sergeant Major Moore was on the set. 'Zero-One-Alpha, confirm still at your present location?'

'Affirmative.'

'Look Tony, Tac HQ say they have received no contact report and are unaware of any other troops in your sector. Police Special Branch will recover the vehicle and attend to the dead. Sorry, nothing more we can do from this end. Best you head back.'

'Will do, thanks Rodney.'

Tony trusted their CSM, if not Tactical Head Quarters back in Wankie. Cover-up or not, there was nothing to be gained from sitting it out any longer.

When Alpha section arrived back at their platoon base on the banks of the Zambezi river that evening Tony was not surprised to find himself under open arrest. He accepted Lieutenant Anderson's half-hearted reprimand, delivered on behalf of Captain Williams, with comparatively good grace. Once back at his makeshift open-sided bivvy, which formed part of the perimeter of their bush camp, he opened a tin of franks and beans and ate them cold. Grateful at least that returning patrols were excused guard duty he settled down to catch up on some sleep.

Awakened by the sound of footsteps, Tony opened his eyes to

find Anderson squatting next to his sleeping bag. Heavily dependent on his corporals, Anderson had no desire to alienate Longdon. 'Sorry to disturb you, Tony but I have just got off the air with Major Young. We now have some clarity on that incident at the village.'

Sitting up and peering out into the moonlight, Tony acknowledged, 'I'm all ears.'

'Apparently a belated sitrep *was* received confirming the contact and that a few locals were caught in the cross-fire. The delay was due to the patrol's radio being damaged in the explosion.'

'A few locals! We counted a couple of dozen. So, were the Selous Scouts responsible?'

'Young didn't say, but he did suggest that a good number of the dead you counted could well have been terrs.'

'That's bullshit. But what the hell, at least I'm off the hook.' After a moment's awkward silence he persisted, 'I have been vindicated for demanding information on other units in our area, haven't I?'

'I tried, Tony, but Captain Williams is still insisting you be brought up on orders for . . . insubordination. It's no consolation but this sector has been frozen and the whole Company has been ordered back to HQ. We are apparently being relieved by one of those new Auxiliary units. As we know these guys are mainly turned guerrillas, so I'm not sure what the top brass are playing at. Sorry I couldn't be more helpful, Williams can be . . . difficult at times.'

'Tell me about it,' Tony agreed, adding as he pulled his cap back over his eyes, 'Thanks for trying anyway.'

Ambush

The warning cough of a hippo reverberated across its watery domain. High above, a fish eagle screeched back in shrill defiance from a cloudless sky. Both calls echoed haughtily along the banks of the river, heralding another stifling day in the forbidding Zambezi Valley.

Tony stood alone among the tropical foliage on the banks of the powerful river, drawing an inner strength from the sweeping torrent. He could think of nothing more exhilarating than the solitude of the bush in the pre-light of dawn.

Detaching himself from the group of men loading the last of the platoon equipment onto the two dilapidated troop carriers, Wells dutifully made his way to the water's edge to summon his corporal. He wisely gave Tony warning of his approach, calling to him over the incessant roar of the Zambezi, 'Hi, Corp. That river sure is something else, hey man! Like it really fucking gets to you.'

His rifle resting comfortably in the crook of his arm, Tony turned to meet the diminutive individual who had given him no end of trouble these past six weeks. He acknowledged the greeting with a weary smile; it was pointless bearing a grudge with so few days to go before they were stood down. As it was, it had been he and not Wells who had ended up in the proverbial mire.

'Foxy, you're right, it grows on you. Africa untamed, one of the few rewards we reap from these crazy jaunts into the sticks.'

Making their way back through the tangled undergrowth to the man-made clearing that had served the platoon as a base camp, Wells scoffed, 'Look at them, one bloody terrorist with an RPG and boom up go the whole fucking lot! I tell you Corp, some guys never learn.'

Tony glanced across at the group of sunburnt men standing around at the back of the trucks, waiting for the order to embus. Wells was right – as territorial soldiers they did tend to possess a weird nonchalance, a kind of it-could-never-happen-to-me attitude.

'We shouldn't be too hard on them, Foxy. The wife and kids start playing on the mind towards the end of a camp. They know this move out of the valley is in the right direction, a step closer to home.'

'Sure Corp, but admit it man we've been dead lucky so far. The guys are getting a bit too bloody Harry casual now. Hell, look at you, man. How many times must I tell you about carrying that fucking rifle like you're on a turkey shoot?' He delighted at catching Tony in an unguarded moment.

Corporal Richard du Preez strode over to the two men as they entered the clearing. Richard was a big man with clean-cut features and a ready smile. He was also impressively turned out, in spite of his weeks in the bush. Wells by contrast had greasy unkempt hair and wore filthy combat shorts and a camouflage t-shirt that looked as if he'd slept in it for a month – which indeed he had.

'Ah, there you are Tony,' Richard greeted his colleague affably. 'My lot are just filling in the latrine pits. Lieutenant Anderson suggests we have Charlie section in the lead vehicle, with our Alpha and Bravo sections in the second truck. He'd prefer the stronger fire force at the rear in case of an ambush, but it's up to us.'

'So what's new,' Tony quipped. 'Either way is fine by me. The gooks can pick their target in this bloody terrain.'

'It's agreed then, we'll bring up the rear. Incidentally, Anderson will be travelling in the second vehicle with us,' Richard concluded, an uncharacteristic note of disdain in his voice.

'Sacrificing comfort for safety,' Tony said knowingly as he moved off to collect his kit. He looked back over his shoulder to catch a final glimpse of the vast brooding river as the trucks nosed their way through the bush to the dirt road which would take them on their winding journey up and out of the valley – out of the steaming, mosquito-infested jungle, domain of the majestic grey and maroon Zambezi parrot, back to the parched thorn scrub above the escarpment, home to the monarch of trees, the baobab.

Rhodesia was a land of contrasts and Rhodesians were another kind of people, Tony reflected. The vast majority of whites remained convinced that the black savagery that once was Africa still lurked threateningly beneath the mantle of civilisation. Obsessed with their heritage, they were prepared to let the younger generation die to preserve a way of life that was no longer defensible in the present day.

The whine of the aged engines fell a few decibels as the trucks lumbered out of the jungle and onto the relatively even surface of the dirt road. Now able to make himself heard in the back of the open truck, Wells turned to Tony. 'So, what do you think they are going to do to you, Corp?'

The mere fact that this brazen, diminutive ex-soldier of fortune professed to give a damn about anybody else would ordinarily have reduced Tony to raucous laughter, but as it happened he was receptive. For he was already contemplating his fate, not to mention that of the country if crimes like the massacre were allowed to continue with impunity.

'Hard to say. If it was up to Williams I have no doubt he would carry out his threat of a court martial. Major Young on the other hand probably knows there's a risk of this whole sordid mess going public if they press charges. Frankly I can't see them taking the chance.'

'Hope you're right, Corp. I was just getting used to you.'

'Thanks for the vote of confidence.' Tony grinned as he turned his attention back to the dense, menacingly close bush and instinctively checked his safety catch was off.

Having reached the initial gradients of the escarpment the front vehicle, with its lighter load, began to gain an appreciable lead.

'Thank fuck for that!' Wells exclaimed, rinsing his mouth out with a swig of tepid water and spitting the brownish liquid onto the protective layer of sand bags at his feet. 'Why the hell didn't the prick drop back earlier and spare us the fucking dust bath?'

'Not exactly an expedient on the driver's part, this old Bedford's so clapped it can't keep up,' Richard du Preez voiced from behind Wells on the bench seats that ran back-to-back down the centre of the vehicle.

Tony lowered his face veil and beat the powdery dust from his hair with his cap before thumbing the grit out of his eyes. From their position, a third of the way up the winding slopes of the escarpment, the panoramic view was breathtaking. The jungle of unbroken treetops, endlessly covering the valley floor, appeared to undulate and dance in the shimmering heat waves. Higher up the rocky escarpment the foliage thinned and the greens gave way to shades of brown, until at the summit the transformation from tropical jungle to dry scrubland was complete.

'That's quite something, the real bloody Africa,' Tony murmured half to himself.

'Screw the view, Corp, this heat's unreal. I'd blow my own fucking brains out if I had the energy,' Wells declared, lighting a cigarette without offering his packet around. Having wedged his rifle between his knees he deliberately left it pointing skywards to antagonise Lieutenant Anderson, who was making wild gesticulations from up front to indicate he wanted all weapons pointing outwards.

The gradients grew steeper and the rear vehicle fell even farther behind, until eventually the two trucks became separated. It was then, as the trailing Bedford rounded a hairpin bend to continue its painfully slow grind up the next slope, that all hell broke loose.

The hot dry air was suddenly alive with the incessant crack of bullets and the whine of ricochets as the guerrillas laid down a withering hail of fire into the back of the open vehicle. The old Bedford lurched and lumbered on, two, three, four seconds and then the ground beneath the right front wheel erupted in a sheet of orange flame, earth and dust. The blast from the landmine reverberated across the valley below like distant thunder.

Tony could only speculate on how the lead vehicle had missed the mine as, dazed and partially deaf, he hurled himself straight over the side of the vehicle, bellowing for the others to follow.

When help finally arrived it was in the form of Captain Williams from C Company HQ and an army doctor and his orderly, flown in by helicopter. 'Doc, over here,' Williams called out. 'It's Peterson the platoon signaller, he's in a bad way.'

'He's dead.'

'Good God man, he's still breathing.'

Major Fenton bent down and with his thumb unceremoniously closed Peterson's remaining eye. The young soldier sat motionless, bolt upright against the mopani tree where he had been propped. The flies quickly re-settled.

'Brain dead, Captain, he's lost half the side of his head.'

'But he has a pulse!' Williams exclaimed, aghast.

'Stranger things have happened. Now, who's in command and what in blazes have they done with the wounded?'

'Anderson, Lieutenant Anderson,' Williams called out cautiously, for this was his first casevac mission and there could still be terrorists lurking about. 'You there, where's your platoon commander?'

The young trooper glared at Williams. 'Have some respect for the dead, man. You fly in here shouting the odds but where the fuck were . . .'

'Easy, soldier,' interrupted Fenton placing a comforting arm around the boy's shoulders. 'What's your name, son?'

'Don, Rifleman Don O'Connor, Alpha section, Sir.'

'Don, I'm a doctor and we're here to help sort out this mess. Now, who's in charge and where have they put the injured?'

The trooper stared at the major, the man's greying hair and reassuring gaze quietening him. 'The Lieutenant's cleaning his rifle at the back of the truck, Sir.'

'He's doing what?' Williams asked in a more civil tone as they all set off around the side of the wrecked vehicle. Anderson sat with legs sprawled in the dirt, oblivious to all about him, feverishly rubbing the barrel of his FN with his jungle hat.

'He's been like that since he saw the side of Peterson's head . . . and realised what the stuff was splattered over his own face and rifle,' offered the trooper, tears streaking his dirt-smeared cheeks.

Williams turned, retched once and vomited violently at the side of the road.

'Where are the rest of the men?' Major Fenton prompted.

'Corporals du Preez and Longdon are up on that rise, where the gooks ambushed us from. They left Riflemen Wells and another chap with me to guard the ammo trailer, the lieutenant and the injured; they should both be around here somewhere. The wounded are over there in cover,' he added, pointing towards a dense clump of undergrowth. 'Sir, I want to go home now, please,' the young trooper concluded, shaking uncontrollably.

'Soon son,' the major replied as he turned to meet the tall burly corporal who had just burst out of the bush onto the road. Richard du Preez came loping towards the small group, rifle held at the ready just off his chest in powerful hands. The big Afrikaner headed straight for the medical officer, his shirt wet through with sweat and bare muscular limbs crisscrossed with bloody scratches from the bush.

'Less than an hour and a half, we did not expect you so soon Sir,' Richard greeted him tersely. 'Over here, Major, behind these rocks,' he directed. 'Three wounded and . . . three dead, if you include Peterson who we left back there rather than risk moving him at the time.' They carried on into the protection of a natural formation of boulders at the side of the road. 'The remaining six of us got off pretty lightly, considering. Although I think Lieutenant Anderson has lost it,' he concluded flatly.

'What of Charlie section in the other vehicle?' Williams interjected.

'They were way out up front, and just lucky I guess. Or the

mine was planted after they had passed, to target us at the rear. The gooks bomb-shelled as soon as we returned fire, so Tony ordered them to sit tight at the top of the escarpment rather than risk hitting another mine on the way back down.'

Fenton stepped over the bodies of the driver and the other luckless trooper, placed discreetly out of view of their buddies, and moved quickly down the line of the three wounded. The amount of blood was deceptive and he relied on their eyes and pallor to assess his priorities.

'Send my orderly over with the drips on the double, please, Corporal.'

Perspiring profusely in the noonday heat Fenton attended the wounded. It soon became evident that whoever had applied the field dressings had done a damned good job of stopping the bleeding in all but one case, a chest wound that still oozed and wheezed. Fenton emptied a second phial of morphine into the trooper's arm, smiled reassuringly into his glazed eyes and moved on to concentrate on the two he was still able to help.

Richard detailed the medical orderly and then walked over to where Williams was standing ashen faced, surveying the wrecked vehicle. He gratefully accepted a cigarette from his Company 2IC and took a long, deep drag.

'What in God's name ... ?' Williams asked, bemused by the carnage.

Richard did not answer. The road and overhanging branches were strewn with strips of rubber, pieces of truck body and personal kit, ample evidence of the devastating effect of the landmine. Instead he asked, 'May I have a couple of your fags, Sir? We've completely run out of smokes around here, and I reckon Tony could do with one as well.'

'Corporal Longdon ... wounded?'

'No, never better and a candidate for a citation if you ask me. After his court martial that is,' Richard added before he could check himself.

Williams flushed scarlet. The whole bloody world had apparently heard of his altercation with Longdon, and there was little doubt who they were siding with. 'Where is he now?' he demanded, getting a grip of himself.

'Up there, where the gooks ambushed us from,' Richard pointed to a spot above the road overlooking the killing ground. 'He patched up our guys; had to use all the morphine. Now he's doing what he can for a *piccanin*. It doesn't have a chance, but you know Longdon.'

'A what?'

'Black baby, a boy I think. We slotted four; two cadres, a walking wounded left to hold the fort and the *umfazi*. Unfortunately she was carrying a kid on her back.'

Williams sneered, 'Camp followers, if they choose to run with the gooks what do they expect?' With that he set off down the road to see for himself.

'Major, Sir.'

'Yes, Ronnie?' Fenton answered looking up from the trooper with the chest wound he had returned to. The face of his orderly was drawn, and Fenton knew this scene would be etched on his young mind forever.

'Sir, the other two wounded and the lieutenant are secure and the chopper pilot's anxious to get off the ground. If this chap's stable they would like us to get him aboard, pronto.'

The major shook his head. 'Let them go, son, this man's in no hurry,' looking down he gently drew the blanket up over the head of the trooper.

The helicopter screamed as it lifted off in a cloud of dust and leaves, and the major called out through cupped hands, 'Ronnie, let's get these other poor devils in the bags, the flies are becoming impossible.'

'They hit us from in there.' Richard indicated a particularly dense patch of undergrowth.

Williams whistled as he stared down the bank that fell away

sharply to the road below. 'Talk about point blank. Those bastards will pay for this.'

Ignoring Williams, Richard called out, 'Keep your finger off the trigger sport, we're coming in.'

Tony looked up, eyes red rimmed and expressionless, his lips set in a tight line.

Williams surveyed the small clearing. The lifeless body of a black woman, clad in rags, lay with arms folded serenely across a gaping hole in her chest. A naked, emaciated baby lay on a threadbare blanket at Longdon's knees. Tony's deft fingers continued to adjust the field dressing, stained dark rust brown, to cover what was left of the baby's buttocks and groin. The sex was indiscernible. Lashing out at the flies, he quickly folded the blanket once, twice, three times over the motionless form. Then, lifting up one of the mother's arms, he tucked the neat bundle up against what remained of her right breast. The child was dead.

Rising stiffly Tony gratefully accepted the cigarette Richard stuck between his lips. He ignored Williams completely.

Placing mother and child into the same body bag, Richard and Tony humped them down to the road. As they set their load down at the end of the row already formed by their four dead comrades, Wells finally materialised from the bush.

'Hey, where the hell did you find the fucking fags?'

'Here, smoke yourself to death,' Tony said, handing over his cigarette and again resolving to kick the habit. He hardly recognised his own voice, it sounded so hollow and distant. Probably not surprising he thought, considering all the screaming he, Richard, and Wells for that matter, had done while launching their counter attack.

Snatching the cigarette with indecent haste, Wells had only taken three quick drags before it dawned on him; there was another body bag on the road at their feet. 'What the hell is this,' he cursed, sending a hefty kick thudding into bag and contents. 'We should leave them for the bloody hyenas,' he snarled defiantly up at the two sweat-drenched corporals.

Tony balled his fist, but he had not bargained on the uncanny reflexes of the wily ex-mercenary. The barrel of Wells' FN was already pointing squarely at his crotch, the front sight touching his fly. Tony had seen that look in Wells' watery brown eyes on more than one occasion in the past few weeks. The dilated pupils supported his view that Wells was probably a bloody psychopath.

Richard moved quickly between the two men, pushing Wells' rifle barrel aside. 'We have work to do, gents. Let's get the other bodies down before the chopper returns.'

Wells' eyes cleared as quickly as they had glazed over. 'What are we waiting for?'

Having elected to be the last to leave, the sun was setting as Tony and Richard watched the helicopter drop down over the escarpment on its final run in. Richard turned for a final look at their wrecked truck as the chopper droned towards them. His jaw was set and his gut knotted as he reflected on the anguish of the loved ones left behind, their loss all the more tragic in the knowledge that, to all intents and purposes, the war had already been lost. Ironically it had been his own countrymen in South Africa who had sold Rhodesia down the river in the end, forcing Ian Smith's government to agree to hand the country over to so-called black moderates. He knew there was no such thing and that in the end no white control meant no law and order, it was as simple as that.

'I don't envy the chaplain his job, telling parents their sons have died after we've already practically surrendered,' Richard said as he made a final check on his kit.

Following his colleague out of cover and onto the road, Tony offered, 'I don't think I was ever that naïve as to believe we were actually fighting a war we could win. At best I saw it as an exercise to buy time for the politicians; only they managed to bungle every opportunity they had for an orderly hand-over of power. The final nail in our coffin is going to be this latest farce, whites sharing power with non-representative black leaders.'

'Tony, that's better than nothing. This one-man one-vote crap is a typically bloody British approach to democracy. Name one country in Africa where democracy has worked. Blacks are inherently incapable of running a country on their own. But what the hell, Rhodesia is getting its independence and that should appease the West.'

'Not for long, Richard. What Ian Smith has conceded can hardly be termed an acceptable settlement and I don't see it working; which means the likes of you and me . . .' But he was drowned out as the Alouette screamed in low overhead.

Shouldering their kit and reversing their weapons the two men exchanged weary smiles, bent double, and sprinted across to the waiting helicopter.

Insubordination

'Good evening Corporal, come on in,' Major Young invited.

'Good evening,' Tony acknowledged. 'Sir,' he added as an after-thought. It was even hotter in the ops tent than out in the stifling September night, but Tony was oblivious to the heat. The sedative Major Fenton had insisted on for the survivors of the ambush was having the desired effect.

Sitting in his canvas camp chair behind the folding table, Young toyed with his lighter. He was contemplating another cigar, his only vice, normally one a day. The shocking events of that after-noon had not made his task any easier. Yet discipline had to be maintained, particularly in an operational area. Weakening, he selected a cigar, clipped the end and lit it. Exhaling a cloud of blue smoke he said, 'Corporal, I'll come straight to the point. You not only disobeyed a lawful command yesterday, you were insubor-dinate. As things stand Captain Williams has every right to proffer charges.'

'Then I suggest he does just that. Will that be all . . . Major?' Tony quipped wearily, savouring a sense of euphoria from the medication while staring fixedly at his commanding officer.

Young shot back, 'Corporal, let me make it clear I have no intention of tolerating this bloody superior-than-thou attitude of yours either.'

It was Young who broke off eye contact, his shoulders sagging as he relented. He could not risk having his hand forced. Com-manding part-time soldiers, many of whom were headstrong executives in the real world, had never been easy. 'Sit down Tony . . . please.'

That's better, Tony thought, as he obliged.

'Tell me, what is it with you and Williams?' Young asked, inspecting the ash on his cigar.

Stifling a yawn Tony made an effort. 'For starters I can't help it if the army chooses to commission half-wits. Secondly, I know what it was we stumbled on out there but Williams refused even to listen. Sure, I lost my temper, but what do you expect after what we had seen at that village? Which reminds me, what is Brigade doing about the massacre?'

Young winced and took another long draw on his cigar. He needed to have a serious talk to Longdon about his offhand attitude towards officialdom. Unfortunately time was not on his side. Brigade had insisted on the withdrawal of all troops from the area and that he put an end to speculation about the incident at the village. He continued with his conciliatory approach. 'Tony, Major Fenton said your first aid probably saved a couple of lives today, while Corporal du Preez says that the immediate action you initiated undoubtedly saved others. Under the circumstances I'm prepared to prevail on Captain Williams to drop this issue.'

Tony had no difficulty in detecting Young's weakening resolve in spite of his own light-headedness. 'Major, it's been a long day, so let's get to the point, like you said. Unless I get some answers I'll goad Williams into carrying out his threat of a court martial, if it's the last bloody thing I do. Only, as a civilian, I will elect to conduct my defence in a civil court of law.'

Young moved forward and placed his elbows business-like on the table. He had taken about all he intended. 'Corporal . . . that could very well be the last *bloody* thing you do. I don't have to remind you of the Official Secrets Act we all signed, do I? Be warned, if you insist on pursuing this issue, either in or out of uniform, they are going to throw the book at you. And I wouldn't bank on a public trial.'

Tony stood up unsteadily to take his leave. What he needed right now was a bath, even if it was only going to amount to a bucket of cold water behind the bowser. 'Threats won't make me forget what I saw. Besides, the newspapers aren't that far from the truth as it is.'

'What papers? What truths?' Young demanded impatiently.

'I'm referring to overseas press reports, like the one that inferred the missionaries that keep getting bumped off are victims of our own forces, pseudo-terrorists.'

'Corporal, that's cheap propaganda and you know it,' Young sneered. 'Next you're going to tell me that you believe our chaps butchered those nuns at the Gokwe Mission Station and went on to execute twenty-odd pickers at the Melsetter Tea Estates.'

'Major, I don't profess to know what other outrages have or have not been committed, but we both know there is no love lost between the army and certain men of the cloth these days, many of whom openly support the liberation movements. We also know that the Selous Scouts regularly cross into Mozambique dressed as Frelimo soldiers or terrorists, depending on their mission. When they do they carry communist AK-47s and RPDs, like those used at the village yesterday.'

'All right Tony, sit down. I would now like to have my say.'

Slumping back into the chair Tony took a pack of cigarettes out of his top pocket, pausing barely long enough for Young to nod his consent before lighting up.

'I don't exactly know what to make of these events, but I don't believe for one minute that the situation has got out of hand to the extent you are suggesting. After Williams briefed me yesterday, and prompted by your Lieutenant Anderson, I had another go at Tac HQ. This time they confirmed there had been a contact. Eleven terrorists and sixteen civilians caught in the cross-fire.'

Tony scoffed, 'Even if I did believe it, how the bloody hell do you shoot sixteen civilians . . . *by accident?*'

'I know, it doesn't look good, but there's a war going on. That's it, Tony.'

'But . . .'

'No more buts, Corporal,' Young cut him short. 'Like the

colonel said, the matter is closed. Longdon, I mean it, or be it on your own head.'

Tony nodded as he got to his feet, a nauseating tiredness coming over him. Young also stood up, but before he could offer his hand Tony came briefly to attention, turned and stepped out into the night. Pausing a few paces from the tent flap he asked, 'Would I be correct in assuming Williams will be dropping the charges, Major?'

'Yes, Corporal,' Young replied resignedly.

Spear of the People

Turning back from the office window, Tony stared blankly across at Reg who had just broken his train of thought. 'Sorry, I can't seem to get the damn army out my mind.'

'I just asked if you would be applying for a deferment from this next call-up.'

'Yes, as a formality, but I don't hold out much hope. As we know there's a lot of speculation about a major offensive after the first rains. The authorities will be taking it seriously, what with this being the terrs' last opportunity to bring the country to its knees before one of the stooges of the Transitional Government is elected prime minister. That's when our troubles really begin.' Making his way back over to the coffee table, Tony offered, 'Cigarette?'

'Thanks,' Reg acknowledged, taking out his lighter. 'For my money I think the worst is over. Whatever one thinks of Bishop Muzorewa the fact remains that within six months the blacks will have the vote, and their so-called freedom, and the gooks won't have any reason to carry on the fight.'

Tony shook his head. 'Come now Reg, who's going to buy into this Zimbabwe/Rhodesia compromise lark? Real independence is not the token handing over of power to black puppets of a white regime.'

'If that's the case, how do you account for literally thousands of terrorists taking advantage of the pre-election amnesty?' Reg countered. 'We can't form these ex-terrs into Auxiliary units fast enough at the moment.'

'Reg, cast your mind back to when they started this Auxiliary business. The headlines heralded the move as one of the Transitional Government's boldest strategies or greatest follies. For the old Rhodesian Front cabinet to sanction what amounts to the formation of private armies is hard to swallow. That is, unless there is more to this radical change of heart than meets the eye?'

'Tony, there's nothing sinister about it,' Reg said reassuringly. 'There are just not enough jobs to absorb all the gooks now laying down their weapons, and to leave them drifting aimlessly around the TTLs or black townships is inviting trouble. What could be more logical than to train them to protect their own people? This way we keep them occupied as well as under our control.'

Tony made a face as he stubbed out a partially smoked cigarette. 'Reg, the locals call the Auxiliary units *Pfumo re Vahnu*, Spear of the People, because that's what they are, the people's militia, not the government's. At best they remain an unknown quantity, like a growth yet to be classified malignant or benign.'

'Tony, contrived or not, independence is just around the corner. Besides, you are the one who insists we shouldn't become like the South Africans, seeing a communist behind every bush.'

'Don't get me wrong, I think it's a marvellous idea to repatriate terrorists. But I can't help but ask where's the logic in re-arming them and sending them back into the bush.' Tony absently tapped another cigarette from the pack on the table, accepting a light from Reg. 'What's more as far as the terrs are concerned we are supposed to be on our last legs, which is not that far from the bloody truth. With ultimate victory in sight, why are thousands of them suddenly choosing to lay down their weapons and come meekly home – home to join the Auxiliaries?'

Reg fell silent. Besides having learnt the futility of arguing against his boss, he could not refute the logic.

Tony pressed the button on the intercom. 'Jenny, please get me Mr Squires on the line.'

'The attorney?' Reg enquired packing up his unfinished papers.

'Yes, maybe he can come up with a new slant for the Exemption Board.'

Kathleen

The summer moon was well above the horizon by the time the aged, pre-sanctions Mercedes drove up the tree-lined drive carpeted with purple jacaranda blossoms. Kathleen Longdon hurried across the patio to meet her husband as he came out of the garage, her short skirt and halter neck top accentuating her youthful figure. Her only adornment was a black velvet choker centred with a pink cameo. Vibrant auburn hair, styled with a gentle flip, brushed her shoulders.

Tony caught her around the waist as she flattened herself against him. 'Slow down girl,' he gasped, pulling back from her kiss to draw a breath.

'I like that! I'm ecstatic at having you home again and all you can say is, down girl.'

'I got home yesterday,' Tony reminded her with a gentle slap on her behind. He was relieved to see her looking relaxed, more like her old self again.

'How was your day?' Kathy asked dutifully, taking his briefcase and falling into step as they walked arm in arm up the path.

'Hellishly long and I'm starving. It's amazing, I get hungrier sitting behind a desk than I do trekking through the bush all day with a full pack.'

'Is that all you think of, your stomach?' Kathy chided, slipping her arm around his waist and squeezing his perceptibly firmer midriff.

Tony stopped, held his wife off at arm's length and looked her critically up and down. 'Which reminds me, how much weight have you lost in the last couple of months?'

Kathy shrugged. 'A few kilograms, I suppose. I don't always feel like preparing a proper meal for one, so I make do.'

Tony knew better, Kathy was far too industrious not to do something because it was too much trouble. The strain of the past weeks had clearly taken its toll.

'Now that you're back I'll soon be my chubby old self again,' she joked. 'Jenny phoned to say you would be popping into the hospital on the way home. How is Mac?'

'Coming along,' he replied, flopping down on the nearest patio lounger without elaborating. Kathy let it go. She knew the last thing he needed now was for her to start on again about the ever-increasing risks in the operational area.

'Are you going to stand there staring at me all night?' he asked, waving playfully in her face.

'I'm sorry. I'll get the drinks and you can unwind a bit before dinner.'

Kathy returned a few minutes later with two glasses of brandy and coke, brimming with ice. Settling herself on his lap she sipped her drink while absently running her fingers through his hair, now curling up at the nape of his neck. He had been twiddling again she noted, wondering if he realised just how much stress she too had been under these past months.

'I know how you feel,' Tony said with uncanny insight. Taking her hand he kissed her palm, 'When we're apart the world seems a pretty lonely place and we take strain, hey kid?'

Kathy's eyes misted over, those few words were worth a thousand unspoken *I love you*'s. While reluctant to dispel the magic of the moment, something was bothering her. 'Love, Jenny sounded upset when she called to let me know you would be late. She sounded, well, almost tearful?'

Tony did not answer immediately. There were all too few of these carefree moments lately and this was not a good time to broach the question of his next call-up. 'Maybe I upset her. You know what I'm like when I first get back. I'm a little short with everyone and my language is atrocious . . . fuck this, fuck that.'

'It's unlike Jenny, she's normally so composed, so businesslike,' she persisted.

'Maybe she has a thing for Mac or something. Who knows,' he said irritably, having unwittingly reminded himself of his own recent infidelity. 'I'm sorry, let me have a quick dip and chill out a bit.' He eased her off his lap. 'Water is the one thing you can't get enough of in the bush,' he continued with the small talk while he stripped off. His buttocks flashed white in stark contrast to the deep tan of the rest of his body as he sprinted across the lawn and plunged into the inviting blue depths of the pool.

Still chuckling at the spectacle as she folded his clothes over her arm, Kathy picked up his shoes and briefcase and went indoors. She needed to check with Maria to see just how long dinner was going to be.

Tony sank slowly to the bottom of the pool, drifting down through the shimmering beams of the underwater lights. He held his breath for as long as he could, savouring the balmy, tepid water. He felt himself starting to relax, memories of his drunken one-night-stand in Wankie soothed away by the blissful sensation of weightlessness.

He was just sinking to the bottom of the pool again when the serenity of his underwater world was shattered and Kathy glided gracefully down to join him. Laughing and touching, they eventually swam to the side and climbed naked out of the pool. They made love in the moonlight on the cool, lush Kikuyu grass.

'Hey, what happened to dinner?' Tony asked rolling over onto his side.

'So much for basking in the afterglow,' Kathy chided. 'Dinner is under control. I turned everything down and let Maria go. She can do the washing up in the morning. Now, tell me that you love me, that you will always love me,' she pouted as she caressed the hairs on his chest.

'You know I do, silly,' he assured her, giving her a long lingering kiss, but he could feel her tension.

Towelling themselves down they made their way silently back

to the patio. Tony noted the clean glasses and ice bucket on the table. As he straddled one of the loungers and reached to pour the drinks, the reason for Kathy's mood became obvious. The familiar *On Government Service* buff envelope was in the middle of the table. With hindsight he should have put the call-up papers in his briefcase, not in his jacket pocket. Berating himself for actually feeling relieved that this was all that was bothering Kathy, he picked up the envelope and tapped it self-consciously on the arm of his chair.

'I'm sorry sweetheart, really I am. I would have got round to telling you. Only this evening just didn't seem like the right time. Besides, I have a good chance of deferment as Reg has already been called up for part of the same period. Someone has to hold the fort,' he concluded, with an optimism he did not feel.

Kathy just sat and stared back at him.

Snapping his fingers, he encouraged, 'Come on girl, stop worrying about something that might never happen.'

Her towel wrapped around her, Kathy sank down onto his lap. Resting her head against his chest she began rocking slowly from side to side. She opened her mouth but no words came, tears flowed silently down her cheeks.

'It's no good', she sniffed eventually, 'we'll never get away from these army commitments. It's always the same. You tell me I have nothing to worry about, that it will all come right in the end, and like a gullible fool I believe you. I'm certain that in your heart of hearts you too must know it's hopeless. How long must I endure these months of waiting, of not knowing, of telling myself that no news is good news? I try, my darling. I really try to be strong, but I honestly don't know how much more of this I can . . .'

Squeezing her even closer, Tony held her while she brought her sobbing under control.

After a while she pushed herself up in his lap, took a deep wracking breath and blurted out, 'I'm not stupid you know. Those four men who died in that last landmine incident a few days before you got out were from your unit. You even mentioned one of them by name in a letter not three weeks ago – Dennis Smith. His wife had just had a baby. Now he's dead, Tony, *dead!* You . . . you either pull the wool over my eyes or simply say nothing, pretending these things aren't happening. God forbid, it could have been you. It might sound pathetic but you are really all I have left since Mum and Dad passed away, and I know the chances you take. Let's pack up and go. Leave the house if we can't sell it; just get out before this next call-up. Before it's too late.'

Normally never at a loss for words, Tony eased round Kathy to finish pouring the drinks. The truth was Kathy had become very dependent on him since the death of her parents, shortly after her eighteenth birthday. The driver of the other car had been charged with drunk driving but had jumped bail, which had not helped with closure. They were married just two months after the funeral. Handing Kathy her drink, he was surprised to see her swallow down half of the stiff brandy without batting an eyelid.

'Kathy, we can't leave Rhodesia without my getting army clearance, and you don't get that while in receipt of call-up papers. It's a vicious circle, as you know. Besides, I have a responsibility to the company and staff. And I suppose to the country as well, after all it's been good to us over the years.'

Kathy had heard it all before. Making no attempt to save her towel, she slipped off his lap. Hands on shapely hips she made one final attempt to get through to him.

'It's not just a question of responsibility, you're obsessed with your career. It comes before our life together, before the baby we keep putting off . . . before every damn thing. My feelings don't seem to count for anything any more.'

Tony stood up and pulled her to him. It was his only defence. Crushing her warm petite breasts to his naked chest he could feel himself coming erect in spite of her anger.

'Tony behave! What am I going to do with you?'

Staring into her entrancing green eyes, now bright with tears but bravely smiling back at him, Tony tormented himself with the notion that now might be as good a time as any to unburden his conscience. Instead he said, 'Kathy please, I really need your support at the moment.'

Kathy knew what that simple *please* had cost him; he was not one to admit to needing anything, from anybody. Wrapping her towel back around her while Tony poured himself another brandy, she conceded, 'I'll try and be strong my darling, but if you aren't deferred I don't think I'll be able to stand losing you to the army again, not so soon, not knowing what I do now.'

'You'll see, in a couple of weeks this will all be water under the bridge. I will have my deferment and we can take it from there.'

Kathy was not listening. 'Is all this really worth it?' She gestured with a sweep of a slender arm, taking in the pool, the vast expanse of manicured lawn and thick hibiscus hedge, the servants' quarters and double garage, the tennis court, the tall shade trees and standard rose bushes; all typical of Rhodesian suburbia. 'All this is quite meaningless with no one to share it with, should anything happen to you.' An involuntary shudder went through her as she continued, 'If you end up in a wheelchair or disfigured, I know you will never be able to forgive yourself; and all for what?'

'Kathy all this, as you put it, is everything we have worked for. What we have achieved in the last seven years is more than most people dream of in a lifetime.'

Kathy took a sip of his drink and made one last stand. 'Darling, admit it, this is not the same Rhodesia we once knew and loved. Things have changed and nobody, not even you or that left wing NUF lot you've got involved with, can do a damned thing about it at this late stage. What about the family we were going to start? First it was your career, then the political uncertainty and now this senseless, endless, bloody war.'

Tony raised his hands in mock surrender. 'I will give the question of a move down south serious consideration, I promise.'

'Thank you,' Kathy accepted graciously, knowing full well what the outcome would be no matter how well-founded his intentions.

'Good. First dinner, then to bed,' he grinned slapping her rump affectionately through the damp towel. 'I've got plans for you,' he chuckled.

'Oh, you must be joking. Not again, you couldn't possibly.'

Stepping back, Tony let his towel fall to the ground. 'Want a bet?'

Exemption Board

Peter Squires slipped the brief into his attaché case and tapped on the interconnecting door to the suite of the ageing senior partner, George Phillips.

'Come in. Peter, thank you for sparing me a few minutes of your time, I simply wish to stress the importance of your getting young Longdon deferred from his commitment. For a month at least,' Phillips concluded, addressing his young colleague over the top of gold-rimmed glasses.

'Naturally I will do my best, George. Although I must confess that until this morning I had no idea you had a personal interest in the man.' Still standing before the huge desk, which was cluttered with law books and pending briefs in tattered buff folders, Squires noted the mounting backlog of work with an obvious look of concern.

Phillips dismissed the chaotic state of his desk with a wave of his hand. 'Actually this matter is of a somewhat delicate nature.'

Squires drew up one of the well-worn, red-leather visitors' chairs; it was apparent his partner intended more than just a few words of encouragement.

'My association with Mr Longdon extends only to a shared political affiliation . . . outside of the Rhodesian Front, naturally. That is to say, outside of Ian Smith's team and his cohorts in their newly formed Transitional Government. I also share with others a high regard for this young man's ability as a negotiator and, when it suits him, diplomat.'

Aiming his spectacle case at Squires, Phillips continued, 'Recently surreptitious negotiations between elements of the external wing of the African National Council and certain Rhodesian moderates, both black and white, reached finality. Matters of far-reaching national significance were agreed upon, and Mr Joshua Nkomo and his executive in exile in Zambia are now preparing the final draft of a proposed peace pact. Embracing as it does a number of meaningful concessions, this document could well form the foundation of an all-party summit conference. I do not have to elaborate on just how desperately Rhodesia . . . Zimbabwe/Rhodesia, whatever we are supposed to call the country now, needs a workable solution to the present impasse.'

Squires fidgeted as he reflected with growing uncertainty on what he had assumed to be a straightforward assignment. 'I appreciate the importance of finding common political ground in our country George, but what does Mr Longdon remaining at large, so to speak, have to do with national politics?'

Phillips spent a good minute lighting up one of half a dozen exotic pipes dotted haphazardly around the desk. He puffed away thoughtfully for even longer before continuing. 'I am led to believe that Longdon's services will be required early in November. Mr Nkomo's proposals will be secreted into the country by one of his lieutenants. The same one who so ably reported back to executives of commerce and industry, and other white liberal elements in Rhodesia, after the all party Geneva conference in 1976. It was at one of these report-back meetings that an accord was struck up between him and Longdon. As this prominent Nationalist risks detention or worse if apprehended in Rhodesia, he has naturally expressed a desire to make the delivery to someone he knows and trusts . . . our Mr Longdon.'

Squires stood and smoothed his trousers. 'Well, Longdon really has got himself involved, hasn't he?'

'Yes indeed, Mr Squires . . .' Phillips again paused for effect, 'and had more people shared those convictions and become involved, our country might have been spared economic suicide and political chaos.'

Squires glanced sideways at his client as they drove back down Abercorn Street. It was a short drive from the District Commissioner's offices in the High Court Building to Longdon's offices, but long enough for him to become extremely uncomfortable at the silence. As they pulled up in front of the building he offered, 'I'm sorry, I bungled it. You were quite right back there, you probably would have been better off going it alone.'

'Please, no apologies. I over-reacted. It was *fait accompli* before you even presented our case. Frankly I don't know why they even bothered with the bloody pretence. As for their argument that without security we wouldn't have an economy to worry about, they will wake up too late to discover that without an economy you can't sustain a bloody army either.' He flicked his half smoked cigarette into the gutter as he got out of the car.

Tony let the telephone ring several times before snatching up the receiver. 'Longdon.'

'*Hoe gaan dit*, Tony? Did you get off?'

'Oh, it's you Richard. I'm fine thanks, and no, it was a complete waste of bloody time. Looks like I'll be joining you and the boys next week after all. I suggest you bring a couple of extra cartons of smokes, just in case we hit another bloody landmine.'

'Don't joke *Meneer*,' Richard replied. 'Seriously, it will be great having you along. I don't think I could face another stint with Williams without some moral support. By the way, I have a message for you. Remember I told you my brother runs the sawmill at Kamativi? Well your girlfriend contacted him.' There was an awkward silence. 'Vicky, that pretty young blonde thing we met at the Baobab Hotel during our one and only spell of R&R?' Richard made light of Tony's apparent discomfort.

Tony remembered, even though it was a night best forgotten; until that day he had not known what it was like to have a conscience. 'Richard, I'm sorry your brother has got involved. We did not even exchange last names, so I can't imagine how she made the connection or why she would even want to.'

63

Richard was not to be put off. 'Perhaps I can shed some light on that. At one point during the evening, when you were off getting drinks or taking a leak, Victoria started asking questions. She was mainly interest in you, but I might have mentioned that we du Preez's settled in Wankie on moving up to Rhodesia from South Africa when we were kids, and that my brother still worked there.' Still reflecting on that memorable night at the Baobab Hotel, Richard went on, 'Anyway the message was, please contact her if you can but she will understand if you can't. She also sends her love. Lucky man,' he chuckled.

Ignoring Richard's mirth Tony said, 'Just give me her number and I'll think about it.'

'She never left one, but I can make some enquiries.'

'Thanks all the same but it is best left. I feel bad enough about that night as it is,' adding in his defence, 'I made no secret of the fact that I was married. Look, I have a couple of urgent calls to make; you can bend my ear all you like at the barracks next week. Don't forget, extra fags.' He rang off. Staring thoughtfully at the receiver he lit a cigarette.

It had been Victoria's engaging blue eyes, dimpled cheeks and youthful exuberance, enhanced by a dozen beers, which had attracted him. Her fresh girlish smell still haunted him. The fact that she had so willingly given herself to him, and that he had been powerless to resist, had left him with a nagging feeling that there had been more to the chemistry of that fleeting one night stand than he was prepared to concede. He knew he had to get her out of his mind or it would only be a matter of time before Kathy sensed his torment.

Stubbing out his cigarette, he made a note to advise Head Office of the outcome of his application for deferment. He then called Pat O'Neil, secretary of the National Unifying Force, to tell him he would not be able to keep his rendezvous with Mr Nkomo's courier, as well as to enquire about progress with the local press in connection with his report on the village massacre.

'Pat, what do you mean they can't touch it?'

'Tony, like I said they got very excited, even verified our statistics on black civilian casualties, but came back to say there was no way round the censors. Having had another look at those numbers myself, it might be just as well. My point being that as a responsible organisation we are looking to rock the boat, not panic the entire country.'

'Damn them,' Tony cursed after O'Neil had finished reading out the stats the NUF had compiled in support of his report. 'They've circumvented censorship before. It's their job to ferret out the truth in the national interest.'

'Tony, the editor is a personal friend of mine and he said that even without a state of emergency, martial law or censorship, they would need hard facts before attempting to expose anything this volatile. He also intimated that, if and when you can substantiate your claims, the story would still need to be leaked to the international press first. Apparently, providing the story breaks overseas the local boys can find ways around the sensors to report on a report.'

Once he had hung up, Tony lit a fresh cigarette and studied the figures he had jotted down. They spoke volumes to anyone prepared to read between the lines. Of the twenty thousand-odd people killed in the war so far, only half, ten thousand, were actually terrorists. The non-terrorist numbers comprised security force losses of just under a thousand, the remaining nine thousand being *civilians*. Of these only three thousand five hundred blacks and five hundred whites were reported murdered by terrorists or killed in landmine explosions. The rest, a staggering *five thousand* people, all black, had been accounted for by the security forces as collaborators, terrorist recruits or simply killed in cross-fire. Tony's blood ran cold as he ringed the figure 5000. And these statistics had been taken from official government communiqués; God alone knew what the actual numbers were.

Nyoni

Jodie awoke as if from a dream, damp with perspiration. As she stared up through the gloom at the poles supporting the thatched roof of the hut, the events of the previous evening slowly came back to her. The empty beer bottles, the steadying hand beneath her chin, her inebriated father and then the trek through the night, the final leg cradled in powerful arms. It all seemed quite unreal.

In spite of the relative coolness of the hut's interior Jodie could see from the beams of sunlight filtering through the cracks in the poles of the crude door that the day was well advanced. Apart from the pungent odour of wood smoke in the hut there was another, less distinctive smell, of wild animals Jodie fancied, before convincing herself she knew better. Absently squeezing the bed covering, a habit from her childhood, the horrifying truth dawned on her. She was lying beneath a *kaross* of black-backed jackal hides – the fox-like creatures she had seen on game drives. A muffled scream left her lips as she cast the hairy blanket aside and scrambled into the centre of the smooth, dung-plastered floor. Standing in the middle of the hut, trying to control her trembling, she was far from over her ordeal, let alone the shock of her own nakedness, when the narrow door creaked and swung slowly inwards.

A young African woman stepped cautiously through the low entrance. Straightening up she revealed her own nakedness save for a leather apron adorned with beads, barely large enough to cover her pubic area. She carried Jodie's summer dress, freshly washed, over her arm.

Jodie's visitor was not tall but nicely proportioned. Her skin was the hue of polished chestnuts and she had the whitest teeth

66

and the most insincere smile Jodie had ever seen. The girl's only other distinguishing features in the half light were her breasts, pear-shaped, unlike the much heavier, more rounded versions of the Zulu maidens Jodie had encountered back at the hotel. Conscious of the younger girl's eyes on her own nakedness, Jodie reached for her dress.

'Nyoni,' the girl intoned, offering up the skimpy garment with both hands but with knees only slightly bent in a half-hearted gesture of respect.

'Jodie Knight, pleased to meet you,' Jodie replied, hastily slipping the dress over her head. 'What about my underwear and sandals?' she asked. She also wanted to know where she was and why what's-his-name was not on hand to allay her fears on awakening in such primitive surroundings, on a grass mat of all things. But all that could wait until she was outside in the fresh air, she decided.

In Jodie's haste to vacate her claustrophobic surroundings she banged her forehead on the low wooden crossbeam of the door. Then, coming up too early, she slammed the back of her neck into the tightly packed thatch of the overhanging roof. Ruffled as well as flustered, she had no sooner got clear of the hut than she found herself hopping from one foot to the other in a most undignified fashion, the sun-baked clay of the compound scorching the delicate soles of her feet.

Taking her hand, Nyoni led her across the compound to the inviting shade of a large mango tree in the centre. The fact that her guide had set out to cross the compound, instead of simply drawing her back into the protective shade beneath the eaves of the hut, did not register in Jodie's present state of mind. Excusing herself with another half-hearted bow and dutiful smile, Nyoni left the white girl propped up against the base of the mango tree, massaging first one then the other of her blistered insteps.

Alone beneath the tree in the centre of the compound, Jodie took a deep breath as she surveyed the half-circle of rustic mud huts in the eerie stillness. This was nothing like the rambling homestead of Robert Redford's 'Out of Africa' fame she had somehow imagined, even dared to hope for! The small kraal complex was completely encircled by an impenetrable jungle of overgrown sisal. The menacing thorn-tipped plants, with three-metre long, thick, fibrous leaves rosetting out from their core, dwarfed the huts, creating the illusion of a flat, animated world with no horizon. The only signs of life were a dozen or so chickens scratching in the dust. Apart from the green of the sisal, the rest of her new world was a kaleidoscope of browns. The hard earth of the compound was a reddish brown, the walls of the huts were dark mud brown and the thatched roofs had taken on a weathered, golden-brown hue. Even the hens were a speckled orange, red and brown.

Jodie was still contemplating her surroundings when her man materialised through the dense wall of vegetation on the opposite side of the clearing. Apart from *veldskoen* boots he was clad only in a faded pair of camouflage shorts; his half-naked body glistened with sweat. The hilt of a large bush knife protruded from its sheath on his belt and he carried an AK-47 assault rifle casually in his left hand. Tarzan, she thought, suppressing a nervous laugh, only to correct her initial impression on registering the gun.

Having come up with a start on seeing her by the tree, the Rhodesian now made his way slowly towards her. Fascinated by the oil-like effect of the sweat on his powerful physique, Jodie was still marvelling at how anybody could emerge unscathed from a jungle of cactus-like plants, half naked, when he stopped a few paces from her. A cry caught in her throat as she noticed the vivid purple burns. Unable to help herself, Jodie's eyes followed the raised scar tissue down over the one half of his chest to his waist, where it disappeared into the top of his shorts.

'Good morning, or should I say good afternoon?' he said curtly. 'The burns are from Frantam, a type of napalm used in bombs dropped by the Rhodesian Air Force. I'm sorry if the sight offends you.'

Dropping her hand from her mouth and lifting her gaze, yet another shock awaited Jodie. The beard was gone. Clean-shaven, his strong jaw looked deathly pale; it was also strangely angular, the chin slightly out of line with the rest of his face. The cause of the disfigurement became apparent when he deliberately turned his head to one side for her benefit. A jagged white scar ran from the corner of his left eye down over a perceptible break in the lower jaw, before tapering off just short of the jugular vein in his neck. His expression was cold and detached.

This was certainly not the greeting Jodie had expected, the man's strange aloofness being even more disconcerting than the scars. She could understand him wanting her to be under no illusions about his disfigurement, but why the hostile attitude, particularly after tenderly carrying her for miles the night before?

'It is I who should apologise. I'm not normally squeamish; it just came as a bit of a shock,' she said, breaking the uneasy silence and wriggling her still painful toes in the dust. 'Besides, it's what a person is on the inside that really counts,' she added, immediately berating herself for such a lame remark. As he slowly turned his head back in her direction she swallowed hard – his gaze was vacant, as if looking right through her. She cautiously waved a hand in front his face. 'Was my coming here so dreadfully wrong?' she asked in a further attempt at regaining his attention.

The Rhodesian's only response was to wordlessly flip his rifle up into the high port and cock his head, as if registering some distant sound.

Conscious of the sweat trickling down the insides of her arms, Jodie realised her plight went beyond the merciless temperature. Peering anxiously about her, in the hope of catching sight of the black girl, she persisted. 'I only wanted an opportunity to thank you for freeing me from that vicious bramble bush. And to try and better understand this nomadic existence of yours.' In spite of apparently talking to herself she continued to play for time. 'It might help if I knew your name?' But again to no avail. She was on the verge of doing an about-turn and heading for her hut, even if it meant risking a bullet in the back, when the man blinked in rapid succession.

69

'*Thank goodness*,' she sighed. 'You were about to tell me your name,' she hastened lest he relapse.

'Tony.'

'Anthony,' she teased without thinking.

'Tony,' he insisted, staring at her intently to retain focus.

'Tony who?' she asked more tactfully.

'Just Tony,' he repeated flatly, shaking his head as one might after a swim.

Smiling uncertainly, Jodie could not help wondering what had become of the man with the gentle healing touch, whose quiet assertiveness had given her such confidence in her hour of need.

'I see. Perhaps once we are better acquainted?' she suggested, clasping her hands behind her back to keep from fidgeting and to prevent the rivulets of sweat from running down the inside of her arms.

'It's not a question of trust but of . . . knowing who one actually is,' he said hesitantly, now looking more confused than angry. 'It was a mistake bringing you here, but we are going to have to make the best of it until first light tomorrow, when it will be cool enough to start back.' He looked away, her striking green eyes playing havoc with his subconscious as vague memories stirred deep within. Over the years such vagaries had come to haunt him, to threaten his very sanity.

Dumbfounded, Jodie shrugged in a gesture of helplessness. It seemed incredible that anyone would not know who they were. It was then that Nyoni called out in a strange dialect from the door of the smallest of the five huts.

'Food is ready,' Tony echoed with an audible sigh of relief. Hobbling along after him it dawned on Jodie that he had not been coming to meet her after all, but was simply returning for lunch.

In response to the other woman's silent gestures Jodie followed Tony's lead and rinsed her hands in the enamel bowl on the stand just inside the hut. Seating herself gingerly on the remaining low wooden stool, she faced her hosts over an array of clay pots simmering next to the embers of the open hearth. As if it were not hot enough already she thought, staring down at the coals inches from her still bare feet. The last thing she wanted right now was food, but she realised she should eat, her last meal being a tuna salad at lunch the previous day. Her knees jutted out awkwardly on the ridiculously low stool, and she was forced to tuck her short dress between her legs to retain some semblance of modesty in the absence of her underwear.

Nyoni ladled a steaming helping of boiled chicken pieces into Jodie's bowl, followed by a watery green spinach-like substance. On completing the serving she motioned impatiently at their guest, who was looking enquiringly about her for the cutlery, and proceeded to demonstrate the art of eating, African style. Plucking a portion of fluffy white maize meal from the communal pot, she squeezed it delicately into a ball in her palm, dipped it into the gravy in her bowl and popped it into her mouth.

The smell was enough to put Jodie off the stodgy maize porridge, and the only part of the chicken she recognised in her bowl was the neck, a wing and some skin. She dutifully plucked a lump of stiff maize meal from the pot, only to let out a soft cry as the scalding porridge stuck to her fingers like glue. The look on Nyoni's face left Jodie in no doubt that she was once again the victim.

Jodie became increasingly uncomfortable at the silence, and the other woman's near nakedness, as the meal progressed. Asking herself again what she was doing out here in the middle of nowhere, she despaired that tomorrow could not come round soon enough.

Nyoni studied their guest through veiled lashes as she toyed sullenly with her meal. She had heard that white women were sexy but she had never imagined anything like this. The woman's eyes were greener than the deepest pool, her hair the rich red-brown of a sable calf, and her skin the creamy hue of goat's milk. As for the way she walked, she would shame a lioness in season. Now staring openly at the other woman, Nyoni recognised her resentment as jealousy, an alien feeling that was making her think and do unkind things. Gone was the gentle, obedient girl who had fled Rhodesia five and a half years ago, risking all to care for the man who had nearly died saving her life.

Looking up, Jodie was taken aback by such open hostility. Turning to Tony for reassurance she found to her dismay that he was eating mechanically, staring fixedly into the smouldering embers. Placing her bowl on the ground she inspected her sticky fingers and wondered how her mother would handle the situation. She concluded that no one in their right mind would have got themselves into such a ridiculous predicament in the first place. It might help, she thought, if she knew Nyoni's status, be it maid, cook or concubine. Probably all three and more, she speculated.

'As for you,' Jodie blurted out at Tony as she got to her feet, 'please don't bother yourself on my account, I'll find my own way back to the hotel.'

'I doubt that,' Tony spoke up, to the surprise of both women. 'This has not been easy for us either. You are the first outsider to . . .' his voice trailed off as he got unsteadily to his feet, grimacing.

'That may be so but that doesn't give you people the right to treat me like . . . like a *leper*,' Jodie retorted, facing the man and doing her best to ignore his obvious distress.

'I'm sorry, it's just that you don't belong . . .' Tony managed before forcing his fists against his temples.

Leaping up, Nyoni helped Tony back onto his stool. Dipping a cloth into the enamel bowl she bathed the perspiration from his forehead, glaring accusingly at the white woman as she worked.

Jodie offered a half-hearted shrug by way of apology, turned, and stormed out of the hut. This time she stooped low when negotiating the exit. Refusing to break into an undignified run as she crossed the hot clay compound, she quickened her pace and made straight for the hut she had seen the little vixen enter earlier. She was determined to find her underwear and shoes, before returning to Hluhluwe, alone if need be.

As Jodie shoved open the frail wattle door of Nyoni's hut the smell of cheap perfume caught in her throat. Once her eyes had adjusted to the gloom of the windowless interior she crossed to the solitary piece of furniture, an ancient chest of drawers. With her hand on the handle of the top drawer, she paused to study an old photograph in a battered chrome frame. Straining her eyes she read the faded gold-leaf caption: *Indaba of Chiefs, Rhodes Matopos National Park, Matabeleland, Southern Rhodesia 1957. On the occasion of the visit of Her Majesty Queen Elizabeth the Queen Mother.* The photo depicted some fifty or so African chiefs seated in orderly rows against an imposing backdrop of enormous granite boulders, some larger than double-storey houses. All the chiefs wore white pith helmets and khaki dustcoats, and proudly sported heavy-looking, half-moon-shaped, brass badges of office on their chests, hanging from chains round their necks. Moving closer Jodie inspected a smaller photo inserted into the corner of the frame. It was of one of the aged chiefs accepting a scroll. The family resemblance to Nyoni was unmistakable. So, Jodie reflected, our little vixen is another Rhodesian and one of breeding. In which case she should have better manners, she mused as she yanked open the top drawer of the dresser with a vengeance. Then again, she wondered how she might feel if the boot was on the other foot. Madam's noble lineage might also help to explain the intricate scarring on her cheeks and chest, Jodie thought, having first noticed them while sitting round the fire.

Jodie's rummaging soon unearthed her bra, panties and one sandal, hastily concealed beneath a host of clothing oddments. Having slipped into her underwear she continued the search for her other sandal, finally discovering it under an exquisitely decorated bead apron. Inspecting the lovely red, white, yellow, black and green garment in the poor light it was evident that, in spite of its relative size, many hours of painstaking labour had gone into this intricate work of art. The apron was new and Jodie guessed it was some sort of ceremonial regalia, being hoarded for a special occasion.

Conscious of her prying, she was about to return the apron to the drawer when a preposterous notion struck her. '*You wouldn't dare,*' she breathed aloud as she tried the garment up against her own waist. The next thing she knew she had slipped out of her dress and bra and was securing the apron at the small of her back with the soft leather thong. Modesty dictated that she retain her panties – bare breasts were one thing, a bare arse quite another. 'Just one circuit of the compound,' she whispered in breathless anticipation as she slipped on her sandals.

Determined to show that brazen hussy she did not have a monopoly on going topless, Jodie stepped boldly out into the bright midday sun.

Having chastised each other for their dismal attempt at hospitality, Tony and Nyoni were leaving the cooking hut to make amends. Still nursing a throbbing head, Tony blinked hard in disbelief. Nyoni simply gasped at the sight of the half-naked woman shamelessly standing in front of her hut. The woman's disrespect knew no bounds! As an educated white person she must know that misfortune would befall the owner of a bridal apron, if it was first worn by another?

Her eyes adjusting to the glare, Jodie froze at the sight of her hosts staring back at her. Such scrutiny was a far cry from a stealthy streak past the half-open door of the cooking hut. In spite of her mouth having gone completely dry, Jodie realised it was too late for a faint heart. Willing one foot in front of the other she headed for the shade of the mango tree. With each step she had to fight the urge to fling her arms protectively about her bare breasts.

His headache momentarily forgotten Tony stood mesmerised, unable to drag his eyes away from the spectacle. Nyoni on the other hand sprang into action, for the challenge was unmistakable. With a guttural scream welling up from the pit of her stomach she charged, going in low and fast like a leopardess.

Bemused by this unexpected turn of events and the speed and ferocity of the attack, Jodie barely had time to raise a hand in self defence before the lithe body of the black girl cannoned into her, bringing them both down heavily. Lying prostrate and breathless on her back, reflecting on those wasted months of judo lessons, panic swept through Jodie as she realised that the clawing at her head was Nyoni's fingers gathering up a fistful of hair. Visualising part of her scalp being wrenched from her head, she desperately groped about until her fingers closed over a smooth, palm-size, grinding stone. She felt her arm rise slowly, as if in a dream, the crude weapon aimed blindly at the spot where she imagined Nyoni's head to be. Too late, Tony rushed forward, only to wince in sympathy as the rock found its mark.

Nyoni's vision exploded in a profusion of coloured lights and a roaring sound filled her ears. Still crouched over Jodie she teetered a moment longer before dropping like the stone with which she had been so soundly clubbed.

The girls lay side by side on the hard hot earth of the compound, connected by Nyoni's outstretched arm, her fingers still entwined in Jodie's hair.

Shaking uncontrollably, Jodie opened her eyes to discover to her amazement, and short-lived relief, that Nyoni was not only alive, thanks to a cushion of tight wiry curls, but already struggling to her feet. Collecting her wits just in time, Jodie kicked out as the black girl pounced again, one foot catching Nyoni in the chest the other in the pit of the stomach, sending her sprawling head over heels. This time Tony was on hand to kick the grinding stone out of harm's way.

Both girls scrambled breathlessly to their knees. Covered in a powdery dust, their firm young breasts rapidly rising and falling in unison, they glared at one another. Seeing the funny side of it, Tony burst out laughing. The girls immediately followed suit, both laughing until the tears were streaming down their grimy faces.

Crawling across to one another they embraced like long-lost friends. Nyoni inwardly acknowledged her newfound respect for the white girl, while Jodie, realising that somebody might have been seriously hurt due to her antics, was grateful to Nyoni for accepting the bash on the head in such good grace.

'You were right to remind me of my manners,' Nyoni said in perfect English.

'No, it is I who should be apologising for provoking you, and for hitting you with that rock,' replied Jodie, gently fingering the egg-size swelling on the girl's temple. Helping her newfound friend to her feet, Jodie turned to Tony to apologise for creating a scene, but he was nowhere to be seen.

Sensing Jodie's concern Nyoni offered kindly, 'Do not worry, he often goes off without warning to be alone. Come, let us go now and bath at the spring.' She took Jodie's hand and led the way over to a barely visible opening in the wall of sisal.

'First let me return your apron and retrieve my dress,' Jodie said releasing Nyoni's hand.

The Path of Darkness

The girls set off in single file down the narrow path that wound through a maze of towering sisal. They emerged five minutes later in a small clearing at the base of a rocky outcrop where a natural spring fed a crystal-clear pool, surrounded on three sides by reeds and ferns. The only access to the pool was over a large, smooth boulder that sloped gently down into the tepid waters.

'It's beautiful!' Jodie exclaimed, taking a deep breath and running her fingers down the silky head of a bulrush at the water's edge. Once again she regretted the suddenness of her departure from the hotel – besides the contents of her handbag and toiletries she now missed her camera. Brenton, not to mention her mother Christine, would swear she had made up the whole incredible story.

The bond between the girls grew as they bathed and inspected one another's grazes and bruises. Nyoni had no idea a white woman could be so caring. For Jodie's part she found the genuine disposition of the new Nyoni most heartening.

Leaving the water at last, they stretched out naked on the smooth rock and let its retained warmth ease their aches and pains. Lying very still while Nyoni sang the praise of her namesake, the birds, Jodie watched in awe as hundreds of the tiny pale-blue creatures flocked to the water's edge for their evening drink. The resident weavers were more boisterous as they flitted from reed to reed, puffing out their brilliant red and black plumage to ward off would-be trespassers from their nesting areas. Once the birds had finished drinking, swarms of bees droned in to alight at the edge of the rock where the ripples lapped. Finally, as if to complete the fairytale world, a family of yellow- and blue-necked terrapins made their way clumsily through the reeds and up onto the rock to sun themselves.

Nyoni rolled over onto her stomach to finish telling Jodie the story of the honey bird – how traditionally it had guided her people to beehives, in exchange for an offering of honeycomb that was always left at the site of the plundered hive by way of reward. With her head in the crook of her arm, Nyoni studied the white girl now staring dreamily off at the wine-red sunset.

'Is it right for . . . for a black girl to be the friend of a white woman?' Nyoni asked uncertainly.

'Why of course it is!' Jodie said with a bemused smile but without averting her gaze from the magnificent sky, which was changing to a darker shade of purple as they spoke.

Encouraged, Nyoni asked, 'Then will you be my friend?'

'I would be proud to be your friend,' Jodie said, turning on her side to meet Nyoni's warm soulful gaze. It was distressing to reflect on how apartheid in colonial Africa had so profoundly influenced even those as innocent and far removed from civilisation as Nyoni, she thought.

'That is good. Now that we are friends I am happy for you to be Tony's woman.'

'Nyoni!' Jodie protested looking into those large almond-shaped eyes. 'It's not what you think. Initially I may have harboured some romantic notions but now my interest is simply professional curiosity, coupled with a desire to help. If I can determine what it is that troubles the man.'

'You also see that he is troubled?' Nyoni asked anxiously, a serious expression on her face.

'It's pretty obvious. From what little I know of him my guess would be he is suffering from post traumatic stress syndrome. He displays a number of symptoms: mood swings, detachment and denial. I gather he was in the army and subjected to some sort of bombing accident; a near death experience judging from his injuries.'

'How can you know all these things?' Nyoni asked suspiciously.
'I studied psychology, but I would need a lot more information and a frank discussion with Tony to be more certain.'

'What is psychology?'

'It's a behavioural science. It reviews the symptoms of people who have suffered some sort of mental or physical disorder. Once we have diagnosed the nature of the problem, we are better able to help the patient understand what probably triggered their anxiety. Then we can prescribe treatment to aid in their recovery.'

'Then you must do this thing for Tony. You must help us before it is too late,' Nyoni pleaded, wringing her hands. 'Each time the spirits possess him he grows more troubled. I do not fear for my own life but I am afraid for his.'

In spite of the clammy heat Jodie felt a shiver run down her spine. She did not need a degree to know that the black girl's fear and anguish were real. Placing an arm around Nyoni's shoulders, she said, 'It might help if you tell me just what it is you think is troubling Tony. But first, would you mind explaining your relationship with him?'

In response to Nyoni's confused expression, Jodie prompted, 'From the picture of the Indaba of Chiefs in your hut I gather you are also from Rhodesia and that you probably travelled to South Africa with Tony? You are a very attractive young woman and you choose to live alone with a man in this secluded place.'

Shaking her head vigorously Nyoni protested. 'I am not sharing his *bed*. I am but as a younger sister to him,' she insisted, stifling a sob. 'I try to help but do not know how to drive out the demons that trouble him and threaten his life.'

Still doubting the relationship was entirely platonic, Jodie decided to give Nyoni the benefit of the doubt, wondering how sincere her own claims about her feelings for the man must have sounded. 'Very well then,' she said, 'tell me what you know of Tony's problem.'

'His troubles started back in Rhodesia, now Zimbabwe. I was twelve or thirteen at the time. There was much trouble in the

Tribal Trust Lands. One night the *gandangas* came to our village and took me and many other children, to carry their supplies and to be their . . . whores,' Nyoni flinched at her own recollection.

'How dreadful! I had no idea. There is no need to go on,' Jodie said.

'I must,' Nyoni insisted. 'You see, once on the march again the terrorists were attacked; ambushed by Tony's patrol in the middle of the night. There was much shooting and many people died.'

'You were caught up in the midst of a battle, on top of everything else? You poor child!' Jodie said drawing Nyoni closer and instinctively prompting, 'What then?'

'There were many, many *gandangas* and the soldiers were all killed, except him. In the morning aeroplanes dropped bombs and more soldiers came in helicopters. They left without finding Tony who was close to death at the bottom of a *donga*. The same one I had fallen into as I tried to escape in the dark. When it was over I went for help and my people took Tony back to our village. It was days before he opened his eyes and when he did he cursed the *sangomas* for helping him cheat death. His wounds were very bad. It was a long time before he could feed himself and even longer before he would bathe, for fear of seeing his face in the water. Long after the fever had left him he would cry out in the night and it was said he travelled the path of darkness, the path of madness. That is how his troubles started.'

'Incredible, but why wasn't his presence reported to the authorities?'

'At first my people thought he was going to die and they would be in trouble. Later, when he could walk unaided, he told the elders he had no wish to return to the city. He said he could not remember his past life and that those he had once known would be as strangers.' Taking Jodie's hands in hers, Nyoni went on to ask in all seriousness, 'Now that you know why he has these symptoms, you can help him?'

'Nyoni, what you have told me helps but you should not get your hopes up. My training has been mainly theoretical, and amnesia, which seems to be what we are also dealing with, simply compounds the problem.'

'Now, what is this amnesia?'

'It's a loss of memory. It can be caused by a blow to the head or some sort of psychological trauma. Sufferers are unable to recall events prior to the incident. In Tony's case it is probably emotional amnesia, due to the violent deaths of his friends and his own horrific injuries. Fortunately this type isn't usually permanent, so memory may return suddenly or slowly over time.'

'Then you can or you cannot help him?' Nyoni insisted impatiently.

'Nyoni I think our best bet is to encourage him to get professional help. I don't understand why he hasn't done so before now. He clearly knows he has amnesia, and must surely associate his other issues, the headaches and dizziness, with what he went through back then.'

'All I know is there are times when he gets very angry and goes off alone, or sits for days without eating or saying anything,' Nyoni said, wringing her hands.

'How often does he have these . . . moods?' Jodie ventured.

'They are coming more often, sometimes every few days. The last time I went to him when he cried out in the night he threw me down, and I thought he was going to strike me. I cannot comfort him, because of . . . what the terrorists did. That is why you must help us,' she sobbed.

'Nyoni, I'm so sorry. Of course I will do what I can, I promise. Now dry those tears,' Jodie said cradling the distraught girl in her arms and gently rocking her.

'Good, then it is settled,' Nyoni confirmed, easing out of the other woman's embrace, her tears disappearing as quickly as they had come. 'Tonight you must go to him, ease his troubled spirit as only a woman can. Lead him back from the path of darkness.'

Jodie swallowed hard. Fantasising over cocktails in a public place was one thing. Actually making out with a virtual stranger in a mud hut, in a bizarre effort to relieve a tormented psyche, was something else entirely. Not to mention the man's dubious state of mind.

'First prize will be to get him to acknowledge that he needs professional help,' Jodie reiterated pointedly, adding before Nyoni could come up with any more bright ideas, 'I will talk to him during the journey back to Hluhluwe in the morning. Tell him that ignoring his condition is not an option. I'll recommend he stays over to get help, before he does himself or anyone else serious harm.'

Nyoni got wearily to her feet, shaking her head, 'Then it is hopeless. He will never agree to that.'

'In which case I will arrange to get help out here to him,' Jodie vowed.

'This is not an easy place to find,' Nyoni pointed out, adding forlornly, 'It could be too late by then anyway. I have seen that look in Tony's eyes again today, it is all the excitement.' She sniffed as she got to her feet and took Jodie's hand in the fading light, 'I fear for him, but I understand you not wanting to get caught up in this thing. Please do not be angry with me.'

Jodie felt a lump forming in her throat as she followed Nyoni silently back up the narrow path.

Arriving at the semicircle of huts in the dark, Nyoni confidently negotiated the way through the unlit compound to her quarters. Once Nyoni had lit the candle Jodie asked, 'Where is Tony now, it's so quiet?'

'In his hut sleeping, I hope. I put strong *muti* in the coffee pot next to the fire before we went to bathe. He drinks much coffee at night.' She settled down on the reed mat and beckoned her friend to sit beside her.

'A sedative,' Jodie nodded her half-hearted approval, given the questionable morality of secretly drugging one's companion. Mesmerised by the shadows that danced about the small room from the flickering candle, she found herself asking, before she could check herself, 'How would my making love to Tony solve anything?'

Staring fixedly into the flame of the candle, Nyoni whispered,

'I do not need this psychology thing to know that Tony sees in you the likeness of another. Why else did he return to Hluhluwe and bring you back to this place where no outsider has entered? Also, when you are near, his eyes show sadness, a strange longing.' Nyoni extended her hand over the flame of the candle, intent on purging her own anguish.

Snatching the black girl's hand back from the flame, Jodie relented. 'All right, I will go to him and try to throw some light on this so-called path of darkness of yours. But I will do it by encouraging him to *talk* through his issues,' she stressed while reflecting on the black girl's uncanny insight. 'Nyoni, do these tribal markings signify an ability to read the bones by any chance?' She pointed at the scarring on the other girl's face and chest.

'Of course not, silly. I went to a mission school, remember. You also have a scar on your cheek so what does that make you?' Nyoni chided back.

'This was the result of a fencing accident, so I guess it makes me careless,' Jodie laughed, running a finger down the hairline scar on her face, now more visible without her make-up but all the better for plastic surgery.

'I do not know what fencing is, but the scar makes you more beautiful – only three on each side like mine would be better,' Nyoni chuckled. 'It is getting late, let us sleep now,' she said snuffing out the candle with her fingers.

Jodie found herself being gently drawn down onto the sleeping mat. Blankets, not skins, she noted gratefully as she tried to get comfortable. 'Nyoni, there are still so many unanswered questions,' she whispered, having second thoughts as she lay in total blackness listening to the sounds of the night.

'Rest now. I will wake you when it is time. Afterwards I will answer all your questions,' Nyoni bargained as she pulled the thin blanket closer about them.

Dozing fitfully on the hard, unfamiliar surface, Jodie's thoughts were of her father hacking his way through a jungle of sisal to her rescue with half of the South African Police Force in tow.

83

Terrorists at Large

When Jodie stole from Tony's hut early the following morning she felt neither joy nor triumph – just used. She was disappointed in herself for allowing emotion to cloud her judgement and for letting things go as far as they had. What could she have been thinking to go along with Nyoni's outrageous scheme in the first place? Standing in the compound on shaky legs, her scant clothing clutched in a small bundle to her chest, she shivered in the fresh morning air. Staring up at the dawn-streaked sky she felt numb, and in desperate need of a bath and a hot cup of tea. Realising she was staring vacantly at wisps of white smoke filtering through the thatch of one of the huts, her spirits rose. She slipped on her dress and made for Nyoni's kitchen.

'He sleeps as soundly as a new born lamb, not the fitful rest of the damned,' Nyoni enthused as she stepped back into the hut after a cursory check on Tony.

Jodie nodded wearily from where she sat next to the fire, sipping a mug of hot sweet tea.

'Is he free of what possessed him? Has he remembered everything? Will he no longer need help?' Nyoni rattled off, barely able to contain her curiosity the moment Jodie finished her tea.

'Nyoni please, can't the prognosis wait until I at least have had a chance to bathe?' Jodie retorted as she got up to leave the smoky hut. Once outside she set off mechanically in the direction of the narrow path that led to the rock pool.

'I'll get the soap,' Nyoni volunteered, running back to her quarters.

The morning sun was already filtering through the uppermost

reaches of the sisal by the time Nyoni rounded the last bend in the path, only to discover the white girl floating face down in the pool. Plunging into the water with a shriek, Nyoni landed with a splash right on top of her friend. Spluttering and gasping to recover the breath she had just had knocked out of her, Jodie scrambled to her feet. Nyoni, apologising profusely, busied herself searching for the soap in an effort to hide her embarrassment.

'I'm sorry. I thought you were drowning!' She had actually thought the worst; that the white girl had decided to end it all.

'No thanks to you – I nearly did,' Jodie reprimanded, wringing water from a long tress of hair as she stood knee deep in the pool. 'Hurry up with that soap and maybe I'll forgive you,' she relented, seeing the funny side of it.

Once back on the smooth rock the girls stretched out to let the sun dry them. Jodie gave a little shudder, the outside temperature still cooler than the retained warmth of the pool.

'I cannot remember the last time I have seen him look that peaceful,' Nyoni said. 'Was it as I said it would be?'

'He was hallucinating most of the time, due to whatever it was you laced his coffee with. A healthy dose of cannabis no doubt! He kept on about something to do with the sun going down?'

'*At the going down of the sun.* He repeats that while staring into the fire when he is troubled,' Nyoni offered helpfully.

'It's making more sense now. Those words are part of the epitaph on the memorial to Allan Wilson and his Shangani Patrol – they perished to a man at the battle of Blood River. *In the morning and at the going down of the sun we will remember them.* Words immortalised by Sir Winston Churchill, Britain's wartime prime minister. It's probably Tony's way of relating to his own fallen comrades.'

'Yes, yes, but that cannot be all!' Nyoni said, obviously agitated. 'When he was coherent he ranted on and on about the intransigence of politicians and the incompetence of the military, blaming them for his predicament. There wasn't much else, apart from him obviously struggling with his conscience – alluding at times to what sounded like more than one relationship. Unfortunately there was no logical train of thought, no names or places to go on as far as I can recall. It's not unusual in cases like his – people block out harrowing events or compromising circumstances.'

'Then why does he rest so peacefully?' Nyoni persisted.

'Exhaustion. You were right about one thing. He was definitely in need of some . . . comforting. Tell me, just what was it you put into that concoction?' The colour rose in her cheeks as she reflected on the night's scandalous conspiracy.

Not certain if she was being praised or scolded, Nyoni apologised. 'I am sorry, I should have warned you that some African potions can make a man very . . . how do you say . . .'

Studying Nyoni's impish expression, Jodie could contain herself no longer and they both burst out laughing in a spontaneous release of the tension that had built up over the deed.

'You will not be going back to your hotel today,' Nyoni said at last, still clutching her sides. 'He will sleep until the sun is high.'

'Sleep is something I also desperately need,' Jodie confessed. 'But first the answers you promised me last night. For starters, what brought the two of you to South Africa and why to this remote spot?'

Nyoni settled down to keep her part of the bargain. 'Shortly after independence it was said that Joshua Nkomo was planning to overthrow the Mugabe government. Tony had been at our village for about a year and was strong again. He told the elders he was leaving the country before there was a bloody civil war. I followed him to the railway siding at Dett, near the Wankie National Park. That is where he caught me and tried to send me back, saying I would never see my people again if I went with him to South Africa.'

'Tony must have made quite an impression on you,' Jodie said good-naturedly.

'Yes, but there were also other reasons for my leaving, after what the terrorists did to me,' Nyoni said, continuing her story without elaborating. 'We stole rides on goods trains and crossed the border on foot at Beitbridge, it was the dry season so the Limpopo river was low. Travelling on more trains we eventually ended up at Mkuze siding, here in Natal. From there we walked through the bush until we found this abandoned kraal overgrown by sisal. Not far from here we came across the first baobab tree we had seen since leaving Zimbabwe. I think this is what made Tony decide it was a good place; I agreed once I found this beautiful spring.'

'Quite a journey,' Jodie acknowledged drawing her knees up under her chin. 'Is Tony his real name?'

'It was written on his army belt, the part not burned by the fire.'

'Tell me what caused the fire and how he sustained those terrible burns.'

'Let us talk while we eat breakfast, then you can rest. The lands are not far and the melons are ripe,' Nyoni invited, getting to her feet.

'*Lands?*' Jodie asked, accepting Nyoni's hand and pulling herself up.

'Where we grow our food – there are no supermarkets out here,' Nyoni chided.

'You grow crops in among this lot?' Jodie gestured at the jungle of overgrown sisal.

'Yes, in a clearing. But you must not go there alone,' Nyoni cautioned as an afterthought. 'Only one is the right path, the others go in circles and have hidden dangers.'

'You protect an allotment miles from anywhere with a booby-trapped maze? Why?'

'Tony knows best,' Nyoni said, not sure what Tony's reasons were for forbidding her to go to the lands without him. When she had ignored his instructions, to collect fruit and vegetables on those occasions when he was unwell, she had come to no harm. Admittedly she had never strayed far and was careful to retrace her footsteps.

Still shaking her head, Jodie followed Nyoni through the reeds surrounding the pool and onto a barely discernable path. She soon lost her bearings in the maze of sisal, which formed an impenetrable wall on either side of the narrow twisting pathway. When they finally stepped out into the full glare of the sun once more, it was on the threshold of a large clearing. Spellbound, Jodie stared out across the field of ripe maize, surrounded by vegetable patches and a variety of fruit trees. It was a veritable Garden of Eden, one in which she could almost pass for Eve, she fancied, having left her underwear drying on the rock by the pool and with her frock that much shorter and revealing since Nyoni's laundering.

As they moved deeper into the clearing, skirting the edge of the tall maize, Jodie raised her hands. 'This is incredible! It's hard to believe two people could accomplish all this. Do you have a tractor?'

'Where would we get a tractor? Tony works the lands with labourers,' Nyoni explained as she motioned Jodie to sit on a large pumpkin she had placed in the shade for her.

Frowning, Jodie sat opposite Nyoni and waited while the girl expertly split a ripe watermelon with a chop of her hand. 'Where do these labourers come from? We must be miles from the nearest town.'

'Tony's captives, mainly poachers but maybe also a few dissidents, I think,' Nyoni elaborated just as Jodie bit ravenously into the cool red fruit.

'You mean terrorists!' Jodie spluttered, choking on a mouthful of watermelon pips. 'Then what in God's name are we doing here . . . half naked to boot?' She was already on her feet, wiping her mouth with the back of her hand. She was no sooner up than she dropped down onto her haunches to take advantage of the high grass surrounding the little orchard. The colour drained from her cheeks, her eyes fixed disbelievingly on her companion.

'Relax!' Nyoni insisted spreading the cool melon juice that dripped from her chin over her breasts. 'Tony only uses the young cadres, cannon fodder he calls them. He keeps them locked in a stockade. If they work hard he lets them return to their homes after a . . .'

'For goodness sake woman, how . . . how secure is this bloody stockade?' Jodie stammered, dropping her melon in the dust.

'Very, I think,' Nyoni said sullenly.

'You *think!*' Jodie snapped back in dismay.

'I told you, Tony has forbidden me to come here alone.'

'You said no such thing,' Jodie hissed, adding in the same breath, 'Would Tony hear us if we screamed?'

Putting her own melon down and folding her arms, Nyoni mimicked, 'For goodness sake woman, why would we scream?'

'Don't be so bloody naive,' Jodie swore. 'A moment ago I saw a couple of black men, possibly more, I cannot be . . .' The words died on Jodie's lips as she watched the look of unbridled horror flood into the other girl's eyes.

'Jesus Christ,' Nyoni blasphemed, her hand clamping vice-like on Jodie's wrist as she yanked her back onto her feet. Jodie was hot on Nyoni's heals as they took flight, her wrist still imprisoned in the other girl's grasp. They were racing back towards the concealed exit, to the safety of the maze.

Long before Jodie's scream rent the still, mid-morning air Nyoni knew they had left it too late. With thirty metres separating them from the secret path, Nyoni looked up to see three black men sprint out from between the tall stands of maize, cutting off their only avenue of escape. Jodie's instincts cried out for them to turn and flee in the opposite direction but her suicidal friend raced on, with her firmly in tow.

The three leering youths could hardly believe their good fortune as their prey continued to charge headlong towards them. Standing their ground while the gap rapidly narrowed, they feasted their eyes on the sleek bodies and firm young breasts, their good fortune all the more incredible in that one was a white woman. The taller of the well-built youths had already taken himself in hand through his threadbare shorts, as if intent on making a presentation of his manhood to the first woman to reach him.

With only seconds before impact Nyoni blurted out breathlessly, 'Go left forty paces . . . then right and right again . . . stop if lost . . . Tony will come.' With that she catapulted Jodie away from her with a violent wrench of the other woman's arm.

With her friend lurching on at full tilt towards the narrow gap now just visible in the wall of sisal, Nyoni launched herself headlong into the group of startled young men. Clawlike fingernails slashed out as she collided with her would be assailants, bringing two of the youths heavily to the ground. Both men were soon preoccupied frantically protecting their eyes and private parts from raking claws, flying heels and stabbing elbows. Nyoni sank her teeth into an ear.

It would have been enough time for Jodie to make good her escape, had it not been for the biggest and surliest-looking member of the gang. Having nimbly side-stepped the charge, he lost only a few precious moments before realising that the black girl's attack had been intended to buy time for her beautiful white companion. Already sweating profusely in his excitement he released his huge erect penis and took up the chase.

With less than ten metres to go to the path, Jodie smelt and then imagined she felt the rancid breath of the sex-crazed man on her neck. It was more than her exhausted body and strained nerves could take. Her legs buckled under her.

So intent had her pursuer been on Jodie's short dress, exposing as it did flashes of her naked buttocks as she ran, that he had not noticed how perilously close they were to the impenetrable barrier of sisal. It was only while in mid air, leaping over the head and shoulders of his fallen prey, that the doomed youngster realised his plight. He barely managed to twist his body sideways before he smashed into the array of spearlike protrusions; his screams echoed on long after he had impaled himself.

Struggling to her feet Jodie staggered on towards the protective sanctuary of the narrow passageway. Edging breathlessly round the partially suspended youth, she gasped as the man lifted his head and his pained, bloodshot eyes met hers. Mesmerised by the agony on that contorted face, Jodie could not believe what she was witnessing. He was slowly drawing one murderous barb after another from his bleeding flesh.

Her breath catching in quick sharp sobs, Jodie realised she was running again. She was on the path and it was only after she had blindly rounded yet another bend that Nyoni's words flooded back: *Stop if lost. . . Tony will come.* Still contemplating the absurdity of dallying while the would-be rapist made good his escape, she stopped abruptly when Nyoni's scream rang out. Only then did it dawn on her that had the savage pursued her into the maze he would surely have been upon her by now. Which could only mean one thing, he had returned to rejoin his comrades. A second agonising scream confirmed her fears; the hairs at the nape of Jodie's neck stood on end.

Jodie was running again, her legs having found renewed strength. She was heading back down the path, back the way she had come, dashing blindly to the aid of her friend. As she ran she harboured a vague notion that being British would be enough to intimidate the gang into leaving them alone.

Having hobbled painfully over to his colleagues who were still wrestling with their catch, the leader of the trio violently kicked the two younger boys aside. Then spitting a glob of saliva and blood into Nyoni's face he dropped heavily onto her chest and stomach with his knees, crushing the breath and fight out of her. With his prize beaten and gasping on her back in the dust, the triumphant youth roughly parted Nyoni's legs, slowly, sadistically, positioning himself.

RHODESIA, 1978

Brady Barracks

Brady Barracks was situated on the outskirts of Bulawayo. It had been a training centre for the Rhodesian Air Force during the Second World War. Thirty-six years on, its narrow streets still echoed with the sound of troops as men of the local battalions of the Rhodesian Regiment were equipped on call-up and de-mobbed on their return from the operational area.

Driving down the road on the other side of the perimeter fence, Tony could see the throng of camouflage-clad men sorting out equipment in front of C Company stores. It was only as they drove in under the raised boom that he chanced a sideways glance at Kathy. She had a fixed smile on her face, and the unnatural brightness of her eyes added weight to the sick, sinking feeling he had experienced dozens of times when crossing this threshold. His throat became tight and he could feel the back of his nose tingling. The goodbyes over the past seven years had never been easy; over the last two they had become increasingly difficult as the tempo of the war increased.

Once they had parked, Kathy slid wordlessly across into the driver's seat and stared vacantly out at the hive of activity while Tony unloaded his kit. It was only when he stuck his head through the window to kiss her goodbye that she attempted a genuine smile. Throwing her arms around him she pressed her face to his neck.

'Hey, come now. What did we agree?' he said kindly.

'I know,' she sobbed. 'I'm sorry darling but . . .' The rest of the sentence was choked off by his kiss. Her hand found the gear lever and she rammed it blindly into first the moment their lips parted. Trying in vain to voice a few words of encouragement, she shook her head in despair and took her foot off the clutch. The car lurched forward, gaining speed as it headed for the exit.

Tony swallowed hard, shouldered his kit and set off in search of the men who would be in his section for this commitment. Just my bloody luck he thought, as he stared down at an ungainly middle-aged individual with glasses sitting in the gravel with his lap covered in straps, pouches and water bottle carriers.

'Your name Jacobs?'

'Yes, Sir,' came the startled reply as Jacobs scrambled to his feet to salute, webbing dangling from him like so much spaghetti.

'You don't salute NCOs you f . . .' But Tony checked himself. What with people leaving the country, getting injured or worse, they had been reduced to calling up just about anybody capable of carrying a rifle. 'Welcome to Alpha section,' he said instead. As he spoke he caught sight of Wells about to duck out of sight out of mind, behind one of the barrack rooms.

'Foxy!' he called, 'Get your arse on over here.'

Rifleman Wells grinned as he ambled across to his corporal. 'I was just on my way to the shithouse, Corp.'

'It can wait, and why the hell haven't you shaved? Get rid of the bloody beard before Williams sees you and has you up on orders.'

'I'll take my chance,' Wells said affectionately stroking the sparse gingery growth.

Tony shook his head. Nothing had changed; the guy still had the mentality of a juvenile delinquent. He let it go, for now.

'Foxy, this is Jacobs. Help him get this lot sorted out.'

Wells pulled his corporal aside. 'You're fucking joking man. He's half blind and old enough to be on pension. Seriously, man, he should be in the stores, not in a rifle stick. At least switch him for something with smaller fucking ears, he's a walking target for Christ's sake.'

'The luck of the draw. Now get his kit sorted for him,' Tony said, suppressing a grin. 'When you've finished find this Nell fellow who's also supposed to be with us. Then collect our rations, sling out the junk but *this time* keep the bloody salt tablets, vitamin pills and crap paper.'

'OK, OK, Corp, take it as done. I'll also get our guys down to the armoury to draw weapons.'

'Great. I'll meet you back here after my briefing and once I've collected our maps and other controlled stores.'

The atmosphere in the sparsely furnished ops room was one of quiet expectation as Major Young entered.

'Good morning, gentlemen. Please be seated. You may smoke.' There was a scuffle of chairs as the small group of officers and senior NCOs sat and lit cigarettes. Continuing, Young said, 'I don't think any of us expected to be back together as a company quite this soon; a sign of the times I'm afraid. Lieutenant Anderson has not made a full recovery, so Company Sergeant Major Moore will assume command of 1st Platoon with Corporal Richard du Preez now acting CSM.'

Walking over to the flip chart, Young explained, 'I collect final orders from Tac HQ on our arrival in Wankie. At this stage I can only give you an overview of where and how I see us operating.' Flipping to the chart headed *Operational Area* he said, 'Gentlemen, our northern boundary will be the Zambezi; to the east the Lukozi and Gwai rivers; to the west the Matetsi; to the south the main Victoria Falls–Bulawayo road. The area west of the Matetsi is under the control of an Auxiliary unit, about a hundred strong. I understand they are still pretty wild and woolly so no one crosses this boundary without clearance, not even in hot pursuit.'

Pausing to light his cigar Young turned to the final chart headed *Mission*. 'We will be tasked in reconnaissance to detect any terrorist build-up prior to the forthcoming elections. In view of the apparent failure of our hearts and minds campaign we are going to have to keep the gloves on, particularly now that the transitional government has undertaken to guarantee the safety of the rural electorate before, during and after the voting. Any questions? Yes, Mr Moore?'

'Just our ETD, Sir?'

'Sixteen hundred hours, so I'll leave you to get back to your men. Thank you, gentlemen.'

Having organised Jacobs, Wells left him in charge of the kit and ration packs and set off in search of the last member of their four-man section still to be accounted for. Skirting the armoury once more, he made his way up the road to the canteen.

It just had to be Nell, the thickset, overweight fellow sitting in the corner of the otherwise deserted canteen, reading the *Chronicle* with a couple of cream doughnuts and a litre of milk in front of him.

'Your name Nell? Hey . . . I'm bloody talking to you man,' Wells raised his voice as he approached the table.

'What if it is?' the stocky man answered without lowering his newspaper.

'The bloody canteen is off limits during deployment. It's a no-no, get it man?'

Nell folded his paper. 'Like beards, hey chum?' he said looking up at the unshaven weasel of a man.

'Don't fuck with me boy! Me and Corporal Longdon don't take kindly to smart arses,' Wells snarled.

'Relax and help me finish these doughnuts, Foxy,' Nell invited, taking the wind out of Wells' sails.

Wells stared intently at the big man. 'Do I know you, Nell?'

'It's Piet. No, but I've heard of you. Tell me, have they finished loading the stores trucks yet?'

'It's safe to come out, if that's what you mean,' Wells grinned for he was beginning to warm to the big fellow.

'Have you found out when and where we're going?'

'We pullout at sixteen hundred, straight to battle camp on Hunters Farm for a bit of revision, then back up to the fucking Wankie area again,' Wells obliged.

'When do we draw weapons?'

'We already collected ours,' Wells said before forcing an entire doughnut into his mouth and reaching for the bottle of milk.

'Who's the poor bastard on the MAG?'

'You are,' Wells spluttered, choking down his mouthful.

'Not a bugger!' Nell exclaimed as he got to his feet. 'No ways am I lugging that fucking beast thing around for six weeks.'

'Luck of the draw man,' Wells said with a smirk from ear to ear. 'We lost our previous gunner in a fucking landmine ambush last commitment,' he added for good measure.

Tony was pleased with his chaps on his return with the section's equipment. Jacobs and Wells were helping Nell load the MAG belts. The rations had been split up equally, the shoulders and pins on the grenades checked and all the water bottles filled. After his introduction to Nell, Tony shared out the one-man gas cookers and spare radio batteries. He gave the medic bag to Jacobs, the flares to Nell, and binoculars to Wells. He kept the radio, maps, compass, claymore, detonators and morphine.

Wells dropped the last of the heavy ammunition belts into Nell's lap before turning to his corporal. 'I see your mate Richard du Preez is acting CSM. Just think, Corp, it could have been you with your bum in butter if you had not got the entire company kicked out of the bloody ops area last camp. Try not to disgrace the fucking lot of us again, OK?' He was still chuckling to himself as they clambered aboard their vehicle.

The three covered stores trucks and six open troop carriers lumbered out past the boom, bulging with men and equipment. The men sat silently back-to-back, rifles between their legs pointing at a cloudless blue sky. A military policeman astride his motorcycle signalled them through the last of the city's traffic lights and the convoy swung out onto the main Bulawayo–Victoria Falls road. Wells busied himself returning the V for victory salutes from passing motorists with his own one-finger variation.

Watching Wells' antics Tony asked himself what the hell he was doing back in uniform. Having always prided himself on being one step ahead of the pack, here he was still in the country and heading back into the bush. The Jewish community, a good barometer in troubled times, had started leaving the country in earnest two years ago. What kind of fool was he to risk his life and Kathy's sanity, for a cause future generations would probably not even remember; and likely condemn if they did? The look of hopelessness in Kathy's eyes still haunted him as he resolved to get the evidence the NUF needed to support his allegations of foul play. Then he'd give serious thought to heading down south as soon as he got out, whether or not the press was prepared to go public on the indiscriminate culling of locals in the Tribal Trust Lands.

Darkness had fallen with ten kilometres still to go to the turnoff to Hunters Farm. Six gruelling days of battle drills then back to the operational area in the Wankie district, fascinating, Godforsaken Wankie! One of the hottest places in Rhodesia with more mopani flies and mosquitoes per square metre than any place on earth, Tony brooded. While little could equal the harshness and inhospitability of the area, he found solace in the fact that this part of the country abounded with baobab trees; stately giants that were so much a part of Africa's timeless mystery.

Tony's mind continued to wander as it often did during these long intervals of inactivity. Normally his imagination would conjure up ambushes and contacts until he had mentally executed dozens of successful offensives. But this evening was different. The warm breeze reminded him of the small coal-mining town of Wankie for which they were once again destined. He closed his eyes and let his thoughts drift back to that fateful evening at the Baobab Hotel, less than two months ago – to his meeting with Victoria Bond.

Victoria

Tony and Richard were in excellent spirits as they drove up to the Baobab Hotel, situated on top of a rocky outcrop on the outskirts of Wankie. All credit for their evening of R&R went to Richard who had pulled strings to get them both on the weekly ration run, their first respite in three weeks of constant patrols.

There were dozens of casually dressed people *braaing* out on the lawn beneath the stars on that warm, midsummer's evening. The public bar was full, mainly with men in uniform, for it was a Saturday night and a surprising number of army and police lads were out on passes. Most of the chaps in uniform had to make do with their own company, for Wankie was a small mining town where men outnumbered the few single, divorced or widowed women at the best of times.

The lounge was also full and the tables, wet with condensation, were cluttered with glasses and empty beer bottles. There was a dance floor with a four-piece band on a raised platform at one end, while rifles, both military and civilian, lined the other walls. The locals had most of the better tables, with the army and late arrivals competing for what was left.

Tony ducked behind some shrubs as he and Richard approached the open double doors of the lounge, reappearing with a set of officers' crowns on his epaulets. Allowing Corporal du Preez to precede him, the newly commissioned major followed his *orderly* into the smoke-filled room. Richard made for a table occupied by three young national servicemen, a fourth having just conveniently vacated his chair heading in the direction of the ablutions.

'Over here, Sir,' Richard beckoned as he ceremoniously pulled back the empty armchair for the *major*, now unhurriedly approaching the table.

'Hey, that chair's taken,' a young trooper protested before receiving a nudge from one of his friends, both of whom were already getting respectfully to their feet. The young man making all the fuss quickly followed suit, saluting for good measure.

'Good evening, gentlemen. Our apologies, we thought we had located a vacant seat. Please carry on.'

'No, that's quite all right, Sir. We were just leaving. You're welcome to the table, Sir,' offered one of the young soldiers.

'What splendid luck, thank you,' Tony acknowledged, while Richard nodded approvingly as the young men gathered up their glasses and half empty beer bottles and head for the veranda.

'Best get shot of these pips in case we bump into some real brass.'

'Oh, come on man they suit you. You're more credible than the real thing,' Richard joked.

'That's not difficult.' Tony grinned, discreetly slipping the crowns off his epaulets and shaking his head at the crazy things one got up to while in uniform.

They were on their fourth beer when, in spite of the din from the band, a perceptible hush alerted their keenly attuned senses. Both men looked round. Not tall, but perfectly proportioned, with blonde hair in a bun, the woman standing in the doorway wore a dove-grey skirt and matching blouse with a loose contrasting maroon waistcoat. She also wore a smile that said it's Saturday night, so let's have fun.

Richard kicked his colleague's boot under the table. Tony was already staring but Richard insisted on kicking him again, harder this time.

'*OK*, I'm not blind,' Tony protested.

'Not her,' Richard countered, 'the gorgeous bit behind mum and dad, next to the jerk in the suit; hopefully her brother. Bugger it,' he cursed almost immediately as a tall good-looking guy in jeans stepped out from the crowd to meet the new arrivals.

Mum's double but lovelier, the young woman wore a white, flared, knee-length skirt with lace trim and a short-sleeved yellow blouse with a turned-up collar. Her blonde hair reached almost to her waist. Slightly more rounded but with the same cute, slightly upturned nose as her mother, she carried herself with equal grace. Tony placed her in her late teens, early twenties.

'Richard, girls her age don't hold hands with their brothers. If she has one it's probably the tall dude now giving her a peck on the cheek.'

'Whatever, she's really something, hey man! Worth travelling eighty kilometres through terrorist-infested bush to ogle.'

'She's a bit chubby.'

'Puppy fat, sweet and innocent, just your type,' Richard goaded.

'How do you know what my type is? Besides she's only a kid and I'm happily married,' Tony came back. 'Right now I'd happily trade her for a couple more cold beers and another steak and onion roll. Believe me!'

Richard obviously did not, judging from his raucous laugh, which attracted unnecessary attention to the conspicuously empty chairs at their table.

Dad was a big lean man with greying hair and the pallor of an underground shift boss. He wore an olive-green safari suit, typically Rhodesian and immensely practical. The good-looking guy in jeans and t-shirt bore a striking resemblance to his father, tall and without an ounce of surplus flesh but not a miner, judging from the tan. The fifth member of the party was a shy-looking character in a dark-blue suit and tie, totally impractical attire for Wankie. He also looked justifiably concerned at the number of eyes unashamedly feasting themselves on his girl.

Tony was not surprised after Richard's outburst to see the tanned individual with long, wavy, fair hair making his way around the dance floor towards their table. In his early twenties, with handsome if somewhat effeminate features, he had alert blue eyes like his sister. He was certainly no soldier with hair down to his shoulders – possibly a rancher or a game ranger, Tony fancied.

'Good evening, gentlemen.' The young man presented himself.

Now that's a reasonable start, Tony thought, a civilian referring to army as gentlemen. 'Good evening,' he replied, equally civil.

'If these chairs are not taken, may I commandeer them for the ladies?' The young man motioned towards the two women now watching expectantly from across the room.

'What about the gentlemen?' Richard countered politely but pointedly.

The stranger's cheeks flushed a shade darker and yet when he spoke it was in a soft, perfectly controlled tone that belied his disenchantment. 'Actually, we had hoped you might consider vacating the table for a mixed party?' The young man made his point with equal candour.

It had been weeks since Richard had sat at a table, let alone in an easy chair, and he was just beginning to get the feel for it again. He was about to protest but Tony beat him to it. 'It will be our pleasure. It's time we got some fresh air anyway. Richard, on your feet.'

The younger man then further surprised Tony by clicking his heels with military gusto, extending his hand and offering very properly, 'Thank you, gentlemen, I . . . that is we, appreciate the gesture.' His handshake was powerful and sincere.

Tony got a whiff of her perfume as he pulled back his chair. For her part she hardly had time to thank him with a curt smile and a flash of perfect white teeth before the young man in the suit edged his way awkwardly between Tony and the back of her chair, muttering that he could manage.

Once outside the crowded lounge the two friends crossed the clinker-covered car park to peer out over the eerie starlit bush, which stretched away like a grey sea from the base of the *koppie* far below. Standing in the shadows they relieved themselves in a flowerbed, toilets being something one soon learned to do without in the army. Besides, as far as Tony was concerned there was a certain magic in standing legs astride beneath a star-studded sky, a welcome breeze ventilating the crotch, crickets screeching and the pungent, sweet smell of mimosa pollen in the air.

Richard tapped Tony on the shoulder with his free hand to draw his attention to a military vehicle, barely visible through the clump of trees into which it had been reversed at the back of the hotel. It was conspicuous by its lack of regimental insignia. 'That's one of the new modified U-1100T Unimogs on issue to regular army units,' he observed. 'I wonder what the hell it's doing back there?' He was already beginning to slur his words.

'No idea,' Tony said dismissively, devoting his attention once more to the three magnificent baobab trees from which the hotel derived its name. The giant trees – one of the largest living things on the planet – rose majestically from the dry earth in which they had stood for a thousand years or more. Their huge boles, twenty metres plus in circumference, were gnarled and creased in great smooth folds. Their naked branches reached up into the night sky in wild profusion, taking on the ghostly appearance of a weird array of roots.

Standing beneath these imposing, unearthly giants of the bushveld, the last thing Tony wished to be reminded of was the army. 'Just look at these beauties. African baobabs *Adansonia digitata*. One of only eight species worldwide and the only one found on this continent.' He shook his head in awe. He had also read that the cavernous openings often found in their great boles were used as shelters by weary travellers and housed the hives of wild bees, while the tree's fruit, the cream of tartar, was used as sweets and made refreshing cool drinks for the children of the bush. It was also said that potions steeped from the bark had healing properties, restored virility and afforded protection against crocodile attacks. 'Baobabs, the source of legends,' Tony proclaimed as he buttoned up his fly. 'A fitting tribute to the resilience of all those who eke out an existence from these arid lands,' he added poetically.

'The bloody land is arid because our black brothers don't have a fucking clue about land husbandry,' Richard corrected him indignantly.

The band was bashing out a rock number when the two corporals ambled light-headedly back into the lounge to secure standing space, just off the dance floor. Everybody possessing a partner was dancing or simply pressing up against one another on the cramped floor space. The young lady from the group that had occupied their table was out there as well, looking more radiant than ever with a smile on her face and a flush in her full cheeks. Her escort was also enjoying himself, having had the presence of mind to shed his jacket and tie.

His foot tapping in time with the music and his eyes on the dancers, Tony leant closer to Richard to make himself heard. 'You were right, Wankie certainly excelled itself with that young lass.'

'I thought you were only here for the beer and steak rolls?'

'Affirmative,' Tony grinned broadly. 'That and just seeing people in civvies and being able to drink out of a glass makes me feel half human again in spite of the bloody uniform.'

The band paused before going on to play a few bars of an American square dance. There were roars of delight and some hand clapping, mainly from the fellows with the less-attractive women. The men formed a circle on the outside while the women, some a little hesitant due to the number of chaps in jungle-green battle fatigues, formed up in the centre. The band struck up and off they danced, round and round, laughing and stamping in time with the beat.

Richard's cue came a moment later when the music stopped to allow the dancers to take their partners. Snatching Tony's glass out of his hand he gave him an almighty shove. 'Now's your big chance, Mr holier-than-thou,' he taunted as Tony went sprawling into the mass of bodies on the dance floor.

As luck or fate would have it, the steadying hand that helped Tony regain his balance belonged to none other than the young woman with the cute nose and long blonde hair, now swept back in a girlish ponytail.

'Thank you.'

'Don't thank me,' she retorted coolly. 'You nearly took my eye out with your cigarette.'

Flushing red as he crushed his dog-end under heel, Tony was

about to apologise and take his leave when the music started up and she took his hand. Having guided him down the dance floor, away from the band so that she could make herself heard, she introduced herself. 'I'm Victoria. Barging in like that was extremely bad manners,' she chastised, the soft, almost humorous, tone in her voice making a mockery of the reprimand. 'The only reason I'm forgiving you is because you were kind enough to give up your table earlier.'

She remembered, Tony reflected, still somewhat bewildered and trying to clear his head. 'I'm Tony, and I was pushed,' he explained awkwardly, trying to pick up the step.

'A likely story, but even if it's true someone else will still have to leave the floor.'

'Two guesses?' He sniggered without thinking.

'David!' she breathed, looking anxiously over her shoulder. He was dancing with an older woman but still there nonetheless.

Ignoring the tempo and simply holding her closer for support, Tony chuckled to himself, for the beer was having a telling effect on his balance as well as his tongue.

The music stopped but no new circle formed. The army chaps were satisfied with the status quo and the locals who had expectantly released their partners, in the hope of retrieving their women, had no alternative but to accept them back as the musicians picked up the mood and played on.

When next the music stopped a few couples left the floor, including David who dutifully escorted his middle-aged partner back to her table. Displaying more courage than one might have given him credit for, he then returned to the dance floor. 'Excuse me,' he said tapping politely on the taller man's shoulder. 'May I, may I butt in . . . please?'

Tony did not resent the intrusion; in fact he almost welcomed it. He was unaccustomed to dancing, let alone this close with a very attractive teenage girl. His weeks in the bush were not helping either, and every time one of her firm breasts or a thigh brushed against him he was compelled to think of something unpleasant, like Captain Williams. Her girlish fragrance, a combination of talc, toilet water and hair spray, coupled with the effect of half a dozen beers drunk in quick succession, had left him both light-headed and embarrassingly amorous.

On the second tap Tony nodded and took a pace backwards. If for no other reason, he needed to prove that the army had not entirely deprived him of his sense of value. But it was not to be, for even with his limited experience of women Tony knew enough to realise that when one squeezed your hand at a time like that she was certainly not looking to be let go. Intoxicated in more ways than one, Tony turned and grinned down apologetically at the anxious young man at his side.

'Sorry mate, not your night I'm afraid.' No sooner had he uttered the words than Tony bit his tongue. Was this really him? He needed a cold shower and a bloody good night's sleep.

'Victoria!' David appealed, taking a precautionary step back from the solidly built individual in uniform.

'I'm sorry, Dave, there will be other dances.' Victoria offered a lame smile and a shrug of feigned helplessness. As David turned and stormed off the dance floor she muttered in her partner's ear, 'That was most unkind. You could at least have been tactful.'

Shuffling back down to the quieter end of the crowded dance floor once more, Tony said, 'You are quite right, I'm uncouth. I will see you back to your table and your boyfriend and call it a night.' Still she did not release him and they danced on. Women, he thought, closing his eyes and resting his cheek against the top of her head.

The lights were dimmed as the evening progressed and the tempo of the band mellowed. Still they danced. There was a lot of smooching and groin grinding going on about them. Tony also found himself pressing up against his partner, while he poured his heart out. An avid listener, Victoria clung to him just as tightly. Even after the band had downed their instruments for a break, it was a minute or two before they sheepishly broke off their embrace and left the deserted dance floor.

Arriving back at her table, Victoria self-consciously did the introductions, 'That's my brother Gerald, and this is David . . . a friend of the family. Gentlemen, this is Tony. And who might you be?' she asked the uniformed stranger now seated next to her brother.

'Richard . . . Richard du Preez,' he slurred, getting unsteadily to his feet. 'Tony and I are together, remember? Your brother kindly insisted I rejoined our old table after your parents left.'

Reluctantly seating Victoria next to David, Tony took a chair opposite Gerald. The younger man raised his glass and they drank to their new acquaintances. David continued to sulk, staring fixedly at the wet tabletop, ignoring everybody.

'Cheers David,' Tony offered anyway, saluting the top of the youngster's downcast head.

'What became of Mr and Mrs?' Tony asked of no one in particular.

'Dad got fed up trying to compete with you lot for his wife,' Gerald laughed.

Victoria knew that while her brother had made light of the situation he was not far off the mark. Mother was a notorious flirt and Dad was as jealous as they came.

'I understand you command a Company with . . . one of the Territorial battalions, based out this way?' Gerald said to Tony.

The restraint Gerald exercised in prying without dropping sensitive information implied that he was well aware of the fact that loose talk cost lives. The statement itself implied that Richard had a loose and mischievous tongue. Taking a swallow of his beer to buy time, Tony decided against compounding the deceit. 'We are not at liberty to discuss operational issues I'm afraid,' he replied, glaring at his colleague over the rim of his glass.

'My apology, it was wrong of me to pry,' Gerald said, casting an eye about the busy lounge, which was occupied mainly by locals now that midnight was approaching.

'Don't officers have stars or something on their shoulders?' Victoria asked.

'Normally, but they don't always wear their pips in operational areas, for security reasons,' Richard answered on Tony's behalf. 'Show the lady,' he invited, his slurring more pronounced than ever.

Tony reluctantly took the set of major's tabs out of his pocket, each embossed with a single crown, and held them up momentarily for inspection, without comment.

'Last round, *Sir*,' Richard grinned apologetically as he signalled to a passing waiter.

David raised both hands. 'Really, thank you all the same but I must get Vicky home, it's nearly twelve. Say, don't you fellows have to be in bed, I mean back at barracks, by twenty-four hundred hours?'

'Other ranks my dear chap, other ranks, and it's one minute past to be precise,' Tony's surrogate orderly confirmed, continuing with the pretence.

Outwardly Richard did not appear that drunk, but his speech and the loss of his fetish for punctuality were a clear indication to Tony that his friend was well and truly plastered. He was not too far behind for that matter. What the hell, the bloody army could wait for once, he decided.

Midnight came and went with Gerald, Tony and Richard engrossed in their debate on the war, failed politics and the deteriorating economic situation; current Rhodesian topics. Victoria looked on quietly, occasionally sipping her drink. Tony appeared to be getting the better of Gerald in the debate, something she found surprising. It was almost as if her brother was deliberately leading with his chin.

'Really Vicky, it's time to go,' David insisted, getting impatiently to his feet.

'As you wish David,' she smiled demurely but remained seated. 'Thank you for coming,' she added when David continued to stand his ground.

'*Good night*,' David said with exaggerated emphasis as he marched stiffly out of the lounge.

Having watched the little pantomime, Tony noted that Victoria was looking bored. Not that there was much he could do about it – the band had packed up and he and Richard were already well overdue back at the supply depot barracks. He also noticed that she was showing a little more leg than she would have liked, the low armchairs making modesty difficult. It was only after she had re-crossed her legs for the second time that he realised he had been staring. Averting his eyes, he turned his attention back to her brother. The man was an enigma, in that his interest in politics and all things military seemed out of charter with his bohemian appearance. He also had an uncanny knack of drawing people out in conversation, while letting nothing slip from his side. It was a discipline that seemed to come easy to the man. Indeed, so guarded and evasive had Gerald been that Tony had still not established what he did for a living. Having previously eliminated miner, farmer and game ranger, Tony asked directly, 'Gerald, what exactly is it that you do in this neck of the woods?'

Smiling, but ignoring the question, Gerald looked at his watch before running both hands through his long wavy hair. 'Gentlemen, a most stimulating evening but you really must excuse me. Hopefully we will meet again some day and can continue where we left off.'

He's done it again, Tony thought, as Gerald eased himself out of his chair and turned enquiringly to his younger sister. Victoria made no attempt at getting up; instead she pouted her lips and appealed to her brother with a feigned look of defiance.

Gerald smiled back. A year or so ago that look would have told him he'd lost the argument before it had started, but he was older and wiser now. Fortunately for his sister he had already decided she was old enough to make up her own mind, now that she was going on eighteen. While not entirely comfortable at the age difference, he had learned enough about their guests to know they weren't your typical army guys; in fact Tony was quite the gentleman.

'Sis, it's up to you. Are you coming with me or would you prefer to have Tony and Richard see you home?'

Victoria sighed, for a moment she had thought she might be losing her touch. 'That depends on Tony. Will I be an inconvenience?' she asked of the two men lounging back in their chairs.

'Not at all,' insisted Richard, again answering for his friend. He could already visualise Vicky nestled between the two of them in the cab of the ten-ton Bedford.

To reassure himself that he was not going to regret leaving his little sister with virtual strangers, Gerald turned to Tony. 'She will be in safe hands with you, won't she Tony.' There was no mistaking the statement of fact.

'Perfectly safe. I'll arrange for a taxi and Richard can follow in the truck.'

'What, no staff car?' Gerald quipped.

'Not appropriate in an operational area; landmines and all that,' Tony countered with a known fact before Richard could come up with something less plausible.

Following Victoria to her feet, Tony and Richard shook hands with Gerald and then stepped aside so he could embrace his sister. He's bloody tall, Tony reflected, realising that in spite of his own six foot two inches he had been looking up at Gerald when they shook hands.

'Thank you for coming tonight, it meant a great deal to the folks. Take care and remember we all miss and think about you constantly,' Victoria whispered a little too loudly in her brother's ear.

Giving his sister a cautioning glance, Gerald hugged her briefly for a second time before taking his leave. He waved as he rounded the door.

'What is it your brother does that he has to take care?' Tony asked.

'That was just a figure of speech.'

'Where does he stay? Obviously not at home with you and your folks?'

'Tony, please, I'm not at liberty to say,' Victoria said, stifling a yawn.

'As you wish,' Tony conceded before taking Richard by the arm and drawing him aside in the almost deserted lounge. They had a real problem with the time but what the hell, why should this camp be any different from the rest. He was just not cut out for this regimental crap, he thought.

'Richard, I'll sit it out with her ladyship until she has finished her drink and then get a taxi and see her home. You had best head straight back. I'll get the cab to drop me at the barracks, whenever.'

'Brilliant, and how the bloody hell do I account for your absence and explain the hour?'

'Here, put these on before you get there,' Tony stuffed the set of officer's crowns into Richard's pocket. 'At the guardhouse simply demand to inspect the duty roster and while you are about it sign us both in, chances are those national service lads at the boom will be half asleep this time of night.'

'What if they . . . aren't?' Richard persisted.

'Then make something up – you've had plenty of practice to-night.'

Richard shrugged and reluctantly bade Victoria goodnight; he was having serious misgivings about having drunk too much and now having to buck the system.

Sitting back down opposite Victoria, Tony found himself marvelling at what a really attractive girl she was, a little buxom but nicely proportioned. Her petite nose, dimples and sexy blue eyes were a delight to behold.

'You're not bad, not bad at all. Do you know that?' Tony nodded approvingly.

'I'm flattered,' Victoria blushed, again attempting to get a little more hem out of her skirt.

'You're welcome. Now tell me, how did a pretty young miss like you end up alone with a guy in uniform, twice her age?'

'I'm here because I trust Gerald's judgement. As for your being twice my age, I'll have you know I will be nineteen next month,' she lied, having added a year before she could help herself. 'While you cannot be much older than Gerald; mid twenties I'd say?'

'Close enough,' Tony beamed.

'More to the point, I'm here because I want to be. I find you interesting and . . . really quite handsome,' she said, blushing while fighting down the butterflies in her stomach as she hesitantly removed the comb securing her ponytail, letting her hair down with a flourish.

Tony reached for his cigarettes; the gesture with the hair had his heart racing. It had also been some time since he had been paid a compliment like that. 'What's so interesting about me?' he asked self-consciously as he exhaled.

'You're different.'

Tony raised an eyebrow.

'You are very self-assured, dominant in fact, when it comes to talking to men. On the other hand you are surprisingly shy when dealing with women, even nervous perhaps. Unless I happen to be an exception to the rule, which I doubt,' she explained.

'Nonsense,' Tony said in response to this uncanny assessment by the teenager now challenging him with large laughing eyes from across the table.

'You deny women make you feel uncomfortable?'

'Yes,' Tony lied, easing himself awkwardly up in his chair.

'I also happen to trust you, in spite of your not really being a major or whatever,' she continued.

'I never said I had a commission.' Tony was exasperated as it dawned on him that she was subtly directing the conversation, just like her brother.

'Your friend did.'

'Hero worship, can't take him anywhere. How did you know we were having you on?'

'I didn't. Gerald discreetly pointed out earlier that your shirt-sleeve is less faded where you've recently worn stripes. He agreed that officers do not always display rank in the field, but he said most are too vain not to do so at functions like this. He also said it was improbable anyone your age could have worked his way that far up through the ranks, even with your ability; *ego*, I think he called it.'

'The cheeky *bastard!* Tell me, what would you do without big brother?' Tony was more relaxed now that the truth was out and he found himself enjoying the banter.

'I'd have guessed,' she laughed. 'For starters, would an officer and a gentleman really allow himself to get quite so inebriated, while escorting a lady? Secondly, if you had some authority Richard would not have looked so concerned about arriving back at barracks after hours. You guys are probably in for the high jump, according to Gerald,' she concluded, stifling a laugh while cautioning herself against saying too much, having been forewarned by Gerald.

'I beg your pardon!' He was about to tease *what lady*, but checked himself, for in spite of her bravado he sensed she might be feeling a little uneasy now that the lounge was almost empty. Instead he said, 'In my defence, Victoria, I was well on my way to getting plastered long before we were . . . introduced. However, you are quite right to remind me that I have drunk too much and I apologise if I have embarrassed anyone.'

'Please, there's no need for an apology. We all know how tough it's becoming out there in the operational areas these days. You're entitled to let your hair down . . . occasionally. Besides, I really don't mind you like this. You're so relaxed; all sort of soft and . . .'

'Lollopy,' he finished for her.

Her laughter rang out. 'Actually I was going to say cuddly.'

'Yes, that's better.' He grinned broadly, getting to his feet and offering her his hand.

It was even warmer in the taxi than it had been out in the night air, and as Tony dozed his head slipped unobtrusively down on to Victoria's firm, full breast. His left arm was snugly wedged between them, his right arm across her lap. The heady, feminine scent of the young woman's closeness added to his intoxication and he felt he was losing touch with reality.

VICTORIA

Intent on the drive, as the taxi made its way down the winding road from the top of the *koppie*, Victoria received a rude awakening when the hand on her lap found its way beneath the hem of her skirt. Every muscle in her body tensed instinctively and she squeezed her legs tightly together. Only to find to her horror that she had simply imprisoned the offending hand between her stocking-less thighs.

Tony remained motionless for what seemed an age before he felt the silky sensation of warm skin peeling slowly back from his hand as Victoria gingerly parted her trembling legs. There could be no mistaking the bold invitation for him to right the wrong he had done her. It was even possible, he thought, that he might be forgiven if he did the gentlemanly thing. Blame the booze and the damn uniform he decided, moving his hand all the way up.

Victoria gasped. She'd clearly misplaced her trust. Instinctively closing her legs again she only succeeded in forcing his hand even more firmly against her womanhood. Panting in short breaths she pressed the nails of her free hand into Tony's face and forehead, warningly.

'Christ, hold it,' he groaned.

'What do you take me for?' she hissed in his ear, not loud enough to unduly alarm the African taxi driver concentrating on the narrow road. 'And stop taking the Lord's name in vain.'

'OK, OK, I'm sorry. I must have dozed off. Just relax your legs a second.'

Victoria did not move.

'I promise.'

Parting her quivering thighs in short jerky movements Victoria grabbed his arm, but the harder she pulled the slower his hand seemed to move, his fingers caressing her inner thigh all the way back to the relative safety of her knee. By the time she had his hand back in her lap, the excited little tremor that had begun in her stomach had manifested itself in an uncontrollable shudder that wracked her whole body.

Feeling Victoria's involuntary rapture, Tony gently snuggled his head and shoulder even closer up against her breast. The mood was reminiscent of his drive-in cinema days, he thought, as he dozed off.

When next he opened his eyes they were parked outside one of the large wood-framed colliery houses with the usual green corrugated-iron roof and wide fly-screened veranda. The big garden was well tended, as were most of the properties in Wankie, the lush greenery being a welcome respite for those who spent much of their waking lives wresting coal from the sweltering, dust-laden, bowels of the earth.

Tony paid off the taxi driver, who had refused to wait around at that hour of the morning even with the meter running. Shouldering his rifle and sidling up to Victoria on the pavement in the deserted street, Tony lit a cigarette while she fiddled in her handbag.

'You really should have gone with him, you'll not get another taxi this time of night in Wankie,' she warned, taking out her lipstick.

Tony leant back against the fence to steady himself. He really should have opted for a good night's sleep at the barracks, in a bed for a change, he thought. If he'd had a dozen hours sleep in the past four days that was a lot; coupled with too much to drink his fatigue was complete.

Having touched up her make-up in the subdued orange glow of the streetlight, Victoria looked anxiously back at the darkened house. 'I really should go in, it's almost two o'clock and Mum is probably listening for the door.'

'Are you often out late?' he whispered, staring down at his cigarette in disgust; the more he smoked the more they seemed to taste like sawdust.

'Most nights,' she teased but quickly corrected herself, realising their time together was fast running out. 'Very infrequently to be honest, as I'm sure you've already guessed, Tony.'

Flicking his cigarette into the night Tony placed his hands on Victoria's shoulders, intent on a polite goodnight kiss. Only to end up in a wild passionate embrace, her mouth smothering his, their tongues thrusting and probing.

114

'Tony,' she gasped finally, breaking off for air.

'Yes, Vicky?' he panted, collapsing back against the fence with her in his arms.

'Tony, there's something I have been meaning to ask all evening . . . but I haven't found the courage. Possibly because I think I already know the answer.' Fidgeting with her handbag she added, 'I realise it's presumptuous as we hardly know each other but . . .' Faltering, she pulled back out of his arms, now more afraid than ever of the truth and the finality of it all.

'Vicky you are very beautiful,' Tony murmured as he looked on helplessly while she dabbed her eyes with a tissue. He had never played on feminine sentimentality and would certainly not stoop so low as to string along anyone as trusting and unspoilt as this. 'What can I say? Yes, I am married. Damn it, happily so.' Slamming the heel of his boot into the fence post behind him in frustration, he added, 'I'm really very sorry. Sorry for getting involved. Sorry for acting the way I did on the dance floor and again in the bloody taxi; for barging into your life. I could blame the bloody army but I realise I should know better.'

Pulling her back into his arms he hugged her to him and blurted out, 'Vicky, it's also true to say that I have never felt for anyone quite the way I do now for you. Hell, this is not making it any easier is it? I really am . . .' He was again in the process of apologising when Victoria pressed a restraining finger against his lips in a very adult gesture.

Easing out of his arms she slipped the latch on the gate and led him by the hand into the front garden. The driveway was lined with flamboyant trees, their spreading branches meeting above them, further defusing the soft orange light from the deserted street. Halfway up the long driveway she turned and flattened herself against him, seeking his mouth and kissing him for all she was worth. Just as unexpectedly she pulled out of his embrace and fled wordlessly across the lawn, trying unsuccessfully to stifle her sobs. At the front door she turned once, waved and was gone.

Tony did not know how long he had lain there. The last thing he remembered was sitting down on the lawn under the trees, rifle across his lap, lighting another cigarette and contemplating the long trek back to the barracks. He must have collapsed into a deep sleep for he found himself coming around ever so slowly, as if out of a dream.

Her voice gradually penetrated his dulled senses, but it was the freshly bathed and powdered smell of her that finally jolted him into full consciousness.

'Oh, Tony, what are you still doing here? What am I going to do with you?' she asked, kneeling next to him on the grass in her short silk dressing gown.

The moon had long gone and it was dark at the base of the tree where he lay. Her hair, brushed out and hanging loose, fell forward to shroud Tony's head in a gossamer veil as she brought her face down over his. Her cheeks were wet and the salt from her tears stung his dry lips.

Powerful arms pulled her urgently down and Victoria squeezed her eyes shut, her heart pounding as he pulled open her gown and undid his belt.

The booze and lack of sleep still clouding his senses, Tony found himself incapable of restraint. The long celibate weeks in the bush fuelling an animal like lust within him, he roughly took his fill of the love she so innocently, so willingly, offered.

Victoria sobbed quietly from beginning to end right there on the lawn, where she became a woman. A little tender but deliriously happy, she clung to Tony as the gentle early morning breeze heralded in the dawn.

Battle Camp

Tony was unceremoniously shaken out of his day-dreaming as their truck shuddered across a cattle grid, at the point where the convoy turned off the main road. Jolting down the dusty corrugated farm track that led to the training camp they were greeted by the shrill screech of a night jay as the headlights swept the dry, rolling grasslands. An owl drifted on silent wings across the night sky and a startled family of ostriches loped down the side of the road, gradually outpacing the convoy.

Ten minutes later they passed the red flag at the entrance to the military facility on Hunters Farm. The vehicles pulled up against a row of whitewashed bricks, demarcating the crude open-sided sleeping quarters of *GaBulawayo*, its Matabele name meaning *the place of killing*. Battle camps were intended to simulate actual combat conditions and the use of live ammunition ensured sufficient blood was spilt to dispel any suggestion of childish war games. The fifth and final day of their training culminated in an advance to contact, with the entire company covering five kilometres of unbroken bush in full battle dress in the heat of the day.

Having showered and washed his kit, Tony settled back on his sleeping bag to read the day old newspaper he had nicked from a ration re-supply truck. He could tolerate the heat, flies, sleeping on the hard ground and tinned food, provided he was able to keep abreast of the news.

His attention focused on the single-column headline on page three: *SOLDIER, TEN TERRS KILLED, Salisbury, Thursday. The terrorist war has claimed another twenty-four lives, a Combined Operations*

Headquarters communiqué reported today. Killed in action was Rifleman Desmond Paul Jackson (20), married with an eight-month-old daughter. He came from Salisbury and was a former pupil of the Ellis Robins Secondary School.

Security forces have killed ten terrorists and six terrorist collaborators. Seven black civilians have been murdered by terrorists in the operational areas.

A total of one hundred and fifty six people died in the war last week, according to military communiqués, of those seventy-six were terrorists and fifty-eight collaborators.

A few years ago, Tony thought, the death in action of one of Rhodesia's sons would have commanded front-page headlines, followed by a comprehensive write-up. Had Rhodesians become so blasé, so inured to death, as to now be unmoved; or was it simply that a small nation could not indefinitely shoulder an ever-growing burden of grief? Tony found the number of black civilians still being wiped out in cross-fire equally disturbing. The fact that trained soldiers continued to eliminate nearly as many so-called collaborators as they did terrorists, supported his view that sinister forces were at work.

Major Young looked thoughtful as he watched his men break camp. They had worked hard but were still civilians at heart. He was concerned that six days of battle orientation were no longer sufficient, in light of current reports that terrorists were now crossing Rhodesia's borders in droves. He knew the time was fast approaching when the enemy, in their vastly superior numbers, with modern weaponry and the support of the locals, would actively seek to engage the four-man patrols of the territorial forces.

Perhaps they were naive, he thought, to persevere with their struggle for the hearts and minds of the rural population. In spite of all their efforts, the terrorists now decidedly had the upper hand. All the mission schools and clinics in the TTLs had been forced to close, every dip tank had been destroyed or abandoned and the district commissioners and conservationists driven off the land. Maybe the Europeans should clear out, let the blacks have their freedom, their famine, their disease and their civil war? But

118

in his heart he knew this was not the answer, he also knew that the majority of blacks hated the war as much as anyone else. In the main the local tribesmen only wished to be left alone to sit around their fires, drinking last week's brew and discussing the condition of their cattle and the fertility of their wives.

The White Man's Grave

The convoy made good time, and four hours after leaving Hunters Farm the familiar landmark of the Baobab Hotel, on top of a rocky outcrop, heralded their approach to Wankie. Skirting the town the convoy passed several black mine-workers' compounds bordering the flat, inhospitable bush scrub, before turning down a short lane and into the military base, itself a converted mine compound. The camp was the tactical headquarters for the North-Western Command. It was from here that Major Young would collect his orders, prior to moving north to an operational base camp between Wankie and the Zambezi river.

While the officers enjoyed a cold beer in the air-conditioned comfort of the mess, some of the men wandered off through the maze of prefabricated concrete huts to renew old acquaintances. Others took advantage of the hot showers and a few wrote letters home.

Having showered and hijacked that day's edition of the *Bulawayo Chronicle* from the officers' lounge, Tony now squatted on a pile of old bricks in a patch of shade opposite the camp's pay telephone. Apart from the heat he was otherwise content with his lot, he was clean and had a call booked through to Kathy. It was almost noon and she should be home after her tennis.

Acting CSM Richard du Preez had guessed correctly. 'Thought I'd find you here sport. I'm going into town on the off chance of meeting up with my brother. He banks and collects supplies on Thursdays, stopping in at No 1 Colliery Club for a couple of pints on his way back to the Sawmill. Coming along for the ride?'

'Thanks, Richard but I'm waiting on a call to the wife, up to an hour's delay. Jaunts into town, hey! Rank certainly has its privileges, *Sergeant Major*,' Tony goaded good-naturedly, for he did not begrudge Richard his new acting status.

'Actually, I bribed Major Young, told him I could probably organise a couple of sacks of game biltong for the guys.'

'What about transport?' Tony enquired, getting up and offering Richard a cigarette.

'An ambulance, that's all the motor pool could spare. Must go though, only have an hour and a half. Thanks for the fag.'

Whistling as he drove into town, sweating profusely in the khaki ambulance, Richard wondered what it was that he had to feel good about. An ex-resident of the area, he recalled how traumatic it had been when his father had died of malaria down on the farm, shortly after they had moved up from South Africa, followed a year later by the shock of losing both his grandparents, on his mother's side, to black water fever. He recalled his mother telling him that the region had been christened *the white man's grave* by early traders and hunters. Had it not been for some of the best hunting in Africa, and finds of rich coal deposits in more recent years, he doubted that anybody in their right mind would have settled in Wankie at all. He stopped whistling as a sobering thought struck him: one day the whole of Southern Africa could aptly be dubbed *the white man's grave*. First Kenya, then the Belgian Congo, Zambia, Angola, Mozambique and now Rhodesia, all had succumbed to majority rule; each successive defeat of colonialism having proved more costly than the last in terms of white lives.

It never ceased to amaze him that in spite of black dictatorships having impoverished all of sub-Saharan Africa, reducing once prosperous nations to beggars of aid, the rest of the world was still hell-bent on championing majority rule. The West put democracy on a pedestal, yet turned a blind eye to the fact that to date not a single change of government in black Africa had been brought about through the ballot box.

Driving slowly past the bank Richard searched in vain for his brother's long-wheelbase Land-Rover. It was already twelve-thirty and he had just decided to try the club when he saw someone he recognised. She looked very chic in her blue uniform. Her blonde hair had been cut short and she had put on some weight but she still exuded all the girlish charm he remembered. She was coming down the wide marble steps of the bank with three similarly dressed young women. On their way to lunch, Richard guessed.

Braking and sliding across the seat he stuck his head out of the passenger window, leaning on the hooter as he did so. The girls, walking off down the pavement in the opposite direction, looked back just long enough to confirm their suspicions; another jerk in uniform making a spectacle of himself.

With the lunchtime traffic building up behind the big ambulance, Richard whipped off his cap and leaned further out of the window.

'Hey, Vicky,' he bellowed. 'It's me, Richard.'

Hooters blared from the rows of stationary vehicles shimmering in the heat waves. Ignoring the commotion a moment longer, Richard waved to the pretty blonde who had turned once more and now recognised him. With a final wave he reluctantly let out the clutch and moved on.

Her arm still held high in greeting, it was all Victoria could do to prevent herself running after the ambulance, now caught up in the flow of lunch time traffic.

Richard sighed, she had looked really great and he could hardly wait to report back to Tony. It would be an easy matter for him to trace her through the bank. The hardest part would be finding an excuse to get into town once they had moved out into the operational area.

Vicky's heart was pounding as she watched the military vehicle out of sight but she was already beginning to regret her over-zealous display of enthusiasm. If Richard was back in the area, then in all probability so was Tony. Having acted rashly once in trying to contact him, after missing her period for a second month, she had vowed to keep her secret; to be confronted by the man now would present more problems than it solved.

'Excuse me Sir, did you book a trunk call to Bulawayo?' the national service lad enquired, sticking his head around the side of the telephone booth.

Tony grinned as he stood up, folding the newspaper. It made you feel old when a kid in uniform called you sir.

'Thanks mate, sorry for the interruption. I'll be as quick as I can.'

'Hello, hello,' he called as he took the receiver.

'Mr Longdon?'

'Yes!'

'Sorry, I am getting no reply from your Bulawayo number. Would you like me to try again later?'

'No, we move out in an hour. Can you try this other number for me, while I wait?'

'Number please?'

'Bulawayo 57728, still reverse charges.'

'One moment, I'll see what I can do. You're through, six minutes only.'

'Hello son, it's wonderful to hear your voice. Are they looking after you all right? Are you getting enough sleep, dear?'

'I'm fine thanks, Mum. How's everything with you and Dad? Played any golf lately?'

'Not for a while darling, it's really so dreadfully hot. Gosh, you must be feeling it too, I bet. It really is wonderful hearing from you out of the blue like this. Everything is all right, *isn't it?*'

'Everything is just fine,' Tony confirmed dutifully. 'I've lost a bit of weight but feel better for it. How's Kathy doing? I tried home but she was out. Is she coming round for meals?'

'She's fine and yes we have had her round,' Helen confirmed, adding after a short but perceptible pause, 'She was round last night in fact, dear.'

'Are you sure she's OK, Helen?' He always called her by her first name when getting serious.

'Please don't worry yourself. She will be fine dear. Oh, she's received your letters, two in less than a week, very thoughtful of you. We also received ours. Dad sends his love and I'll write soon, dear.'

'Does she come round for supper every night?' Tony persisted.

'Well not exactly, dear. Last night was the first time . . . to be honest. But then she has spent quite a few evenings with Margaret and Roger. She seems to get on well with Margaret,' she said without conviction. 'Son, why not write and let's try again to persuade Kathy to move in with us for a while. We have plenty of room. She may feel differently now.'

'Three minutes,' cut in the operator.

'She would also be company for me,' Helen added.

'Why do you feel we should push it? You know how she feels about imposing. You and I know it would not be a problem, but try convincing her. Helen, out with it, what's bothering you, before we get cut off?'

'Dear, it's probably absolutely nothing . . . just your doting old mother again. It's just that I feel Kathy may be spending a bit too much time at Roger and Margaret's.'

Tony noted it was Roger and Margaret now, not the other way around. Should he be reading anything into it or should he be relieved that this was all that Helen was making a fuss about? He trusted Kathy implicitly.

'I see,' Tony acknowledged, slowly tapping a cigarette from the packet; the conversation cruelly reminding him of his own infidelity a few months earlier. 'OK, I will write and suggest she comes and stays with you. In the meantime please ask Mark to keep an eye on that wife of mine. At least I can trust my own brother.'

'Now Tony, stop that talk. Kathy may have been acting a little strange lately but she's a very level-headed young woman, you know that.'

Tony did not know quite what to think. All he knew for certain was that the army was the worst place in the whole goddamn world in which to try and keep a level head at times like these.

'Maybe, but she's not the one I have my bloody doubts about,' he came back, voice raised.

It was his mother's turn to ignore the inference and wisely re-direct the conversation. 'Son, we heard yesterday that Mark, Linda and the children are now seriously thinking of going down south, for good. He's had a job offer and flies to Durban for an interview this coming Saturday. It's in textiles or something. Probably for the best but we are going to miss them of course.'

Mark was Tony's younger and only brother. Like so many others he had somehow managed to avoid military service, in Mark's case by playing on the fact that he had an obscure heart murmur.

'If he's got any sense he won't be too bloody choosy. The way things are going at the moment they are starting to call up the sick, lame and lazy,' Tony advised without malice for he did not begrudge his brother his devious good fortune.

'Nine seconds please,' reminded the girl at the exchange.

'OK Mum, nice talking to you, look after yourself and my love to all. Don't forget have a chat to Mark for me. He's a lot deeper than we give him credit for and I'm sure he'll be able to get through to Kathy for us.'

Women, Tony thought, replacing the receiver after his mother had said her farewells through choked back tears. As he left the booth he absent-mindedly took out his handkerchief and blew his nose, hard.

Tony still had an uneasy feeling in the pit of his stomach as he made his way across to the open-sided canteen. They had been friends with Roger and Margaret since they were kids, a long time, perhaps too long. On leaving school Roger had joined the railways as a fireman; stoking the boiler on a steam train eight hours a day was not everyone's cup of tea but it was an occupation exempt from military call-up. Having since left the railways he had man-aged to continue to dodge the army, and now naively attributed his success as a life insurance salesman to his endearing charm and good looks.

Major Young had done a good job on the camp quartermaster and Tony watched while the rest of C Company tucked into heaped plates of cold meats, salads and as much bread, butter and jam as they could eat. He sat at the end of one of the noisy trestle tables but found he had lost his appetite.

Contact

It was mid-afternoon and nothing stirred as the convoy snaked through the rocky hills and deep ravines beneath a merciless sun. They were moving off the watershed heading towards the Zambezi river – terrorist country. Wells was the first to relax his vigil as they entered a more open stretch of country.

'Was there anything of interest in that newspaper back at Wankie, Corp?'

'Not really, just more propaganda.'

'Like what?' Wells prompted, more out of boredom than genuine interest, as he begrudgingly offered Tony a cigarette.

'Stuff like conditioning the electorate in the run up to the referendum in January next year. The Transitional Government is subtly trying to convince the whites that ratification of their so-called majority rule constitution is the lesser of two evils. If they get the nod they'll go through the *motions* of a one-man one-vote election in April.'

'Give it to me straight man, is that good or bad?'

'It means that Zimbabwe/Rhodesia, for that is what they are planning on calling the country at the end of the day, will have a black prime minister within six months. Bishop Muzorewa, if the Rhodesian Front succeeds in pulling off this farce.'

'Then no more army,' Wells said forlornly.

'I don't think you need worry about being out of a job just yet,' Tony reassured him. 'Unless the guerrilla leaders of the Patriotic Front participate in these elections we could end up spending even more time in bloody uniform, only this time fighting to protect the bishop and his puppet government from their own kind.'

'That will be the fucking day!' Wells snorted. 'South Africa here I come.'

'They're next on the list,' Tony said fatalistically.

Around the next bend the parched terrain flattened out and the thorn scrub gave way to mopani forests. The tall, stark mopani trees appeared lifeless after eight months without rain and would afford little respite from the sun in the days ahead. Even more disconcerting, Tony thought, was the fact that these trees played host to the dreaded mopani fly. He also noticed that every bit of foliage to a height of two metres above the ground had been devoured by the drought-stricken livestock of the locals. It was not uncommon to see goats standing on their hind legs or even climbing into thorn trees to get at what leaves remained. Nudging Wells, Tony observed, 'What an existence, a land plagued with mopani flies and mosquitoes, thousands of starving goats and rivers that flow for only two months of the year and are infested with bilharzia when they do.'

'It's no wonder the fucking terrs are dying to move into the bloody suburbs, hey Corp. Get it man? *Dying.*' Wells was still laughing at his own joke when the convoy arrived at a man-made clearing in the bush.

As the trucks approached the barbed-wire entanglement surrounding the base camp, two sun-blackened troopers in scant green army shorts and sleeveless camouflage t-shirts pulled back a section of the wire from across the dirt road. Inside the camp several other young National Servicemen ambled listlessly over, eyeing their replacements as one might the condemned. It was obvious to Tony that they'd had a gutfull of the harsh inhospitable terrain and murderous heat.

The flies, as well as the heat, had already made themselves felt by 05.25 the following morning. Rousing himself, Tony ducked out from beneath the stifling confines of his mosquito net – a base camp luxury – and slipped on his shorts. The sweat quickly dried on his bare back as he shook out his damp sleeping bag. The best thing about last night had been the two hours guard duty up on top of the water tower, where occasionally he had felt a faint breeze.

'OK, rise and shine you wankers, it's five-thirty, shit, shave and shampoo time,' Piet Nell called out, coming in off the last guard. Stamping noisily as he made his entrance through the doorless opening of the barrack room.

A horrendous fart rent the air as Wells acknowledged the wake-up call as only he could. 'I can't wait until we piss off out on patrol and leave this reveille crap behind,' he announced, sitting up and stroking the day-old stubble on his face with the back of his hand. Williams had personally escorted him to the barber for a haircut and shave back at the garrison in Wankie. Picking up his rifle he set off in the direction of the ablution block, clad only in a pair of sagging, dirty grey underpants.

Tony had just returned from the makeshift showers and was contemplating what Young's strategy would be for the deployment of his three platoons, when Wells came doubling back through the open doorway.

'For the last time Foxy, get that fucking sling off your gun. You are not attached to the bloody Congolese army any more,' Tony reprimanded his charge.

'It's a fucking rifle, not a fucking gun,' Wells corrected as he hastily pulled on his shorts and boots, minus socks. 'Do you guys want to know what's cooking or not?'

Two minutes later Acting CSM Richard du Preez came bounding into the billet. 'Get ready to move out. Major wants all three sections mobile in ten . . .' he paused, noting the advanced state of readiness of the men. 'Let's make that five minutes and well done the grape vine.' Turning to his colleague Richard continued, 'Tony, Acting Lieutenant Moore is still down with jippo guts, Major asks that you head up first platoon for this patrol.'

Once the rest of the men had gathered round, Richard spread a map on the bare concrete floor and began the briefing. 'A patrol of four National Service lads has run into about a dozen terrs somewhere here,' he indicated on the map. 'The gooks have them pinned down with a heavy machine-gun and the lads are understandably concerned. They called for air support but Tac HQ has nothing available at this time.'

'Richard, that's five kilometres by road and a further seven or eight across country, two hours at least, depending on the lie of the land. Can they hold out that long?'

'It's a bitch I know, Tony. Tac HQ has assured us that as soon as a K-Car can be spared they will drop in a fire-force stick. Apparently the RLI ambushed a group of terrorists of company strength crossing the Zambezi last night. All the choppers from Wankie are committed to what has developed into a running contact.'

Richard jogged alongside the lead vehicle to hand up a large brown envelope to Tony as the trucks moved off.

'The company clerk picked up the post in Wankie yesterday. Two letters in there for you, the rest for your guys, OK?'

'Thanks mate, keep the beers on ice.'

'I almost forgot,' Richard yelled at the last minute, 'I saw Vicky coming out of the bank yesterday.'

'Who?'

'Victoria,' Richard bellowed as the second truck roared past, enveloping him in dust.

'Load?' prompted Wells as they drove out through the gap in the barbed wire entanglement.

'Load,' Tony ordered, stuffing the mail into his pack and willing Vicky out of his thoughts.

As they approached their drop-off point, Tony signalled to Wells who banged on the cab. The driver slowed and they debussed on the move. Even with the sun just on the rise the late October heat in the Deka lowlands defied imagination. Mercifully the mopani flies were conspicuous by their absence. Tony signalled a five-minute break after the first hour's march and the men moved into all-round defence at the base of a *koppie*, before lighting cigarettes and sipping water sparingly. Sweat dried in white patches around their armpits.

CONTACT

Longdon and Wells clambered over flesh-searing rocks to the top of a small outcrop to establish radio communications. Making himself heard over the static, Major Young advised that the terrs had pulled back but one of the National Servicemen had been wounded. A chopper had perforce been redeployed for casevac, ETA within the hour. Longdon's patrol was to do its best to reach the rendezvous in time to secure the LZ.

Corporal van der Merwe was now up front and pushing it. There was an urgency in his stride for not even he, a seasoned farmer, could guarantee a better than fifty percent chance of hitting a pinprick on a map after a long trek over featureless terrain. They slogged on for another forty-five minutes before Van raised his hand.

'What's the problem?' Tony asked, sprinting up to the front of the patrol.

'Wells says he heard the chopper and has spotted those National Service lads,' Van was pointing at a spot four or five hundred metres away, to the left of an open expanse of low ground.

'Zero-Two-Delta this is Zero-One-Alpha we have you visual and can hear Cyclone approaching from the west. Over.'

'Alpha my man is critical. I say again, critical. Confirm they have an MO aboard.'

'Copied, Delta wait out.'

Tony swallowed hard. The corporal's speech had been controlled but there could be no mistaking the urgent tone in the younger man's voice. Tony's set crackled just as he caught sight of the helicopter, a couple of kilometres off, coming in low over the dry grey bush.

'Delta, this is Cyclone we copied that. We have a medical officer on board, should be with you in five. Alpha, what is your position? Over.'

'Cyclone, we are on a rise to your southeast. Delta are on the edge of a clearing about half a kilometre to our north.'

'Confirm no sign of CTs and clearing OK for LZ?'

'Affirmative, it looks good from here, putting down smoke. Over.'

131

'Alpha, I have your smoke and the clearing.'

'Delta, I'm making my approach. Do you copy? Over.'

Come on, Tony willed, they will overfly if you don't acknowledge. The voice that followed brought a lump to Tony's throat. 'Copied, Cyclone but hell man, you are too late, Mike's dead.'

Wells looked across at his corporal, his eyes unashamedly bright. 'Fucking terrs,' he snarled.

Fucking war, Tony was about to add. Instead he said, 'We tried.'

The casevac complete, Tony posted lookouts and rested the patrol. Finding a spot with a good field of vision and some shade, he sat and took out the letters he'd stuffed into his pack earlier. From the handwriting he could tell one was from Kathy and the other from Mark. Having saved Kathy's for last, he finished his brother's with a chuckle; it had been pretty much what he'd expected. Mark made reference to how anyone dumb enough to end up in the army deserved what they got and how he knew they all secretly loved it anyway, because what else would all the budding war heroes have to talk about when they got home?

Mark had been good enough to enclose a current newspaper cutting, which he had endorsed with the PS *Things are hotting up old boy so keep your head down. Hope to see you in Durban one day, if you live that long.*

The report under banner headlines proclaimed a massive victory over ZIPRA, Nkomo's Zimbabwe People's Revolutionary Army, inflicted in the very heart of neighbouring Zambia. At 08.30 on that fateful morning the Rhodesian Air Force, operating under the code name *Green Leader*, had delivered a crushing blow to the largest of Nkomo's guerrilla training camps, situated on the outskirts of Lusaka. In the most ambitious raid of its kind in the war to date, Rhodesia's antiquated Canberra bombers and rocket-bearing Hawker Hunters had levelled the sprawling camp. Alouette K-Cars equipped with 20-mm cannons had followed up to deliver the *coup de grâce* as they hovered above the carnage.

Tony slowly shook his head – whether they had killed five hundred or five thousand it was not going to change the outcome of the war. Quite the contrary, this so-called victory would certainly see Nkomo abandoning his agreement to drop the unholy alliance between himself and the Mao-communist co-leader of the Patriotic Front, Robert Mugabe. Nkomo having previously expressed a willingness to ditch the alliance in exchange for his return to legality and an undertaking that he and his party in exile could return home and participate freely and openly in the forthcoming majority rule elections.

Tony scanned the bush once more before opening Kathleen's letter. It was not her customary five or six pages but he was thankful at least that the only reference to Roger and Margaret was to the effect that she had popped in to have dinner with them a few times.

I nearly had a fit, darling. Your Major Young's wife called round on Thursday morning. As you know I have never met her. She simply arrived at the house and asked if I was Mrs Kathleen Longdon. Then she came out with how do you do, I'm Mrs Young and my husband is the officer commanding your husband's unit. Well, can you imagine what went through my mind? I went weak at the knees and had to sit down.

As it turned out she's calling on all the men's wives, seeing if she can be of any assistance and trying to get some of us together to help one another pass the time. We ended up having a nice old chat and agreeing it would be a good idea if she telephoned in advance of any future visits. I'm fine now, dear.

A week is a terribly long time darling. I'm trying to stay busy and keep my mind off it all but my thoughts just keep coming right back to us. You must think me very selfish going on like this but I love you so. Just five weeks more and we will be together again. I can't wait to feel your arms around me. Enough slush, hey?

I received your second letter on the fifth day. Oh, and darling, no I don't mind your sexy letters. In fact I quite enjoy them, even if I do get a little embarrassed, believe it or not. But don't you think you should be more discreet? Gosh dear, imagine if one ever fell into the wrong hands? It must be all you think of, and oh boy, the detail.

Well dear I want to get this into the morning post so will close now. Please take care. Everyone sends their love and we all miss you madly. Keep safe and God bless.

There had been nothing untoward in the tone of the letter that he could put a finger on. In fact Kathy sounded as endearing as ever, having signed off with her customary heart shape of kisses. Why then did he still feel so ill at ease, he wondered?

Indefinite Call-Up

During the weeks that followed it was all C Company could do to keep abreast of events in their area. A white farming family was butchered, after the mother and two pre-teen daughters had been raped in front of the man of the house and assembled farm labourers. A trading store was razed to the ground and the severed head of the black storekeeper impaled on a fencepost. A local chief had his lips ripped off with pliers, and a bus hit a landmine and plunged into the Gwai River Gorge, killing all fifty-seven villagers on board.

In the second week of November the skies opened and the rains finally came, falling in torrents and turning the bush green overnight. The seasonal influx of terrorists followed, only this time they were reliably reported to be crossing in their thousands. The summer rains heralding the beginning of the final onslaught to free Zimbabwe.

The terrorists' propaganda proclaimed that the whites were fleeing the country in droves, abandoning farms and houses – which was not that far from the truth. Further, that victory was imminent and the spoils of war, white women, cars and land, in that order, were theirs for the taking. It was also said that the black soldiers and police were on the verge of turning their guns on their white overlords.

The weekly supply of one day's fresh rations never seemed to catch up with C Company, but it was the resultant dearth of mail and news from the outside world that really got to Tony. Not knowing was a nightmare and his imagination was getting the better of him. Had Kathy stopped this Roger/Margaret nonsense? Had she moved in with his folks? Which of his letters had she received? Were the ranks of the Auxiliaries still growing like a cancer? Were the locals still being indiscriminately taken out in cross-fire? He was particularly concerned about his own suspicion that the rank and file were deliberately being kept in the dark.

Major Young was also a worried man after he returned from his weekly briefing. 'No Peter, they could not even give me a tentative date for our withdrawal.'

'Surely, Major,' came back Captain Williams, a note of disbelief in his voice, 'to say they don't know when we will be stood down is admitting we are no longer on top of the situation.'

'Tac HQ said they should have something for us by next week, and then hopefully we can give the men more encouraging news.' Admitting to himself that the present state of affairs hardly inspired confidence Young added, 'On a positive note we were told we are making significant headway in a number of TTLs. The Auxiliary programme has apparently snowballed beyond all expectations. Thousands of ex-terrs are now coming on side under the amnesty to be trained and redeployed.'

Williams was not convinced. 'I still feel we must be stark raving mad to fatten, train and arm more insurgents to turn loose in the reserves, where they can carry on stirring up the locals with impunity.'

'They are not just turned loose,' Young replied, crossing to the flap of the operations tent to check the evening sky for signs of more rain. 'They remain under the control of the Ministry of Defence as you well know, Captain.' Young's tone ending the discussion.

Following another eventful week, the twin-engine Cessna Lynx that had collected Young at first light that morning returned him to the makeshift bush airstrip at sundown. Captain Williams, Lieutenant Charmers, Acting CSM Richard du Preez and the company clerk were assembled within minutes of their CO's return from his weekly briefing. Lieutenant Slater and Acting Lieutenant

Moore were not present as their respective platoons, deployed in rotation, were still in the field.

Dabbing at his brow with his handkerchief, Young stood behind his folding table to address the small congregation gathered in the ops tent. 'Well, gentlemen, it's finally happened.' He paused and reached for a cigar. 'As of now C Company is committed for an indefinite period. Further, all uncommitted territorial forces and national service units are in the process of being mobilised. Very soon, all ten battalions of the Rhodesia Regiment will be in the field in support of our regular forces.' He lit his cigar while the reality of their situation sank in.

Lieutenant Moore operated his patrols with two sections out and one in, and so it was that Corporal Longdon and his men only received the grim tidings of the indefinite call-up three days after Major Young had dropped his bombshell.

When Tony's platoon finally returned to Company HQ he immediately demanded an audience with Major Young. Knowing Longdon as he did, and already concerned about morale given the circumstances, Young agreed to see him. He could ill afford to have Longdon venting his frustration on the men and further aggravating an already tenuous situation.

Major Young sat patiently smoking while Tony paced the confined ops tent, loudly berating the government, the joint chief of staff, Western diplomats and the South Africans for their collective incompetence. Letting his arms fall to his sides at last, Tony finally flopped down into the canvas chair that had been offered to him ten minutes earlier.

'Feeling better?' Young asked, exhaling a cloud of smoke. Having conceded defeat after his last altercation with Longdon, he had decided against being confrontational in the hope that logic would prevail.

'Yes, a little. I suppose we are all in the same boat and have to make the best of it.'

'That's a very mature approach,' Young agreed, inwardly thinking there was hope for Longdon yet.

Tony lit a cigarette. It was obvious Young was being diplomatic to avoid dissent in the ranks at a time when the patience of the men was growing thin. A win-win situation if he played his hand right.

'Major, I think we both accept this national mobilisation could be the final straw for an economy weakened by sanctions and a chronic shortage of skilled manpower. There is also a danger of foreign controlled business, like the one I work for, deciding to close up shop in our part of the world. Under the circumstances I feel I have a duty to ensure that decisions that can affect the . . .'

Five minutes later Young held up his hands. 'All right, Mr Longdon, you can go into town with the ration run in the morning and call your head office. Should your South African people need to meet with you, a twenty-four hour pass in Wankie is the best I can do. Your leaving the country at a time like this is out of the question. Is that clear?'

Tony left the ops tent feeling relieved and pleased with himself. His concern for the business had been genuine enough but Kathy was his bigger worry. In her case the damage would already have been done, what with the news of the indefinite mobilisation in the public domain days ago. He had visions of her sitting alone watching the evening news, while what little faith she still had in the country was shattered by the announcement.

Kathleen Longdon had not been alone that night but her world *had* come crashing down around her. After the news of the mobilisation that evening she had hardly touched the meal Margaret had prepared. Drinking more than usual she had also been in no fit state to argue when Roger insisted on driving behind her, to see her safely home.

While still in a state of shock her weakened resolve had proven powerless against Roger's calculated advances once he had her alone. What resistance she could muster was bullied out of her and she eventually succumbed to his will – to having her hate of the war and what it had done to her life and her marriage agonisingly purged from her in a selfish act of lust, bordering on rape.

Arriving in Wankie with the ration party at noon the next day, Tony called his head office in Johannesburg. The deputy chairman confirmed they were anxious to discuss the recent turn of events in Rhodesia and welcomed the opportunity for members of the board to meet with him in Wankie the following Friday. Satisfied with his business arrangements, Tony tried five times during the next hour to get through to Kathy; each time there was no reply from the number.

Richard du Preez was in charge of the ration run and had assured Major Young they would be back by last light. 'Tony, we can't delay our departure any longer. You've done what you came for so I suggest we quit while we are still ahead, for a change.'

'Just one last call to my folks, they can let Kathy know to be in Wankie next Friday. The bloody mail's been hopeless lately!'

Helen was home but confessed to not having seen Kathy that week. Having promised to pass on Tony's message she promptly broke down and wept. Recent events were proving too much for her, what with her eldest son on indefinite call-up, her youngest son and his family preparing to leave for Durban for good; and on top of it all her daughter-in-law estranged.

'Helen, pull yourself together, indefinite does not mean forever and I'll be out before you know it,' he tried to reassure her as he ground out the butt of his cigarette under heel, immediately tapping another from the pack.

'Son, I do so want to believe that. But what am I to do about Kathy in the mean time? She was not at home when I telephoned after that dreadful news, and when I got through the next morning she sounded so . . . so strange, almost indifferent.'

'Helen, stop worrying,' Tony said abruptly without even trying to disguise his impatience. 'Just make sure she knows to make it through to the Grand Hotel in Wankie by next Thursday night and that I'll be there Friday morning. I'll take it from there and everything will sort itself out, I promise.'

'Yes, I'm sure you're right, dear. Kathy is probably just a little overwrought. Seeing you again will make all the difference,' Helen concluded with a tremor of uncertainty in her voice.

Saying his farewells, Tony slowly replaced the receiver. 'I don't need this fucking army,' he cursed as he rejoined Richard.

'I know but it sure as hell needs us sport. Can we get going now?'

Operation Quartz

Major Young peered out into the early morning mist while his clerk decoded a radio despatch from Tac HQ. It had been raining on and off all week, making it heavy going for his platoons in the field.

'Sir, the meeting is still on for this afternoon but the fixed wing is grounded due to the weather. They ask if you can make it through today using our own transport.'

Young looked at his watch and then consulted the camp duty roster. 'Tell them affirmative. Then ask CSM du Preez to bring forward Friday's ration run. Let him know I'll be accompanying it. Also alert Corporal Longdon. He's scheduled to be in Wankie tomorrow anyway, for a board meeting of all bloody things.'

The contingent from C Company arrived at army headquarters in Wankie with thirty-five minutes to spare, half of which Young spent declining Longdon's request for permission to go into town that afternoon. 'Damn right I'm serious, Corporal. You're the one who doesn't understand the bloody meaning of the word *reasonable*. I can hardly be held accountable for the camp pay phone being removed for security reasons. The answer is no, and that's final,' Young concluded as he marched off across the muddy parade ground to the officers' mess, where he found his colleagues already in a huddle speculating on more bad news.

Tony was in a foul mood as he stormed off to find a batman to wash and iron some kit, prior to his meeting the next day.

Having accompanied the convoy as part of the escort party, Rifleman Wells lost no time in making himself scarce. Slipping off he went in search of some booze, having drunk the last of his brandy over a week ago. Finding the OR's bar closed until 16.30 he ducked round to the back of the building. His attempt at forcing one of the rear windows was unsuccessful, as was a piece of wire in the back-door lock.

Toying with the idea of going AWOL for the afternoon, to find a bottle store in Wankie, Wells stopped in his tracks as he passed an open window at the rear of the admin block. The door of the liquor cabinet in the office was ajar, and the mirror reflected a healthy stock. He could hardly believe his luck; the boss man was obviously still out at lunch. Somebody up there loved him after all. In his haste to empty his water bottles, while still in their carriers, he drenched both trouser legs.

Once inside Wells filled the first of his canteens with brandy. The second he half-filled with what was left of the scotch and was busy contemplating the compatibility of vodka versus gin when the door open. He dropped down behind the desk just as an African orderly backed into the office. Placing the tea tray on the coffee table in the centre of the room, the orderly left as silently as he had entered.

His heart pounding, Wells screwed on the caps of his water bottles and quickly helped himself to a handful of cigars. He was about to make for the window when he heard voices and the door opened again. This time he made it back under the desk with only a second to spare, cursing his luck under his breath.

'That was an impressive tour and an excellent lunch, Ronald. You don't fare at all badly in this neck of the woods. That South African wine was better than anything we have had at the mess back in Salisbury for ages.'

Colonel Ronald Baker was justifiably pleased with the compliment; the Wankie command was a demanding one given the intensity of insurgency crossings from Zambia. There was one advantage to the command, its proximity to the South African paramilitary police base at the Victoria Falls. His own quartermaster was well connected with his counterpart and the South Africans wanted for nothing.

142

'Thank you, Sir, we do our best. May I offer you a KWV brandy, a cigar perhaps, also courtesy of our South African friends?'

'No, thank you, Ronald, not before my meeting with the company commanders, the tea will do nicely,' Major General Armstrong replied getting comfortable in an easy chair at the coffee table.

Baker settled himself opposite the greying, slightly built general. He was anxious to clarify a point. 'Talking about the meeting, Sir, I must admit the brevity and urgency of your communiqué has left me guessing. As I see it, we are simply to integrate elements of the Territorial Forces with the Rhodesian African Rifles units in this area?'

Armstrong looked thoughtful as he ladled six spoonfuls of sugar into his tea.

'That's perfectly correct but it goes deeper than that, *much deeper*, Ronald. Only a handful of senior personnel . . .' he paused, rose, and closed the window, 'know the enormity of the operation we are planning. The initial phase of the operation, the indefinite commitment of all TF battalions and the mobilisation of all other able-bodied European males under sixty years of age, is progressing well. This we accomplished under the guise of affording protection for the electorate during the forthcoming elections. This strategy will ensure that two thirds of our men in the field, some sixty thousand, are whites.'

Baker moved forward in his chair, returning his cup to the tray, the intrigue was infectious.

'How long will we be able to keep the territorial battalions committed though Gordon, without doing irreparable harm to the economy?'

'Not nearly long enough to eliminate the number of terrs we must if we are to get back on top of the situation. Hence the reason for my visit,' Armstrong said taking a sip of his tea. Baker was sitting on the edge of his seat by the time the general continued, 'You are aware of the training programme initiated to cope with the build-up of the *Pfumo re Vahnu*, the Auxiliaries as we call

143

them. As you know, these auxiliary units are supposed to comprise of terrs that have seen the light and decided to side with us. Well, nothing could be further from the truth. In fact the majority of our so called *Spears of the People* are actually terrorist infiltrators, paying lip service to the amnesty.'

A bemused Baker got uncertainly to his feet, before thinking better of it and sitting down again. 'Sir, that's *incredible.*'

'Yes, it is, Ronald. As it stands we can hardly keep pace with the training and the formation of new auxiliary units. Numerically they number in their tens of thousands and what's more, wait for it, they are planning to incite the locals they are being entrusted to protect and start an insurrection the likes of which has never before been seen in Africa. They intend waiting until after the elections, when ironically they plan to rise up against the new black government; what with their leaders Mugabe and Nkomo being excluded from the election process. Their objective is twofold: to purge the country of liberal blacks and *annihilate* the remaining whites. Their timing could not be better. The country will be in a state of flux during the transition from white to black rule and there will be complacency in the armed forces, what with the war technically at an end.'

Baker frowned, rising once again. 'Well, I don't know about you, Sir, but I think I could do with a drink.'

Armstrong raised a restraining hand. 'What I have told you is only the half of it.'

Baker nodded and sat down again. He was shattered, as a senior officer in the Rhodesian Army he must surely shoulder some of the eternal shame for their gullibility. The logistics of trying to contain a national uprising were mind-boggling.

Bent double under the table, Wells stifled a bout of wind as cramps caused by his tense immobility gripped his bowels. He wished to hell the officers would shut up. He had enough problems of his own without being privy to the secrets of a nation about to be plunged into anarchy by hordes of savages armed to the teeth as a result of bureaucratic bungling.

'I just don't know what to say, Gordon. To think we could actually have fallen for such a plot. It's a bloody nightmare.' Armstrong beamed for the benefit of the junior officer. 'Not quite, Ronald, actually it's more like a pleasant dream. The truth is it was Military Intelligence's covert operatives who put the external wing of our African Nationalists up to the idea of infiltrating the Auxiliaries in the first place.'

The colonel held his breath expectantly. 'Go on, please.'

Armstrong was still smiling. 'As you know we have been infiltrating the terr recruiting drives for years with our own black Special Unit personnel. It was these fellows who we used to sow the seeds of this infiltration plan. The fact that we already had dozens of turned terrorists operating alongside the Selous Scouts made it easier for our chaps to sell the idea.'

'Forgive my impatience, Gordon but where does this leave us? We seem to have nurtured a better-trained and infinitely stronger adversary?'

'Yes, Ronald, but now we have them, tens of thousands of the blighters, just where we bloody well want them, concentrated in the assembly points. We all know the time and cost involved in hunting down and killing a *single* terrorist.' Armstrong paused. 'Need I say more? In view of the need for this exercise to be perceived as authentic, even the instructors putting the *Pfumo re Vahnu* through their paces are under the impression that this is the real thing.'

'It's incredible. Next you are going to tell me that we are simply going to move in and . . .'

'Anything is possible,' Armstrong interjected, nodding knowingly.

'I foresee only one problem, Sir, and that's the government of the day,' offered Baker as he contemplated the strategic implications of a move against the Auxiliary Units. 'Very soon now it is going to be black. Even if we convince our new prime minister in waiting, Bishop Muzorewa, that a pre-emptive strike is advisable to protect his own arse, will he go along with it? I mean it's asking a lot of the man to sanction our . . . *neutralising* a significant number of his countrymen. Even if we prove treasonous intent, will he have the balls to stand up to the inevitable international outcry?'

The army was indeed fortunate to have a few university graduates of Baker's calibre, reflected Armstrong, eyeing the liquor cabinet and regretting his haste in advocating restraint in his junior officer. Choosing his words carefully, Armstrong responded, 'A black government would indeed have difficulty condoning our actions, but that of course presupposes such a government will be in a position to condone *anything!*'

It was a statement of fact and Armstrong studied Baker's face carefully during the seconds that followed.

'I see, Sir. Then this would logically bring us to the final phase of the operation you are alluding to?' Baker was hardly able to contain his enthusiasm.

'Operation *Quartz*, precisely,' confirmed Armstrong, well pleased with the colonel's comprehension and acceptance of the situation.

Baker's respect for his superior now knew no bounds. The fact that he had just tacitly pledged his support for what was destined to be the first white military coup in Africa was of little consequence.

Armstrong looked at his watch and got to his feet. 'The important thing now is to put the proposed merger of our black and white troops across in such a way as not to arouse suspicion or create animosity. This afternoon I'll be prevailing on the company commanders of the RAR to convey to their men the need for a greater show of black-white solidarity on the eve of our independence and a new multi-racial society. As the European troops might not be taken in quite so readily by this sudden burst of pluralism, I propose prevailing on their majors to convey to their men the need to help bolster the morale of our black troops. This at a time when these people feel they face an uncertain future in view of their years of complicity with the whites.'

Baker handed the general his cap. His mind boggled and yet all he could offer was, 'We certainly have an eventful future ahead of us, Sir.'

'Eventful, yes; but at least we are reasonably assured of having one at all.'

Wells landed on rubbery legs. It was no longer fear of discovery that was terrifying him but the knowledge that he now shared an awesome secret, too burdensome for him alone. Striding stiffly off to the front of the building he was unaware that while his departure had gone unheralded, it had not gone undetected.

Absent Without Leave

Tony arrived at the Grand Hotel early on Friday morning and strode purposefully through the deserted foyer to check the register. His directors had arrived from Johannesburg the previous afternoon, but there was no record of a Mrs Longdon. The African night clerk obligingly double-checked, only to confirm there was neither a reservation nor any messages.

His heart pounding, Tony made his way over to the public telephone. There was no delay at that time of the morning and the operator at the Bulawayo exchange came back to him with a polite, 'Sorry, Sir, no reply from the number.'

'Let it ring,' he demanded. 'Please let it ring a little longer, it's very important,' he added apologetically, his voice charged with emotion.

The telephone rang for a further agonising minute before he heard the click and was disconnected. Wiping his damp palms down the side of his combat trousers he placed a second call. This time he waited to be connected without the customary *one moment please*.

'Hi son, it's good to hear from you. I hope it's good news for a change. Look I must run already late for work, just a moment while I get your mother out of bed for you. Hang in there my boy, bye for now.'

The old man was certainly not one for long conversations, Tony thought, which was just as well as he was in no mood for pleasantries.

'What do you mean you don't know where she is, Mum? For God's sake, if she's not in Wankie and not at home the only other damn place she could be is with you.'

'Kathy has a mind of her own dear,' she pleaded. 'Son, have you not received my letter?'

'What bloody letter, Helen?'

'Two minutes, three minutes only,' the operator interrupted curtly.

'Son, I have my doubts whether Kathy . . . will be coming to Wankie.'

Tony held the receiver away from his ear and stared at the instrument in disbelief. His hand was shaking and he had to take a deep breath before he could trust his voice again. 'Helen, let's start from the beginning, shall we. You told Kathy I had a pass for the day and was expecting her up here, right?'

'Yes, of course I passed on your message son. But as I say . . . I have my doubts, dear. I'm really sorry.'

'*You're sorry!* Drop the melodramatics and just tell me what the bloody hell's going on, *please?*'

'Three minutes finish off.'

'Go to hell,' Tony yelled at the operator. 'Helen, out with it.'

'Honestly son, I would only be guessing. Why not try calling the Gardiners? Margaret will probably be able to tell you more,' Helen concluded with a tremor in her voice.

'Time's up.'

'OK Helen, you win,' he managed before the line went dead. Lighting a cigarette he took several long draws before dialling again. Fortunately when he got through to the Bulawayo exchange it was to a different operator.

Margaret Gardiner dissolved into tears at the sound of his voice. This was followed first by one and then the other of her two young children, the bawling in the background providing a fitting chorus to her own hysteria. It was some time before Tony was able to calm her sufficiently to get out of her, '*Haven't you heard?*'

'Heard what, for Christ's sake?' he demanded, coming out in a cold sweat. Slumped against the cowling of the telephone booth, he listened in mute silence while Margaret blurted out something about Kathy and Roger having an affair and running off down south. She was still wailing on about how the ungrateful bastard had just up and left her and the kids when Tony replaced the receiver. The foyer was still deserted when he crossed numbly back to reception and asked, 'Please call a waiter, I need a double brandy.'

Staring at the big man in uniform, with a rifle slung from his shoulder, the clerk shot a glance at the wall clock. It was only twenty past seven. 'I must apologise for the bar, Sir, she only opening at ten am, Sir.'

'You must have bloody room service or something!' He was about to ask what time the management and reception came on duty, when the clerk excused himself and hurried off down the passage.

On his return the clerk found the soldier slumped in one of the armchairs in the lobby, smoking. Handing over the glass, half full of brandy, he beamed when Tony gave him a ten-dollar note and said to keep the change.

Tony's initial inclination had been to go AWOL and head down south to retrieve his wife, sorting Roger out in the process. Having tossed back the brandy, his eyes watering from the raw spirit, he was already having second thoughts. Anything else he could have made allowances for but not this, never this. Dogging his half-smoked cigarette and getting wearily to his feet, Tony helped himself to a couple of peppermints, squared his shoulders and made his way down the passage to the dining room. His hunch was correct; his colleagues from Johannesburg were already at breakfast.

Delighted at Tony's early arrival, Robinson and Goodridge warmly greeted their Rhodesian general manager, only to be treated like strangers in return. Well aware of the stresses that Rhodesians in general, and those committed to military service in particular, were subjected to they made small talk while doing their best to overlook his off-handedness.

'Gentlemen, I have certain time restraints, so if I may I will give you a brief overview of recent events and how I see them impacting the country; more specifically the local branch of the company.'

In spite of his preoccupation with his wife's infidelity, Tony remained reasonably objective during the twenty minutes it took him to give his assessment of the situation.

'Gents, in conclusion, I believe any thought of disinvesting at this juncture would be premature. This indefinite mobilisation issue will blow over. Whether power ultimately vests with Bishop Abel Muzorewa, as head of a token black government, or with one of the more militant leaders of the Patriotic Front, the fact remains the world will continue to demand this country's strategic minerals. While we have mining there will be a demand for our equipment, and a future for the Rhodesian branch of the company.'

Having offered Tony coffee, which he declined as he had the breakfast, Goodridge, the group finance director, cleared his throat. 'Tony, while there is obviously a great deal of merit in what you say, the fact remains we are dealing with shareholders funds. You know as well as the rest of us what happened to capital left tied up in Zambia by those who chose to believe things could not possibly get worse after independence. The real issue now is whether or not an escalation of hostilities, as is indicated by this latest indefinite call-up situation, will weaken Rhodesia's economy to a point where the business is no longer profitable and able to afford to pay dividends. All of which presupposes that the government of the day will even continue to allow dividend repatriation.'

Robinson, the sales director, added, 'I'm afraid I must concur, Tony. Naturally a final decision will only be made once the matter has been put to the full board. Nevertheless, we appreciate your frankness and whatever the outcome you can rest assured your future with the company is secure, although it's probably going to mean a transfer down south by the looks of it.'

Tony shrugged, took out his pen and scribbled his resignation on a paper serviette. 'It's not only *my* future I'm concerned about.

I was hoping the company would give the new state of Zimbabwe/
Rhodesia the benefit of the doubt, for the sake of the staff up
here.'

Folding the serviette and passing it to Goodridge, Tony politely
shook hands with his bemused associates and left the dining room,
rifle in hand and jaw set. He bought a bottle of brandy from the
off-licence adjoining the hotel and set off down the road. Arriving
at a deserted football stadium on the edge of town, he climbed the
long flights of steps and settled himself in the shade at the very
top of the stand.

Weaving his way aimlessly back into town a few hours later,
Tony chastised himself for not having bought two bottles in the
first place. When next he consciously took stock of his situation
there was still no bottle store in sight, and he found himself making his way unsteadily up the marble steps of Barclays Bank. Taking a sideways run at the last few stairs, he arrived at the top not
knowing what he was doing there.

Once inside the bank Tony came up short, swaying precariously while his eyes adjusted to the fluorescent lighting. Letting his
head pivot to the left and staring at the door marked Manager, his
double vision took in the foreign exchange department, the row
of three tellers and the raised accountant's cubicle. 'And now?' he
asked himself, still trying to fathom what was so compelling about
the bank. Discounting the possibility that he could be drunk, in
spite of his inability to focus clearly, he shrugged, staggered and
almost fell as he pivoted on his heels in an effort to re-locate the
door.

Victoria Bond finished thumbing a wad of notes and stamped
the deposit slip. Looking up with a polite smile as she pushed the
duplicate slip back under the grille, she finally noticed the unsteady individual in army fatigues not three metres in front of her.
Rushing through the low swing-gate into the main banking hall,
she found her voice at the same time as a worried-looking commissionaire reached for the telephone. She had one word on her
lips, 'Tony!'

The surprised soldier completed a further half circle in response to his name. And this time would have lost his balance had Victoria not caught him.

'Bugger me, I'm surrounded!' Tony muttered, staring intently at the white-haired commissionaire, then at the burly bank manager and finally back at the cute busty blonde. 'Your hair, what the . . . hell have you done . . . I prefer it . . . *long?*'

'He's delirious, probably malaria,' offered the ageing commissionaire.

'Motherless,' corrected the manager with a scowl as he got a whiff of Tony's breath.

'I know him, Mr Engelbrecht. Please, I'll take him. Get him outside, if that's OK?'

'He looks a bit of a rough diamond, Miss Bond. Perhaps it would be wiser to call the MPs?'

Tony smiled. His head was going back and forth between the two. 'Forget it mate, she . . . always gets her own way mark . . . my . . . words,' he chuckled.

'I'll be perfectly all right, Mr Engelbrecht. If you will just ask Phyllis to stand in for me, I'll make up the lost time.'

'As you wish but be it on your own head. Now get him out of here before he throws up.'

Glaring at the bank manager, Tony fumbled in his thigh pocket for the loaded magazine he'd had the presence of mind to remove from his weapon earlier. 'Vicky, keep this just . . . in case . . . I decide to shoot this . . . son of a bitch.'

Grabbing the heavy magazine, Victoria darted off to collect her handbag. She apologised once more to her boss as she half led, half pulled her charge out through the doors into the sweltering noon sun. Having coaxed him as far as the corner Wimpy Bar, she managed to get several cups of black coffee into him, between repeated demands for a drink.

'I need . . . a bloody drink . . . woman. A real . . . bloody drink . . . you understand. Or else.'

'Or else what?'

'Or else . . . I'm going to shoot . . . every last fucking person in this . . . Godforsaken town.' Pressing a finger to his lips he said, 'Sorryyyyyy,' to the people at the surrounding tables.

When Tony slipped beneath the table for the third time, Victoria realised she was not making any progress. Calling a taxi from the restaurant's telephone, she tipped the waiter heavily and asked for his help in getting Tony up and out onto the pavement. Once in the taxi she suggested they take him back to the barracks to rejoin his unit, but he would not hear of it and threatened to jump out of the cab.

'I don't need the fucking army just a bottle of . . . brandy. Shit, is that toooo much to ask? And I sure as hell don't need a nurse-maid. What I . . . need is a . . . fucking drink.'

Cringing at the language and shedding a tear as she struggled to keep him upright and his rifle safe at the same time, Vicky was grateful when the African taxi driver volunteered to take them to a place where her friend could sleep it off.

'This hotel is on the other side of town near the marshalling yards, Madam. Not the best, but no one is asking questions.'

Victoria had serious reservations when the taxi drew up in front of the dilapidated three-storey hotel, with empty beer bottles and other litter strewn in the gutter. She was about to wave the driver on when Tony opened his door and pitched headlong out onto the pavement. Lurching to his feet he negotiated the half dozen steps leading up from the pavement, crossed the polished red stoop and stumbled into the reception area.

'Great . . . just great . . . the fucking place has character,' he slurred as he slumped over the counter to grin down at the African desk clerk with frizzy grey hair.

'Hey *boy* . . . oops, I mean *governor*. Where's the bleeding bar?' The bespectacled old man just nodded in the general direction without getting up.

Walking as if on the deck of a boat, Tony made his way noisily down the dim corridor, muttering, 'Bad mannered black bastard . . . to think they will be running the fucking country in a couple of months. Still . . . no fucking excuse . . . you mustn't call them *boy* any more,' he chastised himself.

Tony was on his second neat double brandy by the time Victoria had paid off the taxi and located him, propped up at the end of an abnormally long counter in the public bar.

'Really . . . you don't have to hang around, honey. I'll be just fine,' Tony insisted. No sooner had he spoken than his elbow slipped off the edge of the bar and he sent his drink flying. 'Fuck . . . what a waste,' he cursed. '*Fuck*,' he echoed again as he banged his head solidly on the counter attempting to lap up his spilt drink.

'Go for it General!' encouraged one of half-a-dozen equally inebriated individuals seated around the dingy, stale-smelling bar. 'No woman allowed in here General, unless she's going to strip,' said another.

'Take if off, take if off,' the chant was enthusiastically taken up as Victoria turned and fled to a chorus of raucous laughter and hand clapping.

Having paid up front for the only room with a bath, Victoria thanked the clerk as she hesitantly took the key. There had been no questions, no register and no receipt. Just like the taxi driver had said. Peering cautiously over the top of the saloon doors, Victoria noted with relief that most of the motley individuals were once more engrossed in their beers. For his part, Tony now had a fresh glass in his hand and a half empty bottle of brandy clutched in the crook of his other arm as he slouched on the counter.

Blinking hard in disbelief as the bottle was snatched from his grasp, Tony swung off his stool and gave chase. 'You've really done it this time . . . *fucking hell*,' he bellowed as he groped after his tormentor.

Victoria had no problem keeping ahead of Tony, in spite of the burden of the heavy rifle and the bottle. Had the situation not been so serious she might have burst out laughing as Tony finally made it to the top of the second-floor landing, on his hands and knees. Coaxing him on with the brandy bottle, she managed to get him into the musty-smelling room. It boasted a sagging double bed, a telephone and a threadbare armchair. The Bible was conspicuous by its absence. Having reclaimed his bottle, Tony slumped into the old armchair, only to slither onto the floor where he settled with the bottle between his legs.

Victoria drew a hot bath and laid a towel on the linoleum floor to prevent him slipping, tears streaming down her cheeks. This was not the Tony Longdon she had cried herself to sleep over these past three months, the father of her unborn child. To make matters worse she had just lied to her mother on the telephone, telling her she would be staying over at Phyllis's for the night. She would call in at home in the morning for a change of clothes on her way to work.

Tony had finished the rest of the bottle by the time Victoria succeeded in getting him into the bathroom. Unable to get his boots off, she pleaded with him to at least please try and help undress himself. In response he clambered fully clothed into the bath, chuckling as he sank slowly beneath the surface. Screaming as she frantically grabbed a fistful of his hair, Victoria managed to hold his head clear of the water long enough to yank out the plug. Tony coughed and spluttered, roared with laughter, coughed once more and vomited over himself.

Sobbing, Victoria stripped off his clothes and washed him where he lay. She then hauled him over the edge of the bath and half dragged, half carried him to the bed. Mercifully he passed out the moment his head hit the pillow.

The crash and hiss of the shunting steam locomotives in the marshalling yard across the road continued unabated well into the night, not that Victoria had time to notice. Her patient, plagued by fits of violent shaking interspersed with bouts of verbal abuse, kept her busy mopping the perspiration from his forehead and trying to calm him. Around midnight he finally fell into a fitful sleep, his rantings having become progressively incoherent to the point where Victoria had stopped even trying to fathom them. Propped up uncomfortably against the old brass bedstead, Tony's head cradled in her lap, she fretted that he might die of alcohol poisoning.

As the dawn began to break she moved Tony's head back onto the pillow and got stiffly off the bed. Stretching and stifling a yawn, she took stock of her situation. Tony was not getting any better, he'd called out incoherently twice in the past hour. What was more it was nearly six o'clock and if she was to get home, bathe and change in time for work she would have to leave soon. But if she left there was no telling what he might do. Calling the barracks was one option but she was loath to do so for fear of what they might do to deserters, this much at least she had gleaned from his ravings.

Reflecting on her dilemma while mechanically touching up her make-up, Victoria suddenly heard voices in the passage. Thinking it odd that anyone would be about at this hour she moved closer to the door. It was then that Tony chose to slam a fist into the wall next to the bed. Throwing open the door Victoria found herself confronting two equally surprised soldiers, both with rifles slung over their shoulders. The stocky man with greying temples and captain's pips had a rugged but homely look about him. His younger companion was tall and appeared nervous.

The middle-aged man was the first to regain his composure. Smiling, he said, 'Good morning, Miss.' His companion stared at the floor, avoiding both Vicky's gaze and the impatient glances from the two heavily made-up women backed up behind them in the passage. Victoria had not noticed the whores, the officer's pips commanding her full attention. They must have come for Tony she concluded, darting back into the room.

The stocky captain managed to get a foot in the door. 'Please, Miss, I'd like to help.' Easing his head round the door he smiled, 'If I'm not mistaken you could do with some?' He had a teenage daughter of his own back home and the look in those frightened, bloodshot eyes gave cause for concern. He felt the door give a little and said softly, 'Harry Goosen's my name. This is hardly the place for a young lady, is it?'

A moment later the door swung open and Victoria stepped aside, her arms hanging listlessly at her side and her bottom lip trembling from the strain of her ordeal.

157

'What's the matter with him? He's not dead is he?' Goosen asked as he wavered on the threshold, questioning his eagerness to play the Good Samaritan. The naked body lay spread-eagled across the bed, the lower half covered by a sheet and the head lolling precariously over the edge. Wet army camouflage fatigues and boots were piled up outside the bathroom door.

Hurrying back across the room, Victoria grabbed an arm and unceremoniously dragged Tony back into the centre of the bed. 'He's sick. Alcohol poisoning, I think,' she replied holding up her hands in a gesture of defeat. The tears now flowed freely and her breathing came in long choked-off sobs.

'Now, now, my dear, I'm sure we can sort things out,' Goosen offered as he turned to his colleague in the passage, 'Sergeant Drake, get shot of the . . . *ladies*, will you. Or just let them wait in the room if you like. Then come back and give me a hand with this lad, he's army.'

'What have you done with his rifle and dog tags my dear?' Goosen asked as he completed his visual inspection of the bedroom.

Victoria sniffed and dabbed a tissue at her puffy eyes. 'I'm sorry; I'll be all right now. Really, there is no need for you to trouble yourself.'

'No trouble,' Goosen assured her as he crossed the room to open the window. The fresh air rushed in but so did the noise from the marshalling yards.

Returning from the bathroom, Victoria dutifully handed the captain the dog tags and pulled the rifle out from under the bed. 'I have the bullets in my bag.'

'Good thinking,' acknowledged Goosen, moving the solitary armchair up alongside the bed and sitting down. 'Longdon! *It can't be!*' he declared as he got his first real look at the other man's face. Turning the asbestos dog tags over in his hand he said, 'Well I'll be buggered!'

Moving closer to where Goosen sat in the armchair, Victoria asked with renewed hope, 'Is he a friend of yours?'

'Not really, the last time I set eyes on this reprobate was about six years ago. Bloody spunky youngster he was then. I was only thirty-five at the time and I've been grey ever since. How come the two of you are holed up in a joint like this?' he asked kindly without insinuation.

Victoria sat on the edge of the bed and briefly recounted the course of events since Tony had arrived at the bank. She also said that as far as she could make out some sort of family crisis had prompted Tony into going AWOL, then on a drinking binge.

Nodding, Goosen leant forward and without warning slapped the prone figure across the face. Lunging off the pillow, Tony ended up with his head where his feet had been, face down, breathing heavily but otherwise motionless.

'That's Longdon all right. Look Miss, this could take a while. Have you got somewhere you would rather be in the meantime?'

'Please don't hurt him,' Victoria pleaded as she tried to pull Tony back round on the bed. 'He really doesn't know what he's doing. Perhaps . . . I should call a doctor?'

'You have nothing to worry about, believe me. It's going to take more than a good binge to permanently incapacitate this boy. We'll take good care of him and I promise to have him back on his feet in a couple of hours,' Goosen said as he helped her turn Tony over and get his head back on the pillow.

Sergeant Drake had returned and now stood in the open doorway, hands in his pockets watching the scene and shaking his head. He found it hard to believe that after an all-night session on the town, to celebrate their first weekend pass in months, his colleague had just volunteered their services as babysitters.

After further assurances, Victoria admitted she would like to go home and freshen up and let her boss know she would not be coming in. Saturday mornings were the busiest period for a teller but she needed to see this through. Having called a taxi and bundled up Tony's laundry she reluctantly took her leave.

Once the girl had gone, Drake stepped into the room and closed

159

the door. 'Sir, this is fucking crazy, we have two expensive ladies next door and you want to play nursemaid to a bloody alky.'

'Pay them off and then get down to the kitchen and organise some coffee, lots of it. Oh, and Jim, we're not going anywhere until this boy's back on his feet. I owe him, from way back.'

While Drake was off trying to rouse the kitchen staff, Goosen manhandled Tony into the bathroom and shoved his head under the cold-water tap. Once Drake returned they got the best part of three cups of coffee into the patient before starting to walk him, back and forth, up and down, supported on either side. The only pleasure Drake derived from the experience was seeing Tony get slapped in the face every time he closed his eyes or shouted abuse. To Drake's delight, Goosen cuffed their boy almost repeatedly during the first thirty minutes of his ordeal.

An hour later and Tony started fighting back in earnest, willing himself out of the mist. The room took on shape and he could feel the pain in his head and the fur on his tongue. Shrugging off his tormentors he staggered to the toilet and brought up the cups of force-fed coffee and the remaining bile in his stomach. Having rinsed his mouth and washed his face he made it unaided to the open window, where he filled his lungs. Without turning, and still leaning heavily on the soot-covered windowsill, he uttered his first intelligible sentence in nearly twenty-four hours, 'Thanks, who-ever you are.' He paused, took another deep breath and added, 'Reckon I could eat a bloody horse, after a packet of aspirin and a smoke that is.'

'Jim, you heard the man, order breakfast and something for a headache.'

'Harry *please*, you know there is no bloody room service in this dump!'

'Then get your arse back downstairs and organise something.'

'Yes, Sir,' Drake said saluting belligerently as he left the room.

Turning his head slowly, Tony gradually focused on the older man now sitting in the chair next to the bed. It had been the voice. 'Well, I'll be fucked!'

Goosen nodded his head and grinned back; the recognition had made it all worthwhile.

'Company Sergeant Major Goosen.'

'Captain Goosen now, Longdon.'

'Captain, I don't believe it. Not even you can be that much of a glutton for punishment,' Tony tried to smile but the pain hit him behind the eyes.

Having returned with Tony's breakfast on a tray, a disenchanted Drake now sat on the windowsill smoking and staring moodily out across the marshalling yard. Longdon had managed a bath, six aspirin and most of the food in the time it had taken to get housekeeping to send up a maid with a change of bed linen and fresh towels. With Longdon back in bed, Goosen found himself tiptoeing around the room like a broody hen, their invalid having finally drifted off into a deep peaceful sleep.

'Captain, what did this creep do way back when, save your bloody life or something?' Drake asked in a sarcastic whisper from where he was perched on the windowsill.

'Not quite,' Goosen said, still in the armchair. 'In fact, all he ever did was pull the piss out of me and buck the system. It's what I did to him that I owe him for. We were on a training manoeuvre, in Wankie strangely enough, back in 1972. We were based at the airstrip and I was CSM at the time. Most of the lads got passes one Saturday night and after a few drinks at No 1 Colliery Club five of them, him included, dived off the top board into the club swimming pool.'

'Big deal,' Drake voiced his frustration as he checked his watch. It was nine forty-five. What the hell could be keeping the dame, he wondered?

'It was a big deal at the time,' Goosen assured him. 'You see they went in fully clothed, boots, beer glasses, bottles and all. The locals left in disgust and when the MPs arrived there were just the five of them, sitting at a table under the fairy lights looking like drowned rats, demanding bar service.'

'Hasn't changed much has he,' Drake chipped in again.

'I suppose not,' Goosen agreed, suppressing a grin. 'Well, anyway, the following day they marched. The punishment was twenty-one laps of the airstrip, about thirty kilometres. Dress was battle fatigues, full packs, pouches and weapons. As if that was not bad enough, each had two house bricks added to their packs for good measure, courtesy of yours truly. It was a day I shall never forget.' Goosen paused to light a cigarette. 'The heat was murderous. Even the tar on the airstrip started to melt as the morning progressed. First one and then another of the defaulters collapsed, only to be pulled up by their mates and slog on. Feelings were running high that Sunday morning, what with almost the entire company lined up along the fence on the airstrip. By noon it was very bad and instead of the earlier cheers there was an almost reverent silence.'

Goosen leant forward to check on Longdon's breathing. 'Our CO had expected them to drop after about ten laps, three hours at best in that heat. Well, I tell you, six hours later and with four kilometres still to go, we gravely regretted the spleen we had put into the punishment. But the CO and I knew that even if a reprieve was offered it would not be accepted. Egged on by Longdon, all five of them were going to see it through to the end, even if it killed them; just to spite the system.'

'And?' Drake encouraged showing marginally more interest.

'Well, those last four kilometres took them three hours and twenty minutes, three of them staggering along, half carrying, half dragging their semi-conscious buddies. Their hands were raw, burnt black from crawling on the molten tar. I personally lifted the packs off their backs as they collapsed, *en masse*, at the end of the final lap. Our CO had a civilian ambulance standing by to take them to the Wankie Hospital. He insisted I went with my boys, and I was proud to.'

'They all survived?' Drake asked making no attempt at disguising his disappointment.

'Yes, they were put on drips while the nurses cut the dead skin from their blistered hands and feet. I remember the chorus of four-letter words that filled the ward as the antiseptic went to work. The doctor ordered four days of R&R and, believe it or not, they spent it with their feet up around the pool at No. 1 Colliery Club. Excused boots, they were so pampered during the remainder of the camp that they even took to falling in as a separate unit apart from the rest of the company. I have no doubt at whose instigation,' Goosen nodded at Tony, still sleeping like a baby.

'Thereafter, he and his cronies wormed their way out of every bloody camp duty by referring to themselves as the SPCSMBs. Which I later learnt meant the Special Privileged Company Sergeant Major's Boys. The devils even held a private fucking parade, to bestow honorary life membership of the order of the SPCSMBs on me.'

When Tony next came around it was from a natural sleep and he felt half human, if still a little disoriented. Returning from the bathroom with a towel around his waist and his hair wet from the shower, he even managed a smile as he asked sheepishly, 'Harry, I don't suppose you know how I got here or where the bloody hell my uniform and rifle happen to be?'

'A very sweet young thing took you under her wing, nice looking bit of stuff. Vicky, Victoria Bond, she said her name was.'

Tony sat down on the side of the bed, his head in his hands. He vaguely recalled a woman's presence, but how and where they had met remained a blank.

Goosen continued, 'She took your kit to get it laundered and your rifle is under the bed. As for the rest, it's Saturday and you're in a third-rate hotel on the wrong side of the tracks. Now it's my turn. Which company are you with and are you AWOL?'

'Saturday!' Tony exclaimed running the back of his hand over the stubble on his chin. Slowly events of Friday morning started drifting back, the telephone call to Margaret Gardiner and Kathy's adultery, his resignation and then nothing. 'Hell that's enough,' he voiced aloud as the wretchedness of his situation dawned on him and he fought off the nauseating urge to return to the bathroom and throw up again.

'Tony, whatever trouble you're in the sooner you come clean with your CO the easier it will go on you.'

'Got another fag?' Tony asked. 'Major Young and my guys were due to head back with the rations at first light today; the story of my fucking illustrious army career.' He got shakily to his feet. 'Harry, I need one last favour if you don't mind. Drop my rifle off at the guardroom and get a message to Major Young for me. Let him know I have a family crisis and need a few days to pick up the pieces.'

Drake could hardly believe his ears. 'For Christ's sake, Corporal, you don't just take occasional fucking leave in the middle of an indefinite call-up.' Groaning and shaking his head as he got up from the windowsill he added, 'Aren't you satisfied with totally screwing up the one and only bloody twenty-four hour pass the captain and I have had in ages?'

Ignoring his sergeant's outburst, Goosen drew Tony to one side. 'This is important, Tony?'

'Yes, without boring you with all the gory details, briefly my situation is . . .' Having completed his summary of events Tony concluded, 'It's damn important, Harry.'

'OK, I will do what I can. But for what it's worth I think they are bound to ask the MPs to pick you up.'

Tony stuck his cigarette in the corner of his mouth and came noiselessly to attention in his bare feet, slowly raising his left arm in a two-fingered Boy Scout salute. 'To the SPCSMBs, to the memory and the men, I reckon this clears the slate, Captain. Thank you.'

Goosen snapped back a salute, picked up his and Tony's rifles and wordlessly left the room.

Having met her daughter at the front door Gloria Bond demanded an explanation for her puffy eyes and bedraggled appearance. After some soul searching and a few tears, Victoria blurted out the whole story, barring any reference to her pregnancy. While not condoning Victoria's liaison with a married man, Gloria acknowledged that things like this did happen and could not simply be ignored when they did. Having promised her assistance, it was agreed Victoria would return to the hotel and bring her young man back home.

Richard du Preez had been at the guardroom waiting on any news of his colleague, and intercepted Captain Goosen in the process of handing over Longdon's rifle. Goosen confirmed Tony's whereabouts and went on to explain as best he could about his wife doing a bunk and the disastrous meeting with his directors.

Richard in turn confirmed that as luck would have it their departure had been delayed due to engine trouble. Grateful that Tony was at least still in Wankie, he knew that as long as Major Young remained blissfully unaware of his predicament there was still a chance of salvaging the situation. Commandeering the remaining serviceable ration truck and ordering Wells onto the back, to keep an eye on the recently loaded stores, Richard set off for the hotel.

Having returned with Tony's uniform on a hanger just before noon, Victoria could hardly credit the transformation. Not only had he bathed and combed his hair, he'd also borrowed a razor and had a shave. In the midst of explaining about her ordeal with her mother, Tony had taken her gently in his arms and pulled her to him, kissing her until she was faint from lack of breath.

Tony was in the process of tucking his freshly ironed shirt into his pants when Richard barged unceremoniously into the room. '*Excuse me!*' Richard said flushing red and turning awkwardly to greet Victoria, 'Nice to see you again, Vicky, sorry . . . for the intrusion.'

'Hi, Richard. This is not what you think. I can explain.'

'No need,' Richard said to save Vicky further embarrassment. 'Captain Goosen sort of put me in the picture. Are you all right?' he enquired kindly.

'I'm fine now, really. Thank you for coming out of your way like this. He's . . . not in too much trouble, is he?'

'Not yet, but he sure as hell will be if we don't get back before fourteen-hundred hours.'

'Richard, I need a favour . . .'

Richard raised a hand to check his friend in mid sentence. 'Sergeant Drake has already told me you would like a few days leave or something. I agreed with him that you must have finally taken leave of your bloody senses.'

'I just need a couple of days in Bulawayo, to sort a few things out. I'll be back latest next Friday, when they can pick me up on the weekly ration run.'

'Tony, be serious, it just doesn't work like that. Not in any man's army.'

'I am deadly serious, just explain to Young that thanks to the fucking army my wife buggered off and a promising career went to the wall on the rebound. I now need time to close some bank accounts, see a lawyer and initiate divorce proceedings . . . whatever.'

After last night Victoria was convinced that nothing would shock her again. Now, as some of Tony's earlier ranting started to make sense, she was overcome by this new reality. Unable to control the tears welling up in her eyes, she instinctively moved into Tony's arms. Whether they were tears of pity for him, or tears of joy at renewed hope for herself, she was not quite sure.

'All of this is a bit sudden I know, Vicky,' Tony comforted her, adding, 'I don't remember what I might or might not have told you in the last twenty-four hours but I'll do my best to explain it all on the way over to your place. The least I can do is apologise to your mother for involving you.' He smiled as he brushed away a tear and gave her a reassuring squeeze. 'You're putting on a bit of weight around the middle my girl,' he chided.

Leaving the hotel together in an uneasy silence, Tony placed a hand on his friend's shoulder once out on the pavement. 'Richard, I'm sorry for being a bit short back there, reckon I'm still strung out from that bloody binge yesterday.'

'That's OK; I'm not sure what I would have done in your circumstances either. I'm sorry about your marriage and all that. I'll do my best with Major Young, for what it's worth.'

Victoria crossed the road to wait with the taxi, while Tony went over to the ration truck in response to Wells' frantic gesturing. The little man with the cold watery eyes had leapt up from the boxes of rations on which he'd been dozing, and clambered urgently to the back of the vehicle to attract his corporal's attention.

Tony stopped just short of the tailboard and gave Wells a friendly salute. 'How's it, you bloody *scabanga*?'

'I'm fine, Tony. Come on man get the hell up here. I have to bloody talk to you.'

'Not now, chum. I'm taking a few days compassionate leave . . . sort of. Plenty of time for chit chats when I get back. Say cheers to Piet and John for me and keep out of trouble while I'm gone, OK?'

Wells jumped off the truck and pulled Tony to one side. 'No way man, you can't do this to me. I fucking need you.'

It was obvious that the little man had been drinking again, but with his own head still throbbing Tony realised he was hardly qualified to call the kettle black.

'I'll be back, Foxy; latest next Friday.'

Wells stared menacingly up at his corporal, his grip tightening on the younger man's arm.

'Hey, you two back there, break it up. We are late enough as it is. Come on Wells, get back topside,' Richard demanded from the driver's seat.

Wells spun around and glared at Richard but instead of the usual string of abuse he pleaded, 'OK, OK, just give me a minute.' Levelling a half-crazed stare at Tony again he continued, 'Corp, my number's up man. Have I ever lied to you?'

Tony was about to reply *constantly*, but checked himself, for even in his present state of mind it was obvious that something was seriously troubling the little devil. 'What do you mean your number's up? Quick, spell it out man.'

167

'The shit's going to hit the fan and the whole country's fucked.'
'Foxy!'

'OK, OK,' Wells blurted out in a desperate bid to retain his corporal's attention. 'You were right all along about there being something fishy with all those fucking Auxiliaries coming on side. We are now going to have to shoot every last one of the mother-fuckers, before they do us in. Corp, I swear, this is real serious shit man. I'll tell you everything but you must come back with us. No one's going to believe me, but they will listen to you. Everybody listens to you. This Operation *Quartz* thing is big man, really, really *fucking big*. I promise . . .'

'I'll promise you something for nothing, Foxy,' Tony cut in. 'Your bloody number will be up if you don't stop hitting the bottle. You have been at the brandy again, haven't you?'

Wells shrugged. He knew he was not getting through to the bastard.

'Look Foxy, as soon as I get back from Bulawayo, and providing Young does not have me stuck in detention, we will sort out what-ever it is you have got yourself into, alright?'

Wells spat on the road at Longdon's feet and climbed back up on the truck.

Crossing the street to the waiting taxi, Tony could not help feel-ing that perhaps he would sleep a little easier if Wells' number did indeed come up.

Tony got on remarkably well with Mrs Bond considering the circumstances. He confided all in Gloria, by way of explanation for her daughter's predicament, while Mr Bond slept soundly as his underground shift was only due on that evening.

Gloria found it in her to forgive them both. She also commiser-ated with Tony on the outcome of his marriage and insisted he spend the night, before making his way back home to Bulawayo the following day to attend to his errands. She was all heart, all woman and a lonely one at that Tony thought, as he thanked her for her concern.

When Les Bond awoke he hardly spoke to Tony and ate his eggs and bacon in silence. He did not like visitors, especially good-looking young servicemen. Tony found Gloria even more attentive after Les had left for work. Nipping in and out of the kitchen, where she was cleaning up after her husband's breakfast and preparing the evening meal, she had asked him twice how he preferred his steak.

It was just after eight o'clock, with the dinner table barely cleared, when Gloria suggested that they all retire early. 'Victoria needs a good night's sleep after her ordeal,' she insisted.

Having caused her mother sufficient anguish for one day, Vicky protested only lamely. For his part, Tony's hands still shook when he held them out, so an early night made good sense. His mind racing as he lay on the bed in the guest room, Tony found himself fighting off sleep as he tried to come to grips with the events of the past thirty-six hours. Each time he tried to comprehend the depth of despair to which Kathy must have sunk before she gave up on him, something screamed from within, *whore, adulteress*. Another part of him protested there could never be another Kathy. He eventually drifted off to sleep.

The door must have creaked for Tony sat bolt upright, bathed in a cold sweat. His eyes now wide open, he peered blindly into total darkness trying to come to grips with his surroundings, and finding himself naked in a bed as opposed to fully clothed in a sleeping bag under the stars. His imagination getting the better of him he leapt out of bed, only to bash into the wall with a head-jarring thud that left him reeling.

'Tony, what's the matter?'

The light clicked on and Tony found himself blinking rapidly while staring at a pair of ample white breasts, bursting out of the halter of a flimsy negligee.

Gloria Bond placed a restraining finger to her lips. 'I'm sorry if I startled you, my dear. Are you all right now?' she asked, her voice as inviting as her gown was revealing.

Standing there completely naked, the throbbing in Tony's loins was as disconcerting as the speed with which his manhood had risen to the occasion. Gloria switched off the light. She was satisfied that if indeed men had balls for brains then at least Tony's were in the right place.

His bare backside still pressed hard up against the cool wall, Tony felt his heart pounding as adrenalin coursed through his veins anew. It was inconceivable, he thought, that he'd been so painstakingly nursed back to health by the daughter, only to have the love she so rightly deserved lavished lustfully on her mother. But even before he found his voice the woman was upon him. Coming up on her toes she flattened herself against him, the hardness of her pubic area thrusting urgently into his groin.

His breathing coming in irregular gasps, Tony was sorely tempted to bend this voluptuous vixen over the side of the bed and avenge Kathy's fallen virtue and Roger's treachery. But his pain was too new, too sobering. He needed time to wallow in his torment before seeking revenge. In spite of his manhood paying him no heed Tony was about to protest, only to let out an involuntary groan as Gloria grasped his swollen penis in both hands and dropped to her knees.

'*Jesus!*' he exclaimed, grabbing a fistful of hair and mercilessly yanking Gloria's head back, delivering a sobering flat hand across her cheek in the process. The backhand that spontaneously repaid him in kind caught him solidly across the mouth, and his head smashed back against the wall for the second time that night.

Alone once more, Tony got back into bed, but try as he might he could not doze off. He was still wide awake at two o'clock that morning when nature called. Slipping into his combat fatigues he made his way to the toilet. Victoria's bedroom was one room down, on the opposite side of the passage. The door had been closed when he had passed on his way to the bathroom, but oddly enough he found it ajar on his return.

'Come in,' a soft but commanding voice invited. 'And close the door,' Victoria said as Tony entered the room. She sat cross-legged on the end of her bed with its pretty floral duvet, her hands in her lap and eyes downcast. The only light was that from the passage. Closing the door he felt his way over to the bed. As he stood before Victoria she took his hand in hers and caressed it with her cheek.

Feeling the warm wetness of her tears, Tony whispered, 'Vicky . . .'

'Shush. Tony . . . you once said you had never felt for anyone else the way you felt about me. Did you mean that? Do you really love me, the truth please?'

Squatting before her, Tony drew Vicky's head into his shoulder. 'It would be very hard not to love someone as tender and beautiful as you.'

'Please, Tony; I can do without the flattery. I simply have to know . . . one way or the other.'

'Yes, I love you Vicky, very much so.'

'As much as you loved Kathy?' she asked earnestly taking his face between her palms, as if seeing with her hands in the darkened room.

'Yes, as much as I loved Kathy.'

'As much as you still love her?'

'As much as I . . . still love her,' he admitted hoarsely, nodding his head in her hands.

'Thank you for being so honest, my darling. I can accept being loved as much as she, because if your utterings last night are anything to go by, you love her very dearly.'

Standing, Tony drew Vicky to him off the bed and led her across to the window. He was at a loss for words, amazed at the ease with which she had got him to acknowledge something that until now he had been unable to admit to himself. Opening the curtains to stare out at the waning moon, he was still choking on the lump in his throat when Victoria came to his rescue.

'Well, I'm pleased that's settled,' she whispered. 'Now all that remains is the question of my mother.' She raised her voice as if deliberately tempting fate. 'Do you think I will ever be able to look her in the eyes again, let alone forgive her? Tony, I could not help overhearing the commotion. I even got a peek at her as she came storming out of your room. She . . . she looked like an absolute tramp in that get-up.' Sobbing, Vicky went on without lowering her voice, 'I cannot tell you how ashamed, how *disgusted* it made me feel.'

Belatedly placing a finger on Victoria's lips, Tony realised that the damage had probably already been done. Then again, even if Gloria had overheard her daughter he doubted she would be venturing forth again that night. While Vicky cried herself out in his arms he tried to reassure her, 'Vicky, your mother's a lonely person. I . . .'

'Oh, Tony please, it's sickening,' Vicky said, taking several deep breaths to get her sobs under control. Backing out of his embrace she crossed the room and turned the key loudly, pointedly in the lock. Having collected a few tissues from the dressing table, she returned to the bed and slipped out of her shorty pyjamas. She stood naked in the moonlight for a moment before pulling back the bed covers.

'Vicky, I'm screwing up your life. Are you sure this is what you want?' Tony asked as he sat on the edge of the bed. He was about to add that he was not in a position to make promises but ended up asking, 'Are you on the pill?'

'Yes . . . of course,' she replied hesitantly, crossing her fingers and resisting the urge to blurt out *a fat lot of good the pill would be at this late stage.* She was determined to be patient so that when he was eventually able to give freely of his love, it would truly be hers to have.

Kissing Victoria's eyes closed, Tony eased her gently down onto the pillows. The memory of their first night together, when he had unceremoniously taken her on the lawn in the early hours, still vivid in his mind, he resolved to be gentle.

Victoria's back arched and she groaned unashamedly as her strong young body shuddered through one exhilarating climax after another. If this was love and being a woman she had truly arrived.

In Cold Blood

The echo of Nyoni's last scream still ringing in her ears, Jodie continued her headlong dash back down the narrow path through the sisal. It was just as the opening into the lands appeared through her tear-blurred vision that an arm snaked out, encircling her waist from behind. Too breathless even to cry out, Jodie offered no resistance as she was dragged unceremoniously to her knees.

Cocking his rifle as he vaulted over the crouched obstacle in his path, Tony charged on into the clearing. Three shots rang out in quick succession, the retorts echoing through the hills in the nauseating silence that followed.

Her heart pounding against her ribs, Jodie relieved herself where she squatted on the path. She had no idea where Tony had come from or how he had found them, but she offered a silent prayer that he had. They deserved what they got, she told herself, in spite of a fervent opposition to capital punishment. Rape was a dreadful evil, the brutality and terrifying reality all too stark at first hand.

Jodie willed herself up on trembling legs as Tony ushered a sobbing Nyoni back into the maze. Watching her approach, clutching her abdomen and covered in red dust, Jodie was on the verge of tears when Nyoni smiled a tight-lipped courageous smile that said it all; Tony had arrived in time. Mouthing another silent prayer, her third in as many minutes, Jodie quickly forgot the shame of the damp patch on the dry earth between her feet. There were no words to express her gratitude for her friend's incredible bravery.

The girls embraced briefly before being shepherded forward, Tony motioning Nyoni to take the lead. Arriving back at the pool, their grim-faced guardian wordlessly acknowledged their request to bathe. Having washed away the dirt and dank perspiration of fear, Jodie and Nyoni dressed in silence, Tony's mood making them even more uncomfortable.

As they headed back up the path towards the huts, the humidity and closeness of the mid-morning heat only added to Jodie's frustration at Tony's sullen disposition. It was all she could do to stop herself from turning and pounding on his chest. If they had been reckless it was due in no small measure to a trying and sleepless night. On that sobering thought she turned to confront him, hands on hips.

'Before you start,' Tony cautioned, 'let me remind you that your stupidity resulted in three untimely deaths. What's more, I don't think you understand just how very, *very* lucky you both were. Nyoni here can testify to what might have been.'

Jodie winced as Nyoni's nails bit into her upper arm, cutting short her protest.

'It is true,' Nyoni whispered, her eyes tightly closed as if shutting out the memory of some unspeakable horror.

'A thank-you might be more in order,' Tony said as he signalled Nyoni on.

Jodie held her ground a moment longer, it having dawned on her that Tony now seemed more alert and articulate than usual. Had last night's antics accomplished something after all, she wondered?

'Thank you,' she obliged adding, tongue in cheek, 'Do we not also warrant a little gratitude or doesn't last night count?' Jodie heard Nyoni catch her breath and saw the colour rise in Tony's cheeks. She had clearly hit a nerve but the accusing look of disdain was a far cry from the bashful atonement she had anticipated. Still pondering the reason for Tony's contempt, Jodie found herself being pulled urgently off along the path.

On entering the compound Nyoni sent chickens squawking in all directions as she waded through them, en route to the cooking hut. Having deemed it expedient to follow her friend's lead,

Jodie was also about to duck into the protective confines of the hut when a quiet but assertive command brought her up short.

'Wait, we have some unfinished business to address,' Tony said sombrely from beneath the *indaba* tree in the centre of the compound.

Pleased at the opportunity to clear the air, Jodie went over and sat with legs crossed on one of the reed mats in the shade of the tree. There was an awkward silence while Tony absently patted one and then the other of the breast pockets of his bush shirt.

'I guess there was a time when I smoked,' he muttered self-consciously, adding hesitantly, 'About . . . last night, it came as quite a shock, being seduced during what amounted to a drug-induced therapy session. I may well have certain . . . issues which I need help with, but what the hell were you thinking?'

'That's *outrageous* and you know it,' Jodie blurted out. 'For starters, it was Nyoni not I who spiked your coffee, even if she might have overdone it. And while I arrived uninvited it was most definitely you who did the seducing, my friend. Nevertheless if making love to me, if you can call it that, was so distasteful, then I apologise. Rest assured there will be no more attempts at helping you overcome your . . . your damn problems,' she concluded tersely, getting to her feet.

Reaching up and taking hold of her wrist, Tony relented. 'If I've got this it all wrong, I'm sorry. As you say, I have . . . problems.' Releasing her arm as he got up, he pulled back his shoulders to relieve the tension. 'Let's start again then,' he invited. 'Explain how last night was intended to help me with the likes of the nightmares that haunt me and are slowly driving me mad?'

'It is not that simple,' Jodie said, concerned she was being backed into a corner. 'You have suppressed anxieties, possibly PTSD, compounded by amnesia. Given the time that has elapsed not much is likely to change without professional help.'

'Last night was professional help?' Tony persisted.

'No, of course it wasn't. I know this is going to sound crazy,' Jodie capitulated, 'but Nyoni has this theory about my bearing a resemblance to a wife or loved one, and my presence being able to trigger memories from your past. In retrospect, it's somewhat bizarre and I should have known better. But whatever you may think of me, it would be heartless not to acknowledge her courage in all of this.'

'Conspiring to drug me took courage?'

'Not that – inviting another woman to fulfil the role she has been denied,' Jodie shot back, close to tears.

'What *role?*'

'*Men!*' Jodie said, sniffing back the tears. 'Tragically, the abuse Nyoni suffered at the hands of those . . . those terrorists has left her terrified of intimacy. And you thought you were the only one with problems?' She sobbed as she turned on her heels and strode off.

Following in her footsteps, Tony said, 'You're mistaken about Nyoni. Either she has been leading you on or your imagination has been working overtime. She was a child when we met and remains so in my eyes. But believe me she is her own woman; in *every* sense of the word.' He pressed his palm hard against his right temple and screwed up his eyes.

'What do you mean?' Jodie asked, slowing her pace.

'I mean you should better research your subjects before jumping to conclusions,' he muttered, grimacing.

Turning to face Tony in time to witness the familiar tell-tale signs, Jodie relented. 'I didn't mean to get into an argument or upset anybody. Perhaps it would be best if you lie down for a while.' Tony stared fixedly back at her until, thankfully, something high above caught his attention.

'Vultures. I need to bury those boys,' he said, his voice hollow and distant as he set off.

Jodie made her way over to the cooking hut to report back to Nyoni. She could see from the dull embers in the hearth that no attempt had been made at preparing a midday meal, which was just as well for she had no appetite.

'Are you hungry?' Nyoni asked.

'No, what I need is sleep.'

'Come then, let us rest a while; we can eat once the sun has gone down and it is cooler,' Nyoni invited. 'He should be back by then and hopefully in a better mood.'

The Moment of Truth

When the girls finally awoke it was to the crackle of a campfire and the mouthwatering aroma of roast pork. The sun had set and a cursory peek out into the compound revealed that Tony had been busy. Borrowing her friend's steel comb Jodie did what she could with her hair, using a piece of mirror propped up on the old chest of drawers, and working by candlelight. The girls exchanged approving glances before stepping out into the warm star-studded night.

Three stools formed a semicircle around a pit of glowing embers and a warthog piglet was suspended above the coals on a steel rod. Shadows from the fire flickered and danced on the walls of the surrounding huts, the stars above appearing brighter than any Jodie could recall. They had just seated themselves when Tony appeared, as if by some prearranged signal, from beneath the eaves of his hut. He was impressively turned out in a white short-sleeved shirt, faded blue jeans and *veldskoen* boots.

Jodie hardly noticed the bottle of wine he carried in place of his rifle, this being the first time she had seen him in anything but frayed khaki shorts and bush shirt. His hair was slicked back and he looked outwardly relaxed. Jodie self-consciously smoothed down her creased dress.

'Good evening, ladies,' Tony offered. 'Nice of you to join me for a little celebration,' he beamed, holding up the bottle of wine.

Their own cups full the girls waited expectantly while their host filled his. Raising his cup Tony said, 'I have been saving this for a special occasion. Welcome Jodie and thank you for your good intentions,' he offered by way of a toast.

'To new friends,' was all Jodie managed, still marvelling at the change in the man.

'To my new friend,' Nyoni echoed taking a sip of her drink and pulling a face. Putting down her cup she took up the calabash Tony had placed beside the fire and started basting the pig with a mixture of beer and honey.

'That was very nice of you,' Jodie smiled as Tony sat down. 'Hopefully a little more will come of my visit than just good intentions.'

'Who knows,' Tony said non-committally. 'For now let us enjoy the moment, tomorrow we leave at sunrise. We will take a break at midday and complete the trip in the cool of the evening, with a bit of luck pre-empting a visit from the Hluhluwe police.'

'Are you expecting them to come about that ... dreadful incident this morning?' Jodie asked anxiously.

'No, those boys were insurgents from Mozambique and won't be missed. All the same the least said the better. I was referring to your second day on the run, so to speak. But enough speculation, tonight we celebrate to say thank you for taking the time to bring some perspective to mine and Nyoni's existence.'

'If I have helped in some small way then I'm delighted. They say acknowledging the problem is half the battle,' Jodie replied, encouraged by Tony's admission, adding, 'Tomorrow is Sunday so you might consider staying overnight in Hluhluwe. We can then visit the local clinic on Monday to see what they recommend.'

Frowning, Tony nudged a log further into the fire. 'South Africa is evolving and my days of leading this existence are numbered. When the time comes to move on I might take your advice,' he concluded without conviction.

'The meat is ready, we should eat before the rain,' Nyoni interrupted diplomatically.

'Rain, what rain?' Jodie said, glancing up at the cloudless sky in frustration.

'If Nyoni predicts rain, it rains,' Tony said, getting to his feet.

'Tony, you cannot be serious about putting this off any longer,'

Jodie pleaded in spite of Nyoni's ploy. 'I mean a few minutes ago you . . .' but Tony had turned his back and was wordlessly carving the piglet with his hunting knife.

It was Nyoni who eventually broke the awkward silence around the fire, after they had eaten. 'It saddens me that you will be returning to Hluhluwe in the morning,' she said, placing a hand on Jodie's knee, 'We have such little time left.'

'Then we should make the most it,' Jodie replied, despairing of making further progress with Tony. 'Tell me what you remember about when your and Tony's paths crossed. Who knows, your recollections might trigger something in his subconscious.' She nodded towards Tony, now staring moodily into the embers on the other side of fire.

'We met just after my abduction, as I mentioned at the pool. My people were awakened early one morning by the whimpering of the dogs to find hundreds of *gandangas* in our village. When it grew lighter we saw big guns on wheels concealed in the bush. The people were assembled and the comrade commissar told us they planned to blow the security force jackals to hell. He said they were heroes of the revolution and demanded food and beer.' Having paused to toss a few more logs on the fire, Nyoni continued in hushed tones. 'We prepared all the food we had but by late afternoon they had finished everything, including all the beer in the village. It was then that the terrorists dragged our head-man into the compound, calling on the people to witness the fate of the *Toshombi*.'

'Sell-out, traitor,' Tony translated flatly, startling them both.

Staring out into the night to hide her anguish, Nyoni continued. 'They . . . cut off his lips and his . . . his . . .'

'Genitals,' Tony assisted once more.

'And fed his flesh to his senior wife before killing him with the long knives on their guns,' Nyoni managed, before her voice broke again.

Her mouth hanging open, Jodie was half off her stool intent on comforting Nyoni when she felt a restraining hand on her shoulder.

'Give her a moment, she will be all right,' Tony said softly from where he now stood attentively behind her.

Sniffing back her tears, Nyoni continued in a monotone. 'They put all the men into the goat kraal under guard before dragging the women off to the huts . . . or just into the bush. They took all the women, those heavy with child, old grandmothers, the children my age and . . . some much younger. When one had finished, another . . .'

'Oh, how appalling, you poor child!' Jodie gasped, shrugging off Tony's hand and embracing her friend. 'I did not mean for you to relive such torment.'

'Time has softened the pain,' Nyoni insisted, braving a smile and continuing before Jodie could protest further. 'I was one of the lucky ones because the comrade commissar was very drunk and fell asleep on top of me. When he awoke the moon had gone and he ordered his men to move out. They took the young men and boys, some of the women and most of the girls. We were told our throats would be cut if we made any noise on the march. At first the only sound was from the big guns moving over the rough ground, but later, when the younger children got very tired, I heard crying.'

Having returned to his stool Tony asked with surprising eagerness, 'Nyoni, what sort of noise did those gun carriages make being manhandled through the bush?'

Toying with the end of a protruding log with her bare foot, Nyoni recalled, 'The wooden wheels made a creaking sound, but it was the chains used to pull them which the commissar cursed the most. They were bound with rags but still made a . . .'

'A metallic clanking sound?' Jodie offered.

'Like a herd of bloody elephants dragging chains,' Tony intoned. 'We may be making progress,' he enthused. 'What other sounds do you remember that night, Nyoni?'

'There was the thud of rifle butts when those who collapsed or cried out were clubbed into silence, to be left for the hyenas,' Nyoni said flatly, adding, 'Much later there was a boom like thunder and a rushing noise like the wind leaving the hills before a storm. This was followed by shooting at the front of the column and a light in the sky, as I have explained many times before.'

'What she saw must have been a flare,' Tony ventured again for Jodie's benefit. 'Please go on Nyoni.'

'Well, when the flare-thing went out it became even darker than before and many of us escaped into the night.'

'What then?' Jodie asked breathlessly, the suspense getting the better of her.

'I ran until I fell into a *donga*, where I hid. Shooting was coming from everywhere.'

'You were firing at women and children?' Jodie challenged Tony in disbelief.

'If we were stupid enough to initiate a contact against such ridiculous odds, we could not possibly have known there were civilians with them. Nyoni found me on the edge of the ravine she had stumbled into. It remains a mystery how we ended up in the same place what with her being held at the rear of the column, with the cowardly bloody terr commander.'

'I ran your way, being more afraid of the comrade commissar than of the shooting and the fire ahead of me,' Nyoni offered helpfully.

'You've never mentioned a fire before,' Tony prompted.

Nyoni shrugged apologetically, 'It was only a small fire in the grass, burning out from the base of a big tree. But it was bright enough to see many, many bodies piled on top of one another. I closed my eyes at the sight, falling into the *donga*.'

Tony slammed his fist into an open palm. 'Claymore!' he exclaimed.

'A what?' Jodie asked.

'An anti-personnel shrapnel mine, the only weapon that could account for the devastation and concentration of bodies Nyoni described.' But Tony's excitement was short lived as reality dawned. 'I initiated that ambush, killing God knows how many civilians,' he said in dismay.

'You actually remember that?' Jodie enthused.

'Fortunately not.'

'Then how can you be so certain?'

'Because claymores are lethal NCOs are responsible for sighting and triggering them.'

'There was no moon and you did not know there were women and children,' Nyoni reminded Tony.

'Go on Nyoni, there might be something else previously overlooked,' Jodie encouraged her friend.

'I hid at the bottom of the *donga* all night, listening to hyenas feeding on the dead. In the morning I heard what I thought was a hyena sniffing for my scent but as it started to get light I could make out the shape of a body, hanging head down over the edge of the *donga*. The face was black with blood, only the hair showed me this was a European. As the sun came up the flies covering his head became so thick I could no longer hear his breathing and I thought he had died.'

'*You?*' Jodie asked, turning to Tony.

'Yes, unconscious and apparently fortunate not to have fallen prey to predators.'

'Anyway,' Nyoni continued, anxious to finish her tale, 'just then one of the terrorists shouted that he had found the bodies of three *jackals*, white soldiers.'

'Encountering no resistance the following morning the terrs probably started combing the area to retrieve their artillery pieces,' Tony speculated for their benefit.

'There were only the four of you?' Jodie asked in amazement.

'Patrols were reduced to four-man sticks to facilitate deployment in Alouette helicopters, that sort of irrelevant detail has not escaped me,' Tony said, nodding at Nyoni to continue.

'I knew if the terrorists found his body they would also search the *donga* and discover me, so I pulled him over the edge. When he hit the ground one eye popped open and I nearly died of fright, the other was stuck tight with blood.'

'How ghastly! What then?' Jodie implored of them both.

'Nyoni and her Cyclops just stared at one another,' Tony volunteered. 'That is until she heard voices and started scurrying about burying me beneath piles of dead leaves and sticks, before squeezing into an ant-bear burrow in the wall of the gully. I recall no pain, only the suffocating tightness of my skin from the congealed blood, and an excruciating thirst.'

'They obviously didn't look in the gully?' Jodie said, grimacing at his plight.

'According to Nyoni they did, and were still arguing about who should come down for a closer inspection when the RAF arrived and carpeted the area with frantam. I was still buried under my death trap of tinder when the boys in blue scored almost a direct hit. The bush above us mushroomed into flame, enveloping our hiding place – which is the last thing I remember.'

Leaving her stool to kneel at Tony's side, Nyoni took up the story. 'He saved my life by dragging his body over the burrow I was in, his hair and clothes on fire,' she said wiping her eyes with the back of her hand.

'You were bombed by your own forces?'

'I can only surmise that a reconnaissance flight spotted the terrs and their artillery pieces and in the absence of any communications from friendly forces, called in the strike. After the bombing Nyoni tells me there were helicopters, no doubt dropping in infantry to mop up. Fortunately or unfortunately, I'm not sure which any more, we remained undetected in our burnt-out gully.' Giving Nyoni a reassuring hug Tony concluded, 'We obviously both made it, so I suggest Nyoni leaves it there.'

Glancing over at Jodie sitting expectantly on the edge of her stool, Nyoni stoked the dying embers of the fire and continued. 'It was noon by the time I found the courage to roll aside his body and crawl out. To my surprise he was still breathing. I met my father and other tribesmen while on my way back to get help. They had been following our spoor, burying the dead along the way. I took them to the *donga* but they said nothing could be done other than wait for the white man to stop breathing, then cover his body with stones to keep the hyenas from scattering his bones. But he would not die and in the end my father agreed to take him with us. It was on the return journey that I learnt my mother and younger brother were among . . .' Nyoni's voice tailed off into a whisper.

'Nyoni, I am so dreadfully sorry,' Jodie sympathised.

'Enough for tonight,' Tony insisted. 'To cut a long story short they managed to keep me alive.'

'More than enough,' Jodie acknowledged. 'Nyoni, I really am sorry for making you relive such horror. Tony, one last thing,' she asked as an afterthought, 'why didn't someone alert the authorities or why did you not make the effort when back on your feet?'

'They didn't expect me to live and I was out of it for a very, very long time. The only *sangoma* prepared to stake his reputation on my not dying on him kept me drugged for weeks to ease the pain. When finally compos mentis, between the scarring and the amnesia, I had lost my nerve,' Tony concluded flatly, pressing thumb and forefinger into his eyes.

'How different things might have been had you had the courage . . .' Jodie started to reflect before checking herself.

'There was only one reality back then,' Tony retorted, ripping open his shirt to expose the purple mass of scar tissue, all the more macabre in the red glow of the fire. Cocking his head for good measure, he again showed off the unsightly facial scar and disfiguring break in his jaw. It seemed an age before he looked back at his stunned audience, vigorously shaking his head as if to clear it. 'I'm sorry I don't know what came over me.' He was clearly embarrassed, adding almost in the same breath, 'We have a long trek in the morning and there may be some explaining to do, I suggest we call it a day.' As he turned and strode off into the night, a blinding fork of lightning lit up the sky, followed by a deafening clap of thunder as the heavens opened and the rain bucketed down.

Dozing fitfully next to her friend, lightning flashing and thunder roaring, Jodie fretted about Nyoni and Tony's fate should he continue to stubbornly refuse to seek help. There was also the disquieting matter of the youths buried out in the lands, illegal immigrants and would-be-rapists but dead nonetheless.

At first light Nyoni accompanied Jodie and Tony as far as the open bushveldt beyond the sisal. There she kissed Tony on the cheek and gave her white friend a tearful parting hug. Harbouring a dreadful premonition, in spite of Tony's reassuring words as he took his leave, Nyoni waited until they were long out of sight before giving vent to her wretchedness. Dropping to her knees, her ululating pierced the early morning stillness and the song of the birds ended abruptly for miles around.

Civilisation

Jodie marvelled at the variety of animals they encountered as they journeyed back through the bush to Hluhluwe. They walked alongside herds of grazing wildebeest and zebra, craned their necks up at towering giraffe and watched with bated breath as rutting impala rams crashed head-on to lock horns. The whirly bush pig was the most timid and comical of all, whole families scurrying off in single file on stiff stubby legs, tails stuck rigidly up in the air like radio antennae. They gave rhino and buffalo a wider berth, and for once Jodie was not unhappy at seeing no lions. Initially Tony walked her right in among the game, but as the day progressed he became moody and uninterested. When pressed he would not be drawn and they continued on in silence, detracting from Jodie's first real wildlife experience.

They rested during the heat of the day and it was early evening by the time they reached the sisal and pineapple plantations, the first signs of civilisation. With Hluhluwe in sight and Tony still stubbornly non-committal on the question of seeking help, Jodie found herself pleading, 'Won't you at least let me arrange an exploratory appointment, if not for your sake then for Nyoni's?' Her pleas falling on deaf ears she trudged on, more acutely aware than ever of her fatigue and blistered feet.

Brenton Knight's endeavours to convince the police his daughter had been abducted proved frustratingly unsuccessful. Miss Knight was an adult, they argued. What was more this was not her first attempt at absconding with the so-called Rhodesian, according to some of the other guests. Further, a 'manhunt', as Brenton had

187

demanded, could only be sanctioned once a person had been officially reported missing for forty-eight hours. They had tried to reassure him that her escort was well known in the district and more than capable of ensuring her safety in the bush – failing to mention the man's bushcraft was such that in any event he would not be found until it suited him.

When Brenton finally plucked up the courage to confide in his wife, it had taken Christine only six hours on the telephone to accomplish what he had failed to achieve in forty-eight. With the cooperation of the British Consulate in Pretoria and serious crime unit at John Voster Square in Johannesburg, a senior police detective was despatched from Durban to Hluhluwe. Now, late Sunday afternoon on the third day after the alleged kidnapping, the local police were frantically trying to recall their dog handler.

The sun had set by the time an exhausted Jodie and her khaki-clad escort stepped out of the bush and onto the wide expanse of lawn at the back of the Holiday Inn. The bar was closed on a Sunday and the pool deck and grounds were deserted.

'This is as far as I go,' Tony announced sombrely.

'I understand you having no wish to meet my father, but at least sleep over, you might think differently about visiting the clinic in the morning? Besides considering Nyoni, you cannot discount the possibility of family in Zimbabwe,' she reminded him.

'I need more time,' Tony stalled, hands deep in his pockets, his rifle slung over his shoulder.

'More time, after all these years! In your heart you know you have put this off for far too long already,' Jodie encouraged, slipping an arm through his and urging him forward.

Tony felt nauseous as he allowed himself to be led across the lawn. 'It's precisely because it's been years that returning to Rhod . . . Zimbabwe would not be an option even if I miraculously did get my memory back,' he lamented forcing one leaden foot ahead of the other.

'Nonsense,' Jodie insisted. 'It may take some adjusting but you

188

will be surprised just how resilient families can be. The important thing is having the confidence to . . .' her voice trailed off – the unspeakable was happening again. His gaze was fixed and distant, his face contorted in pain.

Tightening her grip on his arm she offered a silent prayer as she led him over to his table, still placed in conspicuous isolation under the fever tree. In her sternest tone she ordered, 'Wait here. I will be back for you just as soon as I have made peace with my father. Do you understand?' In the absence of a nod or smile, Jodie repeated, 'Tony, you *must* wait here for me. *Please.*'

Jodie's fatigue and dishevelled appearance were momentarily forgotten as she entered the hotel. She was intent on getting the melodramatics over with, retrieving Tony and high-tailing it to her room for a long hot bath.

Half an hour had passed by the time Jodie succeeded in talking her way out of her father's clutches and retrieving her key from reception. Had it not been for the raised eyebrows at her appearance as she entered the residents' lounge – the only place where drinks were allowed to be served on Sunday – Jodie had no doubt the interrogation would have lasted much longer. In the end she had insisted, 'No, Dad, *you* involved the police so you make the call and tell them it was all a false alarm. I will call Mother from my room and sort out things on that side. Agreed?'

Slipping out by way of the fire escape in the passage, leaving the door ajar, Jodie hurried round to the side of the hotel. But her charge was nowhere to be found. After scouring the gardens repeatedly calling his name she finally gave up the search. Exhausted and close to tears she closed the fire escape door behind her and made her way up the stairs to her room.

Fumbling for the light switch, Jodie made directly for the bathroom to clean her teeth and run a bath. She had almost finished brushing by the time her jaded senses registered that the bathroom mirror was beaded with condensation. Cautiously returning to the bedroom she stifled a cry on seeing Tony's silhouette out on the unlit balcony. He was naked but for a towel around his waist and there were several bottles of Castle beer on the wicker table next to him.

'Tony! How did you . . .?' But she stopped herself on recalling his connections with the hotel staff. The important thing was he had not absconded and was hopefully his old self again.

'Sorry if I startled you,' he apologised, looking round. 'I could hardly leave without my beer ration, now could I?'

'I'm just relieved that you had second thoughts and decided to stay.'

'The truth is I was well clear of the grounds when it dawned on me that I'd had another of those . . . those attacks. I got to thinking and decided I should probably heed your advice . . . while I'm still able to do so.'

'Tony, that's very sensible,' Jodie commended him. 'Give me ten minutes to phone mum and have a hot bath then we'll talk it through.'

The call to her mother took a lot longer than ten minutes and when Jodie finally replaced the receiver she felt as if she had completed her second marathon of the day. 'I'm sorry about that. I will be as quick as I can in the bath. In the meantime you won't . . .'

'I won't disappear,' he promised as she headed back to the bathroom.

Finishing another beer while subconsciously identifying insect and animal sounds out in the night, Tony jumped at the shrill ring of the telephone.

'I'll get it,' Jodie called out, hurrying from the bathroom in her gown, fashioning a turban from her towel as she went. 'Hello. Yes, Daddy, I'm fine. Yes, I promise, none the worse for the experience, apart from sore feet. Yes, I spoke to Christine and smoothed things over . . . for now, I think. But don't be surprised if she arrives unannounced on the next plane,' she laughed. 'Quite sure, I'm far too tired to eat. I had a nice cup of tea and the most divine hot bath, so won't need any rocking tonight. Yes, that will be lovely. Nine o'clock, breakfast on the terrace by the pool,' she repeated.

'Thank you again for being so understanding. Love you Daddy, goodnight and sweet dreams.'

Replacing the receiver Jodie turned to see Tony framed in the balcony doorway, watching her intently. 'No more calls I promise,' she said averting her eyes from his half-naked body and vigorously towelling her damp hair. When she finally tossed back her head it was to find the room in darkness.

'Tony, what are you playing at I can't . . .' She was still in the process of protesting when an arm reached out and pulled her clumsily down onto the bed.

'Tony! Tony!' she repeated, the pitch of her voice rising. 'Let me up, damn you,' was all she managed before his mouth found hers and he rolled on top of her, pinning her down. Her gown having come undone in the tussle, she was left in no doubt that he had discarded his towel.

'What do you take me for?' she blurted out, twisting her face clear. 'What happened back at the ranch was . . .' Groping frantically for the bedside lamp she brought the heavy porcelain base crashing down against the side of his head.

'You're hurting me,' she repeated tearfully, the remains of the lamp poised for a second blow.

There was a tense silence during which Tony continued to breathe in short heavy gasps. Gritting her teeth Jodie was about to strike again when she felt his weight shift and he moved off her. Dropping the lamp Jodie leapt from the bed and ran for the light switch, pulling her gown about her as she went. Turning she discovered Tony sitting on the side of the bed with his head in his hands, a trickle of blood visible between his fingers.

As she returned from the bathroom with a flannel, Jodie asked tentatively, 'Are you all right?' Picking her way through the fragments of lamp she dabbed gingerly at the cut on his forehead. 'I seem to have developed a nasty habit of clubbing people,' she recalled in an attempt to defuse the situation.

'The light, please turn it off,' he asked. His head still in his hands he mumbled, 'I'm so sorry . . . so ashamed. I don't know who I thought it was I was . . . with then, but believe me I had no idea it was you. That is until you literally knocked some sense back into me.'

Finding the courage to turn off the light, Jodie sat in silence at the dressing table while Tony dressed in the dark. She stiffened as he pulled on his boots and slowly crossed the room. Standing head down before her, arms hanging listlessly at his sides, he said, 'I'm like a demented bloody animal, I belong in the bush.'

'No Tony, you belong back in society. Nyoni and goodness knows how many others depend on your getting help and getting well again.'

'I need time. Maybe one day,' he muttered picking up his rifle and making for the balcony.

Jodie followed him. 'We can still work this out,' she insisted, closing her eyes as he leant forward to kiss her lightly on the forehead. When next she opened them he had gone, having dropped over the railing to land catlike on the grass below. Jodie remained on the balcony until the moon rose and the lone fever tree materialised, stark and ghostlike from the blackness.

'I will not abandon you, Nyoni. I promise,' she vowed.

Seconded

Major Young made the necessary arrangements to second a detachment of men to the Rhodesian African Rifles. He and Williams were in accord for once, and Corporal Longdon's name headed the list of men they could ill afford to lose. Far from acknowledging the relative leniency afforded him on his return from unauthorised leave, Longdon's attitude had become even more belligerent on hearing the news of Rifleman Wells' desertion.

Tony's assertion, that the man had neither the inclination nor motivation to abscond from what amounted to his home from home and meal ticket, fell on deaf ears. What was more, Tony rationalised that Wells would not have left without taking his rifle, if only to sell it on the black market.

Tony would ordinarily have resisted being shunted off to the RAR, if for no other reason than to protest the fact that no logical explanation had been forthcoming for the unprecedented integration of black and white troops. But given the situation at home he protested only lamely. He needed a distraction to get his mind off Kathy and the RAR was where the action was, which would improve the odds of him learning more about the covert activities of the infamous Selous Scouts.

There was no animosity towards the new arrivals and the RAR troops, long accustomed to white officers, actually welcomed the additional manpower. Tony and his colleagues on the other hand were unnerved by the almost casual *modus operandi* of the veteran regulars and it was some time before Tony conceded the merits of their basic, yet effective, routines. The RAR relied on informants, as opposed to trudging endless kilometres on the offchance of intercepting their quarry.

The platoon base, to which Tony, Piet Nell and two other C Company personnel had been transferred, comprised three trucks dotted haphazardly on a barren, rocky hilltop. No attempt had been made at camouflaging vehicles or equipment. The camp was sited in the middle of a Tribal Trust Land, the hallmark of which was an almost complete lack of vegetation due to chronic overgrazing. Apart from the camp being totally exposed to the merciless sun there could be no denying the brilliance of its positioning, a silent approach by night was impossible and by day a rabbit would attract attention from three hundred metres.

The twenty-four-year-old European second lieutenant commanding the platoon had lost all interest in the war since obtaining his degree, with a government grant. While Lieutenant Skinner begrudged every day in the bush, with only his blacks for company, it had not stopped him making himself comfortable. He resided in a three-roomed tent affair constructed from truck tarpaulins and furnished with items 'borrowed' from the many deserted white farmsteads in the sensitive areas bordering the TTLs. He lived in his PT shorts and slops and his life revolved around his armchair and collection of cowboy paperbacks. He kept company only with his radio operator cum batman and his 2IC, Warrant Officer Class 2 Sebastian Moyo. Moyo saw to rations and discipline as well as the day-to-day running of operations.

In the weeks that followed Longdon became as one with the RAR, thinking and operating with the smooth unhurried precision of the professional soldier.

Moyo was a big man and his voice was as imposing as his build. Picking his way through the loose rocks to where his white corporal lay half-naked on top of his sleeping bag beneath a ground sheet strung up for shade, he greeted him. 'Good afternoon, Corporal. You have issued your orders for tonight's patrol?'

Tony was about to get to his feet when Moyo motioned him to

stay put. It was not necessary to salute WOIIs, or for that matter commissioned officers in the field, but in other circumstances Tony would have been happy to do so. The man was a battle-hardened veteran and a born leader.

Although accustomed to his subordinates standing rigidly to attention when he addressed them, Sebastian chose to squat next to the white corporal in a gesture of mutual respect.

'Yes, Warrant Officer I have given my briefing. We plan to move out around eighteen hundred hours, after an early supper,' Tony acknowledged, looking at his watch.

'Call me Sebastian,' Moyo invited, adding, 'when we are alone, you understand.'

'Sebastian it is, thanks.'

'You intend to ambush a known crossing place on the Mlibizi river,' Moyo observed checking his notes.

'That was the original plan,' Tony said, rolling onto his side. 'But we now have it on good authority that Chief Mtetwa's villagers are feeding the gooks, so I am considering ambushing one of the paths leading directly into the village. If we draw a blank we can make a sweep through the kraal before dawn, to see what we can flush out.'

'So, Mtetwa is up to his old tricks again,' Sebastian noted. 'It is good to see we have a blooming white Askari in our midst, making use of informants.' He offered Tony a cigarette.

'*Budding* Askari,' Tony corrected with a grin, adding as he got to his feet, 'I learn fast.'

'I will accompany your patrol, if you have no objection?'

Raising an eyebrow but resisting the urge to seek an explanation, Tony said, 'You are more than welcome, Sebastian. It will be good to have a ranking NCO along to carry the bloody radio for a change,' he added out of devilment, as he offered the older man a light.

Sebastian's spontaneous laughter supported Tony's contention that the man possessed an uncharacteristically keen, Western-type sense of humour. Apart from Moyo's overzealous use of the

English language, he made an excellent impression – Sandhurst material under a black government.

'You have gained weight since joining us Corporal, so in the interest of your health I suggest you hang onto the radio.'

'It's the way you people operate that's making me fat. No trekking through the bush for days on end, on the offchance of stumbling upon the enemy. You wait for a lead, follow up and get the job done.'

Sebastian chuckled. 'Yes, I know how it is with you white territorial guys, heads down, arses up and go like bulls out of hell. You cover plenty of ground and climb a lot of *koppies*, but see very little.'

Unable to suppress his curiosity any longer, Tony asked, 'Is there any particular reason for this sudden urge to go *bundu-bashing* Sebastian or are you just needing a break from our armchair lieutenant?'

Tony knew that black troops had a fetish for authority but he was not prepared for Sebastian's reaction. The man's wide-set dark eyes fixed his own in a steely glare. Realising he had given Longdon no cause to suspect just how much he actually detested Skinner, Sebastian smiled. 'You are only making a joke with me, not so Corporal?'

'Only teasing,' Tony assured him, grateful to be let off the hook.

Sebastian clasped his hands behind his back and lowered his voice, 'The truth is I need to discuss these anti-government sediments of yours.'

'*Sentiments*,' Tony corrected, frowning. He was about to go on the defensive and demand an explanation when Sebastian volunteered, 'My men in your section say you speak harsh words about the Rhodesian Front and this, how do you say, *fruitless* war.'

'Futile,' Tony assisted, still on his guard. It had dawned on him that while he had confided only in Nell these past two weeks there had always been one or more of Sebastian's Askaries hovering nearby.

'Yes, this futile war,' Sebastian repeated. 'You are a strange man, Corporal; you distrust our white government and feel sorry for the local blacks. I am told you have handed out hundreds of our malaria pills to those with the fever in the kraals?'

'Dozens,' Tony corrected, still uncertain if he was being praised or set up.

Squatting down Sebastian picked up Tony's binoculars case and flipped it open before he had time to protest. 'Hundreds,' he reaffirmed holding out the case brimming with malaria pills rifled from the ample medical supplies on the stores truck, that was strictly out of bounds.

'It is good you do not take your field glasses on patrol, Corporal. To use them one must climb *koppies*, and we both know what a bloody waste of time that can be!' Moyo smiled as he handed back the evidence.

This typically African trait of beating about the bush was beginning to frustrate Tony. Closing the binoculars case and tossing it back onto his sleeping bag he led with his chin. 'Benjamin, who has taken over the MAG from Nell in my section, the one you said speaks little English, he understands every word I say doesn't he?'

'Yes,' Sebastian conceded without hesitation.

'You planted him to spy on me?'

'Of course,' Sebastian grinned. 'I needed to be sure about you. I would have spoken sooner but you have been so aloft.'

'*Aloof*,' Tony corrected impatiently.

'Yes aloof, like I said,' Sebastian scowled, annoyed at being constantly corrected when everyone else clearly understood him.

'I was not intentionally distancing myself, it just takes time to adjust to a new environment,' Tony explained.

'I understand. I also needed time; time to make enquiries about you.'

'You . . . you had me investigated?' Tony stammered, finding it hard to credit that this enormous black man, with a cannon-ball-like shaved head, could have some sort of vested interest in him.

'Let us just say, Corporal, I was very interested to learn that you

197

are a well-respected member of a left-wing political organisation, which acknowledges that the fulfilment of fundamental black political aspirations is essential for a just and enduring peace in our beloved Zimbabwe.'

'No shit!' Tony exclaimed, completely taken aback by this gush of perfectly recited political dogma. He felt decidedly ill at ease for the first time since his arrival at the RAR camp. Apart from Moyo's unnerving interest in him, the only other time he had heard propaganda rattled off with such practised finesse was at an intelligence briefing. On that occasion he had been listening to tapes recorded during the interrogation of a terrorist political commissar.

'Well, now that you have me all figured out do you mind explaining what this is all about?'

'I will,' Moyo assured him. 'When the time is op . . . opportune,' he managed surprisingly. 'Right now I have duties to attend to.' He looked at his watch. 'I will be ready to move out with you at eighteen hundred hours.'

Checking his kit in preparation for the patrol, Tony could not help thinking that he was an unwitting pawn in a dangerous game of political intrigue.

Durban in December

The residents of Durban generally avoided the beachfront over the festive season due to the influx of holidaymakers. This December was no exception and the Marine Parade was crowded with perspiring, scantily clad tourists. The Indian Ocean was alive with surfboards and colourful paddle skis and the sun beat down from a cloudless blue sky. Everyone complained about the humidity.

Mark Longdon's two young daughters skipped along beside him as he strolled contentedly down the beachfront promenade in slops, shorts and t-shirt. Having explored the paddling pools and funfair, they were now on their way to the aquarium to see the dolphins. Linda found Durban's humidity unbearable and had elected to remain in the air-conditioned comfort of their hotel room with the weekend newspapers.

An ex-Rhodesian of some six weeks, Mark subconsciously scanned the sea of faces on the off-chance of recognising fellow countrymen – Rhodesians who had taken the gap like he and Linda or who were simply enjoying a break from the stresses of the war at home.

Kathleen Longdon walked listlessly down the wide pavement, her hair blowing in the warm sea breeze, her gaze fixed on the mesmerising rise and fall of the swells, her thoughts miles away.

'Aunty Kathy! Daddy, Daddy, look it's Aunty Kathy,' the girls cried out in unison.

Kathleen bent to hug the excited children to her as they rushed up and threw their arms about her legs. When she looked up her eyes were damp and mirrored the anguish she had suffered since foolishly abandoning all that she held dear. Confronted by her estranged husband's brother, in a foreign country a thousand miles from Bulawayo, thoughts of home flooded back with a vengeance.

Mark smiled a greeting and embraced his sister-in-law. Over the years she had borne the brunt of Tony's determination to succeed at any cost – and all for what, a marriage on the rocks and heartbreak. Mark on the other hand had married a couple of years after his elder brother and had a loving wife and two wonderful daughters to show for it. Admittedly he had never been quite as ambitious as Tony or had to contend with military training and call-ups.

Encouraging the girls to go and feed the hordes of pigeons with the peanuts they had purchased earlier from an Indian vendor, Mark offered Kathy his handkerchief and guided her over to a vacant bench.

'Have you heard from him?' she asked hesitantly, breaking the awkward silence as they sat gazing out at the dozen or more container vessels anchored in the bay.

'The folks got a letter the week before last. Apparently he has been seconded to a black regiment, something to do with bolstering the morale of the African troops. I gather he still intends going ahead with, you know . . .'

'Divorce proceedings,' Kathy concluded for him. 'I received the summons a few days ago and had to read it three times before it dawned on me that I was the defendant.' Wringing her hands she sobbed, 'He cited . . . adultery, desertion, irreconcilable differences, the loss of love and affection and goodness knows what else, as grounds. The whole sordid mess has left me feeling cheap and dirty, just wanting to curl up and die.'

'Kathy, you should not take that legal jargon personally. Lawyers always go for belts and braces to ensure they give the courts enough to act on.'

'Oh Mark, they can say what they like but nothing will change the fact that I still love him with all my heart. What am I to do?' she lamented, taking his hand.

Mark was surprised by Kathleen's touch. Her hands were ice cold in spite of the oppressive heat. There were also dark shadows beneath her eyes. Mark could not ever recall seeing his sister-in-law in such a pitiful state.

'How are things going with you and . . . Roger?' he enquired hesitantly.

'They aren't. The truth is it was over before it started. He's a deceitful, selfish pig of a man. How could I have been so stupid?' she sobbed. Blowing her nose into Mark's handkerchief and sniffing back the tears she concluded, barely above a whisper, 'I walked out on him the day we arrived in Durban, a couple of weeks ago. I have not seen or heard of him since, thankfully.'

'Actually it's going on four weeks since you . . . left home,' Mark noted, massaging her shoulders to help her relax. 'It's for the best. Roger was never going to amount to anything. Not that my dear brother didn't have his faults. I'm actually amazed you managed to put up with his self-righteousness all those years. Then again, who am I to talk? The one time you really needed a friend Linda and I were preoccupied with our plans to get the hell out of Rhodesia. Had we been there for you things might not have got so . . . so out of hand.'

Kathy braved a smile. 'That's very sweet of you Mark but I doubt it would really have made much difference. I was so low at the time that nothing made sense anymore. From the moment I heard the news of the indefinite mobilisation and realised that the army had cheated me out of Tony again, I became emotionally numb. Still, it's hard to believe I actually let something like that happen,' she blurted out ahead of the tears, her first good cry in four agonising weeks.

Ignoring the curious glances from passers-by, Mark encouraged Kathy to let it all out, to release the torment pent-up so dangerously.

'Mark, I'm sorry to be burdening you with all this. I know I brought this upon myself but I dread thinking it's all going to end this way,' she sobbed.

201

Swallowing hard, Mark gave his sister-in-law a reassuring hug and craned his neck to check on the girls. While his brother was far too sanctimonious to lightly forgive and forget, what Kathy needed now was hope, something to cling on to.

'Come now Kathy, it's not like you to throw in the towel without a fight. There must be something we can do? Hell the two of you were together for more years than I care to remember,' he encouraged, adding, 'Would I be correct in saying this . . . this affair was not meant to be – an unforeseen moment of weakness?'

'Yes, compounded by being in the wrong place at the wrong time and having had too much to drink,' Kathy said, nodding into his chest. 'Still, it does not excuse what I did and I must now face up to what I have coming to me.' She sat up and dried her eyes as the girls came running back, their peanut packets empty and with hordes of pigeons flocking after them.

'Right, let's agree then. We will work something out together. But first things first, where are you staying in Durban?'

Kathy choked back a final involuntary sob. 'I have a room at the Lonsdale Hotel.'

'Well we can't have that, not with only two weeks to Christmas. Linda and I have bought a nice three-bedroom place out at Glenashley, that's on the north coast. We move in the day after tomorrow and you, young lady, are coming to stay with us – no buts. Then we are going to sit down and seriously address this problem. Deal?'

Kathleen managed a weak smile, inwardly feeling it was hopeless. 'Deal,' she whispered. There was no fight, nothing left in her any more.

Mark was as good as his word and in the days that followed he and Kathy weighed up all the options. 'Then it's agreed, our initial approach will be a letter in which you spell out exactly what did and, more importantly, did not happen between you and Roger. Include all the slushy stuff, memories from way back when etcetera.'

'Oh Mark, do you really think this has a chance?' Kathy asked, uncertainty getting the better of her.

'Think positively my girl,' Mark insisted. 'As it stands, Tony will not be stood down before the one-man one-vote elections, which means he's not going anywhere in a hurry. He will have time on his hands, so once he has read your letter he's going to stew on it. Hopefully, he will realise just how much his damn conceited pride is going to cost him. It will certainly make him sit up and reassess the situation.' Mark smiled confidently at Kathy across the dining room table. Inwardly he knew that if nothing else the exercise would buy her time, time during which to grow to accept that, if the worst did come to the worst, life still had meaning and a place for her.

Selous Scouts

Arriving in the vicinity of Mtetwa's kraal well before midnight the patrol took up an ambush position on a likely approach route. Nothing stirred for five long hours. Once the moon had waned Tony positioned two men as stops before he, Sebastian and the remaining three troopers began a sweep through the village. They advanced at a snail's pace, rifles cocked, safety catches off with fingers lightly curled around triggers. The mangy village dogs cowered away as the ghost-like figures advanced menacingly between silent huts.

The three Askaris ducked beneath the eaves of the primitive dwellings to feel under the thatch for hidden weapons. They searched woodpiles and chicken coops and checked for tell-tale signs around the dying embers of cooking fires. Tony and Sebastian covered them.

Studying several large mounds of embers in the cooking area of a small, two-hut family unit, Tony turned to beckon Sebastian. To his surprise the man was hovering at his elbow, nodding in silent agreement. About to order a search of the dwellings, Tony's lips had barely parted when Sebastian stepped up to the closest hut and reduced the door to matchwood with a single kick. Having been ordered out, a frail old man shuffled naked into the night, knees knocking, shoulders bent and with trembling hands clasping his wizened genitals. An even deadlier hush had descended upon the village.

The door of the adjacent hut was similarly kicked in, only this time there was no response to Sebastian's commands. An Askari was ordered into the hut and came out prodding two scarecrow-like old crones before him with his rifle. Sharing a filthy grey sheet clutched to their shrivelled breasts, the ancient pot-bellied matrons cowered against the mud wall of their hut. Having re-entered the wives' hut, fingers pinching his nostrils, the trooper dragged out a large cast-iron pot caked with dried maize-meal porridge. Several smaller clay pots containing dry bones were also unearthed.

Responding to a softly spoken question put to him by Sebastian, the *madala* mumbled something about his age and the lateness of the hour, only to have his protest cut short by a backhand that sent him sprawling. The old man's entire being shuddered spasmodically as Sebastian hauled him to his feet by the folds of loose skin at his throat.

'Fuck, is this really necessary?' Tony hissed.

'Yes,' Sebastian said with their suspect already choking on his tongue in his haste to confess.

'There, he admits he cannot afford to eat meat and the food his wives prepared was for freedom fighters,' Sebastian translated for the white corporal's benefit.

'You mean *terrorists!*' Tony corrected dispassionately.

'Terrorists,' Sebastian snorted, inwardly vowing to be more guarded in future.

No sooner had the old man said his piece than his wives started to whine in unison, their low guttural cries raising the hackles on Tony's neck. 'What the hell's the matter with them?' he asked, peering through the gloom at the women still supporting one another against their hut.

'They are cursing the old fool for not holding his tongue. They would prefer he kept his mouth shut and we simply shot him, leaving them in peace.'

'Did he say when the gooks left?' Tony asked, anxious to get on with the job and leave these pitiful people to return to their beds.

'He said they fed them at noon. They will be miles away by now,' Sebastian lied, thankful that his white corporal did not understand the local dialect.

Several other equally barbaric interrogations only served to confirm that half the inhabitants of the village had, at one time or another, been guilty of harbouring and feeding so-called freedom fighters.

'What do you call a man pointing an AK at your guts?' Sebastian asked as the first rays of light flecked the sky. 'You call him *Sir*,' he answered himself, chuckling. Tony was in no mood for jokes but inwardly he acknowledged that the locals really had no choice but to obey the masters of the day.

Arriving at the last and most impressive group of huts, housing Chief Mtetwa and his wives, Tony radioed for Piet and Benjamin to rejoin the patrol.

The white-haired old chief shuffled nervously about urgently directing his household. He ordered his senior wife to arrange stools beneath a wild fig tree for their guests and saw to it that one of his younger, more comely wives served up thick slices of bread – three days fresh – on a biscuit tin lid covered with a piece of brown paper. He had another of his wives brew tea, while a fourth was despatched to milk a goat.

Dunking the stale bread in his hot sweet tea, while listening to Piet's account of what he would normally be breakfasting on at home, Tony could not get the tell-tale cooking fires out of his mind. The more he thought about it the more convinced he was that the ashes would have been more widely scattered had they been lying around since noon the day before.

Finishing his tea, Tony crossed to where Sebastian and Benjamin squatted beside the smoky fire, chatting up two of the chief's newest and youngest wives. Finally coaxing the reluctant WOII away from his new interest, Tony said, 'Sebastian, I'm certain that the old man's cooking area was used more recently than noon yesterday. Either he lied or we misunderstood.'

'Don't worry about the old man's fires, Corporal,' Sebastian said, dismissing the veiled insinuation with an impatient wave of a huge hand. 'He will pay with the rest of these collaborators.'

'What the hell are you talking about? Terrorist sympathisers or not there has been enough bloody head-butting for one night,'

Tony snapped, his preoccupation with the cooking fires forgotten.

'Listen for a change,' Sebastian ordered, thrusting his big head to within centimetres of the white corporal's face and drawing him down onto his haunches, lest their voices carry. 'I did not say we will punish these people. But this village will be made to, how do you say, attune for their sins!'

'Close enough. But what are you implying?'

'Skinner . . . er, Lieutenant Skinner, will report our findings to Company HQ and so on up the chain of command. Then this area will be frozen and we will con . . . conveniently be withdrawn. This village will then be cowardly attacked and many will die, as an example to collaborators.' Sebastian paused before adding, 'You have witnessed such atrocities before, not so Corporal?'

Tony felt a chill run down his spine in spite of the heat of the advancing day. It was uncanny that Sebastian should draw attention to the very type of foul play he and his political allies were hoping to expose. The big man maintained eye contact and Tony instinctively felt the need for caution.

'Atrocities are committed by both sides, there being numerous reports of terrorists punishing villagers for talking to security forces,' Tony pointedly reminded Sebastian. 'What's to stop this gang from returning to take revenge once we've left?'

'Why would they cut off their noses in spite of their faces? This is the only village in the area big enough to keep them fed. Believe me, once the area has been frozen there are those who will engineer a contact at this village. Many will die and it will be said they were killed in the cross-fire. Am I ringing any bells?' Sebastian challenged.

Tony's mind boggled at the man's obvious inference to the massacre he himself had witnessed not that long ago. 'On what pretext will the area be frozen?' he asked, playing for time.

'What do you mean?'

'What *reason* will Tac HQ give for wanting us out of the area?'

'Oh yes, that. The pretext being we are needed elsewhere and

207

that an Auxiliary unit, the *Pfumo re Vahnu*, will be moving in to take over the security of the area.'

His mouth dry, Tony nodded; Major Young had come up with precisely that explanation.

'I think it is time we speak openly about the atrocity you witnessed, Corporal,' Sebastian said, noting the look of bemusement on the younger man's face. Tony simply nodded as Sebastian led him off round the side of a hut for greater privacy. 'You see, Corporal, when Skinner has his nose to his books I listen in on sitreps from other units close to our sector. I was on the air the day your callsign redeployed to check out an explosion. Naturally I listened in.'

Naturally, Tony thought, holding his breath for what might come next.

Secretly allowing himself another self-satisfied grin, Moyo continued, 'Corporal, it was not hard to follow events that day. First you were told there were no other troops in your area, only to discover a military vehicle had hit a mine near a village in which many people went on to die. You bravely spoke out, condemning friendly forces for the massacre. Only to be threatened with a court-martial. Correct?'

Tony gave a soft whistle and lit another cigarette.

'Well, Corporal?' Moyo prompted.

'You certainly have your finger on the pulse, Sebastian, but nothing was proved and the charges were dropped.'

'Do not play games with me Corporal. Together we can expose the Smith government's role in perpetrating these heinous crimes against humanity.'

The government's role, heinous crimes, Tony reflected, no longer in any doubt as to Sebastian's allegiance or just who was using who.

Two days after Tony had submitted his patrol report, Sebastian thrust a message pad under his nose. The area had been frozen and the platoon ordered to relocate, just as Moyo had predicted. As Tony read the order, visions of women and children running and flopping to the ground, cut down in a hail of bullets, came to mind.

Lieutenant Skinner left it to the last minute before boarding the lead vehicle once the platoon was ready to move out. Only then was Sebastian able to supervise the loading of his armchair. The convoy set out for their new location, a distance of twenty-five kilometres as the crow flies but a three-hour drive over corrugated dirt roads.

Having passed through an isolated late afternoon downpour, a blessing for the inhabitants of the semi-arid Manjolo TTL, they arrived at their destination drenched and steaming. Dropping down over the tailboard, Tony landed in mud where for nine months there had been only dust. Shouldering his kit he set off to find Sebastian.

'Sebastian, can you spare a moment, please?' Tony asked as he approached the warrant officer. The man was urgently supervising the unloading of the royal armchair, at the same time instructing the signaller on the best location for the radio aerial.

'Later, I'm busy, Corporal. Get your men dug in, shell scrapes will . . .'

'Suffice,' Tony obliged. 'I'll be brief then. Once we are dug in I would like to take out a recognisance patrol.'

'Back to Mtetwa's kraal?' Sebastian asked knowingly.

'Yes, I'll leave Nell here to get things sorted out but I will need my four Askaris.'

'So you would see for yourself, which is good Corporal,' Sebastian said, suddenly more attentive. 'But you will be returning to a no-go area, not only dangerous but also again risking a court martial,' he cautioned, adding as he sent the armchair on its way, 'I will accompany you to be on the safe side, if you do not object?'

'No objection,' Tony said, realising he had been frowning. 'It's just that I would have thought you had more pressing duties establishing camp.'

'Let me worry about that, Corporal,' Sebastian said, discouraging further debate.

'Then we need to leave shortly if we are to reach the village before first light tomorrow.'

'I will join you as soon as I have posted the guards and let Skinner know I will be joining a patrol.'

So it was simply *Skinner* now, Tony reflected as he left to return to his men.

While waiting with the rest of the section for Sebastian, enjoying his last cigarette of the day, Tony began to question the wisdom of returning to Mtetwa's kraal. The arduous trek and the risk of entering a no-go area were not his only concerns. Even assuming a massacre did take place, and that with the collaboration of a regular army warrant officer a public outcry were to bring a halt to further carnage, there was still the seemingly insurmountable problem of the interim government. A government hell-bent on electing a black puppet prime minister, leaving the ostracised leaders of the Patriotic Front no alternative but to continue their campaign to reduce the country to a state of anarchy.

Tony stubbed out his cigarette in the encroaching gloom. In his heart he knew he would be unable to live with his conscience should he not at least attempt to avert a tragedy. Besides he had little enough to lose, what with Kathy estranged and no job to return to.

'Unavoidable delay,' Moyo said curtly as he picked his way through the puddles to join the group sheltering from the intermittent showers beneath an acacia tree.

'So much for our last precious hour of daylight,' Tony muttered under his breath as he proceeded to give each man, including Sebastian, a good shake to check for loose equipment.

They had been travelling for less than two hours when Moyo whistled a halt. Annoyed at yet a further delay, Tony was on his way back down the line when he heard the cumbersome MAG being set down heavily at the rear, followed by an audible sigh from Benjamin in the darkness. Checking his advance he wiped the perspiration from his forehead, signalled the rest of the patrol to ground and rested up against his pack. Sebastian gave the tireless Benjamin the thumbs up as they squatted in the dark, well pleased with themselves.

The tall, lean figure blended in perfectly with the clump of sparse vegetation in which he stood, motionless yet completely relaxed. Dressed in a dirty dark-green boiler suit, with something resembling a tea cosy for a hat, he had a communist RPD sub-machine-gun slung from his neck and held at the ready. Two similarly clad figures, also uncannily concealed half in and half out of the sparse cover, stood their own silent vigil nearby. The men were on the fringe of the cleared ground surrounding Mtetwa's kraal, two blacks and a white but no one would tell them apart beneath the mixture of fire ash and camouflage cream that broke up their features.

Throughout the night and the early hours of that morning, plagued by mosquitoes and chilled by the dew, the three Selous Scouts had stood their ground in the certain knowledge of the kill. The gooks would come, if not this night then tomorrow or the night after, but return they would now that the RAR had been moved out of the area.

They came in the pre-light of dawn, moving with the stealth of hunted animals as they advanced like phantoms on the ill-fated village. Moving well ahead of the main body, two of their number passed within an arm's length of one of the sentinels. Stopping on the edge of the compound the guerrilla vanguard observed, sniffed the air and listened for ten long minutes before proceeding unchallenged into the outer ring of huts.

Nervously coaxing the embers of their cooking fires into life, the early risers in the village wisely ignored the presence of the intruders. The men who would punish their elders for engaging the security forces, and once again feast unsparingly on their meagre food reserve, going on to drink the village dry of beer and slake their animal-like lust between the loins of the community's terrified women. This was the cross they were expected to bear, in the name of freedom.

Satisfied that their so-called cannon fodder would have sprung any unlikely ambush, the remaining twenty hard-core guerrillas left the thick bush and moved in on the village.

As the band of men came into view through the early morning mist, Gerald Bond's finger tightened around the trigger of his machine-gun. His nostrils flared and his upper lip curled back. His colleagues also readied themselves for the kill.

The *vakomana* – boys in the bush – as the terrorists were paternally referred to by their leaders in exile, were already beginning to relax as they approached the relative safety of the village. Some carried weapons nonchalantly over the shoulder; others broke into nervous chatter as they swaggered across the threshold of the open compound. The village dogs were strangely quiet.

Thirteen terrorists died in the next few seconds, gunned down from all sides as the three Scouts moved in among them, culling methodically.

Instead of turning on their attackers, the only course of action that might have saved them, the surviving terrorists fled into the village, some bleeding to death as they ran. The Scouts sniped as selectively as the pandemonium permitted. Their quarry on the other hand fired indiscriminately, driving screaming villagers before them and cutting down anyone in their path.

Immune to the screams of the dying that rent the air above the stutter of machine-guns and the sporadic crack, crack, crack of rifle fire, the Scouts pursued the survivors. With the defence forces now spread so desperately thin on the ground, they needed no reminding that they could ill afford the luxury of allowing even a single gook to escape to continue his reign of terror.

Twelve minutes into the fire-fight with twenty-odd terrorists and nearly as many locals dead or dying, the Scouts started to mop up. Working their way systematically back through the village they were intent on ferreting out the few cowardly dogs yet to be accounted for. As he moved through the carnage, Gerald Bond inwardly lamented the tragic loss of innocent lives. Yet experience had taught him that ambushing the gooks in dense bush, where they were in their element, resulted in a pathetically low kill rate.

Moyo had called several more halts during the march and the RAR patrol was still a good four kilometres from the village when the first shots echoed dully through the pre-dawn. Instinctively going to ground, Moyo congratulated himself on his timing. It would all be over by the time they arrived. He was again in the throes of giving Benjamin the thumbs up when Longdon came dashing down the line.

'Cache your packs and spare water bottles. Sebastian, continue to bring up the rear with Benjamin. Moses you stay on my tail, Isaac you take the left flank, Joseph the right. Let's move.'

Setting off, Sebastian realised he had badly underestimated the white man's resolve and stamina. But to pull rank now, and countermand the corporal's orders, would only arouse suspicion and destroy the trust he had been carefully cultivating.

Tony set a cracking pace but in spite of their gallant effort the sun had already breasted the horizon by the time the six exhausted men reached the approaches to the village. They would have arrived sooner had it not been for Moyo's insistence that they deviate and approach from the east to ensure they had the sun at their backs as it rose; sound tactics but costly in terms of precious time.

Breathing heavily the men flattened themselves against a small rise overlooking the sprawling settlement. Having picked up the dreadful wailing over a kilometre from the kraal, they were now staring down at its source. The bodies of dead terrorists, stripped of their weapons and wearing oddments of civilian clothing to disguising their telltale overalls, were inconspicuous amidst the carnage. Not that Tony would have registered their presence had they been in full regalia, it being all he could do to stop from retching as the memory of the acrid stench of death, from the last massacre, flooded back.

Benjamin flicked a pebble in his corporal's direction to attract his attention. Following his gunner's keen eye to where a couple of

213

darkly clad figures were skirmishing down the far side of the village, Tony watched as the men methodically cleared one section of scrub after another.

It was Moyo who picked up the third individual, skirting the village on their side. As the trio continued their advance the patrol was able to make out the cylindrical shape of the drum-type magazines beneath their communist RPD machine-guns.

'Those are bloody terrs, not military personnel,' Tony breathed, with an audible sigh of relief that surprised even him.

'Scouts, two blacks and a white,' Sebastian corrected. 'And they are hunting,' he whispered.

'Hunting!' Tony exclaimed uncertainly as he reached for his binoculars case, to find it still contained only malaria pills and boiled sweets.

'For more so-called terrorist sympathisers,' Moyo lied effortlessly. 'They will not rest until . . .' a short burst of automatic fire cut him short. Seconds later another black soul fleetingly broke cover. This time only a single shot rang out, economically despatching the hapless individual.

As the three Scouts converged on a point a hundred metres from the patrol's position the lone tall individual removed his headgear, revealing a band of white skin as he mopped his brow. He raised an arm aloft and his colleagues acknowledged the all-clear signal before continuing on into separate cover.

'We must move back,' Moyo warned, his thick lips only centimetres from the corporal's ear.

'We cannot risk losing sight of them,' Tony countered, breathing through his mouth to avoid another whiff of the man's sour breath.

'They have eyes like hawks and the nose of a jackal,' Moyo hissed.

'We outnumber them and have the element of surprise,' Tony reminded him without too much conviction. 'Surely we are close enough to get the drop on them,' he whispered, easing off his safety catch and glancing back over his shoulder to check the positioning of the rest of the patrol.

Swallowing hard, Moyo was about to tell his corporal, *You must be out of your fucking mind*, when something caught his eye. One of the Scouts was moving off, walking unhurriedly through the bush at right angles to the patrol, heading away from the village. 'We are too late; they have recharged their magazines and are moving out. They will leave at intervals, tracking each other to their next destination,' he volunteered, visibly relaxing.

Flattening his cheek against the stock of his rifle, Tony's finger curled round the trigger as he drew a bead on the departing Scout.

A gasp escaping his lips, a wide-eyed Moyo managed to get a hand to the barrel of his corporal's rifle just in time.

His sights weighed harmlessly to ground Tony's whole body began to shake in a delayed reaction to the carnage. Not to mention his fatigue and the realisation that he'd been about to shoot one of their own.

'Trust me, Corporal,' Moyo pleaded, 'if but one Scout survived it could end very badly for us. Even if we managed to kill all three, claiming we mistook them for guerrillas, the fact remains we would have done so in a frozen area.'

Staring at the spot where the first Scout had melted into the bush, Tony acknowledged, 'I can't believe we are just going to sit back and . . .' a big hand forced his head down before he could finish. Cautiously pulling Sebastian's hand away from the back of his neck, Tony slowly looked up to see a second Scout moving out. It was the tall white member of the band, the absence of his balaclava revealing a mop of long fair hair. Tony blinked in disbelief but there could be no mistaking the individual, even from that distance. This was the unassuming young man Tony had met at the Baobab Hotel. Only now Gerald Bond was the epitome of death, with an RPD machine-gun slung round his neck and a pair of 9-mm pistols on his hips.

Even after the last Scout had followed his colleagues into the bush the patrol remained motionless, intent on the incessant wailing from the village.

215

'Disciples of the devil,' Sebastian spoke at last. 'Murderers of women and children,' he added for good measure.

'You were not so brave a moment ago,' Tony reminded him.

'It is already too late for these people. What matters most is keeping *you* alive, having now witnessed such shocking in-human . . .'

'Inhumanity,' Tony suggested.

'Yes, whatever, but now you can use your influence to save many lives. By exposing this inhumanity you will be furthering the cause of justice and freedom, for all the people of Zimbabwe.'

The political commissar talking again, Tony reflected. 'What about those poor devils down there, we can't just leave them.' He was about to protest more strongly when a soft bird-like call distracted him and both men looked round. Moses was pointing urgently away at three black shapes on the horizon, coming in low over the treetops.

The Alouette Mark IIIs were closing fast. To Tony's relief, as well as his surprise, he was able to make out a distinctive white cross on one of the fuselages. The two escort choppers were K-Cars, 20-mm cannons protruding from their open sides.

'Corporal, without coms we are sitting like ducks in a no-go area. We must go *now*,' Sebastian insisted, setting off into the bush and signalling the rest of his anxious Askaris to move out.

With little option but to follow suit, Tony brought up the rear, more questions than answers on his mind. There was the question of Victoria Bond's brother, a well-balanced, intelligent individual; hardly the type to embark on a spree of wanton mass murder. Another imponderable was the helicopters – only the Scouts could have summoned them, but why call in a mercy mission if intent on creating mayhem?

As the weary patrol neared their base camp, Sebastian sidled up to his corporal. 'We need to discuss your plans for communicating these atrocities to the outside world, once I get you a pass.'

More convinced than ever that Sebastian had a second agenda, Tony continued to hedge his bets. 'Assuming I do have connections, what is there to be gained at this late stage? We are only months away from elections and the end of white rule – and the war.'

'It will expose this non-representative interim government as puppets of the racist Smith's regime. The regime responsible for these atrocities,' Moyo blurted out, unable to contain his frustration.

Steeling his resolve, in what could now be in the national interest, Tony continued to probe. 'Assuming we can get the word out, why should Smith and his colleagues start heeding world opinion now?'

Moyo knew time was running out for the cause and his comrades over the border in Mozambique. It was vital he retained the trust of this important pawn, even at the risk of showing his hand; assuming this astute white was not already on to him. 'Corporal, just as you and the NUF are working behind the scenes to bring peace to this country, I am doing the same as a member of the external wing of the ANC.' Ignoring Tony's slack jaw, Moyo elaborated, 'When I discovered who you were I knew that by helping you I could help the cause. We need to discredit Ian Smith and his propaganda, aimed at blaming our innocent freedom fighters for these atrocities.'

While Tony had suspected Sebastian of playing a double game, he had not imagined anything quite this daunting. What with senior elements within the ranks of the RAR actively supporting the terrorists, it was little wonder the kill-rate of the black troops had fallen so alarmingly of late. There was obviously more, much more.

'You never cease to amaze me, Sebastian,' Tony said truthfully. Realising just how precarious his situation had become he added with conviction, 'Sebastian, far be it for me to judge your commitment to the struggle. Had I been born black, I would probably have been at the forefront of the fight against a system that discriminates against the majority of its citizens.'

The look of triumph mirrored in Sebastian's mahogany brown eyes told Tony he was safe, at least for the time being.

'Yes, from what Benjamin tells me you are indeed a man of

strong liberal views,' Moyo said, visibly relaxing. 'Once we have disgraced the Smith regime this will pave the road for the return of the father of Zimbabwe. His people will then rise up and this government will be forced to concede the transfer of power to the true leaders of the liberation,' he concluded excitedly.

'By the father of Zimbabwe do you speak of Joshua Nkomo or Robert Mugabe?' Tony asked with as much practised calm as his adrenalin would permit, acutely aware that the rest of the patrol was strategically positioned around them.

Sensing the need for caution in spite of Longdon's pledged allegiance, Moyo hedged. 'What does it matter who arrives first? Both are dedicated to the freedom of Zimbabwe and are committed to the Patriotic Front alliance.'

With one subtle difference, Tony mused. Mugabe was a Shona like Moyo and an ardent Mao Communist, while Nkomo was an Ndebele and a capitalist at heart, albeit with a foot in the Russian camp. In spite of having just reminded himself how precarious his situation was, Tony found himself continuing to question. 'When you say his people will rise up, are you referring to the grass roots support of the rural population?'

Lighting a cigarette in cupped hands, for dusk had descended on the bush, Moyo weighed up the risk of saying too much against the pleasure of further amazing his new comrade. Concluding that Longdon would be a fool to tempt fate unless truly committed to the cause, Moyo decided to indulge himself. 'The rural population yes, that goes without saying, but more importantly I refer to the *Pfumo re Vahnu*, thousands of whom have returned under the amnesty and now stand ready in the Auxiliary forces. Then there are those of us among the ranks of the RAR, and some whites who cannot yet speak out openly.'

Pensively tapping a cigarette from his packet, Tony brazenly asked, 'Sebastian, I thought the *Pfumo re Vahnu* were effectively pro-government forces?' He was banking on the assumption that he was worth more alive than dead, and that a true comrade would wish to be fully informed.

Slowly shaking his bull-like head, Moyo could hardly contain his excitement. He had expected nothing less from this white corporal. Making a mental note to question Longdon's lack of a commission, should he survive the acid test he had conveniently invited upon himself, Moyo volunteered, 'Comrade, the truth of the matter is that the Auxiliary units are made up of crack freedom fighters; loyal to the revolution.' Interpreting Longdon's still gaping mouth as a sign that the man was poised to challenge his statement, Moyo hastened to add, 'Admittedly in the beginning a few genuine deserters did take advantage of the amnesty, but they have long since been eliminated.'

Smiling in an effort to disguise the sick feeling welling up from the pit of his stomach, and realising he was a dead man if he baulked at this disclosure, connections or no connections, Tony responded with all the conviction he could muster, 'Sebastian, the whites are blissfully unaware of this phenomenal grass-roots support for the ANC. I agree, credibility must be restored to the leaders of the Patriotic Front so their voice can be heard. The Smith regime is unlikely to get its mandate for a black puppet prime minister once the electorate realises that it could lead to anarchy.' He had chosen his words carefully and was well rewarded by the expression on the mutinous warrant officer's face.

Moyo was a happy man as they filed back into camp. Not only had he been assured of Longdon's support, the man had even gone so far as to pledge his willingness to serve the new state of Zimbabwe. Not that whites were contemplated in the new scheme of things.

Brother and Sister

Captain Gerald Bond disembarked in a deserted side street and watched the olive-green staff car out of sight from the shadows. It was dusk and there was not a breath of air to alleviate the midsummer heat of January.

Urban terrorist attacks on homes of police and military personnel were common enough to dissuade Bond from visiting his family too frequently. This evening was a case of urgently needing to talk to his sister, in private, so he waited until it was completely dark before slipping into the back garden of his parents' home. Relaxed but motionless he waited behind the hibiscus hedge until the lights in the house went out.

Responding cautiously to the tap on her window, Victoria was barely able to contain her delight on peering through a crack in the curtain and seeing her brother.

Removing the finger from his lips, Gerald kissed his sister through the burglar bars once she had opened the window. 'It's good to see you again, my not-so-little sister,' he observed.

'Don't you want me to open up for you?'

'No, I can't stay long. I'll say hello to Mum and Dad next time round. But you can turn off the light, I feel like a hare in the headlamps.'

Victoria switched off the light without question and hurried back to the window. Since Gerald's transfer to the Selous Scouts from the SAS a few years back the family had learnt the futility of being overly inquisitive.

'Sorry I couldn't make it home any earlier. Did you get my telegram?'

'Yes we did and a happy New Year to you too, brother dear.

Hopefully this year will see an end to the country's problems, what with the referendum this month paving the way for majority rule elections in April.'

Gerald fidgeted uneasily as he glanced at his watch. 'Vicky, this is a bit awkward so I'm going to come straight to the point. It concerns Anthony Longdon.'

Victoria's face lit up on hearing Tony's name, but her joy was shortlived as she studied her brother's expression. 'What about him and why this odd visit?' she implored, her grip tightening on the burglar bars.

'I need to know more about your relationship; just how serious is it?' Gerald asked, struggling with his conscience as he considered his lovely sister, six years his junior and seemingly so vulnerable standing there barefoot in her dressing gown. From the tremor in her voice he knew it had been wrong to come, to allow emotion to cloud his judgement. He should have let events take their course; others had been called to account for less.

'Gerald, I happen to be very much in love with him. Now are you going to give me a straight answer or do I scream the house down?'

'Hold on Sis,' he smiled, placing a reassuring hand over hers on the bars. 'We may have been reading too much into this. It's just that our Mr Longdon appears to be going out of his way to buck the system. He has recently added insubordination and absenting himself without leave to a well-documented personal campaign to discredit the government.'

While nothing Gerald had said really came as a surprise to Victoria – Tony having bared his soul to her in this very room not seven weeks ago – her brother's involvement left her flabbergasted. 'Gerald, you said you were going to get straight to the point. I'm your sister for goodness sake, just tell me what it is he's supposed to have done and how on earth it could possibly involve you of all people?'

'Vicky, please, you know better than to ask. Look, now that I know how you feel about the guy, I'll do what I can to . . . smooth

221

things over. Trust me.'

'No Gerald, I don't think I can trust you. Not with your being so evasive about someone so dear to me.' Folding her arms across her chest she glared at her brother through choked-back tears, as if willing an explanation.

Gerald felt decidedly uncomfortable but he held his sister's gaze. Assuming it was not already too late he knew it was not going to be easy getting Longdon off the hook. The bloody fool had involved himself with a black warrant officer, who was presently the subject of a top-priority security investigation. Moreover, the pair of them had violated a no-go area and witnessed a contact but reported nothing.

Sensing her brother's uneasiness, Victoria turned and pulled in her gown, revealing a well-defined bulge.

'Gerald, I love you both dearly but it's Tony's child I'm carrying.'

'Holy shit!' Gerald swore, hardly able to believe his eyes. While he had it on good authority that Tony had spent time with his sister subsequent to their meeting at the Baobab Hotel, some five months ago, and hence the visit, he had not bargained on this. The guy was married and Vicky was not that kind of girl. 'The folks?' he breathed, barely above a whisper.

'I told them just before Christmas,' she confirmed turning back to face him. 'They have been very understanding and supportive – considering.'

'Well, I guess it's congratulations. How long before . . . before it's due?' He managed a smile for his sister.

'*It* happens to be a *he* and you will be an uncle in about four months.' It was Victoria's turn to brave a smile, her intuition warning her that something more sinister than Tony's political views or his intolerance of the system had brought her brother here tonight.

'Gerald, what little I have gleaned of your activities these past few years leads me to believe your authority exceeds . . . the normal call of duty,' she said solemnly. Drawing a deep breath she added, 'If after tonight any misfortune were to befall Tony we, that is the baby and I, would never be able to forgive you.'

Gerald felt a chill go through him. In truth, it was more a question of providence whether or not Tony's luck held out. Sebastian Moyo's fate, he knew, had already been sealed. 'I appreciate how important Tony must be to you, Sis. Believe me,' he conceded sincerely.

'Gerald, he means *everything* to me. For the record his wife left him and he felt obliged to resign from his job due to the political uncertainty. Hardly surprising he has not been himself lately!'

'Then I'm pleased I came tonight. Does he know about . . .?'

'Not yet, and please, I'd prefer he hears about the baby from me.'

Again checking his watch Gerald said, 'I really must be off, I'll give Tony your regards . . . should I run into him.'

'That's very thoughtful. Just tell him I said I miss him and that what will be, will be. He will understand. One more thing, please do not leave it so long before we see you again. We all miss you terribly.'

'I'll try and get back for a weekend, soon,' Gerald promised as he kissed her goodbye through the bars.

Returning the way he had come, Gerald found himself glancing back over his shoulder. The ever-present feeling of prying eyes was accentuated by the sense of unease at finding his sister with child.

Love Child

The time passed slowly for Victoria but the worst of summer was behind her and the cooler days of early March made her pregnancy that much more comfortable. Filling the space at the bottom of the perfumed writing paper with kisses, she touched up her lipstick and imprinted a kiss for Tony. It was another long, tender letter, seeking answers to some of the hundred and one questions she had not got round to asking during their short but eventful courtship. Before returning to his unit, after his spell of AWOL in November, Tony had said he felt it was premature to make long-term plans. That he needed time; time to adjust to his new circumstances.

For her part she had agreed to wait no matter how long it took. What she had not been prepared to confide in him back then – but had now found the courage to commit to paper – was the joy she felt at carrying their child, already stirring reassuringly in her womb.

She was still at her dressing table in the bedroom when an unfamiliar sound startled her. Frowning as she looked over her shoulder at the drawn curtains, blowing gently in the late evening breeze, she was about to dismiss it when she heard the sound again; muffled voices. Recalling Gerald's clandestine visit some two months earlier, she immediately discounted a childish prank in times like these. Alone in the house, she was regretting her haste in declining her parents' invitation to accompany them on their Saturday night outing to the Baobab Hotel. Protectively clasping her protruding midriff she cautiously crossed the room. She would close the window then make a beeline for her father's study, to retrieve the revolver in the desk drawer.

She screamed as an arm snaked through the burglar bars, her cry of terror cut short by a powerful black hand clamping vice-like about her throat. Flung mercilessly back across the room, Victoria did not see the sinister cylindrical object drop heavily through the window.

Special Branch

The January referendum had come and gone, with white Rhodesians giving Ian Smith's interim government a mandate to proceed with an internal settlement, the lesser of two evils. The unspeakable alternative had been to invite the guerrilla leaders – Mugabe and Nkomo – to return to the country to contest free and fair elections. With preparations under way for the April one-man one-vote polls, the short-lived cease fire collapsed and the security situation steadily deteriorated. The armistice, however, remained in force, and daily more and more guerrillas came on side to swell the ever-growing ranks of the *Pfumo re Vahnu* in the assembly points – some sixteen thousand men all told.

Sebastian Moyo's efforts to organise a pass for Corporal Longdon were frustrated by the ever-growing demands made on the security forces. As the weeks dragged by Moyo became increasingly paranoid. He walked a dangerous path; with one attempt on his life already he knew time was no longer on his side.

Longdon, on the other hand, interpreted Moyo's growing anxiety as a sign that the date of the mass uprising was imminent. His concern was now that his continued isolation in the TTLs would prevent him from timeously alerting the authorities to the impending insurrection. Having toyed with the idea of confiding in Lieutenant Skinner, he had thought better of it. The man was naive enough to call in his trusted warrant officer and confront him with these ridiculous allegations.

Inexplicably, in the early part of March, terrorist activity tailed off. Some said it was the lull before the storm. Others ventured that the leaders of the terrorist movement were about to throw

226

in the towel, in the face of heavy desertions under the armistice. Whatever the truth the breathing space afforded Moyo the opportunity to secure a pass for his white corporal.

Arriving at Brady Barracks in Bulawayo, after a monotonous six-hour drive on the back of a ration truck, Tony made his way over to the guard house to show his pass, phone the airline and call a taxi to take him to the airport. There was an urgency in his stride. Having resolved to expose Moyo and his treasonous cohorts, he needed to make the four-hundred-and-fifty-kilometre trip up to Salisbury, the capital. He was determined to meet with senior echelons at Combined Operations HQ to ensure his intelligence did not get bogged down in bureaucracy. No easy task, even with his connections, knowing what he did of the security at Milton Building.

It was only after he had replaced the receiver of the pay phone in the guardhouse that Tony noticed the military police sergeant frowning up at him from the other side of his desk.

'Let me see that pass again, Corporal,' the red cap demanded, arm outstretched.

Handing over the buff slip of paper with a belligerent sigh, Tony found himself simultaneously shaking his head and tapping his foot while the stocky sergeant read aloud. 'Forty-eight-hour pass to visit private dentist in Bulawayo. So what's this crap about a flight to Salisbury? Connecting to Johannesburg; taking the gap are we?'

MPs were the lowest form of army life in Tony's mind and it showed as he threw up his arms and scoffed, 'Not even MPs can be so naive as to believe anyone would make arrangements to duck the country from a bloody guard house.'

Getting to his feet the sergeant squared his red cap and made his way around the desk. 'Watch that bloody mouth, Corporal or I'll shut it for you,' he spat with his index finger half an inch from the bigger man's nostrils.

Tony balled his fists but restrained himself; this was just the provocation the MP was looking for. 'Sorry, one gets a bit bush-happy after a while,' he apologised, gritting his teeth. 'I only found out my dentist had moved his practice after the pass was issued. My wife called ahead and he has agreed to see me,' he lied.

The sergeant nodded. 'Name of dentist?' he demanded, dramatically thumbing his way through to the Salisbury section of the telephone directory.

'Philip Atkins . . . but he only moved recently. Probably not listed yet,' Tony said, cursing his stupidity for not leaving his flight booking until he got to town.

Shaking his head but smiling at last the MP said, 'You're not going anywhere, you cocky bastard. And get your hands out of your fucking pockets.' He dialled the duty officer. Having explained the situation, he was in the process of recommending a month in detention when the duty officer obviously cut him short.

'Yes, Longdon, Corporal AP. That's correct, Sir, C Company Ninth Battalion. You know this joker . . . Sir?' Having already removed his backside from the corner of the desk the sergeant was standing to attention by the time the duty officer had completed his dressing down.

'Yes Sir, no Sir. Yes, I understand, *Sir.*' Gently replacing the receiver the visibly bemused MP confirmed hoarsely, 'You are free to go on your way, Corporal.'

'Who's the duty officer?'

'As if you don't know,' said the disillusioned MP. 'Major van Heerden.'

Tony left the guardroom feeling decidedly ill at ease. The major was their battle camp training officer and the old goat was far too astute to condone him, of all people, flitting around the country on a bogus pass.

Within the hour Tony found himself boarding the half-empty flight RH512 to Salisbury. The plane was a prop-driven Viscount, a sister aircraft to the Hunyani that had been shot down the September before by a terrorist heat-seeking Sam 7 missile. Thirty-eight passengers had died in the crash, with a further ten of the eighteen survivors butchered on the ground.

The critical ascent was perforce at a more acute angle than normal, and the demand for drinks was noticeably brisk once the seatbelt and no-smoking lights were switched off. In spite of managing three double brandies during the hour-long flight, Tony could not get van Heerden's blatant derogation of duty out of his mind. He was still pondering the mystery as he checked in at the plush Monomatapa Hotel, later that afternoon.

A patron of the five-star hotel on his frequent business trips to the capital, Tony received a warm welcome and no eyebrows were raised at his arrival in uniform and with only a rucksack. Making the call on which he was pinning his hopes, Tony managed a shower before the waiter arrived with his room service order of steak, egg and chips and a bottle of South African wine; reserved stock for special guests. With only a towel around his waist he was about to tuck into what promised to be the most exciting meal he'd had in months, when the telephone rang.

'Hi Peter, that was quick! Good news I trust?' he asked swallowing back saliva from the aroma of the steak.

'Yes, excellent news in fact. Thanks to the damnedest bit of luck one could imagine, old boy,' Peter Day confirmed in the exaggerated colonial accent he had cultivated since he and Tony had left school, some ten years earlier. 'Although I must confess to a few harrowing moments after the second of my contacts also reported having been given the run around; something about the top brass in defence not being prepared to meet with anyone without security clearance, which can take weeks.'

'Nevertheless, you pulled it off?'

'Actually, old boy, I'm not at all certain I deserve the credit. I had drawn two blanks, as I said, when out of the blue some officious sounding clerk *called me* and offered to make the arrangements. It's all set for ten o'clock tomorrow morning, believe it or not. Simply present yourself at the security desk at Milton Building. They have your details,' he concluded helpfully.

'You're too modest, Peter,' Tony flattered his friend from the Ministry of Commerce and Industry. 'The next time I'm in town

I promise we will get together for a couple of beers, for old times' sake.'

'I look forward to it, and to hearing why this appointment was a matter of life or bloody death, old boy.'

Slowly replacing the receiver, Tony reflected on the odds of bureaucracy tipping the scales so heavily in his favour twice in one day. He made short work of the bottle of wine and the steak, hardly touching the rest.

Having spent a restless night, in spite of the welcome luxury of the suite, Tony was having second thoughts as he arrived at the drab Milton Building the following morning. He had no actual proof of rogue elements within the RAR, and only hearsay evidence supporting the nefarious intent of the *Pfumo re Vahnu*. Approaching the security desk it dawned on him that his main concern now was the disturbing interest the powers that be appeared to have taken in him.

Unsurprisingly, two Special Branch policemen appeared the moment he announced himself. Wordlessly they escorted him up several flights of creaking, wooden stairs in the old government building. Having been ushered into a deserted sparsely furnished and badly lit reception room, Tony stubbed out his cigarette. One of the policemen rapped on the heavy inner doors. Without waiting for a response he motioned for Tony to stay, before departing with his equally deadpan colleague.

After some sixty seconds of staring at the chipped green paint of the double doors, Tony stepped forward impatiently. His arm was still raised to give the doors a really good hammering when they swung inwards on well-oiled hinges. Poised on the threshold Tony again found himself in limbo. Tiring of the melodramatics he strode into the room intent on giving someone a few pointers in etiquette, only to come up short once again to allow his eyes to adjust to the darkened room. Heavy, full-length curtains were drawn tightly across the only window and a diffused red glow permeated down from concealed ceiling lighting. He was barely able to make out the desk with a single chair in front of it.

Tony's jaw sagged as the absurdity of his situation dawned on him and the reason for his anxiety, and uncanny good luck, became abundantly clear. He was staring at a bare lightbulb, suspended ominously low over the solitary visitor's chair. Even as he focused on the dark-suited individual sitting motionless behind the desk, a black eye patch making his gaunt appearance all the more theatrical, Tony refused to accept that he had presented himself at his own interrogation.

A second individual in short shirtsleeves stood erect next to the desk, powerful arms folded across his chest. Tony only noticed the third individual once the doors had clicked solidly shut behind him and the fellow ambled across the room, taking up a position on the opposite side of the desk from his gorilla-like colleague. All three men stared fixedly at the empty chair in front of Tony.

'*You must be fucking joking,*' Tony snorted. Turning instinctively back to the door he tried the handle. 'Locked,' he chuckled aloud, unable to contain the involuntary laughter. The whole scene was absurd, worse than something out of a cheap espionage thriller. Even if things like this did happen in this day and age, they certainly did not happen to executives of large public companies. And they sure as hell were not going to happen to him.

To his credit he managed to land a solid right hook and two good left jabs as the heavies moved in. Finding himself slumped in the hard wooden chair he was left contemplating the futility of resistance. Yet in spite of this new-found wisdom, a rapidly closing left eye and split lip, he goaded, 'If this third-degree crap is Rhodesian justice it's high time we gave the bloody country back to the blacks. They are a darn sight more fucking civilised.' He at least had the presence of mind to remain seated.

The chap with the eye patch got awkwardly out of his chair and with the aid of a stick hobbled around the desk, swinging his lame leg as he came. With his suspect on the verge of sounding off again he slapped a heavy hand on the younger man's shoulder and bellowed, 'Shut the fuck up.'

'*Fuck you,*' Tony retorted, leaping to his feet. Only to be slammed back down again and to marvel at the uncanny strength of the wiry cripple, now effortlessly restraining him. He realised that what he really needed now, apart from a stiff drink, was a good lawyer.

'It's *Inspector*, and for the record this is not the army so we don't have to tolerate your bloody *bullshit*. Get it?' the inspector yelled in Tony's ear. Pointedly removing his hand from the suspect's shoulder he went on to ask, 'Do I make myself clear, you miserable fucking Kaffir lover?'

True to form Longdon again shot to his feet. This time the fist that slammed into his head came from his blind side, sending him crashing to the bare floorboards. Several well-aimed kicks followed.

Tony was not sure how long he lay on the floor but through bouts of nausea it slowly dawned on him that, while he had been doused with water, neither the wet sack over the head nor electrodes to the testicles had been forthcoming. He remained on the floor, struggling to come to grips with his bizarre circumstances and trying to get his shaking under control.

Having imagined he'd heard the doors open and close, Tony only realised there was a fifth person in the room once they had him back in the chair. 'Reinforcements!' he scoffed through blood-caked lips. Cocking his head at a ridiculous angle, in an attempt to make out the stranger through his good eye, he challenged, 'Come on get on with it then, turn on your fucking light.' Still trying to focus on the new arrival, dressed in camouflage kit and with captain's pips on his shoulders, Tony sensed there was something familiar about the tall individual. Shaking his head to clear his vision, he only succeeded in sending white flashes lancing before his eyes. Cradling his head in his hands he slumped forward onto the desk, where he remained perfectly still for long minutes.

'Sorry about that little episode. Here this should help.'

The words seemed to be coming from a long way off. Raising his head, cautiously at first, Tony discovered the light above him was still off and that he was alone in the darkened room with the young army captain. Mechanically accepting the tumbler of water, Tony drank. Recognition only dawned as he handed back the empty glass. The Samaritan was none other than Gerald Bond.

'Again, my apologies,' Gerald repeated. Adding as a matter of fact, 'This was uncalled-for and could have been avoided. Had I been able to get here sooner.'

Waving aside the offer of a cigarette, Tony tried to block out the throbbing in his head and ignore the discomfort from the soaking he had received to revive him. Looking up at his visitor he wondered why, apart from Gerald's rank, he was not really surprised to see Victoria's brother standing before him in an interrogation room on the second floor of a government building in the centre of Salisbury. Then again nothing was likely to surprise him after today.

Gerald Bond sat down on the corner of the big desk, lit his cigarette and continued in a flat monotone, 'They were to have waited. I was unavoidably detained.' He paused, cleared his throat. 'I have lost count of the number of military funerals I've attended, but when it comes to . . . family it's an entirely different matter. She was so young, so dear to us all. Victoria was like . . .' His voice trailed off.

There was an incessant buzzing in Tony's ears and he grinned uncomprehendingly at Bond as he got unsteadily to his feet and crossed to the window to get some fresh air. Yanking the heavy maroon curtains apart he chuckled as he found himself staring at a solid brick wall. Wandering back across the room he helped himself to one of Gerald's cigarettes. He struck the match but found he needed both hands to steady it. Bending to retrieve his beret from the wet floorboards he grimaced as the blood rushed to his head. The events of the morning were taking their toll. Staring at his watch he voiced aloud, 'Half eleven, can't be!'

'That is the correct time,' Bond confirmed.

'I've been here a bloody hour and a half!' Tony mumbled in disbelief. 'I need to sit down, but not there,' he nodded towards the solid wooden chair as he passed it heading for the double doors. Surprisingly they were unlocked and he carried on through the empty reception and out into the passage. From the window at the top of the staircase he could see the traffic and hear the muffled sounds from the avenue below. People were going about their business on the pavement, oblivious to the ominous happenings only two floors above. Letting go of the wrought iron banister, Tony turned to confront Bond who had followed him out.

'Can I go now, or are they waiting to blow my fucking brains out at the bottom of the stairs?' He was squinting against the bright sunlight through his good eye, while fighting down the urge to burst out in hysterical laughter at the absurdity of it all. He still needed a lawyer he thought, only now to sue the pants off the fucking government.

'Of course you may leave. You made the appointment,' Gerald reminded him with a straight face. 'Then again perhaps we should go back in for a few minutes, try to tie up some loose ends seeing as you are here anyway? Then I'll take you back to your hotel.'

'Fuck you,' Tony managed before his legs buckled. He would have plunged headlong down the stairs had it not been for the quick reflexes of his host.

Although the Monomatapa Hotel was within easy walking distance, Bond had the security desk call a taxi. Having helped Longdon into the back seat he was relieved to see the improvement in the man as they drove off and he took in the familiar sights of the city. With Tony more receptive he again attempted to explain, 'I was saying earlier, I was unavoidably delayed. I was in Wankie yesterday . . . for Victoria's funeral.'

Still shaking his head in disbelief as the taxi pulled up in front of the hotel, Tony only managed, 'Is this another sick fucking joke or . . .' before nausea overcame him and he flung open the door.

When Tony had finished throwing up in the gutter, Gerald said quietly, 'It happened five days ago, in a terrorist attack on our house. She was alone on Saturday evening; the folks were at the hotel. They lobbed a grenade through the bedroom window. She never regained consciousness.' Gerald left it at that. Recriminations about his earlier visit home, to discuss Tony, were not going to bring his sister back.

Once back in his suite on the fifteenth floor, Tony made straight for the bathroom to clean up. When he returned Gerald followed him out onto the balcony, where they stood in silence staring out at the spectacular vista of Salisbury.

Looking across at Gerald, Tony swallowed hard, for the family resemblance seemed more pronounced than ever. He felt strangely numb, the loss of Kathy and his career, the pent-up tensions of the past few weeks, the degrading treatment meted out at Milton Building and now this horrendous news. He was still reflecting on just how cruel fate could be when Gerald broke the silence.

'It would help to know if your intentions towards my sister were . . . well, honourable?'

'*Help you!* Why the fuck would I help anyone in cahoots with those bloody SB goons?' Tony snapped, his grief rapidly turning to outrage. He'd had enough for one day. 'You have the fucking audacity to talk of honour, with the blood of God knows how many innocent civilians on your hands. How do you live with . . .' Tony wavered, turned and headed back to the bathroom.

'Here, this will help settle your nerves,' Gerald said handing over one of the beers he had got room service to send up while Tony was indisposed. 'I took the liberty of ordering a dozen, the rest are in there,' he nodded towards the mini-bar. 'I charged them as you are obviously good for it,' he smiled for the first time that day as he took in the spacious suite with a wave of his hand. 'Now what's all this nonsense about innocent civilians?' he prompted.

Tony downed his beer before replying, 'First you tell me what it was those bastards at Com-Ops were hoping to get out of me?'

'That I am not at liberty to say, at least until you and I have a better understanding.'

'Fine, then explain how the hell you fit into all this?'

'I got involved because I promised my sister I would keep an eye out for you. You see, Victoria was carrying your child,' Gerald said solemnly. He neglected to add that Longdon had actually become a father to a son born by caesarean section on his mother's deathbed. This was not something he wished to share with a man who had yet to come clean on his apparent complicity with known enemies of the state.

Dropping down into an armchair, Tony lit a cigarette with hands that were more unsteady than ever. 'I had no idea, why didn't she say something? Then again, I guess I hardly knew my own mind at the time. Vicky was remarkably perceptive.' Staring intently at Gerald, Tony continued, 'As for my intentions I had toyed with the idea of contacting my wife, once I was stood down, just to convince myself it was over; for good. Either way I would certainly have stood by Vicky had I known she was pregnant.' The tremor in his voice added credence to his words.

'Thank you for being frank with me,' Gerald said sincerely. 'Victoria would have made a wonderful mother,' he said, raising his glass in an unspoken toast.

After a long moment's silence it was Tony who made the effort to get the conversation back on track. 'That you found me, let alone were supposedly coming to my assistance, tells me you must know what that pantomime at Milton Building was all about. In which case it's beyond me how you can be party to bureaucratic bungling that results in innocent, law-abiding citizens being given the third degree? Who the bloody hell authorised this crap? More to the point, what would have happened if you *hadn't* turned up? Which begs the question, how come you ended up calling the shots back there?'

'Not so fast my friend,' Gerald said, holding up both hands. 'For starters there was no bureaucratic bungling in your case. Tell me why you went to so much trouble to gain access to the nerve centre of combined operations, and then perhaps I'll be able to answer some of your questions. Do we have a deal?'

'I went to blow the fucking place up, why else!' Tony fumed, hardly able to credit the irony of the situation. Here he was being invited to confide in the very individual he had been hell-bent on exposing for atrocities in the Tribal Trust Lands, before the treachery in the ranks of the RAR and Auxiliary Units had assumed precedence.

'You really are going to have to trust someone, sometime, my friend. And who else can you turn to?' Gerald prompted with practised finesse.

'There's always the police.'

'Feel free. You met them earlier remember, Special Branch?'

Shaking his head, Tony got up and helped himself to another beer. Time was not on his side. The threat facing the country was real, and undoubtedly more pressing than resolving some ridiculous misunderstanding on the part of the idiots at Milton Building. It was also apparent, judging from the day's events, that Gerald outranked some pretty important people. Perhaps he should be confiding in the man; should convince him of the threat posed to the state by rogue elements in the RAR and the massed Auxiliaries. Then, once he had got the audience he sought, go on to expose the Selous Scouts for their role in fanning the flames of insurrection by annihilating local villagers, effectively killing two birds with one stone.

'All right, you have a deal but with the proviso that you undertake to get me a hearing with the powers that be if you buy my story.'

'You have my assurance,' Gerald agreed, relaxing back in his chair.

The sun had set and the room grown dark by the time Tony finally eased his stiff body out of the armchair to switch on the lights. 'So there you have it. The country's incubating a cancer, what with both the Auxiliary Units and the RAR infiltrated and subverted. Given the unprecedented grassroots support for the ANC, an orchestrated uprising will make the Night of the Kenyan Long Knives look like child's play. If you need further convincing I suggest you get your mates to bring in Sebastian Moyo for a chat,' he concluded.

'Your Mr Moyo was finally . . . *taken care of* yesterday, shortly after your departure for Bulawayo,' Gerald said, helping himself to a cigarette from Tony's pack. He had finished his own pack while listening to the other man's remarkably accurate account of the crisis threatening the country. 'Does the news about Moyo surprise you at all?' he asked once he had lit his cigarette.

'Not after today. Actually, yes,' Tony corrected, 'but not as much as discovering the army dictates to Special Branch these days.'

'We don't dictate to Special Branch. I was granted some latitude in your case, due to your association with my sister. However, that will change very quickly should you not have a plausible explanation for your nefarious activities,' Gerald said in all seriousness.

'Nefarious, what the hell are you talking about?'

'Let's see: there is your political involvement with the left wing NUF and their covert dealings with the ANC nationalist Nkomo; fraternising with a known terrorist collaborator, Warrant Officer Moyo; not to mention travelling on a bogus pass and conspiring to gain access to the Com-Ops nerve centre.'

Tony laughed in spite of his split lip – it was a nervous laugh. 'You guys may be determined to brand me a threat to national security, but the lack of evil intent hardly qualifies my actions as nefarious. On the other hand the massacre of innocent people clearly does qualify.' He got to his feet.

'That's the second time this evening you have made that ridiculous claim. Get it off your chest,' Gerald invited, while discreetly shepherding Tony back into the centre of the room.

Aware that he was compromising his plan to expose the Selous Scouts, Tony proceeded to vent his frustration, 'I happened to have been in the area of Mtetwa's Kraal, that . . . eventful day last December.'

'The day you and your RAR buddies came within an inch of your lives. We usually shoot first and ask questions later in a no-go area, you were just lucky I recognised you,' Gerald said tersely.

Completely taken aback, Tony asked incredulously, 'You knew we were there?'

'We picked up your spoor as we were pulling out of the area and followed you back to where you had cached your packs. Besides being surprised to discover an RAR patrol way out of its area, we were intrigued by a white territorial corporal leading seasoned regular troops, including a ranking WOII. I'm guessing all this has something to do with these wild claims of yours about civilian casualties? I admit that an unfortunately high number of locals did catch it that day but it must have been obvious from your vantage point that the majority, if not all, of those killed in the cross-fire were gunned down by the bloody gooks running amok.'

'It was a contact then!' Tony said hoarsely, slumping back in his chair and reaching for his cigarettes.

'What else! You must have seen . . .' Bond's words trailed off as it dawned on him. 'You arrived after it was over and we were pulling pack. But even so, who in their right mind would jump to the conclusion that we were indiscriminately killing off locals?' Gerald shook his head in disbelief.

'It made sense at the time; playing out just as Moyo had predicted,' Tony protested lamely.

'You mean it played out just as Moyo *intended you perceive it!*' Gerald corrected.

'Knowing what we now do about the man that's . . . a distinct possibility,' Tony conceded, hastening to add, 'That is, were it not for a similar incident west of the Matetsi river . . .'

'Last September, just off the old Tetsi control road,' Gerald interjected. 'The day one of our vehicle patrols hit a landmine.'

Tony nodded silently, staring intently at Gerald as the man continued for his benefit. 'Tracking those responsible for laying the mine back to that village, the patrol came under heavy fire from the gooks. We lost one man that day, another seriously wounded.'

'I'm sorry to hear that. But there were no dead terrs or weapons when we arrived on the scene.'

'After a fire-fight weapons are collected rendered inoperable and cached pending recovery, in preference to just leaving them lying around for the next guy,' Gerald said sarcastically. 'As for the bodies, had you astute territorial chaps checked a few corpses for shoulder strap scars or a second set of clothing worn under the first, you would have found the twelve terrs accounted for that morning. I trust the picture is becoming clearer, Mr Longdon?'

'Part-time soldiers, what more can I say?' Tony offered with open palms, a sick-sinking feeling in his gut; the severest kind of punishment was acknowledging one's own stupidity. 'For what it's worth my exposing so-called renegade Selous Scouts had become a secondary objective. My visit to Milton Building was primarily to alert the authorities to the threat posed by the Auxiliaries and rogue elements within the RAR. A little naive in retrospect, considering all this stuff is general knowledge.'

'Tony, all this stuff, as you put it, is far from general knowledge. What's more, apart from your being blinded by statistics when it came to civilian casualties, you are anything but naive. I'm actually relieved, delighted in fact, that we have put the skeletons to bed,' Gerald acknowledged, getting up and extending a hand to Tony in good grace. Tony met Gerald halfway and the two men shook hands where they stood in the middle of the room, directly beneath the ornate chandelier.

'All that we require of you now Mr Longdon,' Gerald said formally, 'is your word that all this stuff remains strictly confidential. That means no press. Or suing the government for that incident earlier today,' he concluded as an afterthought.

'You have my word, and thanks for being so understanding,' Tony said, genuinely relieved at the outcome. 'What happens next? I mean I can't very well go back to the RAR now, can I?'

'That would be tempting fate,' Gerald agreed.

'What about my joining up with your lot?' Tony joked. 'It could be interesting seeing how you intend coping with this Auxiliary business.'

'You want to join the Scouts, after trying to have us branded as a merciless band of cut-throats?'

'Sure, but I know differently now. The Selous Scouts are actually a fun bunch of guys, right?'

Gerald grinned. 'You have a point Tony, but I think a spell of

240

R&R would make more sense. Give you time to get some semblance of order back in your life. Then we will post you back to your old Company, to see out what's left of your commitment.'

With that Gerald took a buff-coloured envelope from his breast pocket. 'A seven-day pass, with authorisation to leave the country should you so wish. I understand you have family down at the coast in South Africa,' he said knowingly.

Tony stared at the envelope. Just pack up and take a holiday in the middle of an indefinite military commitment? But he now knew enough about Gerald Bond to realise there were certain things he had either to accept without question or not at all. He was tired, mentally as well as physically, and could do with some time out to come to grips with the agony of Kathy's desertion and the raw news of Victoria's death.

'Gerald, the fact that you proactively arranged a pass tells me that you for one were not entirely convinced I was a bloody communist,' Tony said grinning.

'Like I told my sister that night at the Baobab Hotel, I'm a pretty good judge of character.'

'Well I'm pleased to have proved you correct on that score. You are also right about my needing a break. I have been over-reacting lately,' Tony admitted frankly. 'I'll take your advice and look up my brother, see how they are settling down in Durban while taking in some sea air.' Extending his hand once more, he said sincerely, 'Thanks for taking the trouble to help . . . sort things out, by that I mean me. Vicky would have been proud of you.'

'It was the least I could do in her memory,' Gerald said, shaking Tony's hand.

Once out in the deserted passage, Gerald paused only long enough to tap three times on the door of the room adjoining Tony's suite. Three equally soft answering knocks came back. Satisfied, he made his way to the lift. The Special Branch boys would in all probability wrap up their tapes for the night. Their *Communist* was no more than a self-opinionated, overzealous Rhodesian. Who, to put it mildly, had made a complete bloody nuisance of himself. Hopefully counter intelligence's most closely guarded secret, their feigned ignorance of a conspiracy, would remain just that, classified. As would the ingenious plan to permanently remedy the situation once the time was right.

Reunited

Tony stopped over in Bulawayo just long enough to collect his passport, pack a suitcase and say hello and goodbye to his parents. There was nobody to meet him on his arrival at Louis Botha airport in Durban but he knew there would be no problem arriving unannounced on his brother's doorstep.

The taxi drivers plying the airport were predominantly European – in contrast to their all-African counterparts in Rhodesia. The fact that South Africa had managed to get away with its system of grand apartheid for as long as it had never ceased to amaze Tony. North of the border economic evolution had seen job reservation in such menial occupations as postmen, bus and taxi drivers scrapped twenty years earlier.

'Just off the Air Rhodesia flight, man?' the perspiring over-weight cab driver asked in a broad Afrikaans accent.

Tony nodded as he cast a disapproving eye over the man's half-open, sweat-stained shirt as he made heavy work of loading his suitcase into the boot.

Self-consciously fastening a couple of buttons the driver muttered, 'The humidity man, this March is the worst in years.'

Tony gave the driver Mark's address then settled down in the front passenger seat and closed his eyes. The hot clammy coastal weather was in complete contrast to the more tolerable dry heat back home.

Not to be deterred the driver again tried to engage his fare in conversation once on the freeway into the city. 'That was a marvellous bloody country, hey man. But you can forget it once they hand it over to the *munts* – not so, *Meneer*?' Undaunted by his passenger's apparent deafness the driver continued, 'You people should burn everything to the ground when you leave, hey man. Give the bloody country back to them the way the whites found it, nothing but bush.'

'A scorched earth policy, obviously the most intelligent thing we could do,' Tony scoffed without opening his eyes, in the forlorn hope that his sarcasm would do the trick.

'This independence crap is never going to happen in South Africa, hey man,' the driver continued, encouraged by the response. 'We treat our blacks firm, firm but fair, hey. That way they don't get confused or start getting too *white*. You know what they say, hey? One-man one-vote, once! Ha, ha, get it man? Once! Then it's a one party state. Have you heard the one about what they are going to re-name Rhodesia after independence; Zimbabwe – *Zimbabwe Ruins*, ha ha ha!'

'Real funny,' Tony acknowledged, suppressing a chuckle as he reflected on the name – the great ruins reminding the Shonas of their people's grandest cultural achievement; the whites on the other hand perceived the name as epitomizing the potential ruin of a previously prosperous country. Turning to look out of the window he absently took in the dry-dock and yacht basin as they drove along the Victoria Embankment, paying marginally more attention to the throngs of holidaymakers and colourful rickshaws as they proceeded on down the Marine Parade. It was only once they had passed the last of the pristine Whites Only beaches, heading north out of the city, that he really sat up and took note. Sure enough, three hundred metres further down the road they passed the Coloureds Only bathing beach, then two hundred metres further on the beach reserved for Natal's Asian population and finally the inevitable; the signs demarcating the Africans Only bathing area.

'Typical!'

'What's that, hey man?' the driver asked eagerly.

'I was just thinking how cleverly you people have managed apartheid with the whole country, including the waterfront, divided into sectors for blacks and whites and all shades in between.'

'*Ja* absolutely, hey man. It's the only way, hey! Let them on our beaches and they would just ogle white women all day. But can you believe it the rest of the bloody world is too blind to see it. It's the same with our buses, can you imagine riding in one with a load of those sweaty buggers? Man, they should put all those bloody loudmouth liberal British politicians on a *black* bus and then see who's still shouting for integration. Not so, man?'

Tony was not surprised that it took the driver fifteen minutes to find the correct address, once in the suburb of La Lucia itself. His brother's house was set well back atop a high grassy bank, only the roof visible from the road. Closing the wrought iron gates quietly behind him, Tony made his way slowly up the steep paved driveway. The only sound was that of a couple of Indian Myna birds squabbling in a palm tree. It was just after two-thirty and Tony suspected that Linda and his nieces would be taking an afternoon nap, it being too hot and humid for much else.

Drawing level with the lawn and swimming pool at the top of the driveway, Tony stopped in his tracks. Not five metres from him was Kathy, curled up on a pool lounger reading in the shade of a flamboyant tree. There could be no mistaking the young woman in the bikini, even with sunglasses and her hair partly obscuring her face, but still Tony did a double take.

Although she had not heard the gate or Tony's approach, something compelled Kathleen to look up just as he put his suitcase down in the driveway. Whipping off her glasses she froze in the process of reaching for her towel, her book falling to the grass.

The estranged couple stared at one another for a long moment. It was Kathleen who regained her composure first, getting to her feet and wrapping the towel around her. Had it really been five months, she asked herself, since that fateful day when she had kissed him goodbye at Brady Barracks, possessed by a dreadful sense of foreboding?

Leaving his suitcase, Tony crossed the lawn on leaden legs. Placing a hand lightly on either of her shoulders he proceeded to do what only a few months ago would have proved impossible, kiss her on the forehead.

Kathleen responded instinctively, trembling hands coming up to rest on her husband's hips. But as the guilt flooded back her eyes misted over and she snatched her hands back.

'It's good to see you, Kathy. Sorry for barging in like this but . . .' Tony managed before the lump in his throat choked off his words.

His presence, the sound of his voice and hearing him speak her name all proved too much for Kathleen. Stepping back unsteadily she turned and fled to her room, joy, fear, guilt and a hundred and one other emotions overwhelming her.

Mark Longdon arrived home just after six o'clock. He kept long hours but was happy with the progress he was making at his new job. He encountered his elder brother on the pathway leading from the double garage. 'Greetings stranger, don't they have telephones up there any more?' Mark chided, delighted to see Tony again and only mildly taken aback by his unannounced presence.

'I missed you too,' Tony laughed as they embraced. 'No suit!' he remarked on his brother's smart but casual white slacks and open-neck shirt.

'This is Durbs, man,' Mark said with a smile. 'It's great to see you, even if something of a surprise under the circumstances. I trust you have seen Kath?'

'We sort of said hello when I arrived. I think she is giving Linda a hand in the kitchen at the moment. Nice of you to have taken her in,' Tony said awkwardly.

'She's been no trouble at all,' Mark said before changing the subject. 'Can I assume you finally had the presence of mind to resign from the bloody army, like I suggested?'

'It's not quite that easy,' Tony said with a broad grin. 'How about you, are you surviving in the big city without me to hold your hand?'

'Like you say, it's not easy. But we seem to be managing so far,' Mark said, gesturing towards the large ranch-style house with its magnificent view of the Indian Ocean – situated in one of the more upmarket suburbs on the north coast. 'What news of the folks? Still in there pitching for good old Ian Smith, while the country grinds to a halt? Reckon some people will never learn.'

'The folks are fine, apart from being a little peeved with you for spiriting their only grandchildren down south,' Tony said as they made their way over to the patio. 'As for Smithy, I think even Mum and Dad are ready to admit the man has lost touch with reality.'

'I reckon I'm well out of it,' Mark agreed, continuing on into the house to greet his family and Kathleen.

While waiting for Mark to freshen up, Tony strolled to the edge of the grass bank to take in the panoramic view. In the foreground below lay the rest of the neat wooded suburb, bordered by a mangrove forest skirting white sandy beaches. Beyond was the iridescent green of the Indian Ocean stretching to the horizon. When Mark rejoined him in shorts and slops and carrying two cold beers, Tony took up the conversation. 'You may be out of it for now sport but for how long is another story; South Africa is next.'

'Sure but why should I worry, the South Africans don't. They think like we Rhodesians did before Mozambique fell, that things will simply carry on as they have forever. Anyway, it's going to be a good few years before their black nationalists start flexing their muscles in earnest to shake off the shackles of apartheid. It's already started of course, the odd bombings, urban terrorism, landmines, farmers getting ambushed; the whole crazy Rhodesian scenario repeating itself.'

'What happens in the meantime?' Tony asked, opening his beer.

'Well, there's no shortage of young South Africans to combat the so-called *total onslaught*. I can make money while they fight the bloody war for a change. Hell, we have protected their arses from incursions from the north long enough. Not me personally, but you know what I mean,' Mark conceded with a cocky grin and a shrug.

Colour television – a novelty for new arrivals and visitors alike from Rhodesia – proved its worth in passing a few awkward hours that evening. The ever-present danger being another embarrassing silence, should someone say something that triggered memories of happier times.

Excusing herself before the end of the evening's viewing, Linda hurried off to the guest room. She needed to collect some sheets and a blanket from the linen cupboard, for the divan in the study for Tony. Her heart skipped a beat on entering the room to find her brother-in-law's suitcase, as yet unpacked, on Kathy's bed.

A bundle of nerves all day, Linda was almost beside herself as she ushered Mark urgently into the kitchen. '*His suitcase is in the guest room!*' she whispered, her facial contortions adding weight to the gravity of the situation. 'How in blazes did it get in there, of all places?'

'So, what's the problem?' Mark countered lamely, his expression giving the game away.

'Mark! You didn't! Oh, how could you?'

'It wasn't easy,' Mark said, making light of his wife's frustration.

'Mark . . . Tony has been in the bush for months. Anything could happen!'

'*Precisely,*' Mark grinned. 'They are adults and still man and wife, until a court of law decrees otherwise. Now stop being such a prude and make some coffee for our guests.'

'*Mark!*'

'I'm telling you it's no big deal, my love. Besides, they must sort out their own problems. End of story.'

Shortly after finishing her coffee Kathleen quietly said her goodnights and retired to her room. Her legs still felt as if they were made of jelly. Linda in turn lost no time in scurrying off to the master bedroom, only to flatten herself breathlessly behind the door.

A few minutes later the epilogue began and Tony rose and stretched. 'Been a long day sport, reckon I'll have a shower and hit the hay. Where do I bunk and what have you done with my suitcase?'

'Spare room, second door on the left down the passage, your

case is on the bed,' Mark replied as calmly as his adrenalin would permit.

'Thanks again for everything. I'll see you in the morning then.'

'Sure thing, and there's no rush to get up early. I'm going to take a day's leave. Then you can tell me how you really got that black eye and thick lip. There are also a couple of domestic issues we need to address, if you know what I mean?'

'Mark believe me, my walking into the tailboard of a truck is a lot more plausible than the truth. As for the rest, it might be best if I check into a holiday apartment in the morning, given the circumstances.'

'As you wish brother dear,' Mark conceded graciously. 'Sleep on it anyway,' he added out of devilment.

Mark made it into the kitchen with the tray of empty cups just as his brother let himself into the guest room. He heard the door click shut and instinctively grit his teeth, still clutching the tray. The suspense-charged minutes passed in deafening silence and Mark had to resist the urge to bellow *yes, yes, yes*. Putting down the tray he turned off all the lights and high-tailed it to bed, on tiptoes.

Mark finally roused his brother and sister-in-law around nine o'clock the following morning. He had prepared a late breakfast, set-up out on the veranda overlooking the pool where a faint breeze offered some respite from the humidity.

The tension of the previous evening had nothing on the mood around the breakfast table that morning. The children had left for school and apart from the uncomfortable silence there was a general reluctance to make eye contact. Deciding it was make or break, Mark cleared his throat and asked with all the seriousness he could muster, 'So, how was the second honeymoon?'

'*Mark!*' Linda gasped. She held her breath for a long moment before the bubble finally burst and the four of them roared with laughter.

The rest of the morning was spent in festive mood, lazing

around the pool, snacking on biltong and drinking ice-cold beer and chilled Cape red wine; just like in more settled times back home. As noon approached Mark fetched a bag of charcoal from the garage, in readiness for the afternoon *braai*.

While the conversation remained light and civil, it was obvious to Mark that the one topic that really needed to be aired was being avoided. Although still a little early to light the fire, Mark crossed to the *braai* and put a match to the kindling. 'Keep an eye on that until it takes hold, please,' he asked Tony, before casually extending a hand to Kathleen as he passed her recliner. 'On your feet my girl, I need your *pap* and gravy skills in the kitchen.'

Once in the house Mark headed for the master bedroom, a bemused Kathleen in tow. Closing the door quietly behind them he warned, 'Brace yourself my girl.' Opening his bedside drawer he handed her a letter. The well-travelled blue envelope was still sealed, with the sender's return address scribbled across the front in red ink. The enquiring smile on Kathy's face faded and the colour drained from her cheeks. With unsteady hands she fumbled the letter Mark had helped her compile just before Christmas, some three months earlier.

'But, Mark . . . I don't understand.'

'Kath, I'm sorry. It came back a few weeks ago but I did not have the heart to tell you. I thought Tony was being a bigger bastard than I gave him credit for, simply endorsing it return to sender. But now I gather he was seconded to the RAR and that there was a lot of confusion with mail and parcels. That would account for this being returned.'

'Then what is he doing here, if not in response to my begging forgiveness?' Kathleen implored hugging her shoulders and shivering in spite of the summer heat.

'Good question.'

'For all he knows I could have spent months, not days, with Roger,' Kathy continued, on the verge of tears. 'How did he even know where to find me for that matter?'

Mark drew her to him. 'Take it easy my girl, one thing at a time.

Let's start with last night? The two of you must have discussed something?'

'We hardly spoke . . . just . . . made love. That's all,' she breathed into his shoulder.

'That's all! But that's good, very good.'

'No Mark, I think last night was simply a release for Tony,' she sobbed while staring at the letter in her hand.

'Kathy, that's my brother we are talking about and he wouldn't give you the time of day, unless he was weakening. If he made love to you last night, thinking the worst, then that my dear was a major breakthrough. What's more I think I can prove it.' Kissing her reassuringly on the forehead, Mark eased the letter out of her grasp. 'Wait here. It's time to put an end to this bloody nonsense, once and for all.'

No sooner had Mark left the room than Kathleen collapsed face down onto the double bed, sobbing into the pillows. She did not know what to believe any more. When she finally lifted her head, red-eyed and damp-cheeked, it was to see Tony standing silently at the bedside. He was holding the now-opened letter clenched in his hand and tears rolled unashamedly down his face. Needing no further invitation, Kathleen flew off the bed and into his arms.

The days that followed passed in a whirl of joyful reunion, filled with sun, sand, surf and sex, visits to the amusement park, rickshaw rides, wine, beer and more sex. They proved to be some of the happiest times Kathleen and Tony had shared in years.

The real turning point came when Tony plucked up the courage to confess his own infidelity with Victoria. While not being easy to accept, the news at least went some way to lightening Kathleen's own burden of guilt. She had even shed a tear when Tony recounted the circumstances of Victoria's death. Not wishing to distress his wife with the knowledge that Vicky had been pregnant, he had left the story there; inwardly conceding that his selfishness in denying Kathy a child had contributed to her loneliness and subsequent breakdown.

Arm in arm, Kathleen and Tony gave a final wave as they

boarded the aircraft at Durban's Louis Botha Airport. Tony was not unhappy to be returning to Rhodesia. He was going back to the army but in the knowledge that this would likely be for the last time, given the advanced stage of settlement negotiations. The country had been good to him and he was determined to see it through until Rhodesia's so-called independence.

For her part, Kathleen did her best to ignore press reports suggesting that the imminent birth of Zimbabwe/Rhodesia could see the economy finally collapse, unless immediate recognition and financial aid from the West was forthcoming. The prospects of which were not encouraging given the generally held belief that the proposed new state of Zimbabwe/Rhodesia was an ill-conceived compromise, like its name. Most disconcerting of all was the fact that emigration had peaked, due to the escalation in hostilities resulting in record numbers of Rhodesians, of all races, dying daily in the conflict.

Helen Longdon spent the next two weeks keeping her daughter-in-law occupied and helping to give her the courage to face each new day.

'Helen, I cannot thank you enough for the company these past weeks,' Kathleen said as she helped the older woman clear away the breakfast things after Alf had left for work.

'It has been a pleasure having you stay with us my dear. How long is it now before we have our boy home again, providing this phased stand-down thing proceeds according to plan?'

'Twenty-one days,' Kathleen confirmed excitedly. 'I can hardly believe it and to think this time it's for good. No more army, *ever*. What a fool I have been all these years, letting my silly pride stand in the way of taking you and Alf up on your offer to stay here during Tony's camps. I'm sorry if I seemed ungrateful at the time, Mum.' It was the first time Kathleen had actually plucked up the courage to call her mother-in-law Mum. It felt good and from the smile on Helen's face, it meant a great deal to her as well.

252

Having done the washing up, Kathy did an impromptu whirl in the middle of the kitchen. She had enjoyed keeping busy, thanks to Helen being one of the few housewives who chose to make do with only a part-time maid. The garden-boy came in to clean the windows and wash the kitchen floor when needed, which went without saying.

'Shall I start on this bit of ironing, Mum?' Kathleen called out, having stuck her head into the laundry.

'I think we should leave something for Betty tomorrow morning dear. At this rate she is going to suspect you are after her job! But you could run the Hoover over the carpets for me, if you are feeling energetic.'

It was pleasantly mild now that the worst of summer was over and Kathleen made good time with her vacuuming. There was a bounce in her step for she knew she would soon be sitting out by the pool, working on her daily letter to Tony. Fortunately, the mail was moving well in both directions since Tony had rejoined C Company under Major Young.

The Last Patrol

Two weeks before the April elections and just three weeks before C Company was due to be stood down, one of the bloodiest battles of the war took place. Over one hundred guerrillas had made a night crossing of the Zambezi river, manhandling an arsenal of 75-mm recoilless rifles and 82-mm mortars.

Since rejoining C Company the feud between Corporal Longdon and Captain Williams had intensified, so it was not unexpected when Alpha section drew the unenviable task of clearing an arid area between the Deka and Gwai rivers, both of which had long ceased flowing.

Williams was adamant, in spite of Longdon's near mutinous insistence that a five-day patrol into a barren wasteland was senseless if not suicidal. The fact that at least one regular army unit had opted to give the area a wide berth, even when the rivers were flowing, had not deterred him either. Indeed, with C Company in the final phase of its commitment, Williams could think of no one more deserving than Longdon to take out the patrol; the more arduous and pointless the better.

The first twenty-four hours were bad enough, with the patrol resorting to digging for water in a dry tributary of the Deka, without success. During the morning of the second day John Jacobs had taken to discarding items of kit, in a demented state of heat fatigue. Thirst was a psychological killer at the best of times, and to make matters worse Alpha section had lost coms within hours of their drop off due to the terrain.

It was shortly before dusk on the third day of the gruelling patrol, the patrol that Tony had dubbed *Williams' Final Fucking*

Folly, that he was forced to call a halt. On the move since before dawn, he had spurred the men on through the treacherous midday heat in a final desperate bid to find water. Shielding his eyes from the glare of the setting sun, Tony scanned his limited horizon in search of a high feature from which they might regain their bearings or better still re-establish radio communications. Their situation was desperate and he knew it would end in tragedy if they did not find water or get airlifted out before long.

'Have you found out where the hell we are, Corp?' Nell asked as he ambled listlessly across to where Tony stood, again studying the map. His lips were cracked and encrusted with dried blood and saliva, his shirt stained white with salt like those of the rest of the patrol.

'Piet, until we can find a feature with a trig-point on top, I can only guess. The iron in these rocks is still playing havoc with the bloody compass. We could be about here,' he stabbed at the map, 'so we should hit the Gwai river before much longer if we keep going in an easterly direction.'

Leonard Phelps, the diminutive postal technician who had replaced Wells in the section, made it to his corporal's side before sinking to his knees, head bowed. 'Sorry Corp, I can't go another fucking metre.'

'Hang in there sport, I recon it's only another couple of kilometres to the Gwai river, where we should find subterranean water,' Tony said before anxiously setting off back down the track to where Jacobs now lay prone on the scorching earth. Lifting the man's pack off and rolling him onto his back, Tony placed a hand on his forehead. He was no longer sweating, not a good sign. Moistening his handkerchief with the last few drops of precious water remaining in his second canteen, Tony dabbed at Jacobs' cracked lips; his face was a mass of sun-blackened blisters. In retrospect they should have been more concerned with finding Jacobs' bush hat than his empty water bottles, when last he had abandoned kit on the march.

'Just ... just leave me,' John stammered, his voice barely audible as he struggled for breath in the furnace-like heat.

'We'll call it a day now then. It will start cooling down in a while and you will feel better.' Propping John up against his pack, Tony asked Piet to stay with the other two while he went to check out a patch of cover in the midst of a clearing up ahead. The clump of dry scrub he had singled out would not afford much practical protection, but it would be cooler than holding up in one of the heat-saturated ravines. Besides they had the machine-gun and a claymore for defence, in the unlikely event of there being any other suicidal life-forms in the vicinity, Tony mused.

Returning for the rest of the patrol Tony squatted down next to Piet. 'I will try for higher ground to establish radio coms at first light tomorrow. Right now we need to move these two into cover and get some grub in them. Then you can give me a hand to set up the claymore next to that dead tree over there. At least it will cover this exposed approach to our night ambush position.'

Nodding, Nell attempted a smile as he asked, 'How are you faring Corp?'

'Lousy,' Tony admitted. 'But if I could get my hands on that fucking idiot Williams, I'd still have the strength to choke the life out of the bastard.'

Having helped John and Len into cover, Tony and Piet trudged back across the clearing with the claymore. The shrapnel mine was the deadliest anti-personnel weapon in the section's arsenal. Lethal up to a range of one hundred metres, it would flatten everything for fifty metres in a radius of 180 degrees, the explosion alone being enough to wake the dead.

Getting Piet to steady the device while he inserted the detonator, Tony looped the wire around one of the support legs; a precaution against dislodging the detonator while playing out the reel back to their position. His hands were shaking by the time he had finished but it was more from fatigue and frustration than from toying with high explosives. He kept telling himself he should have known better than to have attempted to cross this waterless, Godforsaken, wilderness. At worst, the moment they had lost coms he should have returned to the drop-off point and sat it out under a tree for the next five days until their pickup, spiting Williams in the process.

'How about a last fag before we move back into cover for the night?' Piet asked wearily.

'Sure,' Tony replied rolling his head to get the tension out of his neck and shoulders. 'We can also chance using one of the gas cookers just now, to heat up whatever tins we have left with any liquid in them. We have to inject some life into those boys before they completely give up the ghost.'

Piet lit both cigarettes between cupped hands and passed one to Tony. 'Assuming we survive to see it, do you think things will come right once we have a black government?'

'I have my doubts, Piet. Bishop Muzorewa is the likely candidate but without genuine grassroots support I don't give much for his chances once Mugabe and Nkomo and their boys come marching home. Unless that is, the whites who remain are prepared to fight to the bitter end to keep him in power.'

'Always fancied having my name engraved in granite, beneath some glorious inscription like *at the going down of the sun, we will remember them,*' Piet joked.

'Most Rhodesians I know prefer to get pissed at the going down of the sun. Besides, even if we were in the same league as Allan Wilson and the Shangani Patrol, I can't see a Nationalist Government putting up any memorials to *white* Rhodesians.'

Stubbing out their cigarettes they started back, wordlessly playing out the detonating wire.

Tony was rudely awakened less than an hour after he had handed over the midnight guard. Willing himself into consciousness, he slowly sat up as the tugging on his boot intensified. There was no moon and it was a few seconds before he was able to make Nell out.

'Corp, do you hear that?' Piet whispered, drawing in closer behind the machine-gun, trained menacingly at the dark expanse of open ground in front of their position.

Creeping forward, Tony gave Piet's shoulder an acknowledg-ing squeeze. He could hear what sounded like a herd of elephant in the distance, steadily making its way towards them. No harsh sounds, just an incessant dull creaking and crunching as the dry bush parted in the wake of the browsing animals.

'Jumbo, we have been crossing their spoor all day; obviously also on their way to water,' Tony said. 'I'll alert John and Len, just in case they have a mind to walk right on through here.'

As the rumbling, like distant thunder, grew louder and louder, Tony forced back his shoulder blades to help shake off the apathy induced by lack of water and sleep. It was then that he heard it, a metallic clunk, followed by another; unearthly sounds in the bush in the dead of night. He slipped into his webbing where he knelt, instinctively checking his ammunition pouches.

'If those are elephant, they must be dragging bloody chains or something!' Piet ventured from behind the MAG.

Adrenalin pumping, Tony cautioned Piet to keep his voice down before checking on John and Len. Both men still sat hunched over where he'd positioned them, staring listlessly out into the night.

Taking up his own position, Tony willed himself to concentrate. If the sounds were human in origin there were a lot of people out there, and probably a darn sight closer than he imagined. One thing was certain they were on a collision course with the patrol's position, given that the game trail he had been following afforded the easiest going.

With renewed urgency Tony took up the battery box for trig-gering the claymore, deft fingers checking that the negative wire was still connected before tearing back the insulation tape cover-ing the positive terminal. He estimated that the vanguard of the army of insurgents, now clearly visible in his mind's eye, would be in the killing ground within minutes. The choice was his, detonate and take out as many as possible before being overrun, or lie low against the unlikely odds of going undetected.

Instead of Tony's whole life flashing before him, all he could think of was the absurdity of it all. A few dauntless whites presumptuous enough to insist that even if majority rule was inevitable, it would only come about through the patronage of black leaders of their choice, and then subject to constitutionally entrenched minority rights, guaranteed by Great Britain and the United States.

Tony hesitated; there was always that nagging doubt in night ambush situations. Not that he could see friendly forces moving in such numbers this far off the beaten track in the dead of night. As for local villagers, fleeing possible terrorist intimidation prior to the imminent general election, he could hardly see them venturing this deep into an arid wasteland.

'Piet, I'm going out there. I'll only detonate if I'm certain it's terrs, don't get trigger happy or prematurely put up a flare.'

'You're crazy . . . the back blast!' Piet breathed the warning in his corporal's ear.

'I'll make for one of the gullies if it comes to that,' Tony acknowledged as he gave Piet the thumbs up in a gesture of confidence he did not feel. Turning to John and Len, both now marginally more attentive as they peered through the gloom in his direction, he mouthed, 'Hold your fire.' With that he slipped out of the scrub and moved stealthily into the clearing, rifle in one hand, the battery box with the trailing detonator wire clutched tightly in the other; his nerves on edge.

Tony only managed thirty or so paces before they materialised, ghostlike, out of the blackness, scores of heavily armed guerrillas. Their front ranks were already passing the faint silhouette of the dead tree which marked the claymore's position. Tony could smell the quarry now and realised he'd had the pungent scent of unwashed bodies in his nostrils for some time.

He was still fifteen metres from the nearest gully when a cry went up from the vanguard of young black cadres. The alert was simultaneously followed by a blinding flash that illuminated the night. The deafening explosion adding to the mayhem as a hail of jagged metal bearings and shrapnel cut through the advancing mass of humanity like a scythe through ripe wheat.

259

The echo of the exploding claymore still ringing in his ears, Nell instinctively loaded his third ammunition belt and continued laying down a deadly barrage in long sweeping bursts. The initial two-hundred rounds had taken a heavy toll of insurgents caught in the open, and individuals continued to drop in grotesque postures as the machine-gun traversed blindly on fixed lines.

Slammed to the ground by the devastating back blast, Tony groaned with the effort of trying to focus on the dead tree, now ringed by flickering yellow flames as the grass burnt slowly outward from its base. Through blood-blurred vision he made out a contorted mass of humanity and watched men still flopping to the ground, as if at the end of some weird ritual dance.

Dragging himself painfully towards the gully he felt a comforting warmth oozing down his neck and heard the gushing of his own blood in his ears. As his eyes closed he imagined he saw the mighty Zambezi river rising in Central Africa, flowing leisurely across the floodplains of Barotseland, becoming increasingly fretful as it swept through Zambia to thunder over the Victoria Falls, only to rest briefly between the distant shores of the great Kariba Lake before moving swiftly on through the hostile heart of Mozambique to drown eventually in the vastness of the Indian Ocean, its dark waters staining the sea a reddish brown as if with the blood of a dying land.

While the guerrillas may initially have imagined they had encountered the might of the Rhodesian Army, Nell was under no illusion as to who possessed the superior firepower. The surrounding bush was alive with muzzle flashes, the deafening crescendo of automatic rifle fire sounding to him like the opening of the gates of hell.

'*At the going down of the sun, they will remember us,*' Piet bellowed, now on his feet and firing his last belt from the hip. John stepped over Len's lifeless body to stand at Piet's side. They blazed away at real and imaginary targets until the end.

A reconnaissance plane, into the second day of its search for the lost patrol, spotted the exposed artillery pieces and regrouping insurgents at first light the following morning. Having called for an air strike, the Provost left the field of battle to the ancient Hawker Hunters of No. 1 Squadron. After their cannon attack they carpeted the arena with frantam to burn, suffocate and flush out the remaining insurgents from the rocky outcrops and ravines; softening up the quarry for the approaching helicopter-borne fire-force sticks.

Operation Lights Out

Police Special Branch and Army Intelligence worked around the clock to establish how such a large contingent of insurgents had infiltrated so deeply, undetected. By the time General Armstrong arrived in Wankie the following morning, Colonel Baker, Officer Commanding the north-western area, was in a position to confirm Special Branch's initial findings.

'No doubt about it, Sir, after they crossed the Zambezi they covered their tracks by passing through two Tribal Trust areas, both of which are under the control of Auxiliary units,' Baker paused to indicate the sectors on the wall map in his office. 'They escaped detection for a further thirty-odd kilometres by moving through this arid, uninhabited region. They travelled at night, which is when we believe they ran into the territorial force patrol we had been trying to locate.'

Armstrong was about to acknowledge the obvious complicity of the Auxiliaries when there was a rap on the door and a tall, lean individual strode into Baker's office, brandishing a communist RPD sub-machine-gun. Dressed in a grimy green boiler suit and black hockey boots, the young man's unusually long hair fell to his shoulders as he whipped off his knitted cap and came to attention. The sweat-streaked camouflage cream on his hands and face made him look more like a motor mechanic than an army officer; but then he had just been flown in from the sharp end.

Startled by the intrusion, Baker was about to demand an explanation when Armstrong extended a hand to shake that of the new arrival. 'At ease Captain, I'm pleased they were able to locate you.' Armstrong beamed as he turned to make the introductions,

'Ronald, this is Captain Gerald Bond. He commands the Scouts who have been operating so successfully in your area for some time now.'

Baker stepped smartly forward and offered his hand. 'It's a privilege to finally meet the man behind the voice,' he said sincerely.

'Thank you, Sir. I . . .'

'Hold on,' Armstrong cut in. 'You two can reminisce some other time, we have work to do.'

Following the general's lead they crossed to the conference table.

'But first, what news can you give us from the ground, Gerald?' Armstrong prompted.

'The situation is looking good, Sir. A few gooks slipped the cordon but follow-ups are in progress. The boys in blue did a thorough job yesterday. The bodies that weren't burnt to cinders are being flown out now, in nets suspended from the choppers. The pilots are flying at treetop height over the TTLs, which should leave the Auxiliaries in that part of the world in no doubt as to who came off second best in this little melee.'

'They will get the message all right,' Armstrong said. 'This is precisely what we have been waiting for,' he concluded through clenched teeth, his ginger moustache twitching in anticipation.

'To justify another strike into Zambia, Sir?' Baker speculated.

'That goes without saying, but I'm referring to Operation Quartz and the reason for my visit. But more about that in a moment.' Drumming his fingers on his attaché case Armstrong turned his attention back to Bond. 'Captain, were we able to establish beyond doubt that it was those territorial chaps who engaged that gook column?'

'Yes, Zero-One-Alpha, Sir. We recovered what was left of their weapons but only three sets of dog tags; there were no identifiable remains. It must have been an inferno down there during the bombing.'

Colonel Baker cleared his throat, 'We put in an air strike with our lads still on the ground?'

263

'A calculated risk,' Bond replied. 'From the number of gooks air reconnaissance sighted milling around yesterday morning the odds were heavily stacked against a four-man patrol. I was able to confirm as much, regrettably. In spite of the effectiveness of their killing ground, they had little chance against odds of some thirty-to-one. Had it not been for the gooks walking right onto their position, I wouldn't have blamed them for sitting that one out. They were to have been stood down permanently in a few weeks.'

There was a hollowness in the junior officer's voice, which Armstrong found disconcerting. Bond was after all more accustomed to death than most.

'In which case we are fortunate circumstances dictated they elect to do their duty,' Armstrong said pointedly. 'Now, what of your men Gerald, will they have enough in reserve after Operation Lights Out, and can they make it back across the border within the time frame?'

'Operation Lights Out?' Baker interjected again.

'An imminent pre-emptive strike into Zambia. I'll get to Operation Quartz in a moment. Well?' Armstrong prompted again, addressing his battle-hardened captain.

Bond nodded pensively. Since his chat with the now late Mr Longdon at the Monomatapa Hotel, less than a month ago, he had had his doubts. Longdon's feedback was at odds with intelligence reports maintaining that the grassroots support for the Mugabe/Nkomo alliance was limited at best. Should that support be stronger than army intelligence suspected, or were prepared to admit, they could end up biting off more than they could chew.

'Well?' Armstrong repeated impatiently.

'I don't foresee any problems on the Zambian side. And yes, within twenty-four hours of our return we can have reconnaissance units in the vicinity of all major Auxiliary concentrations around the country, ready to talk in air and ground strikes,' Gerald confirmed, before adding with uncharacteristic reserve, 'However, I am concerned about SAS and RLI estimates that they will be able to neutralise eighty percent of the opposition in the initial fire-fight. As ex-terrorists most of the Auxiliaries are hardened bush fighters, if security is breached or if our chaps are the least bit sloppy, the gooks will bombshell. What's more, if they enjoy anything like the degree of support from the locals, as suggested in some quarters, we could find they are able to regroup before we have . . .'

'I think that will do,' Armstrong said, frowning. That one of his most highly decorated officers should even imply that total victory was anything but a certainty was disconcerting. 'In the final analysis the Auxiliaries are nothing but a bunch of ill-disciplined ruffians, in spite of our training. Besides, having grown complacent in their own treachery and the mistaken belief that all the whites are fully committed to the internal settlement elections later this month, the last thing they will suspect is foul play.'

'That may be so, Sir, but as a precaution we should reconsider the wisdom of scrapping contingency plans for the evacuation of the country's European population. The South Africans have already undertaken to secure an exit route via Beitbridge,' Gerald persisted.

Armstrong clenched his fists on top of the conference table. The attitude of the man upon which so much depended was out of character and exasperating.

'Really, Bond, as you well know time and distance renders the evacuation of the entire white population logistically impractical. But enough pessimistic talk,' Armstrong insisted, getting to his feet. 'Gentlemen, there can be no turning back for the reasons I am about to confide in you.'

Ten minutes later Armstrong sat down again. 'So there you have it. On my return to Salisbury I expect to receive orders putting into effect the course of action I have outlined. These plans are obviously strictly on a need to know basis. Understood, gentlemen?'

'Yes, Sir,' Baker and Bond replied in unison, in spite of it taking a certain presence of mind to acknowledge that they were now party to a conspiracy that could change the course of history –

party to what would be the first white military coup on the African continent.

'Sir, given how thin we are on the ground, is this raid across our northern border wise on the eve of a move against the Auxiliaries; and indeed the state?' Baker enquired gravely, his hands like the general's now firmly clenched in front of him on the table.

'It's imperative,' Armstrong confirmed in the slow calculated drawl that had become his hallmark. 'As you are aware Mugabe has thrown just about everything on two legs into the field against us from his bases in Mozambique. Nkomo on the other hand has committed only a fraction of his forces to the fray. The strength of that column those territorial lads clobbered yesterday gives some indication of what that sly old dog is harbouring in reserve on the other side of the Zambezi. We have to neutralise Nkomo's forces in Zambia to pre-empt an attack against our rear, once we have gone on the offensive.'

'I agree with the general,' Bond said. 'While the elimination of the Auxiliaries amassed in assembly points is feasible, it's precisely because we are so thin on the ground that we cannot afford the luxury of looking over our shoulder.'

Armstrong beamed, pleased to hear Bond sounding more like his old self. 'Ronald, I think I would now like to take you up on that South African brandy you so kindly offered during my previous visit.'

'Certainly, Sir, and a cigar?'

'Yes, why the hell not.'

'What about you, Captain?' Baker offered, crossing to the liquor cabinet, now permanently locked since the mysterious disappearance of half of his precious bar stock and imported cigars a few months back.

Bond shook his head, but then changed his mind. 'A scotch on the rocks, thank you, Sir,' he said joining the others.

'Thought you were strictly a beer man?' Armstrong challenged lightheartedly.

266

'Normally, Sir, but whisky better suits my mood. I actually knew one of those territorial chaps, a Corporal Longdon.'

Baker passed round the drinks. 'My condolences, Captain. Did you know the man well?'

'Well enough to know that while he may have died for his country he probably would not have condoned our actions.'

'*Good God, man!*' Armstrong exclaimed. 'Was this fellow not a patriotic Rhodesian?'

'He certainly had the interest of the country at heart.'

'Well, then?'

Bond took a sip of his drink as he considered his response. He could not help brooding on the strange allegiance he felt he owed the man, his nephew's father, after his death. 'I think he would have argued that we should never have let the situation deteriorate to the point where a coup d'état offered the only solution. He contended that Western powers had tacitly been prepared to underwrite an agreement between Nkomo and the white minority all along, in return for stability in Central Africa. He believed Nkomo was pragmatic enough to forgo socialism and adopt . . .'

'Poppycock! The West has advocated nothing short of total white subjugation. They want to bring us to our knees in return for declaring UDI, for having the audacity to survive fourteen years of punitive bloody sanctions,' Armstrong asserted.

'Gentlemen, with respect, whatever Corporal Longdon's views may have been the fact remains he and his men made the supreme sacrifice in the line of duty,' Baker reminded them sombrely.

'You are absolutely right, Ronald,' Armstrong hastened to agree. He was already regretting his short-sightedness in antagonising such a vital pawn as Bond. 'A toast; to brave men and Rhodesia.'

Once they had lowered their glasses, Armstrong went on to elaborate, 'Ronald, during our pre-emptive strike we are also aiming to take out the ZIPRA command centre in its so-called safe house in Lusaka; terminating the fat man himself, Joshua Nkomo, in the process.'

Dutifully saluting the Rhodesian flag alongside his fellow officers, Gerald found himself reflecting on one of Tony Longdon's more profound sayings: *desperate measures, in desperate times.*

When Death Knocks

Kathleen Longdon happened to glance out of the window as she crossed the lounge to unplug the Hoover. She had not heard the aged Volkswagen Beetle draw up in front of the house and was surprised to see a tall, well-dressed woman standing hesitantly at the gate. The visitor looked vaguely familiar in spite of the dark glasses and Kathy felt she should know her.

The stranger was intent on the gate, placing first one hand and then the other on the latch, before removing both and half turning; as if having changed her mind. Kathleen stifled a chuckle, a saleswoman on her first assignment, she speculated. Finally opening the gate the woman strode up the garden path with renewed purpose.

Kathleen refrained from opening the door on the first knock, so preoccupied was she in searching her memory for the name she was now convinced she should know.

'Kathy dear, is that someone at the front door?'

'Yes, Mum, I'm getting it,' she called back, slipping off her apron and brushing a wisp of hair from her forehead. Their visitor removed her sunglasses just as the door opened and an involuntary shudder went through Kathleen as recognition dawned. It was Yvonne, Major Young's wife. As the two tall women nervously appraised one another, Kathleen's smile faded until her expression was as deadpan and fearful as that of the woman confronting her.

Yvonne Young did not feel the nail of her forefinger snap back and break against her handbag, so intent was she on trying to control the tremor of her lower jaw. For Kathleen's part, the porcelain-white hands clutching the handbag and sombre brown tweed suit said it all. Her eyes becoming unnaturally bright, she bit painlessly through her bottom lip, her head moving slowly from side to side.

The tea plates Helen was drying crashed to the floor as Kathleen's anguished cry shattered the tranquillity of the house, sending the senior Mrs Longdon reeling back against the kitchen table.

By the time the family doctor's car braked urgently in the driveway, Kathleen's eyes had rolled back in their sockets. Her face was a mass of bloody welts where she had raked her nails down her cheeks before the two older women had managed to wrestle her down and restrain her. There were also dark traces of blood at the corners of her mouth from the damage to her lip.

Even after the sedative, Kathleen continued to rock rhythmically back and forth on the floor, talking gibberish, and it was some time before Doctor Lewis was able to coax her to her feet and lead her through to the bedroom.

Returning to the lounge the doctor lost no time in attending to Mrs Longdon senior who, now that the initial crisis had passed, was allowing herself to drift into a state of shock. Having got the major's wife to repeat her dreadful tidings, Helen had been unable to accept that her boy would not be coming home; not now, not ever.

Ashen-faced, Mrs Young mechanically swallowed the pills Doctor Lewis had also prescribed for her. The suddenness and violence of Kathleen's reaction had totally unnerved her. She resolved then and there that this would be the first and last time she let the army chaplain prevail on her to assist with these heart-rending next-of-kin calls, no matter how hard pressed he was coping with the rapidly escalating number of bereavements.

Nine Lives

Operation Lights Out resulted in the total destruction of Nkomo's command centre situated in the heart of Lusaka, the capital of Zambia. Yet the guerrilla leader had miraculously eluded his would-be assassins. Some speculated that Nkomo had escaped through a toilet window; others deemed this impossible in view of the sheer bulk of the man. There was even talk of a breach of security. Only one man, the mission commander, knew the truth and Captain Bond's lips were sealed.

In the months that followed, Nkomo's apparently charmed life continued to stave off the white coup. Bishop Abel Muzorewa went on to win the April elections and was sworn in as Prime Minister of Zimbabwe/Rhodesia on 1st June 1979. He went on to form his historic multi-party Government of National Unity. Significantly for Bond, a black uprising was averted, when ultimately Muzorewa wisely elected to hand the country back over to British rule on the eve of renewed talks at Lancaster House in London; talks that at long last included the exiled leaders of the Patriotic Front, Joshua Nkomo and Robert Mugabe.

Just ten months after Abel Muzorewa had been sworn in as Prime Minister, genuine one-man one-vote elections resulted in comrade Robert Mugabe being swept to power by an overwhelming majority. Lt. General Peter Walls, supreme commander of the armed forces, blamed Special Branch intelligence, or more pointedly the lack thereof, for the country's rude awakening on ignominiously learning of Mugabe's unprecedented grassroots support.

Even as Lord Soames, the temporary British Governor of Rhodesia, was in the throes of handing over the new democratic

271

state of Zimbabwe desperate moves were afoot behind closed doors. Moves intended to beat the deadline for the disbandment of certain military units and the integration of the remaining security forces with their compatriots in the guerrilla army. Those generals bent on the preservation of white rule worked frantically to devise a last-ditch strategy to wrest their country from the jaws of tyranny.

Following yet another unsuccessful attempt to eliminate Nkomo, the majority of whose guerrilla forces were still inexplicably harboured menacingly on the other side of the Zambezi river, the white coup was finally aborted. In the interest of public safety, Lt. General Peter Walls publicly denied that a coup had ever been contemplated, asserting that a military takeover could not possibly have succeeded. Yet historians would record that a coup could and would have taken place had it not been for Nkomo's charmed life and the man's uncanny sixth sense in delaying the return of his 20,000 strong ZIPRA army from neighbouring Zambia, until long after the legitimate one-man one-vote elections.

Recently promoted, Major Bond's final task before Mugabe officially took office on 18th April 1980 was to destroy what was left of his unit's intelligence records, the bulk of which had already been ferreted to the authorities in South Africa. The Selous Scouts were disbanded with immediate effect and Bond prepared to go under cover for his new masters, the Civil Cooperation Bureau. The CCB was the covert security division of the Military Intelligence arm of the South African Defence Force; the equivalent of the old Rhodesian Special Branch.

Joshua Nkomo's relationship with Mugabe had soured rapidly after his defeat at the polls and ironically Bond's first task, given his knowledge of the man, was to ensure his safety and advise him militarily. The lesser of two evils, it was deemed imperative that Nkomo be kept in the wings and groomed until such time as Mugabe met with an accident or was taken out in a coup; the generally accepted method for a change of government in Africa.

Bond had one personal matter to attend to before devoting himself to his new responsibilities, a visit to Tony Longdon's widow of twelve months. Having discreetly kept tabs on her since her bereavement, he was aware she had been treated for depression and was presently in the care of her parents-in-law.

Adam

Doctor Lewis, the Longdon family's physician in Bulawayo, refused to discuss his patient outside the immediate family. It was only once Gerald Bond had explained Tony's relationship with his sister Victoria, and the existence of little Adam, their illegitimate and orphaned offspring, that Lewis even agreed to see him.

'My condolences on the loss of your sister, those were trying times,' Lewis said, before asking, 'How old is young Adam and who is caring for him now?'

'He's a year and . . . seven weeks. My parents took him in but to be honest it's not working out as well as I . . . we had hoped,' Gerald confessed. 'Don't get me wrong, we all love the little fellow. It's just that Adam is a constant reminder of the cruel blow fate dealt the family. I think my folks also harbour a nagging belief that Vicky's life might have been spared, had it not been for the added complication of the child in her womb. They are not getting any younger either,' he offered in their defence.

'Neither Kathleen nor her parents-in-law have ever made mention of a child fathered by Mr Longdon. Am I correct in assuming Adam would be news to them as well, Mr Bond?'

'Yes,' Gerald confirmed without elaborating.

Lewis nodded. 'I see, so this interest in Kathleen concerns your nephew?'

'Yes,' Gerald agreed once more.

'Under the circumstances it's only right to warn you that in spite of treatment Kathleen has yet to come to terms with her husband's death. His body was never recovered as you undoubtedly know.'

'I realise this is a sensitive situation, but I also understand

274

Kathleen was released into the care of her parents-in-law a while back now. Which would indicate she is at least on the road to recovery?'

'Admittedly she has made some progress. However, their child-less marriage left her fixated on her husband and she is finding it difficult to cope in the absence of a focal point in her life.'

'A focal point like young Adam, for the sake of argument?' Gerald hastened to suggest.

'I suspected you were leading up to something like this, Mr Bond. I'm not a psychologist and I am sure there are those who would deem it ill advised, even disastrous, to attempt to foist a deceased husband's illegitimate child on an unsuspecting widow, however . . .'

'It could be worth a try?' Gerald interrupted in his excitement.

'I did not say that,' Lewis insisted. 'I was simply going to mention that over the years Kathleen made no secret of her desire to have children. It was also general knowledge that they intended to start a family once Tony was demobbed. Tragically it was not to be.'

'Doctor, surely the prospects of renewed hope for Kathleen and a brighter future for young Adam can justify some risk?'

'What of Mr and Mrs Bond senior?' Lewis asked without committing himself.

'To be honest, I felt it more important to run this past you first.'

'Then I suggest you give me a call once you have talked it over thoroughly with your parents, young man.'

A surprised but receptive Gloria and Les Bond finally agreed to a trial introduction between Adam and Kathleen Longdon. Gerald promised to abandon his harebrained scheme and return home immediately with the boy should there be the slightest concern as to his welfare.

Tucked snugly up in his carry-cot on the back seat of his uncle's car, Adam made the 335-kilometre journey from Wankie to Bulawayo the next day. Anxious to get on with the deed before his parents had a change of heart, Gerald decided against the formality of reverting to Doctor Lewis. He would personally guard against any unrealistic expectations or premature commitments, backing out graciously in the event of anything not going to plan.

Gerald had hoped to complete the three-odd-hour drive before Adam's lunch was due, not to mention a nappy change, but the youngster's biological clock was running fast that morning. He awoke wet, hungry and irritable fifteen minutes before journey's end. When they finally arrived at the Longdons' address the chubby-cheeked, normally contented Adam took it upon himself to let the world know of his discomfort as only he could.

The front door opened as they reached it, thanks to Adam's healthy lungs, and Gerald found himself staring into the wide iridescent green eyes of a frail, yet still exceedingly attractive, young woman.

'My name is Gerald . . . I'm an old friend of Tony's. This is my nephew, Adam. He's quite a handful,' Gerald blurted out, his carefully rehearsed introduction forgotten thanks to Adam's persistent bellowing.

'I'm Kathy, but I am afraid my husband is . . .'

'I know, I'm terribly sorry,' Gerald cut in to spare her anguish. 'Tony was a great guy, my condolences. Ah!' he groaned as Adam pistoned his knees into his ribs. Clumsily transferring the boy from one hip to the other, he went on, 'We were . . . in the vicinity when he started performing for his lunch. I just need somewhere to warm up his bottle and change him, if it's not an imposition, Mrs Longdon?'

There was a strange, almost distant look in the young woman's eyes as she replied, 'I'm so sorry, how rude of me to leave you standing there like this. Do come on in. And please, call me Kathy.'

Breathing a sigh of relief at having made it this far, Gerald said hesitantly, 'I need to . . . nip back to the car for a few of his things. Would you mind holding him for a moment, please?'

'Well, help the gentleman, dear. Go on, the child's not going to bite,' encouraged Mrs Longdon senior, having entered the lounge in time to overhear the introductions.

'Thank you,' Gerald acknowledged gratefully, smiling round the door at the older woman, who he immediately recognised as Tony's mother.

'I wouldn't hold him too close, he's drenched,' Gerald warned as he bundled Adam into Kathy's arms, now nervously outstretched to receive him.

When Gerald returned with a hold-all stuffed with enough nappies, jars of baby food and bottles to last a week it was to find Kathy and her mother-in-law doting over a preoccupied but still disgruntled Adam.

Helen raised an eyebrow as she took a nappy from the bulging bag and draped it over her daughter-in-law's shoulder. 'Why don't you change him while I warm his lunch,' she suggested starting Kathleen off in the direction of the bedrooms with a gentle shove. 'You will find some Vaseline in the medicine chest,' she called after her. Selecting a jar of mixed vegetable purée and one of the bottles of pre-mixed milk she waited for Gerald's nod of approval before setting off to the kitchen, giving their guest a strange sideways glance as she left.

Having returned from the car after fetching yet another bag, containing Adam's clothes and spare blankets, Gerald quietly closed the front door and sat down on the edge of the nearest armchair. He was about to chance lighting a cigarette, in spite of the absence of ashtrays, when Mrs Longdon senior reappeared.

Standing half in and half out of the lounge, with an ear for the sound of the kettle, she offered belatedly, 'I'm Helen Longdon, Tony's mother.' She then enquired pointedly, 'You were saying you were a friend of our son?'

'Yes, ma'am we were military colleagues, of sorts,' Gerald replied, getting respectfully to his feet and glancing round the room for an ashtray at the same time.

'I see. And you are just passing through, from . . . to . . . ?'

It was uncharacteristic of Rhodesian hospitality to interrogate visitors and Gerald felt ill at ease as he continued to play for time. 'From Wankie . . . we're not so much passing through, more like planning on stopping over in Bulawayo for a while. Visiting,' he added for good measure. Give him a military situation any day he thought, easing the second hold-all in closer to his chair with his heel as Helen eyed it suspiciously. The carry-cot would just have to wait.

Helen was about to continue her cross-examination when Adam started yelling again and she was forced to scurry back into the kitchen, to see to his lunch.

Events were moving faster than Gerald would have liked. His strategy called for time in which to get better acquainted with Kathy, using her late husband as the catalyst. He had certainly not bargained on an overly protective, very inquisitive mother-in-law.

Helen returned from the kitchen with Adam's lunch and wordlessly set off down the passage, a set expression on her face. Gerald was left in no doubt that Helen Longdon was a troubled woman, one unlikely to waste much more time beating about the bush.

Adam's crying stopped abruptly and Gerald began counting the seconds. Having got to his feet in anticipation of Mrs Longdon's return, he stood dutifully until she had seated herself. The fact that the elderly woman's face was now as white as a sheet was added cause for concern.

'I think it's time for an explanation, don't you, young man?' Helen said impatiently, motioning their guest to sit down.

'Yes, well . . . perhaps I do have some explaining to do,' Gerald said, clasping his knees to keep from fidgeting. 'To be honest I was hoping things would sort of play out in their own time, if you know what I mean?'

'I'll tell you what I think young man. This *is* your destination and this visit has everything to do with young Adam. You say Adam is your nephew, so his mother, your sister, must be Victoria. Which makes me Adam's grandmother.' Helen closed her eyes as if fighting back the tears.

Gerald sat motionless, speechless.

'Yes, Victoria . . . Victoria Bond,' the older woman recalled, opening her eyes and slowly drawing herself erect in her chair.

Having regained some of her composure she went on in a soft monotone that belied the effort of her every word. 'Young man, my son confided in Kathy shortly after they were reunited in Durban. He told her about his relationship with your sister. But he never said. . .' was all she managed before her voice cracked with emotion. 'He never said anything about having fathered . . .' This time Helen's voice simply trailed off in mid sentence.

Gerald turned to follow the distraught woman's agonising gaze. Kathleen was standing in the doorway leading from the passage, a contented Adam in her arms clutching his bottle.

Without taking her eyes from the face of the fair-haired little boy, blissfully guzzling his milk, Kathleen boldly answered Helen's unfinished question. 'Yes, Mum, Adam is a Longdon. There are just too many wonderful little likenesses for it to be otherwise,' she murmured tenderly. Looking up for the first time, her eyes bright with tears, she continued, 'I know you also recognised the likeness in the bedroom a moment ago, Mum.'

Helen and Gerald got to their feet at the same time.

'Now, now my dear, let's not jump to conclusions. I'm sure Mr Bond has a more . . . *plausible* explanation,' Helen prompted, her eyes wide and pleading as she glared at their guest. 'Too much excitement,' she hissed under her breath as she passed a mute Gerald on her way to her daughter-in-law's side.

'Adam is Tony's son,' Gerald blurted out, relieved to get it off his chest.

'Mr Bond, my son would certainly have told us about anything as important as this,' Helen protested with flagging resolve.

'He is Tony's son, Mum. I know you might wish it otherwise, to protect me, but . . . I think I'm going to be all right, I really do,' Kathleen insisted, the words catching in her throat as she drew Adam closer to her bosom lest Helen attempt to relieve her of her charge.

With emotions running high all round Gerald went on to explain about Adam's birth and why it had remained a secret. 'The reason Tony never mentioned having a son was because he never knew he had fathered one.' He was addressing Kathy and paused while she used her tissue.

'Go on, please,' she encouraged him, anxious for the truth.

'Tony was apparently very unsettled after your . . . separation, so much so that my sister took it upon herself not to confide in him; not to burden him about her condition. I think she was waiting until she felt the time was right, until she knew how things stood between the two of you. Unfortunately that time never came for Victoria. I told Tony of Vicky's pregnancy, shortly after her death. For reasons that are academic now, I never got round to correcting the assumption that the baby had perished in its mother's womb. Tony probably chose not to mention the pregnancy to avoid unnecessary distress.'

'Thank you,' Kathleen said swallowing hard and taking another tissue from her sleeve. 'Now if you will both please excuse us, I think this young man is in need of another change.'

As Kathleen turned to make her way back to her room, Gerald felt Helen take hold of his arm for support. Helping her back to her chair he did his best to reassure her. 'Believe me Mrs Longdon, Tony could not have known about Adam. He left for Durban on compassionate leave the day after I had given him the news in Salisbury. He returned to active service directly after that and well . . . you know the rest; you have my condolences.'

'That's not what's bothering me young man,' Helen smiled bravely as she released Gerald's arm. 'My concern is for Kathy and what bringing Adam to this house is going to do to us all. It can only end in heartache.' Stifling a sob Helen continued, 'While I already feel I know and love our grandson, I can't help thinking that all this would have been best left well enough alone.'

'Mrs Longdon, this was not a spur of the moment thing and I'm more confident now than ever that this will work out for the best.'

'You don't know what you are saying, Mr Bond. You have *no idea* what we have all been through this past year. My daughter-in-law is not a well person.'

'I'm led to understand that people suffering from depression can, and do, benefit from a renewed sense of purpose,' Gerald encouraged stopping short of compromising Doctor Lewis.

'My daughter-in-law is not simply depressed, and whatever it is you are playing at can only have dire consequences in her present state of mind, Mr Bond.'

'Please, call me Gerald,' he requested awkwardly.

'Mr Bond, surely a letter, a phone call, would not have been asking too much? Don't you see Kathy is not a strong woman? Even if she says she is able to come to terms with all this, how do you expect us to rest easy knowing that a part of Tony is growing up out there somewhere? In Wankie, was it you said? Did you give this any thought at all?'

'Mrs Longdon, I obviously discussed this with my parents. Perhaps I should have mentioned earlier that they brought Adam up. I also took the liberty of talking to Doctor Lewis, to see how Kathy was coping.'

'*He put you up to this?*' Helen said incredulously.

'No, this was entirely my idea,' Gerald insisted. 'I had hoped that introducing Adam to Kathy would work out for the best, for all concerned.' Glancing towards the passage and encouraged by the continued silence, he went on to explain, 'My parents have had their share of problems adapting to parenthood again, particularly under the circumstances. And my own commitments keep me away from Wankie for months on end. Still, I apologise if you feel it was presumptuous of me to have imposed.'

'I am sorry for your problems young man but you should have realised this harebrained scheme of yours was likely to backfire. Can't you see the girl is already forming an attachment to the child . . . to Adam? There's no telling how she will react when it's time for the two of you to leave.'

'Mrs Longdon, I don't think you have fully grasped what I have been trying to say. If Kathy, and of course you and Mr Longdon, feel you can come to love Adam, as we have, then there is no reason why he cannot stay. Stay until one day, perhaps, Kathy chooses to offer him a permanent home?'

281

'*Adoption!*'

'Yes, in time. Why not? But shouldn't we also be involving Kathy?'

'All this excitement young man, quite frankly it might be best if you left with the boy now; before further damage is done. We all need more time. Time to think this thing through, thoroughly,' Helen insisted, twiddling a strand of greying hair.

Gerald shrugged helplessly. He had known there were inherent risks, but at least he had tried. Lighting a cigarette, in spite of the absence of ashtrays, he conceded. 'You know your daughter-in-law better than I, so obviously I will respect your wishes. If Kathy has finished changing Adam, we can be on our way,' he said, adding as Helen made her way to the door, 'Please tell Kathy how sorry I am for the intrusion and for any upset this has caused.'

When Helen returned alone a few minutes later, Gerald's heart skipped a beat. There were tears streaming down her cheeks as she wordlessly took him by the hand. Not sure what to expect he allowed himself to be led off down the passage. Only once they were in the doorway of Kathy's room did it become apparent that Helen's tears were tears of joy.

Kathy lay on a large pink duvet on the floor with Adam cradled in her arms amid a pile of protective pillows. Both were sound asleep. Adam held one of Kathy's fingers captive in his tiny fist and there was a look of peace and tranquillity on the young woman's face, which Gerald ventured nobody had seen in a long, long time. He fought hard to control the tightness in his throat and the tingling sensation at the base of his nose. When at last Helen squeezed his arm they quietly withdrew together.

Gerald Bond made the return journey to Wankie alone, in the certain knowledge that a team of wild horses could not separate Adam from his newfound foster mother. He was pleased, not only for Adam and Kathy's sake, but also for his parents. They could now start to put the pieces of their own lives back together, without an ever-present reminder of their grief. For his part, he was now free to apply himself to the clandestine task of protecting and grooming Nkomo; while his colleagues in the CCB – many of whom were also ex-Selous Scouts – worked at facilitating Mugabe's downfall.

With tribalism already raising its ugly head in the fledgling state of Zimbabwe, it was in the interest of the entire subcontinent that the situation be normalised before it degenerated into all-out civil war. It was also important to replace Mugabe before he got round to tearing up the Lancaster House agreement and set about entrenching a one party state; the hallmark of black Africa.

Coup d'état

Two years after South Africa had commenced covert operations to weaken the Zimbabwean economy, Mugabe's government was teetering on the brink. The well orchestrated international publicity campaign, portraying Nkomo as a moderate and the Matabele people as victims of a corrupt ruling class, had proved so successful that the time was deemed opportune for the Matabele leader to stage the long-anticipated coup. Unfortunately for Nkomo and his handlers, the powers-that-be had once again hopelessly underestimated Mugabe's resourcefulness. Within hours of the planned takeover of the national broadcasting facility and other key installations, Prime Minister Mugabe unleashed his notorious Fifth Brigade on an unsuspecting nation.

In the weeks that followed, an unprecedented orgy of interrogations and slaughter saw the annihilation of thousands of so-called dissidents, and the indiscriminate killing of entire families. Rebel arms caches around the country were systematically pin-pointed with uncanny speed and accuracy, over thirty in all. The true brilliance of Mugabe's Korean military advisers became apparent when strategically they left the best for last, the routing of Nkomo's main arsenal. It comprised dozens of tanks, heavy artillery pieces and huge ammunition dumps, spread over a vast area of dense bush on one of Nkomo's isolated farms in the Gwai river district. This enormous cache was painstakingly exposed bit by bit, maximising international publicity.

The message to the world was clear, the slaughter in Matabeleland was a justifiable means to an end, and before long the cries of genocide were reduced to mutterings about excessive force and ruthlessness.

Making it across the border, just one jump ahead of the closing net, a badly shaken and disillusioned Gerald Bond bitterly conceded the first round to Mugabe. Lookout Masuku and Dumiso Dabengwa, Nkomo's former military commander and former KGB-trained intelligence chief respectively, were not so lucky and both were arrested and charged with high treason. Mugabe's cunning, not to mention his formidable spy network, had again proved to be a force to be reckoned with.

Thanks to the seemingly bottomless pit of funds at the disposal of the CCB, Major Bond and his colleagues were back in business before the dust had settled. Only this time Bond wisely opted to set up shop on the South African side of the Limpopo river. While the loss of thousands of tons of arms, ammunition and heavy equipment was a setback, it had been a small price to pay for the cardinal sin of underestimating one's enemy. With upwards of one thousand specialist trained men, mainly black ex-Selous Scouts, having slipped the net with him, Bond was confident that the next time around they would succeed.

Nkomo, for his part, spent some time in self-exile in Botswana, from where he was able to test the water. The sly old Elephant of Zimbabwe eventually had the audacity to return home in the certain knowledge that evidence to convict him was inconclusive. Surprisingly, his ploy worked and Nkomo was spared prosecution and summary execution, due in part to pressure from the West but mainly due to the very real threat of civil war should the Shonas dare to lynch the leader of the war-like Matabele nation.

Zululand Safari Lodge

Brenton Knight was obliged to end his binge on his daughter's safe return from her impromptu jaunt into the bush. Sober, he found the sniggers and snide remarks voiced in the public rooms of the Holiday Inn insufferable. Insisting they leave at once to catch up with their tour party he found Jodie equally intent on staying put. She needed time to recover from her ordeal, she said. They eventually compromised, relocating to the Zululand Safari Lodge down the road the next day.

The Lodge, with its towering thatch roof, was the focal point of a cluster of chalets in natural bush surrounds. Wild animals roamed the grounds and the wildebeest, impala, zebra, ostriches and timid nyala were a constant delight to visitors. The arrival of the Knights' courtesy Kombi was met by a group of bare-breasted Zulu maidens, singing and gyrating as they beat rhythmically on cowhide drums.

Entering the reception area, where the thatched interior reached to cathedral heights and the walls were adorned with trophy horns, Brenton said vociferously, 'Well I'll be damned, this is the very place from our travel agent's brochure, which they assured us we would be staying at!'

Having signed the register, perspiring profusely in spite of the relative coolness of the thatched interior, Brenton lost no time in familiarising himself with the opulence of the Assegai Cocktail Bar. In keeping with its name the bar was decked out with an array of Zulu stabbing spears and ox-hide shields.

The bar's main attraction for the weary male traveller, apart from the air-conditioning and red velvet bar stools, was Samantha, the pretty barmaid. Samantha's daytime attire was short-sleeved khaki shirt and shorts. Her blonde hair was intricately plaited into long ethnic braids.

Having feigned a headache from the heat and retired to her room, Jodie spent a frustrating hour soliciting telephone numbers from uncooperative operators in Zimbabwe. She was determined to keep her promise to Nyoni and find a way to help Tony, before having to return home to England.

Working on a long shot that someone among the dwindling European population in Zimbabwe would know of Tony, she was following up on the only leads she had, a name 'Gerald Bond' and a town called Wankie. These random snippets of information were all she had managed to wrest from Tony during their time together. Fortunately there were not that many Bonds in Wankie, now renamed Hwange according to the operator, and on her third attempt she found herself speaking to a Gloria Bond who guardedly admitted having a son named Gerald.

Initially disclaiming any knowledge of her son's whereabouts or acknowledging an acquaintance named Tony, Gloria's curiosity finally got the better of her when the English girl proved equally evasive about the reason for the call.

'Our dear departed daughter once . . . knew a Tony,' Gloria confirmed irritably as she reflected on what she believed had been a doomed relationship, and one that had cost Victoria her life.

'Can you recall Tony's surname?' Jodie prompted.

'What is this all about?'

Jodie remained silent and Gloria relented, 'Longdon, Tony Longdon.'

'Longdon,' Jodie echoed. 'Does he still have family or relatives in Hwange?'

'No, he actually came from Bulawayo but the question is academic; he died during the war . . . seven or so years ago. Look, my girl you are freaking me out, tell me what this is all about and perhaps I can be more helpful.'

287

'I'm simply trying to establish if Mr Longdon had family in Zimbabwe,' Jodie said.

'A wife . . . Kathleen, and his parents,' Gloria volunteered, on the offchance that the call might have something to do with Adam, her grandson. 'They moved up to Salisbury, *Harare* that is, a few months ago.'

'You say *they?*' Jodie continued to probe.

'She has been living with her in-laws since her husband was killed; her own folks died many years ago. They all moved to Harare when Alf was transferred by his company. I may be able to lay my hands on an address,' Gloria offered.

'That would be marvellous, thank you,' Jodie enthused inwardly, congratulating herself on achieving her ends without compromising a potentially sensitive situation.

Gloria Bond smiled to herself as she challenged the caller. 'First I think you owe me some sort of explanation, my girl.' In response to another awkward silence, Gloria continued angrily, 'Then at least tell me what my son Gerald has to do with all this. Is he still down there in South Africa? Nothing dreadful has happened to him, has it?'

'No, it's nothing like that I assure you, Mrs Bond,' Jodie said, surprised to hear that Gerald Bond was actually down in her part of the world. 'Mrs Bond, I have not actually met your son, his name was given to me by . . . a third party,' Jodie conceded, regretting having alarmed the poor woman.

'Well at least tell me your name and where you are calling from.'

Jodie willingly traded the information for the Longdons' address in Harare; with Gloria convinced of Tony's death she was in any event unlikely to pursue the matter.

Jodie must have dozed off, because when next she opened her eyes the sun was going down. She showered and changed and rushed off three postcards to her mother, two of which she backdated. She was about to leave her room to join her father for cocktails, and start working on him for a trip to the Victoria Falls, via Harare, when the telephone rang.

'Jodie Knight, good evening,' she answered cheerily, gazing out through the screen door at another spectacular mauve and orange sunset.

'That remains to be seen,' the caller said tersely, adding equally officiously, 'What business do you have with the Longdons?'

'Who is this?' Jodie demanded.

'Never you mind, miss. Tell me why you have gone to such lengths to trace the family or I will need to have words with your father.'

'Really?' Jodie huffed. 'Please, be my guest.'

'Look here, my girl, cooperate for five minutes and we won't have to bother your old man.'

'I'm not your girl and you may talk to my father until you are blue in the face. Now who is this, before I hang up?'

'You're English aren't you?'

'And you're a Rhodesian!' She surprised even herself.

'A lucky guess,' he said.

'No, the chauvinistic manners,' Jodie retorted. His accent was the same as that of the only other Rhodesian she had met, Tony, Tony Longdon.

'All right you win. I don't have all night to play games. My name is Gerald Bond and I'm a friend, trust me. Now, what is your interest in the Longdons and more importantly, how did you know to try and get in touch through me?'

That's better Jodie thought, delighted to have *the* Gerald Bond on the line; even if the speed with which Gloria Bond had exposed her was cause for concern. Tony's existence was going to come as a shock to many and she owed it to his family to be the first to know. On the other hand, the more she could learn about Tony and his past, the better equipped she would be to deal with his newly revealed wife, Kathleen.

'Why should I trust you, when a few hours ago your mother made out she had no knowledge of your whereabouts?' Jodie stalled.

'That happened to be the truth, Miss Knight. I'm . . . constantly on the move and can only be contacted through third parties, and then with some difficulty.'

'Sounds like a terribly important position,' Jodie chided.

'That's flippant but true. Now please, who gave you my name?'

'It sounds like you are more concerned about Mr Bond than the Longdons,' Jodie observed.

'That's rich coming from someone who knows next to nothing about them or me.'

'For starters I know you were a Selous Scout or something,' Jodie said, again surprising herself with this gem of intelligence, salvaged from the mine of unrelated information gleaned from Tony.

'You are doing much better than I'd have given you credit for, Miss Knight,' Gerald conceded, adding in all seriousness, 'You are correct about my past. And whether you realise it or not you are by association unwittingly putting Longdon's widow and his son in serious danger back in Zimbabwe.'

'Tony has a son?' Jodie asked before she could check herself.

'Yes, Adam,' Gerald confirmed, adding, 'that you need to ask supports my contention that you are groping in the dark. Whatever it is you are up to could do more harm than good, believe me.'

This time the man's quiet, earnest tone got through to Jodie. 'Mr Bond, I find it hard to imagine what sort of danger I could be putting people in, but if you can convince me you have Kathleen and Adam's interest at heart I will happily cooperate.'

'All right, you win, again. For starters, Adam is my orphaned nephew. The late Tony Longdon and my sister had a thing going for a while. Victoria died giving birth after an attack on our home; ironically Tony was killed in a terrorist engagement a month later. Kathleen has since adopted Adam.' In response to a gasp on the end of the line, Gerald added, 'You should not judge them too harshly, those were difficult times and for what it's worth Tony and his wife were reconciled before his death. Are you now satisfied that I have a vested interest?'

'Yes, indeed,' Jodie said as she wiped a tear from her cheek. 'What was it again that you wished to know, Mr Bond?'

'Just what your interest is in the Longdons and where I fit in.'

'Mr Bond, your story is amazing but not quite as extraordinary as what I can reveal; so I need you to promise you will not resort to some sort of unilateral action.'

'You have my word. I am trying to avert a situation not create one.'

'Well then, in short, I arrived in Hluhluwe ten days ago with a tour group from London. Staying at the Holiday Inn at the time I made the acquaintance of a strange individual who I encountered drinking alone in the hotel grounds . . .'

Several minutes later, Gerald interrupted impatiently, 'What in blazes has a recluse with amnesia and your studying psychology got to do with anything?'

'Everything,' Jodie came back excitedly. 'The local people have dubbed the man *The Rhodesian;* and he's one and the same person your mother claims was lost in action, assumed dead, seven years ago.'

'Longdon? Alive?' Gerald blurted out, a long whistle carrying over the line. 'Miss Knight, this is truly remarkable. If you are not mistaken it's a chance in a million that he survived. Yet there was one person who never gave up on him, his wife Kathleen – in spite of it nearly costing her sanity. Where the hell is he now? Why didn't he go to the authorities? Does he know what you are up to? Amnesia, you say?'

'One at a time, and please, it's Jodie.'

'Jodie, describe this fellow for me. I would hate to think we are barking up the wrong tree.'

'Tall, six foot plus, broad shouldered, brown hair and blue-grey eyes, looks to be in his late thirties but probably younger. In his present state of mind he is withdrawn and moody, but there are layers beneath the veneer that show him to be affable and com-passionate. I suspect he was once demanding and self-confident, even extroverted.'

'Sounds like our man. Apart from the amnesia and some old wounds, you say he's fine?'

291

'No, it's more complicated than that,' Jodie cautioned. Having explained the extent of Tony's injuries and the collateral damage in the form of migraines, recurring nightmares, blackouts and depression, Jodie added, 'I think he's also had malaria and periodically suffers relapses.'

'And he lives in a hut in the bush outside Hluhluwe?'

'More like an assortment of huts and they are a good day's walk from town,' Jodie said without attempting to explain Nyoni's presence over the telephone.

'He must be able to remember something to have put you onto me,' Gerald said sceptically.

'It was I who made the connection. At best he recalls vague glimpses of his past. He is terrified of awakening from his nightmare to discover he deserted family and loved ones, his own words.'

'If that's the case why is he refusing to get help?'

'Denial and fear of what he might discover from all accounts. And if a precarious state of mind and blackouts were not enough, his hobby is rounding up dissidents and poachers!'

'Not good,' Gerald agreed. 'We need to bring him in.'

'I tried to persuade him, really tried, but . . .' Jodie's voice faltered.

'Take it easy, the cavalry is at hand, we *will* get him sorted out,' Gerald encouraged.

Jodie blew her nose, 'It's easier said than done, which is why I have been trying to contact family.'

'We should meet to review our options. How does tonight suit you?'

'Tonight! Are you here in Natal?'

'Not quite, about five hours drive so I could be there before midnight.'

'I'll wait up,' Jodie acknowledged, asking as an afterthought, 'Is Kathleen involved with anyone else at the moment?'

'Not as far as I know. Last I heard she was still clinging to the vain hope that one day Tony will come marching home; a real possibility now from the sound of it.'

'The fact that Kathy saw fit to adopt Adam also tells us something,' Jodie noted, more for her own benefit.

'Precisely, so chin up and I will be with you shortly,' Gerald said, ringing off.

Touching up her lipstick, Jodie attributed the unsteadiness of her hand to the toll extracted by the past week in Zululand. Offering a silent prayer that she was not going to find her father in a state she set out to join him.

There was an authoritative air about the tall, lean young man who strode into the busy cocktail bar just before closing time. Even Samantha, who had received advances from most of the unattached game rangers, farmers and policemen in the district, did a double-take at the deeply tanned individual with wavy, shoulder-length hair.

Edging his way down the length of the bar to where a young woman sat chatting to a greying, portly gentleman, Gerald mouthed, 'Cold Castle,' at Sam, well aware that he already had the attractive blonde's attention.

Pausing behind the leggy young woman elegantly poised on a bar stool, Gerald bent round and kissed her on the cheek. It had been three months since he had been this close to a woman, let alone one that smelled and looked every bit as good as he had imagined. The sleek black cocktail dress accentuated her waist and petite breasts, while her vibrant chestnut hair made her green eyes appear even more striking.

'Really, Mr Bond,' Jodie guessed, feigning indignation as she swivelled around on her stool to confront the tall, denim-clad individual with alert blue eyes and a disarming boyish grin. Giving him the once over, before she could help herself, she was struck by the long but well-groomed hair, slender build and narrow hips; nothing like the hardy Rhodesian war veteran she had expected.

'I trust I meet with your approval!' Gerald beamed outrageously, equally in awe of her captivating beauty.

'I'm sorry, it's just that you are a lot younger than I expected,'

Jodie said, a genuine note of surprise in her voice. Finding it hard to hold his intense, enquiring gaze she took a sip of her drink before saying the first thing that came into her head, 'How did you know it was me?'

'You're the only woman in the room whose looks matched the cultured, incredibly sexy voice on the telephone,' Gerald said, un-ashamedly nodding his approval.

Still blushing Jodie turned to introduce her father.

'Pleased to meet you,' Brenton slurred over the top of his glass as he half-heartedly extended a hand, which he quickly withdrew as the young man's steel-like grip threatened to crush his fingers.

'Thank you,' Gerald acknowledged as Samantha placed a frosted glass and a beer in front of him with an enticing smile. Downing the beer, he wiped his mouth with the back of his hand and said, 'That's better. Now down to business, Princess.'

'I'm not a princess,' Jodie said dismissively.

'Sorry, can't help it if you look the part.'

'You Rhodesians are impossible,' she relented.

'Tell me about it,' Brenton Knight interjected, stifling a yawn. 'But if it takes one to catch one, so be it. Then hopefully we can get on with our damn holiday; what's left of it that is.' Belching discreetly Brenton got to his feet. 'I'm going to retire. Don't be too late now, *Princess*,' he teased, before waving Gerald's outstretched hand aside and setting off unsteadily in the direction of the foyer.

'Princess,' Gerald persisted, 'the way I see it I need to get Tony to accompany me back here, while you prepare the ground on the Zimbabwean side. Given what Kathy has already been through I think it's important you contact her in person, putting some of this psychology training of yours to good use. We then have our boy checked out by a shrink in Durban, en-route to flying him home and into Kathy's welcoming arms.'

Shaking her head at Gerald's ridiculously simplistic scenario, Jodie said, 'I thought I made it clear on the telephone, Tony is a troubled individual. He will see you as a complete stranger and is certainly not going to allow anyone to march him off to a psychiatrist or bundle him onto a flight to Zimbabwe, unless it suits him. Which presupposes you are even able to locate his retreat? What's more he's armed to the teeth.'

'I could arrange to dart him from a helicopter,' Gerald suggested straight-faced while Samantha refilled his glass. 'Seriously, what choice does he have if he's in such bad shape? As for locating him, I have done a bit of tracking in my time. Which reminds me, what in blazes were you doing out in the back of beyond in the first place, or shouldn't I ask?'

'It was nothing like that,' Jodie came back a little too defensively. 'As I mentioned earlier, I viewed him as a potentially interesting case study.'

'Considering the lengths you have gone to for his welfare, he must have proved . . . very interesting?' Gerald said, raising an eyebrow.

'Men!' Jodie exclaimed. 'I was simply trying to assist someone in need and you can help by telling me all about the Longdons.'

Gerald made himself comfortable on the stool vacated by Brenton. 'There's not much more to tell. Vicky's pride, coupled with a suspicion that Tony might not be over his wife, meant he never learned of my sister's pregnancy from her. Adam was delivered prematurely on his mother's deathbed and spent several weeks in an incubator. When Tony returned from South Africa at the end of his compassionate leave, it was with a reconciled Kathleen in tow. He went on to rejoin his unit and while on a routine patrol, shortly before hostilities ended, he heroically or stupidly initiated a contact against overwhelming odds. You know more than I about what happened after that. As for Kathleen, her road to recovery started in earnest once introduced to Adam, who she took to as her own from the start.'

'What a tragic story; I'm so sorry about your sister.'

'Thank you. It's been seven years, although one never gets over a loss like that.'

'Tony never knew he had a fathered a child then?' Jodie prompted.

'Yes and no. Shortly after Vicky's funeral I told him of her pregnancy, so he knew he had fathered a child. But for reasons that are no longer relevant I chose not to dispel the notion that the pregnancy had terminated with her life. To this day he does not know he's a father,' Gerald concluded, taking a long draught of his beer.

'There is obviously more to Tony than meets the eye. I would never have imagined him as the type to carry on behind his wife's back, let alone with a teenage girl,' Jodie observed out loud.

'In his defence there were extenuating circumstances. Although I'm not so sure I can say the same in your case, young lady. You chose to go traipsing off into the sticks with an older, married man with issues and prone to violence.'

'Reckless and impulsive perhaps, but I certainly did not know he was married or the extent of his problems.'

'You Tarzan, me Jane,' Gerald teased before adding in all seriousness, 'Is there anything else I should know?'

'Just that Tony has a . . . companion.'

'What? I thought you said he was a recluse?'

'I didn't want to say too much on the telephone. Nyoni is a charming girl who has sort of adopted Tony. She also happens to be a Matabele and I know what bigots people in this part of the world can be.'

'Don't stop now, this is getting really interesting,' Gerald encouraged. 'Just for the record, I'm no racist,' he hastened to add.

'Nyoni attends to the domestic chores and nurses him through bad patches. As for the rest she has her own quarters and it's all very platonic.'

In response to Gerald's snide chuckle, Jodie went on to explain, 'Nyoni was abducted by terrorists as a child and brutally raped, leaving her paranoid about sex. It was while on the march with the terrorists that they were ambushed. In the confusion she stumbled into a gully where she discovered a badly injured solider, who she went on to conceal from the terrorists. Tony subsequently shielded her from the incendiary bombs, getting badly burned in the process. Whatever you might think, I believe that in Tony's

296

eyes she is still that twelve-year-old little girl. I am not sure what prompted her to follow him to South Africa, hero worship possibly, but she has been with him ever since and is desperate to help. She even drew a map for me before I left. It's very rough and I'm not sure how much use it will be.'

'No need for a map,' Gerald dismissed.

'Excuse me! Father did mention something about Selous Scouts supposedly being expert trackers and able to survive off the land,' Jodie said, looking down her nose in feigned indignation.

'Their reputation does them justice,' Gerald confirmed with a self-assured smile.

'Well, assuming you can find and bring him in, there is still the question of a wife he cannot remember and a son he has never known.'

'Let's cross those bridges when we get to them,' Gerald said getting to his feet and taking her by the arm.

'Where are we going?' Jodie asked uncertainly.

'Onto the veranda, I'm not accustomed to all this second-hand smoke.'

'Also one less distraction,' Jodie said as Samantha smiled her goodnights.

'She's cute but not a patch on you, Princess,' Gerald said pulling back a chair for her once outside. 'Just one for the road, we can firm up our strategy in the morning,' he said, signalling to a waiter.

Finding it hard work getting Gerald to open up about his own circumstances, Jodie stifled a yawn and got to her feet the moment they had finished their drinks. 'It's late and we have a busy day ahead of us so I'll say good night. And thank you again for coming to my assistance so promptly.'

Damp with perspiration from a fitful night's sleep, Jodie was awakened by a persistent knocking. Blinking herself awake as she crossed the room, she had no sooner turned the key in the lock than Gerald swept into the room; accompanied by the mouthwatering aroma of bacon and eggs, toast and coffee. Setting down the tray, he proceeded to close the windows and turn on the air conditioner.

'In Africa we sleep with the air-conditioning on and windows closed, not the other . . .' his voice trailed off as he turned. Jodie was still standing in front of the open doorway, the early morning sun streaming through her short cotton nightshirt. Gerald cleared his throat and mouthed an oath.

'Cat got your tongue?' Jodie quipped drowsily as the seconds ticked by under Gerald's intense scrutiny. It was only once her predicament became apparent that she mustered the presence of mind to nudge the door closed with her heel.

Finally able to avert his eyes, Gerald apologised, 'I'm sorry, guess I'm in pretty bad need of some shore leave.' Hands thrust self-consciously in his pockets he turned back to the window.

'You can say that again,' Jodie said grabbing her robe and making for the bathroom.

When Jodie reappeared, properly attired in her gown and with her hair brushed out, it was to find the table by the bay window set for two and Gerald on his second cup of coffee. She was delighted to see he'd also had the presence of mind to include a pot of tea.

'That little display earlier was childish,' Gerald confessed. 'Please excuse my uncouth manner.'

After a moment's silence Jodie murmured, 'No harm done. Thank you for the breakfast and for remembering we English drink tea. I think I could eat a horse this morning.'

'Shame on you,' Gerald said nodding towards the window and the herd of Burchell's zebra browsing not five metres from the chalet.

'The stallion seems to have lost his tail,' Jodie noted.

'A lucky escape judging from the scars on his rump,' Gerald said, adding as he reached across the table to run a finger lightly down her cheek, 'How did you come by yours?'

'Oh that,' she said blushing at his touch, 'A parting gift from my ex-boyfriend, literally *foiling* around after removing our fencing

masks. Fortunately it's only this noticeable first thing, before foundation and make-up.'

'You don't need make-up, my girl. Besides, the scar adds
character.'

'That's sweet of you,' Jodie said, returning his smile. She was
about to add that Nyoni shared his charm appeal for scars, when it
dawned on her that Gerald was not only wearing the same clothes
as the night before, but they also looked slept in. 'Forgive me for
not asking if you were able to get a room; did you get any sleep?'

'I managed an hour or two in the staff accommodation,' he
said with an impish grin.

'Sam, the barmaid? How could you? I mean you said this was
your first . . .'

'Hold your horses, Princess. I was referring to the black staff
housing behind the Holiday Inn, where you first met Tony.'

'That's one to you,' Jodie said self-consciously, chalking up
an imaginary board. 'But what on earth were you doing in the
African quarters?'

'Like I said, I'm no racist.' He could have added that he'd
been sharing digs with his black colleagues for years, instead he
explained, 'I spent the early hours sounding out some of the locals
about Tony and his routine. He is certainly well known in these
parts for his vigilante exploits. As for the rest I'm still not sure if
they love him or fear him. All I got was a load of mumbo jumbo
about him being touched by the spirits; a convenient excuse for
being evasive without giving offence.'

'It is not just superstition,' Jodie warned, 'one minute he's
behaving normally, the next something snaps and he becomes
irrational. Nyoni even spikes his coffee from time to time, to knock
him out.'

'I obviously won't be darting him but I will arrange to have a
chopper on standby, just in case,' Gerald said in all seriousness.

Before Jodie had a chance to question Gerald's resourcefulness, he continued outlining his plan. 'I suggest you fly up to
Harare tomorrow, Thursday, to break the news personally. Ideally

getting to Kathy's mother-in-law first. Helen's a wise old dear and well worth having in your corner. You can then upfront Kathy together. Once it has sunk in I don't foresee any difficulty in persuading her to return with you to SA to help with Tony's convalescence. Once you are on your way I will make arrangements and set out on foot to round Tony up.'

'What arrangements might these be?' Jodie asked, finally getting a word in.

'Setting up a radio link through . . . associates of mine, so we can keep in touch should anything unforeseen arise. I will also arrange to have a doctor on call to check Tony over if needs be. All going well we should be able to meet back here Saturday evening, latest. We can then take it from there. How does that sound?'

'It's an improvement on last night's plan,' Jodie acknowledged, 'but it still sounds a lot like wishful thinking.'

'In my experience the simpler the plan the more likely the chance of success,' Gerald said.

'Well, if you are confident you can manage Tony, I guess I will be able to cope with Kathleen, with mother-in-law's help. There is just one proviso.'

'What might that be?'

'That you feel free to use my room while I'm gone.' In response to his knowing nod she blurted out, 'It's got nothing to do with Samantha,' adding as she fought down the colour rising in her cheeks, 'it's pointless leaving the room empty when it's paid for.'

'Then I accept on condition that you promise to hurry back. I'm going to miss bringing you breakfast, and seeing you framed in the doorway, Princess.'

'Really, you are impossible,' was all Jodie managed before Gerald came round the table and kissed her full on the lips.

After a lively scene at the bar Brenton reluctantly handed over some travellers' cheques. 'All I agreed to last night was a trip up to the Victoria Falls, *myself included,*' Brenton protested. 'God alone knows what Christine will say if she phones and finds you have now jetted off to Zimbabwe, on a fool's errand.' He threw up his hands in frustration.

Jodie booked her flight, departing Durban at 09.00 the following morning and arriving in Johannesburg in time to make a noon connection to Harare in Zimbabwe. Gerald undertook to drive her the three-hundred-odd kilometres through to Durban that afternoon, where she would sleep over.

Her legs curled up beneath her on the unyielding bench-like front seat of the Land-Rover, Jodie studied the secretive individual beside her. It was over a three-hour drive; time enough to get better acquainted, she reasoned.

'You are the most devious and evasive person I have ever met, Mr Bond,' a frustrated Jodie fumed an hour later. 'We have come full circle and apart from my knowing you were in the army, and the wonderful thing you did in bringing Kathleen and little Adam together, you remain an enigma.'

'A hangover from the good old days, when loose talk cost lives,' Gerald shrugged. 'Must be hell from a psychologist's perspective though, not being able to join all the dots, *all the time.*'

Ignoring the snide remark, Jodie said, 'Very well, tell me about the good old days then.'

'Unfortunately those days ended with the disbandment of my unit on Zimbabwe gaining its independence.'

'Well, what is it that you do in South Africa now then?'

'I suppose you could say I am in the travel business, sort of.'

'Sort of, meaning what exactly?'

'We cater for those with a passion for the great outdoors.'

'Rubbish, anyone can see this is not a safari Land-Rover; it's some type of government vehicle.' Jodie declared, folding her arms across her chest and turning to stare out of the window at Natal's monotonous, seemingly endless rolling hills of sugar cane.

'We buy them at state auctions, long wheelbase, ideal for *bundu* bashing,' Gerald said finding it hard to keep a straight face.

'Does the government continue to service the vehicles?' Jodie asked pointedly tapping the logbook, emblazoned with the South African Government crest, which had worked its way out from beneath a pile of old newspapers under the dashboard. 'I thought we had some sort of understanding?'

'We do,' Gerald conceded, 'and I would have confided in you earlier but for a real concern that I could be inviting the beginning of the end of a promising relationship. To my mind you Brits generally have a very parochial view of democracy and don't really understand the extent to which it is abused in third world countries.'

'Try me, and there is no need to hold back on my account,' Jodie challenged, perking up on her seat.

'OK, but don't say I didn't warn you. From a nucleus of ex-Selous Scouts and former guerrillas, from Nkomo's old command, my associates and I have put together a formidable unit; suitably dubbed Super-ZAPU by the press. We are tasked with helping to . . . facilitate an orderly transition of power in southern Africa. Had it not been for complacency, coupled with an unfortunate run of bad luck, we would have wrested Zimbabwe and neighbouring Mozambique from the lap of dictatorship years ago. We now operate out of bases on this side of the Zimbabwe and Mozambique borders.' He could have added, *our paymasters are the Civil Cooperation Bureau, a covert unit of the South African Defence Force* but that would have been an even more outrageous breach of security. Pausing to rummage under the dashboard with one hand, he promptly received a slap on his wrist.

'I threw out the packet when we stopped for petrol. It's your own fault for having lied about giving up smoking.'

Shaking his head, Gerald asked, 'Have you heard a single word of what I just said?'

'Yes, you and a band of mercenaries are intent on destabilising defenceless African countries. Next I suppose you are going to . . .' but Jodie's scorn ended abruptly as Gerald's powerful fingers clamped down on her wrist.

'We are not *mercenaries*,' he said with contempt, adding in an equally disarming tone, 'The only defenceless things about African states are the millions of peasants who are beaten, raped, starved and butchered into toeing the party line. The sooner these corrupt dictatorships are brought to an end, the sooner millions of dollars in foreign aid will go to fill empty stomachs instead of Swiss bank accounts.'

'Please, you are hurting me,' Jodie cried. 'If it's such a sore point I'm sorry for calling you a mercenary, but I'm not naive and I do read the news,' she said, still struggling.

Releasing his grip Gerald took a deep breath. 'No, it's I who should apologise. I just lose it when intelligent people choose to make light of a very serious state of affairs. Newspapers won't tell you that the government of South Africa accepts apartheid is indefensible. Nor that it knows its chances of convincing the white electorate to accept majority rule will be zero, once millions of starving refugees start flooding into the country from *so-called* independent states to the north. Am I making any sense at all to you?'

'Yes, according to your logic it's acceptable to destabilise an already independent Zimbabwe so as not to impede the progress towards independence and majority rule here in South Africa. Which makes perfect sense, of course,' Jodie concluded sarcastically, folding her arms and pointedly turning to look out of the window.

Still smarting from the tongue lashing, it was some time before Gerald chanced a sideways glance in Jodie's direction. When he did he could not help smiling to himself, she had dozed off with her head propped up against the door jamb and a scowl on her face.

Jodie was still asleep when they pulled up in front of the Elangeni Hotel on the Durban beachfront, only now her head rested comfortably up against Gerald's shoulder.

In Pursuit of Salvation

Jodie arrived in Harare tired and on edge, having spent a restless night suffering Durban's humidity and wrestling with the vagaries of the task ahead. The two-hour delay at Jan Smuts airport in Johannesburg, occasioned by the late arrival of the incoming Air Zimbabwe flight, had not helped her disposition either.

Throughout the drive from the airport to the Jameson Hotel in a hired car, Jodie was struck by the predominance of black people on the roads and pavements. It was the same inside the hotel, hardly a white face to be seen. Even in the relative safety of her own room, she felt oddly vulnerable in her white skin. After her bath she ordered a chicken and mayonnaise sandwich and a glass of milk; chicken being all that the kitchen had to offer in spite of the extensive room service menu.

Jodie drank her milk and ate the chicken, discarding the butterless bread in the absence of any mayonnaise. Having studied her map, she set out with some trepidation to make Kathleen and Adam's acquaintance, hopeful of having an opportunity to confide first in Helen Longdon.

Driving past the well-kept property in a quiet suburban avenue of Highlands for a second time, Jodie found herself fretting over the dozen and one awkward questions that had manifested themselves these past few days. Three years studying the social, cognitive and biological dimensions of behaviour hardly qualified one to deal with the complexities of a long-lost loved-one returning from the grave. There was also always the daunting possibility of a new relationship in Kathleen's life to compound the problem.

Jodie pulled into the Longdons' driveway on the third pass,

prompted by the sobering thought that it had been five days since she had left Nyoni to journey back to Hluhluwe with Tony; the risk to them both increasing with each passing day.

The door opened on the first ring, catching Jodie with her finger still on the bell.

'I'm Helen Longdon. Please do come on in, Miss Knight,' the stately grey-haired woman invited. 'You must be tired after your journey,' Helen commented absently as she ushered her visitor into the lounge.

A bemused Jodie crossed the threshold wondering how on earth Helen could have known who she was, let alone have anticipated her arrival. 'Good afternoon,' Jodie managed as she obediently sat in the chair Helen had indicated.

Acknowledging the greeting with a curt nod and half-hearted smile, Helen sat down opposite her visitor. 'This has something to do with our daughter-in-law, hasn't it, my dear?' She came straight to the point, making no attempt at disguising the concern in her voice.

More perplexed than ever, Jodie simply laid open her palms as if soliciting an explanation.

'Two days ago I was called to our neighbours' house for the telephone. It was Adam's other granny, Gloria Bond, calling from Wankie. I should say Hwange,' Helen corrected herself before adding, 'She said a Miss Knight had gone to some lengths to trace Kathleen, our late son's wife. Alf and I have been expecting a telegram or visit ever since. I put two and two together when I saw you driving up and down.' Wringing her hands, Helen went on pensively, 'I suspect that whatever has brought you all this way from South Africa must be important and probably not good news. You see, unannounced visits have proved traumatic for this family in the past. First there was a Mrs Yvonne Young, informing us of our son's death, then Mr Gerald Bond to introduce us to a previously unknown grandson, and now you. Although for the life of me I cannot imagine what business you could possibly have with Kathy.'

'I am very sorry for barging in like this, Mrs Longdon. The least I could have done was send a telegram. Mrs Bond mentioned you were still without a telephone,' Jodie apologised wondering how she might have worded one: '*Tony alive. Has amnesia. Living in mud hut in Zululand. Will pop in to discus homecoming.*'

'Yes, yes I can see you are sincere my dear but in the meantime the suspense is not good for my blood pressure.'

'What of Kathleen and Adam?' Jodie enquired willing herself back to the task at hand.

'They are not here at the moment, I'm afraid,' Helen said, adding, 'If this matter concerns them both, might it also have something to do with our late son?'

Amazed at Helen's uncanny foresight, Jodie swallowed hard and blurted out, 'I met a man while on a game viewing holiday in Northern Natal who I have good reason to believe is your son, Tony.' So much for breaking the news gently, Jodie thought, poised for a reaction.

Helen closed her eyes and bowed her head, the colour draining from her already pale cheeks. It was as if she was seeking divine intervention, a sign, something to lend credence to what she was hearing.

'Are you all right, Mrs Longdon?' Jodie asked anxiously as she crossed the room to comfort and reassure her, 'You mentioned Adam's uncle Gerald a moment ago. Well I met up with him recently in South Africa. From the description I gave he was as convinced as I am that the man I met is your son.' Placing an arm around the old woman's shoulders, Jodie again asked, 'Are you all right. Is there anything I can get you, a glass of water perhaps?'

Holding up a hand which shook with emotion, Helen implored, 'Please go on, I'm just having a little difficulty taking all this in, you understand. There have been other reported sightings over the years, all ending in more heartache.'

'Mrs Longdon, this is not a case of mistaken identity. Your son was injured in a terrorist engagement. He stumbled into a ravine where he remained until local tribespeople found and nursed him back to health. While he has recovered physically he still has no cohesive recollection of anything prior to the incident. Amnesia has prevented him making contact all these years.'

Helen was shaking her head as if in denial. 'How did he come to be in South Africa? Why has he not accompanied you home? You say Gerald recognised him from your *description*, has he not seen our boy then? Is there something dreadful you are . . .'

Conscious of the lengthening shadows out on the front lawn as evening approached, Jodie interrupted, 'Mrs Longdon, I will do my best to answer all your questions, but first what time are you expecting Kathleen home?'

'She has insisted all along that our boy was still out there somewhere, you know. Kathleen was adamant that one day he . . .' Helen's voice trailed off in mid sentence, her attention focused on the picture of her son and daughter-in-law prominently displayed on the mantelpiece.

'Mrs Longdon,' Jodie tried again, raising her voice a little.

'It's Helen dear, do call me Helen.'

'Helen,' Jodie echoed before rephrasing the question, 'Should we not be giving some thought as to how best to break the news to Kathleen, before she gets home?'

'Home? Oh, no child, she no longer lives with us. Do you know, I think I could do with a nice drink right about now. How about you my dear, or would you prefer tea? I am sorry, how rude of me for not having offered you something earlier.'

'A gin and tonic would be nice, if you have one. Thank you,' Jodie accepted amid concerns that her worst fear was about to become a reality. 'Am I to understand Kathy has found someone else?' she asked while Helen was busy at the cocktail cabinet.

'Oh no, it's nothing like that. She moved into a nice flat at the beginning of the year to be closer to the city. You see, she took a morning-only job when Adam started junior school. Now where was I? Oh yes, ice. Jodie, be a dear and fetch an ice tray from the kitchen. Run it under the hot tap for a few seconds.'

Splashing ice into both glasses and taking a deep swallow of her stiff brandy and ginger ale, Helen looked more composed by the time she handed Jodie her G&T. 'We still see them at least once a week. They are due tomorrow evening in fact. Kathy does a bit of shopping for me at the supermarket on a Friday, after fetching Adam from school. I no longer have the patience to queue for the odd imported items that actually make it onto our shelves these days.' Returning to her chair, Helen offered as an after thought, 'They usually stay for dinner and Paul occasionally pops in. You are more than welcome to join us, my dear.'

'Paul?' Jodie said nearly choking on her drink.

'He's just a friend of the family, nothing more.'

Taking another long draught of her drink, Helen cleared her throat, businesslike, 'Now then, my dear, I think it's time you levelled with me. How grave is our son's condition, if indeed this is our boy?'

Jodie put her glass down and crossed to kneel at Helen's side, taking the other woman's free hand in hers. 'You are a very insightful lady, Helen. Yes, he has a few issues but none he should not be able to overcome with help and some tender loving care,' she encouraged. 'Perhaps I should start from the beginning so you are fully in the picture. But first humour me, when did Paul come on the scene and what part does he play in Kathy's life?'

'Like I said, just a . . . friend,' Helen said hesitantly. 'Although at times I thought it might be better if there was more to it than that. We first met Paul shortly after we arrived in Harare. He and a few others called round from the Anglican Church to invite Kathy to join a fellowship group. He's a nice enough young American, an acquaintance of Gerald Bond in fact. The group meet a couple of evenings a month for tea and coffee, which has been beneficial for Kathy. I'm quite sure that's all there is to it.'

Jodie had barely finished her story when Alf Longdon arrived home from work and she was obliged to start over. Again she refrained from mentioning Nyoni, the situation being sensitive enough without inviting speculation.

The elderly Longdons having completed their cross examination, Alf said kindly, 'Miss Knight, thank you for bringing us this marvellous news. While Helen and I might not yet fully appreciate the significance of all you have told us, I am certain nothing in this world will keep Kathy from accompanying you back to South Africa. As I understand it you believe our son's rehabilitation could take some time. What I am trying to say, Miss Knight, is that we would certainly understand if you wished to continue on with your holiday. As it is, we can never repay all you have done for this family.'

'Mr Longdon, just seeing Tony reunited with his loved ones will be reward enough,' Jodie said sincerely. 'As for my holiday, I am sure father won't mind persevering a few days more to enable me to see this through,' she said with fingers crossed.

'Please drop the Mr, my dear,' Alf invited. 'You have already endeared yourself to us like one of the family.'

'That's very kind of you, Alf. As one of the family am I at liberty to ask how long you have been in Africa? You both still have very broad British accents, unlike Tony?'

'It's been. . . thirty-four years now. We came over just after Tony, our eldest, was born. We came out on one of the Castle Line ships, the Edinburgh Castle. I think after a certain age you retain. . .'

'Please excuse the impertinence my dear,' Helen interrupted on downing her drink, the fifth of the evening, 'but I simply must ask. What interest could a beautiful young woman possibly have in an older man, a recluse I think was how you described our son. Are you in love with him?' She surprised even Alf with her frankness.

Blushing, Jodie admitted, 'A few romantic notions perhaps but no, not love.' Having explained her initial interest in Tony she went on to point out, 'It was actually your son's curiosity that prompted his return to my hotel. I was of the view that he had come back to check on my recovery after my ordeal but . . . a friend firmly believes he subconsciously recognised in me a likeness to another, someone very special. That person could only have been Kathleen, and from what you have told me he must love her very dearly,' Jodie concluded, her eyes bright.

During the silence that followed, Helen dried her own eyes and Alf discreetly blew his nose. With a final sniff Helen said, 'That was most sincere and very reassuring, my dear. You really are a remarkable young lady and I think it's time we shared our little secret with you. You actually do bear an uncanny resemblance to Kathy, in her late teens. Besides the uncommonly green eyes, you share the same hair colouration and are both tall girls with lovely figures. I think I also speak for Alf when I say that, like Kathy, you too have won a special place in our hearts.'

Once they had all dried their eyes Alf refilled their glasses, discreetly halving Helen's measure, and recapped, 'Then, as I see it, Jodie will accompany Kathleen back to South Africa, tentatively the day after tomorrow, Saturday. Helen and I will contact Mark with the incredible news and arrange for him to meet you both at Louis Botha airport; as luck would have it the family live in Durban now. Mark was very close to his brother and is terribly fond of Kathy. Nothing will be too much trouble for him. Which just leaves the million-dollar question, how and when to break this fantastic news to Kathy?'

Having completely overcome her initial scepticism, Helen could not wait to give Kathy the good tidings. She argued her daughter-in-law was far stronger emotionally than she was given credit for. What was more, she believed it was inconceivable that Tony would not recognise his wife or brother.

'I think Miss Knight believes we might be overly optimistic,' Alf cautioned, having paid more attention to what the young English woman had been preparing them for. 'After all these years one more day is not the end of the world. I also agree with Jodie that it would be best if she could first contact Gerald in the morning, to confirm his progress in locating and returning Tony to the hotel in Hluhluwe.'

It was eventually decided that Jodie would return with Kathy's ticket around noon the following day, in good time for a final chat before Kathy and Adam's regular Friday evening visit. It was also decided that Adam should remain with his grandparents, to unburden Kathy and give her time to prepare Tony for the news that he had a son who she had adopted.

It was only during the drive back to the hotel that Jodie began to have second thoughts. Having sided with Alf she was now plagued by a nagging sixth sense; a feeling that every moment's delay was fraught with untold danger.

'Gerald, thank goodness! I have been calling the number you gave all morning, only to have your *associate* keep promising you would call me back. So much for keeping in touch! Now tell me, what news of Tony, how is he taking all this?'

'Calm down, Princess. I have just this minute set foot back in your room. The trip took longer than anticipated, thanks to someone neglecting to mention wandering off their line of march a dozen times; game viewing.'

'But you finally got there?' Jodie demanded anxiously.

'Yes, eventually.'

'Thank goodness. Was he agreeable to return with you? Is he there in the room with you now? You have got him?'

'No, no and no again, which is why I asked my guys to say I would call you once I got back. I did not want to alarm you unduly.'

'Should I be alarmed?'

'Can't I have a quick shower and a cold beer and then call you back?'

'*Gerald!*'

'All right, I'll get to the point. To start with it was Nyoni who actually found me, after I had again lost your tracks. She was on her way home from visiting family and friends in a local village.'

'What village? What family?' Jodie interrupted, adding before he could reply, 'Why didn't she take you straight to him?'

'She couldn't do that, because she has no idea where he is.

Apparently he never made it back to his part of the world after seeing you home.'

'What the hell do you mean?'

'I suggest you sit down, Princess.'

'*Oh my God*, I knew it, he was attacked by a wild animal . . . wasn't he?'

'No, it's nothing that dramatic. To cut a long story short I called in at the Holiday Inn on the way back, on the off-chance he had turned up around there. The good news is he had. The bad news being he is on his way up to Zimbabwe. He left Wednesday morning. He could even be there by now, or about to pitch up at any moment.'

'Gerald, this makes no sense. What could possibly have inspired him to return, and why now after all these years?'

'He was motivated by the same thing you were, to locate his wife. Now he knows he has one.'

'That's ridiculous; even if he has remembered something he would not even know where to start looking. Kathleen moved from Bulawayo up to Harare with the Longdons when Alf was transferred, as you know.'

'He knows just as much as you, because believe it or not you were the source.'

'Me! Impossible! I last set eyes on him at the Holiday Inn on Sunday evening and was only aware Kathleen even existed on the Monday, after my call to your mother.'

'Precisely, but you are forgetting Tony's informal intelligence network in the region, which includes the black clerks at the telephone exchange in Hluhluwe. Beer, ammunition and information being his main reasons for coming to town, you said. Apart from more congenial pursuits of late,' Gerald added in spite of himself. Prompted by the stony silence Gerald continued, 'Anyway, he blacked out or something after leaving you at the Holiday Inn. It was while the old Zulu housekeeper was caring for him that one of the operators from the local exchange reported your conversation with Gloria. Africans have an uncanny ability to remember things parrot fashion, so Tony would have got a verbatim account of your chat with my old lady.'

'*Unbelievable!* What are we to do now?'

'I'm not sure. More to the point, how has Kathy taken the news?'

'Gerald this . . . this is not good at all,' Jodie stammered. 'I was unable to meet with Kathy yesterday after I arrived. She has moved out to be closer to work. But I met with Helen and Alf and we decided, that is Alf and I decided, it would be best if we waited to break the news to Kathy this evening after having checked in with you first.'

'Not good indeed,' Gerald agreed, adding, 'It could get messy if Tony pops up out of the blue. Kathy will think she has seen a bloody ghost, even if she has been in denial. You had best give Alf and Helen a call and alert them to the possibility of their son pitching up on their doorstep.'

'They are still not on the telephone but they are expecting me for lunch. I will leave now, right after you tell me who Paul is. Helen mentioned his name and that you know him.'

'Oh yes, Paul. He's just another . . . *associate*. Good to hear he has kept in touch.'

'You are not the type to have churchy chums, but it will keep,' Jodie said curtly. 'One last thing before I go, how is Nyoni holding up?'

'Apart from being upset at Tony's disappearance, she seems happy enough getting on with her other life.'

'What other life?'

'It's a long story but suffice to say there is no need to worry about her. You on the other hand have some explaining to do. Correct me if I'm wrong but psychology is about getting into the patient's head, not his bed.'

'She told you . . . *everything?*' Jodie gasped.

'I doubt everything and in her defence I had to bribe her with a promise to return with news of Tony.'

'Gerald . . . I'm sorry, I realise now I should have been more forthright with you from the start. It's just that everything has been moving so fast. The situation with Tony was, well it was extremely awkward, almost surreal in fact. I can only . . .'

'Hold your horses, Princess. I gathered it was pretty bizarre. I will keep your bed warm as agreed, and if you are still of a mind to do so when you get back you can bare your soul then. The clock is ticking and you should be on your way, good luck, Princess,' Gerald said kindly.

Face to Face

Having lost consciousness in the bush on Sunday evening, Tony was discovered the following morning by an old herdsman. Abandoning his cattle the old man had run the ten kilometres back to the Holiday Inn and summoned Grace, the buxom black housekeeper. Taking charge of his rifle, and with the help of the off-duty kitchen staff, she had managed to get the dehydrated and feverish white man back to her quarters behind the hotel.

Thanks to copious drafts of herbal *muti*, which Grace forced down him, the fever broke the following afternoon and Tony slept on into the night. He awoke at dawn, naked and ravenous, in a small badly lit room. By the time he had finished a second bowl of sweet maize porridge, Grace had returned with his laundered shorts and bush shirt. Only once her charge had dressed did she give the nod to the bespectacled, middle-aged African who had been waiting patiently outside the confined quarters since late the previous afternoon.

Sidling into the cramped stuffy room, the clerk knelt and bowed his head until his gaze was at a respectful level below that of the white man, now sitting in a chair next to the bed.

'Speak now Jeremiah,' Grace commanded amiably, herself none the worse for wear from having slept two nights on the floor. 'Tell the *Nkosi* what is so important that it kept you from your bed and that new young wife of yours this night.'

Clearing his throat the studious ex-schoolteacher, ex-terrorist, repeated word for word the conversation he had eavesdropped on at the telephone exchange the previous day. He omitted nothing, having gone over his story a dozen times during the long hours of darkness.

315

'You have done well, Jeremiah. It is good I spared your hide and got you a job at the Post Office.'

Stepping out to get some fresh air and shake off the heady effect of the *muti*, Tony realised he had always known a time would come when he would have to confront his destiny. Thanks to the persistence of a prim English girl, who had somehow pieced together his past, that time was now.

Rewarding Jeremiah with a handshake and a pat on the back, Tony turned to Grace, 'And you Mamma, I cannot thank enough,' he smiled, clapping slowly in a sign of gratitude.

'You go now to Zimbabwe, to find your people?' the big comely woman enquired fondly.

'Yes Mamma, I have been away too long. Should I not return, please hand my rifle in at the charge office.'

Accepting a packet of aspirin for the journey, Tony took his leave. He planned to hitch-hike across country to Messina and ford the Limpopo river down stream from the border post at Beitbridge, before heading north to Harare via Masvingo.

Having made it to the border in under twenty-four hours, Tony forded the drought-stricken Limpopo before sunrise to avoid detection. Tourists gave him a wide berth once back on the highway, and it was late afternoon before a long-distance removal van finally stopped for him.

Arriving in Harare shortly before dawn on Friday morning, Tony dropped down from the cab of the removal van. Dishevelled and bleary eyed he waved goodbye to the African driver and his assistant. Moving into the light of a shop front on the deserted pavement, he took stock of his situation. Apart from a still-damp two-Rand note, four of the original two-dozen aspirin and three loose rounds of ammunition, he possessed only the grimy clothes on his back.

Having trudged out to the plush northern suburbs, only to learn from the domestics in the still sleeping neighbourhood that Mrs Longdon junior had recently moved to a flat in town, he was left with a dilemma; look up his parents while in the area or continue on with his quest to find his wife. He concluded that coming face to face with a wife he would not know was marginally less daunting than meeting parents he had no recollection of.

Oblivious to his unkempt appearance and fighting off nauseating exhaustion and a persistent throbbing behind his eyes, Tony cursed the early morning motorists who passed him on his long hike back into the city. It was mid morning before he finally made it to the block of flats he had been directed to, only this time to be informed by the Madam's maid that Kathleen was not expected home until late evening.

'Friday the Madam she does the big shopping at Haddon and Sly,' the maid obliged. 'She is then going over to Madam Helen, her mother-in-law, for the dinner.' About to close the door the maid stood her ground a moment longer, critically eyeing up the big unshaven man now slumped against the passage wall. 'The boss he is sick?' she asked before disappearing back into the flat, to reappear a moment later with a tumbler of water.

Accepting the water, Tony swallowed down the last of the aspirin before wordlessly setting off again. Making it to the supermarket on a second wind he took himself off to one of the less busy side aisles, vaguely aware of his vagabond appearance.

The effort of focusing his attention on every European woman who entered through the turnstiles, in a vain attempt at recognising a feature or a familiar gesture, soon took its toll. As the stabbing pain behind his eyes intensified he found himself wavering on the spot. During periodic bouts of nausea and dizziness he missed several new arrivals, including a tall, well-groomed woman with chestnut-brown hair and unusually green eyes, a handsome, fair-haired little boy at her side. Had it not been for a sudden commotion kicked up by a group of excited housewives, converging on a particular shelf at the end of the aisle in which he stood, Kathleen Longdon would have come and gone without him knowing it.

Gritting his teeth Tony strained to focus on the unruly throng now milling boisterously around the black shop assistant, only a few metres from him. The women were bent on clearing the shelf as fast as the poor girl could stock it. When a tin was knocked to the floor, he recognised the bonanza as a consignment of white pepper.

Preoccupied, trying to control the sporadic shivers that racked his body, Tony was slow to register the demure young woman standing discreetly back from the rabble, calmly waiting her turn at the spoils. As the wave of enthused shoppers swept by, in search of other post-independence scarcities, the young woman unhurriedly approached the shelf. There was something about her poise that held what little concentration Tony was still able to muster.

Looking up after placing her purchase in the trolley, now being ably manoeuvred into position by the self-confident little boy, Kathleen stifled a cry. Although not loud her muffled scream sufficed to stop the unsightly individual, now bearing down on them, in mid-stride. Throwing an arm about her son's shoulders, as he moved purposefully closer to protect his mother, she spun the trolley and the plucky youngster around, away from the vagrant now blocking the aisle.

Even with her back to the unsightly individual, Kathy could not escape those haunting eyes or the vision of the gruesome scar beneath the greyish stubble of his beard. She had not gone five paces when, on impulse, she half turned to look back over her shoulder. The vagrant had not moved and those anxious, troubled eyes remained fixed on her. Slowly, involuntarily she turned to confront the stranger.

It was at that moment, with fatigue, coupled with the bright lights and unfamiliar hustle and bustle, threatening to overwhelm him, that Tony subconsciously started to twiddle a lock of hair at the nape of his neck.

With tears of disbelief misting her vision and with Tony's lips moving wordlessly, the couple continued to stare at one another, memories telescoping the gulf between them.

It was Adam, perturbed by this silly staring game, who eventually broke the spell. 'Come along Mummy, we are keeping Grandma

318

waiting. You also promised me an ice-cream, remember?' The youngster was insistent and pulled urgently at his mother's arm, now hanging listlessly at her side.

Although Adam had barely spoken above a respectful whisper, the word *Mummy* resonated through Tony's numbed senses as if boomed from a megaphone. Reeling, he took a few faltering steps backwards. Rooted to the spot, Kathleen managed only a quick horrified glance down at Adam, before the man who had lived in her heart all these years turned on his heels and lunged drunkenly away down the aisle.

With images of virgin tracks of African savannah looming ever larger in his mind's eye, Tony crashed through a display stand in his bid to escape the claustrophobic confines of the supermarket. In full flight by the time he reached the exit, he hurdled the nearest turnstile and charged on out through the front doors. Cutting a swathe through the pedestrians on the pavement as he went, it seemed as if nothing could stop his desperate retreat.

There was a screech of brakes, followed by a sickening thud and the sound of breaking glass. The agonising scream on Kathleen's lips was drowned out by the hysterical wailing of the African women on the pavement, who had witnessed the white man's suicidal dash into the path of the municipal bus.

Sobbing uncontrollably as she clawed a path through the throng, now converging at the scene of the gory accident, Kathleen thrust Adam bodily into the arms of an unsuspecting fellow white shopper, with a plea, 'Hold on to him for goodness sake.'

Tony lay on his back in an ever-growing pool of blood, only the upper half of his body protruding from beneath the large green vehicle. With the crowd forming ghost-like above him, he managed a weak smile as Kathleen entered his blurred vision and slowly descended, as if out of a dream, to kneel at his side.

'Tony!' she sobbed lifting his head and placing it gently onto a threadbare cardigan, which a faceless old Shona gentleman had thoughtfully handed down from the crowd. 'Tony,' she repeated, taking up a bloody hand and giving it a gentle, reassuring squeeze.

'You came back, my love,' she whispered as his eyes focused on her. 'Who knows what horrors you have suffered, and now this. *Oh my God*,' she breathed, a trembling finger tracing the cruel, jagged scar down the side of his face to where it met the dull purple tissue of the burns on his neck and chest.

As he tried to speak, a red froth oozed from between his lips, followed by a hollow gurgling sound.

'Don't speak. I understand my darling,' Kathleen comforted as she wiped away the crimson spittle with the hem of her skirt and placed a finger gently on his lips to seal them. 'It was those terrible scars, wasn't it my darling . . . that kept you from me,' she sniffed, her handbag and tissues abandoned with the trolley. Still blinking back her tears she felt the weak but perceptible pressure of Tony's hand in hers. It was as if he was satisfied that she had come close to the truth, in part at least.

'I have shared your scars all these years, my love. After everything we had been through together I could not accept that God could be so unkind as to take you from me, not like that, not without so much as a goodbye, my love.' It was only as she wiped the tears from her cheeks with the back of her hand that she noticed with dismay that his eyes were no longer open. It was then, above the buzz of the crowd, that she heard the wail of a siren.

A moment later the crowd eased back, as if on some invisible signal, leaving Kathleen alone in a small island of space at the side of the bus. Looking up she fully expected to see a white-coated ambulance attendant; instead Adam strode boldly up to her from out of the crowd.

A serious expression etched on his handsome face, the six-year-old, going on seven, placed a comforting arm about his mother's neck, right there in the road where she knelt. Looking down at the dark, sticky pool of blood on the tarmac at his feet, Adam asked with knitted brow, 'Has the man gone to heaven, Mummy?'

Blinded by tears, Kathleen beseeched the sea of black faces above them, in the hope that someone would come forward and take charge of the boy. But it was not to be. The grip suddenly tightened on her hand and she was amazed to see Tony peering intently up at them both, his face contorted but his eyes attentive. He was struggling to focus on the child with the fair hair and bright, intelligent blue eyes, standing next to his mother. Adam in turn craned his head round, to better see the upside-down face of the man at his feet.

'Oh, my God, Tony it's not what you think,' Kathleen cried, pulling Adam down onto his knees at his father's side. Although alarmed by his mother's tears and fearful of the blood on the ground now soaking into his jeans, which he had managed to keep clean since changing in the car after school, Adam gritted his teeth and resolved to be brave – brave like the soldier father he had never known but of whom his mother so often spoke. There were even occasions, he remembered fondly, when she would let him hold his father's medals, awarded posthumously, she had explained.

'Tony, listen to me,' Kathy pleaded as she took his head between her hands and gently tilted it in an effort to help him better see the boy. 'This is Adam, your son, my darling. Do you understand? He is your son, yours and Victoria's, Victoria Bond.' Kathleen thought she saw Tony's frown deepen, but before he could respond she found herself and Adam being unceremoniously hauled to their feet. Ignoring her protests, the two African ambulance attendants ushered them firmly out of the way.

To her horror they then proceeded to manhandle Tony out from under the bus and onto a stretcher. Turning to the medical orderly, hovering at the back of the ambulance, dispassionately surveying the scene with a half-smoked cigarette dangling from his lips, Kathleen pleaded, 'Aren't they first going to check him over, stabilise him, insert a drip or something?'

'These boys are not paramedics and I can only do so much,' the surly individual shrugged, hands in the pockets of his grubby white dustcoat.

'Only do so much . . . you haven't lifted a finger! So help me, I'll report . . .' but she was cut off in mid sentence as the orderly shouldered his way past her. Having eagerly descended upon the articles that had fallen out of what was left of the casualty's torn bush shirt the orderly had a self-satisfied, evil smirk on his face as he stood up.

Unaware that the officious individual had surreptitiously pocketed a crumpled, blood-stained two-Rand note and three rounds of 7.62-mm ammunition, Kathleen desperately tried a different approach. 'We are family and wish to accompany the ambulance. Please?'

'Out of the question,' scoffed the orderly. 'We have another accident to attend to; a truck of farm labourers at a level crossing, bad news that one. Then we must collect a maternity case, if we have room.' Prodding Kathy in the chest he added, 'You whites can thank the bloody racist apartheid regime in South Africa for our shortage of ambulances, fuel and spares.'

'Then just give us one minute, please,' Kathy begged as she drew level with the stretcher, urgently seeking Tony's hand beneath the threadbare red blanket. Putting her lips to his ear she whispered in desperation, 'Adam is your son. Victoria gave birth . . . before she died. Gerald brought Adam and me together and I have loved him as my own ever since. Don't you see he's *our son* now?'

Tony's cheek twitched but his eyes remained closed. His complexion had taken on a greyish pallor, the bleeding having started afresh while he was being bundled onto the stretcher.

'My darling, we will follow you to the hospital. I love you and Adam really is . . .' But Kathleen stopped mid-sentence, Tony's grip tightening on her hand; as if in silent acknowledgement. Her joy was short-lived as the belligerent orderly pulled her away from the stretcher.

As the double white doors slammed shut behind Tony, Kathleen drew Adam to her and prayed. They watched the ambulance weave precariously through the traffic, until it was out of sight, its siren wailing into the distance.

Once the crowd had drifted away leaving them alone on the

pavement, Adam tugged at his mother's hand. 'Was that man a solider, Mummy?' he asked studiously, the big bullets that the nasty man in the white coat had picked up not having gone unnoticed by sharp young eyes. 'A soldier and *my daddy?*'

.

Cheating Fate

It was dark by the time a distraught Jodie Knight made it back to her hotel. She ran up the two flights of stairs to her room, rather than risk the lift that was prone to getting stuck between floors. Everything had happened so fast, the accident, the dash to the hospital with Alf and Helen, followed by her introduction to a near hysterical Kathleen and a very tired Adam. Then the police, half a dozen of them, milling around the casualty ward demanding non-existent papers, levelling accusations and repeatedly insisting that Tony was a foreign agent, a spy from South Africa.

They had ignored the European doctor's protest that the patient could die without surgery to remove his spleen. The African detective in charge of the case going so far as to insist that the unconscious spy be revived long enough to sign a confession.

'National security is paramount,' Jodie had heard the man bellowing at the doctor as she fled the hospital to find a working public telephone and seek help, eventually having to resort to returning to the hotel in desperation.

Receiving no reply from the British embassy at that hour, Jodie held her breath while waiting to be put through to the Zululand Safari Lodge. Barely able to hear Gerald above the din once connected and with her nerves at breaking point, she screamed, 'What's all that commotion?'

'You are through to the bar, Princess. I'm having a couple of beers with your father, while we wait to hear back from you. He's not a bad old . . .'

'Gerald, for God's sake, *something dreadful has happened.* Tony's going to die.'

324

'He's what?'

'*Dying*,' Jodie shouted into the mouthpiece. 'They are refusing to let the doctors near him. God, it's unbelievable. I tried the embassy . . .'

'*Quiet!*' Gerald bellowed and a deathly hush descended over the happy hour crowd in the Assegai Bar. Removing his hand from the mouthpiece, he encouraged, 'Take it easy, where are you calling from?'

'Back at the Jameson Hotel.'

'Good, now just relax and tell me what's happened.'

Jodie explained as best she could about the accident, the accusations and the fact that Adam had said something to his mother about the man at the scene finding bullets where Tony had lain. Sobbing, Jodie concluded, 'Gerald, I just know these . . . these bastards are going to sit back and let him die if they don't get their trumped-up confession signed. It's quite unbelievable, they cuffed Alf about the head several times, and just *laughed* at us women. They were like a pack of hounds baying for blood and . . .'

'Let's not get too carried away, we don't want to *upset anybody* now do we?' Gerald cautioned, adding, 'We half expected something like this.'

'That there would be an accident?' Jodie said in disbelief.

'No, that someone without papers could fall foul of the authorities. The police are understandably cautious; a few months ago saboteurs blew up half of their military air capability on the ground at Thornhill airbase. The authorities are only doing their job and it's not for us to question their methods.'

'You can't be bloody serious,' Jodie said shaking her head in disbelief. 'The man's *critical* I tell you,' she screamed for the second time that night.

'I have never been more serious Miss Knight. Just calm down and *let events take their course*. This is Africa,' Gerald hissed.

'Africa be damned!' Jodie shouted, continuing to vent her spleen. 'As far as I . . .'

'One more thing, Miss Knight,' Gerald interrupted calmly,

ignoring her outburst, 'There has been a change to your *travel arrangements*. Someone from Flame Lily Tours will drop off a revised itinerary later this evening. Please stay put and get ready to move on, we don't want you missing the boat now, do we.'

'What boat? What's with all this . . .?'

'No need to fret, Miss Knight,' Gerald cut in. 'The Flame Lily people are very professional and will *take care of everything*,' he said hanging up before she could protest further.

Jodie slowly replaced the receiver; the penny had dropped. She felt a chill run down her spine as she crossed to the window and instinctively closed the curtains. Having checked the latch on the door she hurried though to the bedroom to pack. Resisting the urge to phone the hospital, she prayed they were not all going to live to regret the blind faith she was placing in Gerald.

She had dozed off in the armchair and awoke with a start at the rapping on her door. Fully dressed and packed, she glanced at her watch as she cautiously crossed the room. It was just after three o'clock in the morning, far later than she had expected anyone to be calling; considering the apparent urgency.

'Who . . . who is it?' she whispered.

'Paul, and I have your revised itinerary,' came the urgent reply in an unmistakable American drawl.

'Paul?' Jodie questioned as she deliberately fumbled the lock.

'Flame Lily Tours and we don't have all bloody night.'

'*That* Paul?' Jodie persisted.

'Kathleen's friend, one and the same, lady,' Paul grumbled bursting into the room the moment the latch clicked.

'Two suitcases, fuck,' he muttered under his breath as he checked the room to make sure nothing had been left behind.

'One is a vanity case,' Jodie protested as Paul grabbed the luggage, motioning with his head for her to follow.

'The stairs are this way,' she called out, letting the door slam shut in her haste to redirect him.

'Keep it *down* lady; we leave the way I came in.'

'No checkout,' Jodie mouthed lamely.

'Missy, this place could be swarming with bloody cops any minute from now.'

'I still think I deserve an explanation,' she protested as she was bundled out of the passage window onto a dark, windswept fire escape. Once on the landing it was all she could do to keep her skirt down.

'Nice legs, should appeal to the local plain-clothed sleuths,' Paul whispered. 'They don't give explanations either so what's it to be, sit around and wait for them or get the hell out of here?'

Jodie managed to hold her tongue until Paul ducked into an unlit alley, two blocks down from the hotel. 'What is this then?' she demanded pulling up short and staring at the ominous-looking police car in the shadows.

'It's on *loan* and will not be missed. Police vehicles are about the only semi-reliable means of transport in Zim these days, what with the spares and fuel crisis. The cops in Harare drink like bloody fish, generally on the house and more than usual on Friday nights. As a result vehicles get written off or misplaced with monotonous regularity,' Paul said in lighter mood, encouraged by their having made it this far.

Once they had cleared the city lights and were speeding into the country along a dark, deserted highway, Jodie cleared her throat. 'Perhaps now you can spare a moment to explain all this cloak and dagger stuff? What's to become of the Longdons and where are you taking me?'

'Relax,' Paul grinned. 'Everything has been taken care of, remember. I am not at liberty to say more right now.'

'Why can't you say, the police don't bug their own vehicles do they?'

'No, missy, but interrogations go well beyond thumbscrews in this part of the world. Should we not make it for any reason, we could jeopardise the mission and the lives of your friends.'

'Relax, everything's taken care of, but we might not make it and could be tortured!' Jodie recapped sarcastically. 'Do you treat everybody like mushrooms?'

'What I can tell you is we were the last to leave and have less than three hours to cover some three hundred and thirty kilometres to the rendezvous.'

Jodie consoled herself checking the mileage odometer every few minutes, to mentally update the estimated time of their arrival. They had been travelling for little over an hour when a flashing red light in the road ahead caught her attention. Turning in alarm as the police car decelerated, Jodie watched in astonishment as the slightly built American, with close-cropped ginger hair, drew a huge silver pistol from an ankle holster and laid it across his lap.

'Just a precaution,' he explained as he caught Jodie's expression in the green light from the dashboard. 'We are expecting company but you can't be too careful.' With that he took a packet of king-size Rothmans filter cigarettes from his shirt pocket, 'Cigarette?' he offered.

'Do you have to smoke in the car?' Jodie asked as he tapped one out and lit it anyway, using an expensive-looking gold Ronson.

As the squad car caught up with the ambulance, Paul flashed his headlights and pulled out alongside. Getting a glimpse of the white face behind the wheel, he acknowledged the driver's thumbs up and pulled ahead of the ambulance. Both drivers then switched off their lights and the small convoy sped on, the first signs of dawn streaking the eastern horizon.

'Your friends, Tony Longdon and family,' Paul nodded back over his shoulder as he re-holstered his gun.

'You snatched them . . . all of them?'

'There would have been no stopping Kathy, even if we had considered it safe to leave her and Adam to follow by more conventional means. Alf and Helen opted to sit it out rather than slow us down. They should be OK if they stick to their story of mistaken identity. State records in Zimbabwe never lie and will show their son, the spy, is long dead.'

'But Tony's condition . . . surely he's in no fit state to travel?' Jodie voiced her concern.

'Sure, the journey could kill him,' Paul acknowledged dispassionately. 'He was dead anyway had he stayed. We had no choice but to extract him before he lost more blood or they got round to transferring him to a maximum-security facility. Hopefully the doctor we hijacked as well can keep him alive, until we can get him proper medical attention.'

'Hopefully!' Jodie echoed, finding it hard to associate the nonchalant individual next to her with the supposedly caring, God-fearing person who had befriended Kathleen through the church.

'How well do you know Kathy?' she asked.

'Well enough, but not in the way you are thinking,' Paul acknowledged with characteristic bluntness. 'We are just friends. Part of my assignment has been keeping an eye on her, but for her sake I would not like that generally known.'

'Assignment!'

'Simply making sure no harm came to her and Adam,' Paul said as he lit another cigarette from the stub of the last, ignoring Jodie's frown. 'She has no idea I'm part of this caper and that's how it has to remain, this time for my sake. OK?'

'I don't believe the half of it.'

'That's your prerogative, *Princess*,' Paul said smiling for the first time since they met. 'General Gerry suggested I call you Princess, should you need convincing of my credentials.'

'He has some nerve and he's certainly no general!'

'True, but it won't be long at the rate he's going.'

'What is he now then?'

'That's classified.'

'Naturally,' Jodie nodded. 'What of Kathleen's . . . surveillance, is that also classified?'

'Nothing untoward there, missy, just something I volunteered to do while based in this country. Personal favour to the general while he's . . . committed down south. I guess the man's a little paranoid since he lost his sister to terrorists. Anyway, I reckon the arrangement has worked well for all concerned; it's not easy meeting decent folk in our line of work.'

Detecting the sadness in the older man's voice, Jodie let the matter rest, making a mental note instead to add Paul to the growing list of questions she was storing up for General Gerry, when next they met.

As the sky turned from red to pink in the east, Jodie stretched and stifled a yawn. 'Are we getting close to our hush-hush rendezvous point yet?'

'We are still about half an hour out; get a bit more shuteye while you can. I'll wake you in good time to powder your nose. With less than fifty kilometres to go I reckon the odds have improved to about four to one, in our favour,' he encouraged with a smile.

'*That good!*' Jodie exclaimed, shuddering as she tucked her feet back under her on the seat.

When next she opened her eyes it was daylight and she found herself sitting bolt upright, the wail of sirens piercing the tranquillity of the morning. Glancing in the side view mirror she saw the ambulance still on their tail, only it was silent.

'Where . . . what in blazes?'

'I'm afraid the shit's hit the fan, sweetheart. The fucking flying squad is in hot pursuit, less than a kilometre back. The bastards were waiting for us ten kilometres this side of Masvingo, Fort Victoria in the old days. Home of the famed Zimbabwe Ruins,' Paul explained.

'Bugger the geography lesson, what now?' Jodie demanded pulling down the sun visor before realising just how ridiculous she must look, checking her make-up at a time like this. Even before Paul had given her a pained sideways glance, she had closed the visor. 'Any bright ideas?' she persisted.

'Wait until the vehicle is stationary before applying lipstick,' he laughed.

'I meant the flying squad, you *moron!*'

'Pray, failing which we shoot it out,' Paul suggested, slowing down and pulling over to let the ambulance pass. Four blue and white squad cars now filled their rear view mirror, two abreast and closing fast.

'Holy shit,' Paul cursed aloud as they crested the next rise and the roadblock loomed ominously into view. 'The language gets bad from here on out, sweetie,' he warned reaching round and hauling an AK-47 assault rifle out from under the travel rug on the back seat. Cocking the weapon while steering with his knees, he thrust it into Jodie's lap. Reaching back he grabbed a second rifle.

'Your safety is off and the weapon is set on semi-automatic, just point and squeeze, *short bursts*, got it,' he explained, the tension in his voice discernible for the first time.

'It's moving!' Jodie cried out as the huge obstruction they had taken for a roadblock came hurtling down the road towards them, its port and starboard lights flashing red and green respectively.

'Thank fuck for the marines!' Paul rejoiced as the enormous camouflaged Super Frelon screamed overhead, its 20-mm cannon ripping holes in the macadam in the path of the hapless posse.

'Who in blazes are they?' Jodie asked, swivelling around in her seat, and sending a burst of automatic fire through the windscreen in the process. 'Jesus Christ!' she gasped.

'Not quite Jesus Christ but those boys are just as welcome, lady,' Paul replied as he snatched the rifle from her and made it safe, before tossing it onto the back seat. 'Watch yourself with all this glass,' he warned as the chill morning air rushed in and they were showered with chips from what was once the windscreen. Adjusting the rear view mirror to watch the action behind, Paul was in time to see both of the leading police vehicles peel off and crash headlong through the bush on opposite sides of the road.

Looking back, Jodie was about to cheer when the car on the left came to a neck-breaking halt against a culvert, catapulting the passenger through the windscreen in a crimson spray. Simultaneously, the car on the right launched itself off a termite mound, somersaulted in mid-air and land on its roof, exploding seconds later in a sheet of yellow flame.

'Oh . . . my . . . God!' Jodie exclaimed, throwing her hands up over her eyes. Peering through her fingers over the back of her seat she saw the remaining two patrol cars brake violently and execute tyre-burning U-turns, only to collide in the centre of the road. Having completed half a dozen gut-wrenching revolutions locked together, as if in some grotesque mating ritual, they skidded off into the bush in a shower of dust and gravel.

'He's letting them get away!' Jodie yelled as the helicopter banked sharply and came windmilling back to catch up with the convoy. Its undercarriage of six wheels, grouped in three pairs, resembled the spread talons of a huge bird of prey.

'I should hope so, missy. Hell, we are not here to start a bloody war, leastwise not just yet.'

'Who is flying that thing?' Jodie shouted as the helicopter screamed back overhead. She was still waiting for a reply when she found herself slammed against the door, the car having swung off the main road to shudder down a corrugated dirt farm track in frenzied pursuit of the ambulance, which in turn was lumbering after the helicopter.

'My guess would be your boyfriend, Princess,' Paul shouted to make himself heard above the noise of the wind whistling through the shattered windscreen as the car came back on an even keel. 'Reckon he'll be grounded for a spell after this though. His bit of fun with the cannon is likely to spark an international incident, not to mention half the population of Masvingo now cowering under their bloody beds. But that's his problem. This is the end of the line for me.'

'You're not coming with us?' Jodie shot back in disbelief, slipping on her shoes and frantically gathering up her belongings.

'Not this time,' Paul confirmed, adding soberly, 'Remember, not a word to Kathy about my involvement.' With that Paul floored the accelerator and pulled ahead of the ambulance once more. 'Hang on,' he warned this time, before swerving off the road and crashing the squad car through a barbed-wire fence, forging a path through a ploughed field for the ambulance as they went.

Paul brought the battered vehicle to a halt thirty metres from where the massive helicopter was already setting down in a cyclone of its own dust. Reaching across Jodie to open her door, Paul encouraged, 'Cheer up sweetheart, we made it didn't we? They will have a medical team on board; Tony now at least has a fighting chance.'

'But . . . what about you,' Jodie choked emotionally, her eyes brimming as she squeezed his arm and planted a kiss on his cheek. 'Are you going to be all right? What about the . . . police?'

'I'll be just fine if you're a good girl and get the hell on out of here, pronto. And the police aren't the problem any more, honey. Thanks to General Gerry this area is going to be crawling with fucking Fifth Brigadiers before long.' With that he pecked her back on the cheek and unceremoniously shoved her out of the car, just as the back door was flung open and someone dragged her cases off the seat.

Jodie managed a final wave as Paul wheel-spun the car in reverse, all the way back to the breach in the fence. Her cry of good luck was lost above the piercing whine of the gyrating rotors.

Staggering over the uneven ground behind the fellow with her suitcases, Jodie saw two other men already loading a stretcher through the gaping rear hatchway of the helicopter. A third man was helping Kathy and Adam over the rough terrain, while a fourth carried their luggage. All the men were blackened up, wore battle fatigues with commando-type balaclavas and had machine pistols slung over their shoulders. The abducted white doctor stood wide-eyed next to the ambulance, abandoned where it had come to a permanent halt in a particularly deep furrow.

Willing hands pulled Jodie aboard and by the time she had been strapped in behind the forward bulkhead, the turbine engines were screaming at peak pitch. The ungainly machine bounced once on its uneven footing and lifted off. Dropping its nose, it droned across the open field like a giant dragonfly, rapidly gathering speed as its six rotors cut through the heavy morning air.

They were still hedge hopping to avoid radar detection when they crossed the Limpopo river. The blackened-up gunner relaxed his vigilance and waved to get Jodie's attention. Slipping off his headset he passed it to her, indicating the button she should press to speak into the mouthpiece.

'Hello, General Gerry, please,' she said depressing the red button.

'Hi, Princess,' he replied with a laugh. 'Welcome aboard. My apologies for the enforced radio silence while out of SA air space. How did you know it was me flying this baby?'

'Sorry, that's classified,' Jodie mimicked as she poked her head round the bulkhead and looked up into the elevated flight deck. She immediately recognised Gerald grinning down at her, in spite of his helmet. She also noticed Adam for the first time, sitting between his uncle and the co-pilot.

'I never thought I'd be this happy to see anybody again in my whole life Gerry. Actually, I still prefer Gerald,' she confessed. 'I trust you kept the bed warm in my absence,' she chided light-heartedly now that the danger had passed. 'Cat got your tongue?' she giggled. 'All right, changing the subject then, what have they done with Kathleen and how is Tony doing?'

'We have them back here with us in a makeshift ward, Miss Knight,' a stranger with an Afrikaans accent confirmed, adding obligingly, 'Tony's stable and his vitals are improving. I'm confident he can hold on until we get him into surgery. Once we have sorted out the immediate problems, we should also be able to tidy up the burns and other scarring with a few skin grafts.'

'That's marvellous news. Thank you, Doctor,' Jodie said before enquiring sheepishly, 'Gerald, can . . . everybody hear me over this thing?'

'No, only me, the rest of the crew and the medical team, Princess,' Gerald chuckled.

'I see,' Jodie said blushing but undaunted. 'Hi everybody it's me again. Kathy, how are you holding up, dear?'

'She can't hear you I'm afraid Miss, she's out for the count but resting comfortably. We gave her a sedative earlier. Is there anything we can do for you?'

'I think I will be all right, thank you, Doctor. Just a little light-headed due to all the excitement, I guess.'

'Understandable. Sorry we can't offer you a hot cup of tea but we left at pretty short notice.'

'Please, no apologies, I hate to think what might have been had you not arrived when you did. Back over to you Gerald. Are you permitted to say when we are likely to get wherever it is we are going? I think I might be in need of the little girl's room before long.'

'We land in about twenty minutes. They have cleared us through to Louis Trichardt, the closest town with an ICU. I imagine they will have a loo,' he joked. 'There should also be a fixed-wing charter standing by to take you back to Hluhluwe.'

'Will we be parting so soon?' Jodie asked, unable to hide her disappointment and conscious of the lump in her throat.

'I'll get the Longdons settled and meet up with you in a couple of days, after I have returned this baby and sorted out the paperwork. That's about it for now, Princess. I need to check in with air traffic control for our approach. Why don't you put your head back and catch forty winks.'

'No thanks! The last time I tried that I woke up with half the Zimbabwean police force in hot pursuit.'

'You were never in Zimbabwe, my girl,' Gerald cautioned. 'It's important you remember that. Your passport will receive the necessary attention as soon as we land. Over and out.'

The moment the Super Frelon touched down, Gerald's voice crackled over the headphones, 'Good news folks, just received word from a safe house in never-never-land. The bloody Yank made it home in time for brunch.' The spontaneous round of applause was heard above the dying whine of the engines and Jodie finally succumbed, sobbing openly into her hands.

The days that followed passed slowly for Jodie while she waited for word from Gerald. She had taken to reading the local newspapers, convinced that their audacious Zimbabwean escapade would make the news given its dramatic humanitarian appeal. It was on the third day, while scanning a copy of the *Natal Mercury* in the lounge, that she noticed a brief statement from the South African

Ministry of Defence on page four and made the connection. *A spokesman in Pretoria has denied President Mugabe's claim that South Africa has again violated Zimbabwe's airspace. The government has disclaimed all knowledge of a military offensive, supported by helicopter gun-ships, which is reputed to have resulted in the deaths of five members of the Zimbabwean Security Forces and an as yet unconfirmed number of civilians.* Jodie shook her head as she reflected on Gerald's words: *this is Africa.*

The chatter in the Assegai Bar dropped perceptibly as Gerald Bond made his entrance during the cocktail hour, the locals having been bellowed into silence not a week earlier. As he made his way across the room to where Kathy sat with her father, Samantha followed him down on the other side of the bar pouring a cold Castle. It was apparent from his tight-lipped expression that his disposition had not improved.

'He's still with us but it's not good news I'm afraid, Princess,' Gerald said as Jodie turned to find him at her side. Shaking hands with Brenton, who looked genuinely pleased to see him, Gerald kissed Jodie on the cheek and whispered in her ear, 'You did very well back there. And all is forgiven in respect of that earlier matter.'

'Thank you,' Jodie acknowledged coyly before asking, 'Just how bad is it then?'

'They removed his spleen but it will be touch and go if they can save his left leg.'

Finally taking the beer from a very patient Samantha, Gerald drained his glass before continuing grimly, 'They flew in a specialist surgical team from Johannesburg just as I was leaving this afternoon.' Placing a comforting arm around Jodie he added, 'We should hear later this evening, one way or the other.'

Thankful at least that Gerald was prepared to put the matter of her indiscretion with Tony behind them, Jodie still felt a lingering sense of guilt. 'Had I not got involved none of this would have happened,' she lamented, moving closer into Gerald's arms. 'I should have left well enough alone.'

'That's unfair, Princess, you did what had to be done. Tony was

336

becoming a danger to himself and others the more confused and depressed he got. At least now he will receive the help and support he needs. Kathy tells me there was definitely a breakthrough of sorts in the supermarket and then again while waiting for the ambulance. There is obviously a long road ahead but at least the signs are encouraging. His brother Mark is also at his bedside now and if anyone can get through to Tony it's that guy; what a character.'

'He's right, my dear,' Brenton interjected helpfully. 'From what I gather this fellow could have fared far worse if left to his own devices. And on the bright side, were it not for him you would not have met Gerald,' he said with a smile. 'As for you young man, I cannot thank you enough for bringing my girl back safely from . . . you know where.' He grinned. 'We are truly in your debt.'

Taking the older man's outstretched hand once more, Gerald noticed how comparatively steady it was. 'I don't have the foggiest idea what you are talking about but you are welcome anyway, Sir,' he said, acknowledging his newfound ally. 'Once again my apologies for sticking your head under the tap last Friday.'

'I should be thanking you for sobering me up, a timely reminder of the futility of trying to drown one's problems with alcohol,' Brenton said proffering his glass of red grape juice. 'This time I am determined to remain a teetotaler, for Jodie and Christine's sake, as much as my own.'

'That will make us all very proud Daddy,' Jodie said, giving him a hug.

'Talking about Christine, didn't you intend giving her a call this evening. It's gone six o'clock,' Jodie said pointedly. 'Give mother my love and say I will talk to her in the morning.'

'It's still afternoon back home but I'll leave you two to your catching up, Princess.' Brenton teased as he finished his drink.

Once her father had left, Jodie turned to Gerald and suggested, 'I think we would be more comfortable outside.' Slipping her arm through his she steered him out of the busy, smoky bar.

Leaning over the railing on the rambling thatched veranda, they watched the setting sun bathe the horizon in a blaze of colour. It was Gerald who broke the silence. 'The war killed or crippled thousands of Rhodesians; hopefully Tony is not destined to become just another bloody statistic.'

'We will know soon enough as you say, until then we can only pray. We also need to spare a thought for poor Nyoni stranded out there all alone, she must think we have abandoned her.'

'I assure you there is no need to concern yourself on that score, Nyoni is going to be just fine,' Gerald said. 'As I started to explain on the phone the other day, having the burden of caring for Tony lifted from her is a blessing in disguise. She is at last free to devote herself to her own family.'

'Are you suggesting we send her back to her people in Zimbabwe?'

'No, nor is that an option, Princess. Let me explain a few home truths about your friend. Firstly, her tribal scaring signifies her vocation; she was born to be a rain-goddess.'

'Gerald please, where on earth did you conjure up such nonsense?'

'In rural Rhodesia, knowledge gleaned over many years in the bush. In most tribes rain-goddesses inherited their status, along with the gift. The only proviso being that they remain a virgin. The likes of Nyoni would go up into the hills at puberty, as an initiate, only returning to her people once the existing incumbent had passed on or was dispatched for incompetence, which is more usually the case. Nyoni's defiling at the hands of the terrorists would have effectively ended her career, before it began. In all probability she was encouraged to run off with Tony to spare her life.'

'Gerald, that's preposterous, this is the twentieth century for goodness sake.'

'Not in Zimbabwe, Princess. Africa has always had its witch-doctors, circumcisions, *muti* killings and rain-goddesses. Practices that will survive well into the next century and beyond,' he concluded, beckoning a wine steward.

'Assuming you are not delusional, surely if she is unable to return home that compounds her predicament – hardly a blessing in disguise?'

'Secondly,' Gerald announced pointedly, 'Nyoni has been holding out on you. I mentioned that when I went looking for Tony she ran into me on her way back from a local village. Well, after the customary pleasantries and some subtle probing, she volunteered that she had a family; a girl of two and boy of six months, still being wet nursed by an aunty.'

'Well I'll be darned! Tony did mention something about Nyoni being more woman than she let on. Who is the father?' Jodie asked with bated breath.

'He's an African game guard, working for the Umfolosi National Parks Board. A very understanding chap from the sounds of it, having resigned himself to Nyoni caring for the white man who saved her life, and putting wedding plans on hold indefinitely.'

'Wedding plans,' Jodie mused aloud as she reflected on the ruckus caused by her parading in Nyoni's special bead apron. 'Thinking back, the little hussy really had me bamboozled.'

'Don't be too hard on her, after all her relationship with Tony turned out to be platonic like she said. Her only crime was feeling sorry for the guy and coercing a college graduate to jump into bed with a near perfect stranger, and all without so much as a school leaving certificate to her name!'

'That's below the belt,' Jodie said, glaring at Gerald across the table. 'Take it back.'

'I apologise, but I could really do with a Nyoni in my corner right now, Princess.'

'That's the nicest thing you've said all evening,' Jodie said, adding as the waiter served another round of drinks, 'I'm actually very relieved to learn that Nyoni will be all right, a blessing in disguise indeed. Which just leaves a gullible post graduate and a young man intent on starting civil wars to worry about.'

'Soldiers fight wars. Greed, corruption, intimidation, one-party dictatorships and starvation are what start them,' Gerald said, adding in a more conciliatory tone, 'I'm sorry for sounding off again but you saw what conditions were like in Zimbabwe. A typical example of a potentially great country slavishly following the likes of Kenya, Angola, Zaire, Zambia and Mozambique, to name a few, down the path of impoverished dictatorship.'

'My dear Mr Bond, we seem to be overlooking the role of white colonial governments. Their withholding of a universal franchise fanned the flames of insurrection in the first place. What's more, can you name one colonial government that actually bothered to school their black population in the art of democracy, prior to independence?' Jodie concluded triumphantly, delighted at the timely opportunity to put the past few days of research into African politics to good use.

'Well put, even if an oversimplification.'

'I'm always willing to learn.' Jodie shook her head at the offer of another drink.

'Princess, it's complicated. Why don't you stay in Africa and marry me, help make it a safer place to raise our kids?'

'A nice thought,' Jodie said, smiling broadly. 'You do realise if that was a genuine proposal you are obliged to run it by my parents first?'

'I do and I already have. I spoke to Brenton while you were . . . up north,' Gerald said, leaving his chair and moving round to Jodie's side of the table.

'What did he say?' she asked breathlessly as he drew her to her feet and into his arms.

'He said yes, naturally. But to be perfectly honest, it was only after he had spent quite some time on the telephone to your mother. So young lady you are now obliged to try this on for size.' He handed Jodie a red velvet ring box and went down onto one knee. 'Will you do me the honour of becoming my wife?' he asked formally, while Jodie slowly opened the box.

'It is absolutely beautiful,' she murmured, savouring the moment as she studied the oval gold setting, shaped like a Zulu shield, inlaid with a huge emerald, the colour of her eyes, and edged with brilliant diamonds.

Gerald was still staring up at her expectantly when they were loudly interrupted. 'Mr Bond, telephone,' Samantha called out from the entrance to the Assegai Bar. 'The trunk call you are expecting.'

Gerald jumped up and loped off down the veranda. As he darted into the cocktail bar the crowd within fell silent without prompting. The seconds ticked by with only the chorus of night insects to be heard.

When Gerald reappeared in the doorway a few moments later, the silence was all consuming. Tears streaming unashamedly down his cheeks he stood on the threshold for what seemed an age, before his right hand shot up, thumb held proud as he blurted out, 'Our boy pulled through – with both bloody legs.'

The spontaneous applause that had started in the cool confines of the Assegai Bar swept down the veranda. But Jodie's *yes* was all Gerald heard as she ran into his arms. They were still locked in a warm embrace when the huge silver orb of a hunter's moon breasted the horizon, heralding the end of another day in Africa.

341

Glossary of Words and Abbreviations

Askari: African solider serving in armies of colonial powers.

Auxiliary forces: Ex-guerrillas formed into pro-government counterinsurgent units.

Cadres: Terrorist rank and file.

CCB: Civil Cooperation Bureau, covert special forces under the South African ministry of defence in apartheid era.

Com-Ops: Combined Operations comprising Air force, Army, Police and Internal Affairs.

CTs: Communist terrorists.

Donga: Gully.

Fire Force: Crack forces dropped into contacts by helicopter.

FN: Belgian self-loading infantry rifle.

Frelimo: Mozambique's ruling liberation forces.

Frozen or No-go areas: Areas denied to general security forces as under control of Auxiliaries or Special Forces.

Gandangas/Gooks/Guerrillas: Terrorists.

Indaba tree: Meeting place.

K-Car: Helicopter gunship.

Killing ground: Focal point in an ambush area.

MAG: Belgian FN general-purpose machine-gun.

Munts: Unsavoury slang for local blacks.

Muti: Traditional medicine.

NUF: National Unifying Force, a liberal opposition group.

NCO: Non-commissioned officer.

Nkosi: Chief or leader.

Pfumo re Vanhu: 'Spear of the People' in the vernacular.

PVs: Protected villages, fenced in with night curfew.

RAR: Rhodesian African Rifles.
RF: Rhodesian Front ruling party.
RLI: Rhodesian Light Infantry.
RPD: Russian hand-held machine-gun.
RPG: Rocket-propelled grenade launcher
Sangoma: Traditional healer.
SAP: South African Police.
SAS: Special Air Service.
SB: Police Special Branch, trained as paramilitary.
Selous Scouts: The elite anti-terrorist tracking unit.
Sitrep: Situation report.
Sunray: Company or Platoon Commander.
Tac HQ: Tactical Head Quarters.
Terrs: Terrorists.
TF: Territorial Force soldier.
TTL: Tribal Trust Land, marginal rural land where most of the
    African population lived.
UDI: Rhodesia's unilateral declaration of independence.
Veldskoen: Suede leather shoes or boots.
Wag-'n-bietjie bush: The Buffalo thorn bush dubbed the Wait-a-
    minute bush for its hook-like thorns.
WOII: Warrant Officer Class 2.
ZANLA: Zimbabwe African National Liberation Army, military
    wing of ZANU headed by Robert Mugabe.
ZIPRA: Zimbabwe People's Revolutionary Army, military wing
    of ZAPU headed by Joshua Nkomo.